PAINTING *the* LIGHT

PAINTING
the LIGHT

a novel

SALLY CABOT GUNNING

𝓌𝓂

WILLIAM MORROW

An Imprint of HarperCollins*Publishers*

PAINTING THE LIGHT. Copyright © 2021 by Sally Gunning. All rights reserved. Printed in the United States of America. No part of this book may be used or reproduced in any manner whatsoever without written permission except in the case of brief quotations embodied in critical articles and reviews. For information, address HarperCollins Publishers, 195 Broadway, New York, NY 10007.

HarperCollins books may be purchased for educational, business, or sales promotional use. For information, please email the Special Markets Department at SPsales@harpercollins.com.

FIRST EDITION

Designed by Bonni Leon-Berman

Library of Congress Cataloging-in-Publication Data has been applied for.

ISBN 978-0-06-291624-2

21 22 23 24 25   LSC   10 9 8 7 6 5 4 3 2 1

For Tom, always, for everything

There is only one way to have light. Have dark to put it on.
—WILLIAM MORRIS HUNT, 1876

If you tell the truth you don't have to remember anything.
—MARK TWAIN, 1894

Let me tell you what I think of bicycling. I think it has done
more to emancipate women than anything else in the world.
—SUSAN B. ANTHONY, 1896

Massachusetts women as a rule adhere too
strongly to old-time conventions.
—JULIA WARD HOWE, 1900

PAINTING *the* LIGHT

1893

THE MUSEUM OF FINE ARTS SCHOOL, BOSTON

Ida Russell brought her heels down hard as she walked past the closed door of the life drawing class. She wanted that roomful of promising young men to lift their heads, to suspend their pencils, to ask themselves who was passing and wonder if it was someone important who might have helped their careers more than Mr. Wirth, the instructor of the class they were attending. And of course it would be someone important, they'd think—only an important person would dare to walk by with such a commanding stride—and here they were listening to the renowned Mr. Wirth, who despite his reputation was imparting very little and very poorly. Or so Ida fantasized.

Childish, yes, but it burned, burned like a careless hand on a hot iron, that when she'd tried to enroll in the class she'd been told by the Museum School registrar that it "wasn't for ladies." She'd gone straight to the dean, and when he'd said "unthinkable" in response, she'd foolishly interpreted it to mean that it was unthinkable for a woman to be barred from the class; what it really meant—and what had been made humiliatingly clear soon after—was that it was unthinkable for a young woman to enter any room where a male model posed without his clothes.

Fueled by that remembered burn, Ida reversed course, stopped before the offending door, and cracked it open. She could see only a slice of the model—one long, glorious line of elevated heel and sinewy leg rising into a clenched buttock; just looking at that reaching, striving form Ida could feel the pencil in her hand as it flowed over the paper, perfectly capturing that line. But the renowned Mr. Wirth had seen her; he was marching toward the door making shooing motions with his hands; and the look on his face made Ida want to laugh and cry at the same time: *A lady ruined!* Ida moved on.

Inside her own classroom Ida found her space, set up her easel, pulled her smock over her knees, and picked up her charcoal. Her instructor, the less renowned Mr. Morris, had taken up a position between her and the stuffed owl they'd been told to sketch, but as he was more interesting to look at than the owl, Ida didn't mind. She allowed her charcoal to take a quick likeness: attenuated form topped by long face and bulbous forehead, paralyzing eyes, a sparse beard that he drew to a point under constant, probing fingers.

"Let me give you a few simple rules for learning to draw," he began. "First, establish the fact of the *whole*. Next, put in the line that marks the movement of the whole. Don't have more than one movement in a figure!"

And what movement was there in a stuffed owl? Ida wondered, already grieving for her nude runner down the hall. She slid her sketch of Mr. Morris under a clean sheet of paper, turned her charcoal on its side, and had just roughed in the shape of the whole bird when Mr. Morris surfaced behind her to bark in her ear.

"Is that what you see as the whole? Just the bird? What of the rest of the paper? The white shapes? What shapes have you left around your bird? Do you see how ignored your white spaces are?"

Remarkably, Ida did; this was what she loved most about the Museum School—that she was learning to *see;* shapes, spaces, lights, darks, textures, values. She amended her owl shape until it had divided the paper better, but now the bird had lost some of its owlishness, particularly in the wings and tail. "I'm afraid I've turned my owl into a roast chicken."

Morris didn't smile—he never smiled—and yet something perverse in Ida's nature persisted in attempting to change *his* nature. "Don't paint a thing as it is," he said now. "Paint it as it *seems*."

But once Mr. Morris left, Ida saw at once where she had gone astray with her shape, and better yet, how to amend it; she worked busily until he returned. It struck Ida that over the last few classes Mr. Morris seemed to loom over her particular easel more often than some others, but she wasn't sure if this was a good sign or a bad.

"Good, good, but go on! Don't be afraid. The moment you're afraid you might as well be in Hanover Street shopping." Mr. Morris crossed in front of her and bent down till his eyes rested level with her own. His eyes always appeared blackest when closest. "Do you want to be in Hanover Street shopping, Miss Russell, or do you want to learn to draw?"

Ida had *been* in Hanover Street shopping, too many times, taking the carriage from the family town house on Beacon Hill and stopping for tea at the Parker House on her return. It was what idle rich ladies did on the long, dull days of winter. Or spring. Or summer. Ida had likely bought as much silk and drunk as much tea as any lady on the Hill until one day she happened to read about the Museum School in her father's newspaper and experienced a sensation much like a luffing sail as it caught a fresh wind. She'd collected her sketches and watercolors—the other thing idle rich ladies did—and laid them out on the table in front of her father. She picked up the portrait of her mother. "Is it like?"

Ida's father possessed one of those faces that looked stern no matter the underlying emotion; his mouth under its mustache twitched in the way it did whenever he humored this odd, restless daughter of his, but—give him his due—he studied the likeness with care. "There are elements that are quite like."

"And elements that aren't like. Which? Why?"

"I'm sure I don't know, Ida."

"Neither do I. But I want to. I want to go to the Museum School. I want to learn to draw."

And this was what Ida said to Mr. Morris now. "I want to learn to draw."

"Then draw!" Morris cried. "Go on! No, no, no, don't stop! You'll look at this picture in two years and see what's good and bad in it, you'll see right through it to its center, you'll see what's *true* in it. And do you know what will happen then? You'll take up another work, and in it you'll leave off the false and take up the true."

"And in the meantime?"

"You spoil a lot of paper, Miss Russell. But I beg you, spoil it cheerfully. Boldly. And do it again and again until you make no line that isn't true."

1

November 1898
VINEYARD HAVEN, MARTHA'S VINEYARD

Ida Pease, formerly Russell, looked out the window at dark ocean against darkening sky and worn-out grass dotted with sheep. It was wrong. All of it. The water should still be reflecting the idea of sky; the sky should still be reflecting the idea of sun; the sheep should be crowded around a full rack of hay. But Ida's husband hadn't gotten around to filling the hayrack before he left, and according to his logic that meant the sheep could get by on dead grass until he got home. And the only reason the colors were wrong was because Ezra should have been home hours ago to eat a Thanksgiving goose that had been roasting way too long for its own good or anyone else's.

So perhaps the only thing wrong was Ezra. Ida looked at the clock again. Quarter to five. Not that she needed to wonder where her husband was—his usual route home ran through the back room at Duffy's where he played cards and "did his part to fill the spittoon," as he told Ida back in the days when she'd bothered to ask what took him. But today was Thanksgiving, and Ezra's aunt Ruth and his cousin Hattie had been sitting in the parlor for two hours, Ruth casting looks at Ida that implied it was her fault Ezra was late, that Ida should have learned to herd her husband the way their sheepdog herded sheep. But in truth the old woman was looking at Ida the way she always looked at Ida.

Two years ago at her wedding Ida had gone up to her and said, "I'm pleased to know you, Aunt Ruth."

"Ruth will do," she'd said.

Ruth's daughter Hattie worked at the telephone exchange and was friendlier to Ida but with a telephone exchange kind of friendly, as if she were more concerned about where Ida was going than who Ida was. Ida preferred Ruth's severe gray suits to Hattie's blousy shirtwaists, and at least when Ruth spoke, she said something with a little wind behind it; Hattie preferred to blow wisps of smoke at Ida's eyes.

"We'll eat now," Ida said. She crossed to the stove, pulled the potatoes off the heat, and, as if he'd smelled the earthy steam, Ezra banged through the door with his partner Mose Barstow. Mose smelled of whiskey; Ezra did not. Ezra saved his drinking till he got home, believing—truly believing—that if kept his mind sharp he could make his fortune at cards. At Duffy's.

"Sorry to be late," he said.

"Not late enough."

Ezra paused on his way to the pantry. "What's that you're saying to me, Ida?"

"She's saying she enjoys your absence more than your presence," Mose said. He pushed into the room and kissed the women, first Ida and then Ruth and last Hattie, the only one who seemed to appreciate it. Ezra kissed Ruth and Hattie, but after meeting Ida's eye he left her untouched and moved around her to the pantry.

Ida followed. Inside the pantry it smelled of yeast and cornmeal and dried apples, smells that had once given her comfort when faced with a long island winter ahead. "Out of useless curiosity," she said, "what time do you think it is?"

"It was Mose. He was winning."

"And this is how you keep time. By whether or not Mose Barstow is winning at cards."

Ezra whipped around. "You know, Ida, you've worked up quite a tone of late. Mose wanted me to leave for the Boston office today and I said no, it's Thanksgiving, I'm not leaving my wife to eat alone on Thanksgiving. I told him we'll just have to leave in the morning. And Mose having nowhere to go to eat Thanksgiving dinner, I told him to come along home with me. I'm pretty sure now he's sorry he did."

From the other room they could hear Ruth mumble something to which Mose barked out a laugh. Ezra snagged a bottle off the shelf and went for the door, but he paused there. "And in case you were too busy carping at me to hear what I said, I'm leaving for Boston in the morning. I don't know when I'll be back. Maybe you like that way of keeping time better."

"Go," Ida said. "Stay there forever if you like. But first feed your sheep."

IDA LOOKED OUT THE WINDOW the next morning and watched the steamer *Monohansett* with Ezra and Mose on board glide toward the horizon over an ocean as smooth and pale as ice. As she watched her mood ricocheted between relief and resentment—relief because Ezra's voice pounding at her all evening had left her feeling physically bruised; resentment because over the course of the evening it had come out that Mose hadn't tried to get Ezra to go to Boston at all, that in fact he'd been expected for Thanksgiving at his brother's in New Bedford and that Ezra had waylaid him at the boat.

"Why didn't you just say so?" Ida had asked Ezra later in bed, nothing of her body touching anything of his body, a maneuver that required some effort considering the way the bed sagged. "It would be better if you'd just said so. 'I saw Mose at the boat and wanted company for a quick game.' Or 'I wasn't in the mood for Aunt Ruth and Hattie.'" Or *I wasn't in the mood for* you, *Ida. That* tone *of yours.* Which might not have been a tone at all if Ezra had just told the truth. But Ezra hadn't answered either Ida's spoken or unspoken questions. Instead he'd rolled farther away from her in the bed and snuffed out the lamp.

Now Ida shifted her eyes from the distant water to the closer-at-hand flock: a Cheviot ram, twenty-three ewes, and eighteen lambs had spread themselves over ten acres of rock-strewn, walled-in hillside, as if convinced the grass would be better over the next rise or down the next gulley. Ida had once viewed her marriage in much the same way, but nowadays she saw nothing beyond the next rise but another barren gulley. Even so, as Ida stood at the window looking at the sheep, she had to admit they were a handsome flock, solid-bodied with upright, pink-lined ears and intelligent black eyes set off by dense, snowy fleece. The lambs were now six months old, their bodies grown into their knobby joints but still good for a frolic; Ida watched them chase one another over the rocks, but even as she watched she saw a phenomenon that Lem Daggett, the part-time hired man, had taught her to interpret: as a rule the Cheviots grazed individually or in small groups, but now, as one, they turned and headed for the lee side of the hill. Weather coming. Ida tapped the glass on Ezra's barometer. It nosed downward.

By early afternoon a businesslike north wind had dropped down over the island and within the half hour it had roughed up the sea and flipped over the remaining beech leaves, the usual calling card of a classic northeaster. Two years on the Vineyard and Ida knew what came next.

Ida went out to the dog yard and whistled up Bett; the dog leaped up and planted her feet on Ida's chest to have her ears tugged, a thing Ida wasn't supposed to allow in a working dog but did anyway because they both liked it. She rubbed Bett's ears, undid the gate and sent her off, using the commands Lem had taught her that would send the dog counterclockwise around the flock and drive them back toward the barn: *Away to me! Hold 'em! Bring 'em! Walk in!* Bett lit out like a sable flame, and the sheep knew better than to argue; Ida barely reached the barn door ahead of the flock. But as she lifted the bolt one of the lambs veered off, forcing Bett to circle behind it and nip at its heels, sending it after the others with noisy complaint.

Ida followed the lamb in, dropping the bolt behind her, thinking as she did so that Ezra would have told her she should have left the sheep out—they'd been bred to withstand the rough English hill weather and cooped up inside they would only fret—but the ram had kicked out the east wall of the field shelter and the hayracks were again empty. It would be quicker for Ida to fork hay from barn loft to barn floor than to hitch up the oxcart, especially the way the wind was coming up. Ida hauled the back of her skirt through her legs and jammed it into her belt. She climbed the ladder to the hayloft, pitched down the hay, and dreamed of being in the Parker House in Boston drinking sherry and eating little cakes frosted in lemon ice.

Ida had just finished herding the chickens into the chicken house when Lem came up the track in the wagon. He swung to the ground and greeted Bett. "I saw Ezra at the boat. How's my dog? Still teaching you tricks?"

Ida smiled. Lem had raised and trained Bett and sold her to Ezra, but Lem was no fool—after Ezra had been off on a job for the better part of a month Lem had figured out he'd best train

Ida as well. Ida was never sure if it was her accomplishment or the dog's, but she was proud of how they'd begun to work together.

Lem set in helping Ida fill the wood box, piling extra on the porch. Lem was built like Ezra, square and solid, but with close-cropped gray hair and a weather-creased face. Ida had often speculated how the thirty-eight-year-old Ezra might age into the fifty-two-year-old Lem, and the thought had never bothered her, but lately she'd begun to think with dread of all those years she'd be lying beside Ezra as he creased and grayed and of how old she'd be by the time he did it. She'd been twenty-nine when she'd married Ezra; she already felt twice that.

"I've got coffee," Ida offered.

"You hang on to it. Ruth needs a door hinge reseated." Lem turned around and looked up at the house. "Still no shutters," he said, as if he were keeping score on Ezra. Or maybe Ida only thought so because she was.

Ida went inside, stirred the fire, and made herself roasted cheese, the kind of supper she preferred but only got to indulge in when she didn't have to cook for Ezra. After she'd washed up she spread the *Gazette* under the lamp and began to read, another thing she could only enjoy when Ezra wasn't home because he'd always have to read it first, and if the paper hadn't already disappeared by the time Ida got around to it, Ezra would find some way to disrupt her reading, as if *her* knowing a thing made him not know it. *Ezra.* Again. Perhaps that was the thing Ida resented most of all—that he used up so much of her time even in his absence.

In Ida's first life she'd been a painter. She'd attended Boston's renowned Museum School and had been making good progress, particularly in watercolor; one of her still lifes—although not Ida herself—had been accepted at the prestigious all-male

Boston Art Club, and Mrs. Percival McKinley herself had commissioned a portrait. Mr. Morris had even asked her to teach a class once when he'd been called away. But once Ida arrived on the island, Ezra and the farm had somehow managed to get in her way. Even on a day alone, if she set up a bowl of fruit and sat down with her sketch pad, she found herself unable to focus, as if Ezra were still hovering, as if he'd walk in any minute to divert her to a torn coat or a sick lamb or a storm threatening the harvest. Of course, her inability to focus even in Ezra's absence was not his fault, but so many other things *were* his fault that sometimes that one leaped aboard unnoticed.

THE TEMPERATURE DROPPED. The wind kicked up. It began to snow. Ida took another trip outside to collect the shovel from the barn and prop it next to the back door just inside the kitchen; good thing too—by the time the grandfather clock chimed eleven the world outside was white and howling. She collected her lamp, climbed the stairs to her bed, undressed down to her skin and then added things back in layers: flannel nightgown, shawl, wool stockings, a pair of Ezra's wool socks. She would have to say of Ezra he did keep her warm nights. She would also have to say he kept her sleepless. He slept as if he'd died, without worry, but that trait never comforted Ida; instead it left her to take on the worry herself. Like now. Too late, she thought of Ezra's salvage company down on Main Street and wondered if the old roof would hold. She got out of bed and looked out the window at nothing but white swirling by like smoke in hunt of a chimney. She returned to bed and listened to the wind shriek and moan and roar till morning.

*   *   *

IT SNOWED AND BLEW all the next day, easing just enough before dark so Ida could get out to scatter corn for the chickens, lug water, muck out the livestock, and spread fresh hay. She stamped off the snow on the porch but might have saved herself that bit of trouble—a pane on the east front window had blown out and snow covered the floor as far as the hearth. She snatched the quilt off the downstairs bed and stuffed it into the window, swept the snow onto the hearth to melt it, repeated the previous night's routine down to the roasted cheese, and went to her bed.

By morning the snow had stopped. Ida looked out her bedroom window and saw drifts piled four feet high, almost burying the chicken house. She crossed the hall to look out the front window and saw her favorite old beech measuring its length on the ground alongside random other tree limbs and pieces of fence. Beyond the road she saw the soupy, heaving Sound. But what of Ezra's salvage vessel, the *Cormorant*? And what of the office and warehouse on Main Street?

Ida pulled on her heaviest skirt and accessorized it with Ezra's rubber boots, wool sweater, and oiled jacket. She went downstairs, picked up the phone, and was unsurprised to get nothing but silence. Ezra had been proud of that phone line, one of the first to branch off the main trunk in town, no matter it went dead in every blow. Ida tended the animals, collected the office keys from the desk, and started down the hill, picking her way around the drifts. She was sweating and breathing in rough gasps by the time she reached the town center, the lower foot of her skirt weighted with clumps of half-frozen snow. A dozen men and boys were just starting to work on the road, but past experience told her it would take a day to clear a mile and she was glad she hadn't waited.

Ida looked toward the water. At first she couldn't take in what she was seeing along the shore: boats piled up like children's abandoned toys; a schooner impaled in the middle of the Union Wharf, rendering both boat and dock useless; another dozen two- and three-masted schooners run aground or sunk with nothing but their masts showing; one large coastal trader sitting like a hen on a nest high and dry on the beach; on another a cargo of lime smoldered. Farther out, a group of men had managed to reach one of the schooners and was attempting to extricate something in the rigging. Ida was about to turn away when she saw that the thing was a body, so stiff the men were forced to handle it like a severed dock piling. Beyond that boat another was engulfed in flames, but no one was troubling to put out the fire.

Ida spied Lem standing among the rowboats talking to Chester Luce, the owner of the grocery and operator of the telephone and telegraph, the place where all news either began or ended. As Ida approached Lem, his eyes traveled to the burning vessel at sea. He pointed. "The gasoline for the compressor must have exploded."

Ida whirled around and took a closer look at the burning vessel: Ezra's *Cormorant*. She started to walk in its direction but stopped; even in those few short minutes it had listed farther, and no matter how angry she was at Ezra, she could take no pleasure in seeing the *Cormorant* go down.

Lem and Chester Luce resumed their conversation, Lem angling his body to include Ida too, Luce making no note whatsoever of her presence. The local news was grim but should have been grimmer; eight men had been lost off ships taking refuge in the harbor, but some local men had made a series of runs in the height of the storm and saved dozens more. Fifty schooners had either washed aground or sunk at anchor; the man they pulled out of the rigging was the captain of the *Thurlow* out of

New Jersey, his crew and many others now packed into the Seamen's Bethel at Union Wharf, where they would be given food and clothes in addition to shelter. Phones and telegraph were down but news was going out from the Cape on the undersea cable to France, back to New York, and from there by land to Boston. The latest news—the biggest news—had just come in from Boston off the steamer, and Luce's voice took on a minister's pall as he rolled out the words: the steamship *Portland* had sunk off the back side of Cape Cod, the beaches there littered with its wreckage.

Others lifted their heads, moved close. "The *Portland*?" asked John Cottle. "Boston to Maine?"

"The same. Bodies are washing up from Wellfleet to Chatham. The funeral homes are full."

The words rippled down the beach. *Steamship. Portland. Bodies.* The crowd grew. "Anyone come in alive?" Bert Robinson asked.

"None's I've heard of," Luce answered.

"Alive? In this sea?" Cottle laughed, saw the looks, cut off.

"Anyone know anyone on her?" Most heads were shaken, but some others offered up distant connections as if they were badges of honor: Ira Briggs's cousin lived in Maine and always came up to Boston and back for Thanksgiving; Chester Luce recalled the Chilmark Hardings saying the Edgartown Hardings were going to Portland to stay with their family for the holiday season; Bert Robinson said his nephew often traveled from Boston to Maine . . .

Ida drifted away, the old, familiar horror rising in her. Her father and brothers had gone down in a coaster off the Carolinas, the news sending Ida's mother into such a state of melancholia that a month later she'd walked off an old dilapidated wharf with her pockets full of stones. But as horrific as her mother's death was, the two of them waiting for news of her father and brothers had been as bad—the weeks stretching to months with no word, no certainty. As Ida trudged the beach she could think only of the Chilmark Hardings and Ira Briggs and Bert Robinson's niece, of their faces growing tighter and tighter just as her mother's had grown tighter with each long, news-less day, until the day the news did come that melted her face into an endless pool of weeping.

Ida pushed on, giving a nod to the rare islander who lifted a hand, most of them too busy giving and receiving their own news to take any notice of someone who was still considered "off-island." When she reached Main Street, she dropped into one of the slushy wheel tracks that ran down the middle, the snow piled two feet high on either side of it. She slogged ahead in Ezra's boots, heel to toe, until she reached Ezra's building. The sign PEASE & BARSTOW MARINE SALVAGE was gone; the window on the right-hand side had been pierced by somebody's dislocated awning; the roof was missing a whole swath of shingles.

Ida kicked down a drift, unlocked the door, and stepped inside. The office held the usual books and papers and safe and telephone along with the unusual: a heap of rusted chain, a bracket for a ship's lantern, a dented spittoon. Most of the junk sat in front of the broken window, but Ida decided none of it could be harmed by a little more weather. She examined the ceiling and saw no stains; books, papers, desk, cabinets, all seemed free of wet.

Lem stepped into the office behind her, tracking snow and sand and the smell of wet wool, carrying Ezra's sign. "Found it in the snow in front of the cobbler's. When's Ezra due back?"

Ida's cheeks burned, remembering their parting words. *Go. Stay there forever if you like . . .* "I don't know."

"Come along," Lem said. "I have the wagon."

"I need to check the warehouse."

Lem went with her. The warehouse roof and walls were intact, the contents—more salvage—dirty and rusty but dry. She followed Lem and climbed into the wagon. "I should check on Ruth."

"Already did. Nothing but a fence amiss. And I'll fix that window of yours. I've got the glass in the back."

So he'd checked on her too. A wave of affection flooded Ida, which she quickly checked. Lem Daggett did not need her—either figuratively or literally—wrapping her arms around his neck.

As they drove past the beach Ida looked for the *Cormorant,* but it had already dived below the surface.

2

WHEN IDA FINALLY SAW her husband's dark shape coming
up the track from town, she wasn't ready to face him. She dove
into the pantry and began hauling jugs and boxes and bags
from the shelves as if she'd been midway into a good clear-out.
She'd just set his whiskey bottle on the floor when she heard
the knocking and straightened up. Ezra wouldn't knock. She
went to the door and flung it open on Chester Luce.

"Letter for you," he said. "Just off the boat. From your husband. Thought I'd run it up in case you were waiting on news."

Ida looked at Ezra's sloppy writing on the envelope and wondered that Luce had recognized it. How many letters did Ezra
ever write? She opened the envelope. The letter was dated Saturday, the day of the storm.

> Ida—I'm writing you in a hurry Mose and I are about to
> board the *Portland* for that Maine job I'll be back by weeks
> end Call Lem if you need help with the sheep—E—PS
> Sorry

The word that struck Ida first was the word *sorry*. He'd used it
twice in a week now and it wasn't as a rule a common presence
in his vocabulary. And why the mention of Lem and the sheep?
Didn't Ida always turn to Lem when she needed help with the
sheep? She read the letter again, and this time she stopped at the
word *Portland*. That word was as strange as the word *sorry*. Ezra
couldn't have boarded the *Portland*. The *Portland* went down.

Ida looked at the date on the letter again, read it again, sure she'd taken some particular word wrong, but none of the words had changed into other words or clarified their meaning. She dropped the letter on the table and raced out the door down the track; no matter how old she might feel, Ida was still young enough to run, a skill she'd picked up since she'd moved to the island and begun to chase sheep. She caught Luce just as he was about to take the turn onto Main Street. He heard her and swung around, cautious on the ice, as slow as if she were dreaming him.

"What news of the *Portland*?"

"She went down."

"I *know* she went down. Still no word on survivors? Ezra was on her. And Mose Barstow."

Luce blinked, looked up, spoke to the clouds. "None's I've got wind of. They've piled the unidentified at the Lifesaving Station at Cahoon Hollow, over in Wellfleet."

"I'm talking of the passengers. The passengers on the *Portland*."

Luce gave Ida an odd look. "Like I told you. Piled up in Wellfleet."

"I don't mean the bodies, Mr. Luce. I mean the passengers."

Luce took his eyes from the sky and brought them down to Ida's level. "One and the same, Mrs. Pease. All one and the same. I'm sorry as can be, but that's the thrust of it. Terrible thing, I know. Whatever Mrs. Luce and I can do . . . You'll be wanting to get to Wellfleet, I imagine. If we can help with any of the procedures—"

Ida fought down a wave of hysterical laughter. "I'm familiar with the procedures," she said. She turned and started back up the hill. She made it as far as the kitchen stoop when her knees began to tremble. She sat down hard on the cold and the ice and this new truth that she couldn't seem to wrestle to earth. Ezra. Drowned. On the *Portland*.

Ida sat on the stoop until the rest of her began to tremble from the cold.

LATER, crouched before the fire, Ida still felt frozen—her body and her mind. What to do? Ezra would have told her, and she'd have ignored him more like, but even so, right now she'd have welcomed the telling. She sat some more, wishing something would thaw out so she could at least think if not feel, and when her brain did thaw the first thing she thought of was Chester Luce. *You'll be wanting to get to Wellfleet.* Ida straightened. Yes, that was first. Or rather, second.

First was Ruth.

IDA CLIMBED the uphill track to Ruth's with greater ease than she'd managed the downhill slide after Chester Luce. As she reached the house she stopped to gather herself, to bundle up her own inner turmoil and pack it away someplace out of reach until a later time when she could pull it out and sort through it in privacy. Now was Ruth's time. Hattie's time. But still, Ida hovered on the step, turning to look out over the farm. Ezra's farm.

Of the two farmhouses Ruth's was the newer, built when Ezra took over the farm, perched on the top of the rise so that Ruth would remain part of the place where she'd been born and raised but at enough of a distance to keep her nose out of the actual workings. Of course it was never possible to keep Ruth's nose out of anything, but Ruth's house held the best view: the scope of pasture and hill demarcated by the serpentine stone walls, a wide swath of sea beyond, an even wider patch of sky.

From that vantage point nothing appeared changed, as if Luce had never climbed the hill and handed Ida the letter, as if Ezra had never written the letter, as if he and Mose had never sailed off for Boston. She peered down the hill at the pastured sheep, the old house, the barn. Any minute Ezra could walk out of that barn door knocking manure off his boot and cursing, most likely at Ida, but still . . .

Still. There should have been something more after that *still*. Ida waited, but nothing came. She knocked, opened Ruth's door, and stepped inside.

OF THE TWO WOMEN, Ruth seemed to adjust to the news more quickly; Hattie looked blankly at Ida, but in due time the tears came. Ruth's face looked as if it were meant to cry, the tracks already worn, but Hattie's wasn't yet laid out for it; Ida watched the tears flow willy-nilly over Hattie's smoother cheeks for a time, but after a while she stood up.

"I need to go to Wellfleet and look for Ezra's body."

Hattie's tears stopped. She stood also. "I'll go with you."

"No, you need to look after Ruth."

Ruth snorted. "Who looks after who around here, I'd like to know?"

But Hattie dropped into her chair without argument.

LEM WAS WAITING at the fence when Ida returned. He was about to speak but Ida cut in first.

"I'm off to Wellfleet to look for his body. Will you mind the farm? I should only be a night."

"I'll go to Wellfleet."

"No, I need you to mind the farm."

"Ida—"

"I guess I know what you want to say but I think I'd do better just now if you didn't say it. Is that all right?"

Lem peered hard at her. "I'm taking you to the boat."

"All right."

IDA WENT INSIDE, climbed the stairs to her room—Ezra's room—and fumbled in the closet for her travel suit and travel boots, feeling under water. She looked down at the scuffs on the boots in disgust. Ida had been raised with pretty things; she liked pretty things; she painted—back when she'd painted—graceful still lifes and elegant portraits of men and ladies clad in their finery. But after her first soggy winter on the farm she'd returned her own silk dresses and satin shoes to the trunk where they still sat at the back of the closet, and—somehow—stopped even polishing her boots. But polish them for whom? Ruth would have missed the opportunity to cast a disapproving eye, and Ezra wouldn't have noticed.

LEM HELPED IDA into the wagon and threw her bag in the back. They stayed silent the length of the ride until the wharf came into view, the schooner *Newburgh* still embedded in the middle of it; a crew worked nearby, taking the easiest route of rebuilding the wharf around the vessel. In the meantime rowboats still set off from shore to ferry the passengers to the steamer, and when Ida's turn came she was glad enough of Lem's hand, but not just because of the restriction of her corset. Oh, the dread she felt, sitting in that rocking boat, feeling every ounce of her own weight! Even without her mother's stones, it would be a fast trip to the bottom.

"You call when you get back!" Lem hollered.

Ida nodded and could only hope he saw it because she couldn't wave; she gripped the dory's gunwale with both hands and stared at the crewman's back as it strained, the past flying in and out of the waves around her.

FOR THE BETTER PART of a year after Ida lost her family, she'd sat in her parents' town house on Beacon Hill, pinned down under the sheer weight of her grief. It was too much; too many; how to pry apart one face or voice or heart from the solid mass of dead to register its loss? How to separate a single memory? She was unable to think or form a plan. Whenever she saw water it had seemed to press on her, suffocate her, much as it had suffocated her mother. The house, frayed and fading around encased treasures her shipmaster grandfather had brought back from China likewise oppressed her. She couldn't seem to break out of the track she walked from room to room, dusting and redusting lifeless objects that had lost all meaning for her. When she finally attempted to paint even a simple floral it came out too dreary, too full of umbers and ochres; when she tried a portrait of a neighbor's child, the poor boy came out looking like *he'd* drowned, so pale had she made him. Such was Ida's state at the end of that first year that she might have taken up with any man who chose to notice her, even one far less charming than Ezra.

And Ezra *was* charming. Ida had met him at a schoolmate's wedding and had noticed his taking her in from top to bottom: hair swept high and loose in keeping with the current fashion, mourning silk enlivened with French lace collar and cuffs, her mother's diamond and pearl encrusted locket hanging between her breasts. At the time Ida had believed it was her face and figure that had captured Ezra's eye; later she suspected that in fact it had been the locket. But when Ida intercepted that look of appreciation she'd felt a little spark of life for the first time since she'd lost her family; she smiled, and that was all it took to draw Ezra across the room to her. And, she would admit it, Ida had liked the look of him too: the well-cut suit, the strong shoulders, the confident smile. And she'd liked it even more that he'd apparently asked around about her and knew of her tragedy yet refused to tiptoe around it as if it were contagious. "Are you truly all alone now?" he'd asked. "There's no family left at all?"

Later in their acquaintance, after he'd discovered she was an artist, Ezra had talked of his island home as an enchanted place; he'd described a rising tide of affluent tourists always on the lookout for art, an acclaimed summer institute that offered classes in the arts, more flowers than she could paint in a lifetime. But more important than all of that, Ezra was a man of the land. A sheep farmer. A man who would never be swallowed by the sea. And perhaps there lay the greatest evidence of Ezra's charm: the fact that he'd managed to talk Ida into island life, that a woman who abhorred the idea of water now lived surrounded by it. But when Ezra showed her his Martha's Vineyard farm—the rolling green hills dotted with sheep, the water at a picturesque distance, a late-day glow pinking the stone walls, she'd thought: *peace.*

When had that peace washed away? Perhaps when Ezra and Mose started the salvage business that would not only take them to sea but to "meetings" at Duffy's at every odd hour. Perhaps when Ezra leased office space in Boston that seemed to serve more as an excuse to leave the island at will and without warning. Or perhaps, more simply, when he stopped trying to charm her. However it happened, one day Ida woke from her long fog of grief to find that the island tourists were looking for island landscapes, not portraits and still lifes; that the famed institute was nothing but a summer school for teachers; that the flowers growing wild along the road and in the meadows drooped thinly when imprisoned in a vase; that most months of the year the water and sky and even the farm itself pressed in and down and around Ida like a grave; that she was trapped in a life that she could never claim as hers and from which she could never escape.

And now Ezra was dead. An unexpected wave of anger hit Ida; Ezra had drowned and left her here to sort for him among the bodies—again, a thing that wasn't his fault, and yet somehow she could blame him for it.

IDA CLAMBERED ABOARD THE FERRY and found a seat inside, fixing her eyes on the horizon. The surface of the sea appeared calm enough, but she could feel the swell and roll of it below, the remains of the storm washing in from farther out. Was it still washing in bodies? They'd never recovered the bodies of her father and brothers, but there were times when Ida had thought of that as a gift, especially after she saw her mother's crab-eaten face and those stones in her pockets. For a time Ida had dreamed of her father and brothers still alive, shipwrecked on a remote barrier island, but she wanted no such fantasies with Ezra; she wanted to find his body, to bring it home, to enclose him in the ground along with this terrifying, unwelcome anger. That she should feel this, that it should rise up and wrestle down the grief she should have felt only made her angrier.

The Woods Hole harbor, as compared to the Haven, seemed to have suffered little damage; the wood pilings on the dock stood upright, the steamship office, warehouses, and train station all possessed their original roofs; a few tall trees still hovered starkly in the background. Ida stepped gratefully onto ground that didn't shift under her and hurried to the train station; she purchased the latest *Atlantic* to shield herself from unwanted conversation and secured a window seat. But as the train labored its way down the length of the Cape, she found herself ignoring the magazine and gazing out the window at flat fields, marsh, stunted black pines, ponds skimmed with ice, a bedraggled cluster of houses, and finally, the wind-blasted dunes of Wellfleet

At the station Ida negotiated a hack without difficulty, but as they drew closer and closer to the shore, her composure left her. It was still bitterly cold, which meant Ida would find no rotting flesh awaiting her, but she began to imagine other things that could happen to a body after it had been pummeled by the sea. She began to imagine her mother.

The Lifesaving Station sat perched on the edge of a dune, its roof steeply pitched to deter the wind, a lookout turret standing defiantly above it. The Atlantic stretched out long and seemingly calm beyond, but Ida could hear the rumbling of surf at the foot of the bluff and wasn't fooled. She stepped out of the carriage onto ground that now seemed as unstable as the sea and strode toward the building. The lifesaving boats were lined up outside; Ida considered why and pushed the thought aside, but inside the cavernous space it was as she'd feared—the entire floor was covered with bodies draped in blankets.

Ida stood still and waited as three others completed a ponderous circle of the room. One couple could have been the Chilmark Hardings. A single man could have been a relative of Ira Briggs's cousin or Bert Robinson's niece. She didn't want to draw too close to them, to find she was recognized, to be forced to speak, but even more, she didn't want to get close enough to read the details of their grief. Only after they left the building, the man and woman holding each other upright, the single man striding fast, as if to outpace his disappointment, did Ida approach the surf man on duty and show him the picture of Ezra she'd brought with her.

Ida's single image of Ezra was one he'd commissioned for a wedding portrait: Ida sat stiffly in lilac silk, again wearing her mother's locket; Ezra stood with a knee cocked, looking into the distance, already focused on his exit. The surf man studied the photo at length but as if out of politeness, not wishing to dismiss it without at least feigning attention; in the end he handed it back and gestured to the rows of bodies.

"Best look for yourself, ma'am."

Ida began at the nearest corner and paced the rows, looking for anything of Ezra, even among the Negroes, even among the women, distrusting the sea, distrusting her senses. At first she wasn't able to see anything; next she was able to see nothing but death. At last she was able to see this beard or that coat or a slant to a nose, but nothing she could join up to form Ezra. When she reached the end she stood and breathed to settle herself, then started again, slower this time, holding up the picture, lifting the blankets, remembering to look for Mose too, but she could make no single piece of flesh into either man. She returned to the surf man, who now stood leaning against the wall. "Are you still collecting bodies?"

"Not since the wind shifted."

"How many are still missing?"

The surf man shrugged. "Nobody knows. The passenger list was on shipboard. They're guessing they shipped close to two hundred, it being a holiday weekend."

Ida made a quick survey of the room, estimating not more than forty bodies, which grew the odds against her finding Ezra.

She turned and saw the driver had waited for her at the door with what appeared to be real empathy shadowing his face; he held out his arm and she took it, allowed him to walk her to the carriage. It was well beyond dark when he left her at a rooming house at the center of town that he insisted was clean and safe for women alone; he tried to refuse the money for the fare, but Ida pressed it into his hand. She was not the grieving widow he believed her to be.

But odd as it was considering that Ezra's wasn't among them, seeing those rows of dead bodies in Wellfleet and hearing the groaning of the sea beyond confirmed for Ida the fact of her husband's death. Ezra wasn't going to walk out of that barn. He wasn't going to walk up that hill. He wasn't going to barge into the kitchen with Mose, jabbering about whatever it was he chose to jabber about at the moment. He would not now, ever, age into Lem Daggett. He was dead.

Ezra, dead. Ida got up and paced the room, repeating the words aloud: *Ezra, dead. Ezra dead,* waiting for that overwhelming crash of grief that she knew so well. Around and around she went, seeing nothing but the worn rug under her feet, but no matter how many turns she took she felt nothing but hollow, blank. That fact and the long night itself wore away at her in turns; she'd imagined nothing could ever be as difficult as grief until she came upon its absence.

3

IDA STOOD AT THE PASTURE FENCE and looked over the sheep. It was something else Lem had taught her—stand and look, get to know your flock, spy that gimpy leg or overgrown hoof or restless ewe *before* the leg twisted or the hoof rolled or the lamb was cast. The only trouble with sheep was that they were too stoic, Lem said; by the time they complained it was too late to do much good.

Ida had spent enough hours at the fence by now that she knew her charges: the one she called Queen, who posed like a statue whenever she saw anyone watching; the one born with a twisted leg that ran with an odd hop; the one with the nick in her ear. Queen; Hop; Nick; those she always knew and some others besides, but even if she couldn't name every member of the flock she could pick out the drooping head and hollow back of a sick sheep from halfway across the field. As she did now.

It was one of the older ewes. Ida pondered whether to call Bett to cull the sick sheep from the flock but feared the dog would stress it, cause it to use up too much of its diminished strength. It stood up against the mottled stones of the wall as if to camouflage itself, and Ida determined she should be able to draw close. Ida collected Ezra's crook and a halter, opened the gate, and walked into the pasture, setting off a chorus of noise and a parting of the sea of thick bodies as she walked. As she drew closer she noted the ewe's sides heaved as if laboring to breathe. Ida hooked the sheep and haltered it without difficulty, led it into the barn, and called Lem.

IDA WATCHED Lem's practiced hands examine the sheep, feeling for pulse and respiration, pulling back the eyelids, opening the mouth. Ida had once asked Ezra why Lem didn't have his own sheep farm, knowing everything about sheep the way he did.

"He had one," Ezra had answered. "Burned to the ground one night and his wife with it. It took all the starch out of him; he never could face building again from scratch." There Ezra had paused. "Although once he asked me did I ever think about selling this place."

"What did you tell him?"

"I laughed and said 'Take it!' Told him my price. He never mentioned it again."

Now, Lem straightened. "This looks like pneumonia." He fetched the hollow drench horn; Ida went inside and fetched the brandy. She filled the horn while Lem secured the sheep between his legs, then tipped its head back and funneled in the brandy. She knew the rest. Watch and wait. Either the sheep recovered or there'd be mutton for dinner.

IDA RETURNED to the house thinking of the calendar, of the long winter ahead, followed by the spring lambing and shearing, the summer haying and weaning, the fall breeding and livestock sale, back around again to another long winter. As absent as Ezra had come to be, he'd always made sure he was on hand for lambing, shearing, haying, the sale in October. How was Ida to manage it? Lem would do the shearing, but she'd have to find the money to pay him; she'd have to find the money to pay Bart Robinson, who harvested the hay. Come to that, she didn't like the look of the hayloft—those sheep would eat through eight tons of hay before the grass greened again, and if she had to buy hay . . . Ida knew the farm account had been dangerously depleted when Ezra bought a prize ram in September, but it hadn't worried him because of the Maine job, he said. The Maine job he'd never finished. But now Ida remembered hearing Mose and Ezra, sitting at the kitchen table, gleeful after the purchase of the *Cormorant,* making some sort of list. She'd barely listened, it not being a favorite subject, but she'd heard one particular word: *insurance.*

THE SNOWMELT CAUSED a new problem in town; now Ida's hem was coated in mud by the time she reached Main Street, and once again she cut down onto the beach. Some of the boats had been refloated, a couple had been left to rot, more flotsam had washed up from the wreckage, the cargo of lime still burned. The news of Ezra being aboard the *Portland* must have gone out; she passed a group of three men she recognized by their faces but couldn't sort by name, and they fell silent with that awkward attention death always brought forth. As she moved on she heard the low rumble of their voices behind her, made out the words *artist* and *gone soon,* spoken in a flat tone in which Ida heard no regret.

Ida continued up to the street, watching her footing more than the surroundings, and almost missed the fact that someone had replaced the office windowpane. Lem, she guessed. As she drew closer she could hear noise from inside: the clank of the stove door, something scraping across the floor, the *ping ping ping* of water dripping onto metal. She opened the door expecting to see Lem's economical form crouched at the stove and took a step back as it straightened up and kept rising. Not Lem.

Ida shut the door forcefully and the man whirled around. "Good Lord, you startled me."

Well, he'd startled Ida too, even though she knew him well enough: Mose Barstow's brother, Henry, a man she'd first met long before she'd met Mose, or come to that, Ezra.

THE OPENING EXHIBIT at the Boston Art Club was an event of which people took notice: artists, art patrons, politicians, and most valued of all, society. Mrs. McKinley had allowed the loan of her portrait, and it and a golden bowl of lilies Ida had been particularly proud of occupied a corner of a wall crowded with works of other undiscovered artists. At first Ida had bemoaned that positioning, but after a half hour she realized that it allowed her work to stand out as perhaps a rung above her neighbors'. She lingered as unobtrusively as she could until Mr. Morris spied her and came dashing up just as he dashed at her in the studio. He pointed at the portrait. "Yes, yes, yes, Miss Russell, now you've got the ground just right."

A couple standing just the other side of Morris swiveled to look, the man an unusual combination of light hair and dark eyes, the woman a shimmering redhead who seemed unsurprised by the number of eyes that swiveled her way.

"Is this your work?" the man asked.

Ida nodded.

"Extraordinary." The man looked again at the portrait. "Do I know this lady?" He bent down to read the label and a pair of vertical lines sprang up between his eyebrows. "Perhaps not."

Ida studied the man, who continued to study the portrait. "Was Mrs. McKinley pleased with your rendering?"

"She was."

"Her eyes are so remarkably—"

"Empty? I painted them as they were. An utter void."

There the man lifted his own eyes to meet Ida's, and in them she saw an understanding that surprised her, as if they'd talked about this before, as if they shared a secret knowledge of this woman or this painting or this day. Had Ida lived it before? But now the man was smiling at her, and it was the kind of smile that could only draw up the corners of Ida's mouth in answer. "And yet she was pleased with the portrait," the man said. "Which perhaps speaks to another void."

"Oh, for heaven's sake, Henry," the redhead cut in. "She was made to look beautiful, which is all any woman wants. Isn't that so, miss? But she couldn't have been *this* beautiful; so few women are."

"She wasn't," Ida said. "But she thought she was. Hence, she was pleased with my work. The eyes were my sole bit of honesty."

Now the man—Henry, it would appear his name was—grew pensive. "Ah, honesty. We think it an absolute, don't we? We think a thing or a person is honest or dishonest, and yet there are these shades, these times—" The man's pensive gaze turned to his wife.

"Henry, we should have my portrait done," she said. "In the style of Sargent. Wouldn't that be lovely, a portrait in the style of Sargent?" She addressed Ida. "You could manage that, surely? Take a study of his scandalous Madame X. I could be your scandalous Madame Y."

"I'd hate to rob Mr. Sargent of his next scandal," Ida said. "Or his next letter."

The man—Henry—turned a delighted gaze on Ida. He spoke quietly. Intently. "Best you leave Sargent to Sargent and work on the next Russell," he said.

As they walked away Ida could hear the woman's surgically clear voice trailing behind: "Obviously that woman has a lot more free time than I do."

* * *

BETWEEN THAT DAY and the present one Ida had run into Henry Barstow a number of times and had always been compelled by those eyes. If she were to paint those eyes she'd use something warm, like burnt sienna, and she'd put a touch of the sienna in that wheat-colored hair. Perhaps a touch of that wheat in the eyes . . . But it wasn't so much the colors that always drew Ida to seek out Henry Barstow's eyes—it was the invitation in them, to laugh, or to live, or to share some bit of knowledge or thought or feeling or . . . *what?* Ida collected herself. Right now the eyes were nothing but solemn.

"My sympathies, Mrs. Pease," Barstow said.

"How did you get in here?" Ida asked. "What are you *doing* in here?"

Barstow reached into his pocket and withdrew a key. "Right now I'm trying to get this stove to stop smoking. But in fact I'm my brother's executor." He paused. "And your husband's. Did you not know of that?"

"I did not." But Ida conceded to herself it was possible that Ezra might have mentioned it during one of those conversations where, in the interest of self-preservation, Ida had stopped listening much.

"Is there a convenient time we might meet?" Barstow asked. "There are things to discuss. I've come over from New Bedford."

When Ida made no answer, those two small, vertical lines Ida remembered appeared between Barstow's brows. "You understand you're heir to half this business?"

Well, Ida hoped so. And no doubt Henry Barstow was heir to the other half, which was likely why he was here—to secure his assets. And just what were these assets? Ida looked around. The sign that now leaned against the wall had cracked down the middle; two sodden ledgers had been opened and spread on a crate in front of the stove to dry; a tin bucket had been placed on the top shelf where the ledgers had been stored to capture the steady drip from the roof, new since the thaw; and the stove did indeed smoke badly. Behind her was a pile of junk and behind that was a warehouse full of more junk, upstairs were two rooms full of mice, and on the seafloor sat the charred remains of the *Cormorant*. But Vineyard Haven was becoming a popular destination, not just for members of the marine trade but for tourists; the two less than prime buildings still sat on a prime Main Street lot and had to be worth something.

"Now," Ida said. "Now would be convenient."

Barstow laid the wet ledgers on the floor and upended the crate to serve as his own perch, leaving the desk chair to Ida. She sat down. "You knew they were on the *Portland*?"

Barstow nodded.

"I came here to try to find out if the *Cormorant* was insured."

"Yes. I've been looking for just such a document."

"Meaning, *no*?"

Barstow nodded again. He rose from his crate, but before he reached his full height he returned to his seat. "One of the things we need to discuss is a potential complication."

"What." It pushed out of Ida's mouth untempered, impatient, leaving Barstow to peer at her in mild alarm.

"Perhaps this isn't the best time."

"*What*," Ida said again.

"First, we have to wait for the courts to declare the unrecovered *Portland* passengers dead. I went to Wellfleet—"

"As did I."

Barstow dropped his head down and to the side in a silent gesture that Ida took to mean acknowledgment of their shared torture. He lifted his head. Continued. "Second, when Mose and Ezra formed this company they drew up papers declaring fifty-fifty ownership, but if one were to die before the other, the other became full owner."

Well, that was nice, Ezra. "They died together."

"I'm fairly confident a court would say so, but again, we have to wait on that determination." Barstow looked closer at Ida but must not have seen anything approaching emotional collapse.

"You mean we can't sell today."

"This is how you see the future of this property? Sold?"

"I'm not planning to open an ice cream store, if that's what you mean."

There it was—the laughter in waiting. Barstow pointed at the ceiling. "If you have no objection, I thought I'd stay in Mose's apartment for a few days while I meet with a lawyer. Do you have one?"

"We need two?"

Barstow cleared his throat. "I don't know if you're aware of the Married Women's Property Act."

"No."

"It grants you title to half your husband's assets. I can't say which would take precedence here—the contract or the act, but you'd be wise to secure your own representation."

Well, that was fair. So why did Ida feel so unsettled? Because after two years of Ezra she wasn't used to fair.

"If you have no objection to my staying in the apartment—" Barstow continued.

"I don't, but you will once you see the apartment."

This time Barstow full-out smiled, and the smile rearranged his features so dramatically it startled Ida. She attempted to smile back, but her face resisted—she could feel it and see it in how quickly Barstow's own smile faded, could hear it in his next words: "Again, Mrs. Pease, my sympathies."

4

IDA PUSHED OPEN THE DOOR at the only *attorney* shingle she'd ever spied in Vineyard Haven. Malcolm Littlefield was not engaged, which was good and bad, Ida decided; good because she wanted this done with; bad because he didn't look overloaded with clients. He had the distracted air and indirect focus of one looking to get back to his papers, but Ida decided that was good; she sat down opposite him and told her tale with as few words as possible, which were more words than she'd realized; Littlefield answered her with even fewer.

"There have been no *Portland* survivors. The court will move to declare the missing dead, and barring any extenuating circumstances, it should be ruled they died at the same time. Your husband's property would then pass to his nearest kin in accordance with the law. Children?"

"No."

"Parents? Siblings?"

"An aunt only. A cousin."

Littlefield waved away Ruth and Hattie with a flick of the wrist. He wrote some words on a pad of paper. "Well then. Any children would share half the estate, but as there are none, your husband's property will be yours in the entirety. A farm, you say. And half of the business assets as you describe the terms of your husband's contract. But you'll have to wait on the courts."

"How long?"

Littlefield pointed to the wall behind him and an embossed

sign that Ida had overlooked. RULE YOUR IMPATIENCE; DON'T LET YOUR IMPATIENCE RULE YOU.

If Ida had noticed the sign when she'd entered, she'd have called it a *bad* sign.

IDA WAS OUT with the ox and wagon, forking up storm litter, when she looked up to see Ruth coming down the hill, alternately stabbing the ground and beating back the stray bull briars with her cane. She kept her eyes fixed on the track, an old woman unsure of her footing, and never saw Ida or the oxcart. She walked up to the house, twisted the doorknob without knocking, and let the wind push her in. Ida threw the pitchfork into the back of the wagon, hopped onto the seat, and *gee-ed* the ox back to the barn.

When Ida opened her kitchen door she found Ruth peering into her stockpot, her hair thrust into a halo of gray spikes by the wind.

"Nice of you to pay a call," Ida said.

"Family doesn't pay calls."

And since when were we family? thought Ida. She held out her hand for Ruth's coat, but Ruth pulled it tighter. "It's cold in here."

"It's always cold in here when there's a north wind."

"So you're leaving, are you?"

"Who told you that?"

"Didn't you just?"

"No, I didn't. Come nearer the stove, then."

Ida walked to the stove and after a moment Ruth followed. She sat down, pulled off her gloves finger by finger, shrugged off her coat, and unbuttoned the top button of her suit jacket, as if each move were part of a religious ritual.

"Tea?" Ida asked.

"I didn't come here to be fed. Sit."

Ida sat, relieved about the tea—one less thing for Ruth to find fault with.

"I came to see how you were managing."

"I'm fine."

"I know *you* are. Why wouldn't you be? I'm asking about the sheep."

"The sheep?"

"How you're managing the sheep."

"The same as I've managed them all the other times Ezra's been away."

"Except now Ezra's dead."

Yes. Now Ezra was dead. And so was any connection Ida may have had to Ruth, which had been not much of a connection in the first place. By Ruth's own admission on the day they'd met, she was not Ida's aunt. Thinking this, Ida felt something in her loosen.

"Which I mention only as a way of reminding you," Ruth went on. "Now there will be no end to Ezra's absence."

"Thank you," Ida said.

Ruth peered at her. "I never thought you one for . . . sheep."

"If you mean to say you never thought me one for Ezra, say so."

"Very well, Ezra then."

"But it doesn't matter now, does it?"

"The sheep do. You don't pretend you can manage them."

"I have been. More than I'd like."

"You see? That's just what I mean. It makes no sense you trying to keep it up. Lem Daggett knows his sheep; he can manage the farm for me."

"For you? Haven't you heard of the Married Women's Property Act?"

"No, and I don't need to, since this farm wasn't Ezra's property. He signed over the deed to me in January of ninety-six." She waited, watching, as if to see if Ida caught the significance of the date.

Oh, Ida caught it. In January of ninety-six Ezra had requested Ida's hand in marriage. But before or after he signed away the farm to Ruth?

Ruth peered at Ida. "Oh, don't fret so, dear. I've no intention of evicting you out of hand. Take your time. Make your plans. Find your place. Of course it would be nice to have Lem in by lambing."

Ida held up a hand, signaling the need to back up. She knew Ezra. He wouldn't have worked the farm for nothing. "If you own the farm, what did Ezra get for working it?"

"A percentage of the profits—wool sales in July, livestock sales in October. I confess I'm surprised Ezra hadn't told you, but apparently he felt farm matters didn't concern you."

When Ida said nothing Ruth stood up, eyes on Ida as she pulled on her coat, picked up her gloves, and worked each finger over her swollen knuckles. "As it doesn't concern you now."

IDA WENT TO THE WINDOW and watched the old woman up the hill, every stubborn vertebra stacked up tight. Fury roared through her. She wasn't so big a fool as to believe what Ruth told her outright, and the more she thought of it, the less likely it seemed that Ruth could be right. Never once had Ezra said . . . so many times Ezra had said . . . But just what *had* Ezra said? And what hadn't Ida heard—or cared to hear—in that sea fog of grief?

Ida went out and killed a chicken, bled it, plucked it, and hacked it up for a stew. She felt better. Of course it wasn't true. Ezra wouldn't. Ezra didn't. She could recall it now, the words *my farm* being uttered repeatedly. *I want to show you my farm . . . I get away whenever my farm lets me . . . This farm of mine . . .* But had he ever spoken those words after he proposed in January?

Ida went to the pantry for potatoes and onions and came face-to-face with Ezra's whiskey bottle, which brought her face-to-face with Ezra. What had started with *Ezra wouldn't* now turned into *why did he,* at worst outright lie, at best misrepresent, or far worse, plot. Ida was not a mercenary being, but neither was she a fool; to agree to marry a penniless man she barely knew was far different from marrying a propertied man at least able to keep a roof over her head.

Ida picked up the whiskey bottle and carried it into the kitchen. She sat down in front of the stove and poured herself a glass. She could feel her anger as if it were a thing, as if it were the whiskey burning down her throat. She remembered her wedding night and the freedom she'd felt at being able to relax into Ezra's touch, no longer worried about all those consequences for ruined women that never seemed to trouble a man. There had been a certain haste to the thing—it wasn't their first time, after all—but afterward Ezra had lain back and talked of his dreams: a bigger boat, a building on Main Street, maybe one in Boston. He talked of *their* farm, she was sure he did—of the prize-winning flock *they* would raise. "Wool's come to nothing," he'd said. "But good breeding stock, there's the market. We'll do well next fall, I promise you. And the fall after that, even better. I've got my eye on a ram that will put us on the top of the pile." *We'll. Us.*

Staring at a cloudy image of her face in the whiskey bottle Ida remembered another conversation. Ezra had wanted Ida to paint their portraits, portraits that would hang side by side over the mantel. Ida had disliked the idea of a self-portrait, but she'd intended to paint Ezra; she'd sat him in the chair in front of the bookcase wearing his best coat and tie and done a series of sketches, but none of them pleased her. She'd gone so far as to study her own face in the mirror, but she'd done it in the middle of a workday, with the unraveling topknot, the smoky eyes, the fire-reddened cheeks, and could only think of the portrait she'd done of Mrs. McKinley, how proud Ida had been to capture the iciness of her silk and the warmth of her pearls. How few qualms she'd felt at taking a vain, exceedingly rich woman and painting her exactly as she wished to be painted. The Mrs. McKinleys were the people who had portraits done; what business did a farmer's wife have sitting inside a frame over the mantel? Yet Ida had liked that Ezra wanted her portrait hung there, and for a time she'd even believed it meant love, but later she came to see it was nothing but camouflage, deflection, an easy trade of words for what he really wanted, which was . . . what? Well, her money.

For there were the facts. Either just before Ezra had proposed marriage to Ida he'd been forced to sell the farm and was desperate for the money—her money—to buy it back; or just *after* he'd asked Ida for her hand he'd made sure the farm would stay in the Pease family should something happen to him. And if the latter were the case, it got worse; soon—too soon—after their marriage, Ezra had arranged the sale of the town house in Boston, effectively leaving Ida without a home on this earth.

Could it be true?

Ida set down her glass, got up, and slashed at the potatoes and onion. She put the stew on the stove. It couldn't be true. She forced herself to call up what she'd believed to be real gentleness in Ezra's eyes as he'd asked her about her parents, her brothers; she dug out a moment when a Boston hack had splashed her skirt and he'd mopped her up with his handkerchief; she stood waiting until she could recall the feel of Ezra's strong arm around her as they made their way back to the house in a sudden

hailstorm. She remembered his greeting: *Well, my lovely girl . . .*
But why would Ruth lie about something that would come to
light as soon as Henry Barstow executed the will?

Henry Barstow.

Ida fetched her whiskey, took another swig, and put in a call
to the salvage company, or rather, put in a call to Hattie, as Hattie seemed to see it.

"How are you faring, Ida? Are you managing all right?"

"Managing fine."

"It's hard, I know."

"Everything's hard. Are you ringing the salvage company?"

"If you're looking for that Barstow, he's gone back to New
Bedford. Or going. I'm not sure which."

"Well then, why don't you put through the call and we'll find
out?"

Silence. It had never been Ida's way to pick a fight with Hattie,
and Ida felt she could hear something like shock in the silence,
but eventually Hattie put through the call. Even so, the idea of
Henry Barstow in New Bedford had worked its way into Ida's
head so successfully that she was startled when a voice said,
"Henry Barstow."

"This is Ida Pease."

"Mrs. Pease! I was about to ring you. I'll be leaving for New
Bedford in the morning and I wanted to drop off some funds in
case of an emergency expense. Is there a convenient—?"

"Now," Ida said. "Now is convenient."

SHE WATCHED HIM come up the track and stop at the pasture
fence to stare out at the sheep, the animals ghostly in the near
dark. She opened the door babbling.

"You like sheep?"

"I'm not sure *like* is the word."

"Then you don't like sheep."

"I don't mind them singly, but in the aggregate—" He held wide the lapel of a wool jacket and smiled. "I don't mean to sound ungrateful."

Perhaps it was the fact that his hair had lost its part in the wind, but for the first time Ida saw a flash of Mose. The brother walked to the kitchen table, dropped an envelope onto it, and gave it a tap.

"Something for the day-to-day. I'm afraid for anything more significant you'll need to apply to me."

"You leave in the morning?"

"I'll be back as soon as I can." He paused. "I wondered while I'm here if I might ask you a few questions."

"If I'm allowed to ask one."

"Of course."

Ida led the way to the parlor, forgetting that she'd left the whiskey bottle sitting on the table; she picked it up as if she'd set it out in expectation and said, "May I offer you a drink?"

"Thank you."

They sat on either side of the stove, the shadows exaggerating the planes and angles in Barstow's face, turning him back to the stranger. He took a drink.

"I've just received some upsetting news from Ezra's aunt." Ida explained and watched those double worry lines that Mose never seemed to have sprouted resume their place.

"I'm afraid—"

"Don't be. Tell me. Did Ezra own the farm or didn't he?"

"The farm isn't listed among his assets. But I'll check into it, Mrs. Pease." Barstow took a long swallow. Ida reached over and refilled his glass. She filled hers; if Barstow was shocked at this, it didn't show in his face. But something did.

"You had questions?"

"I did. But if you have others—"

"One other, yes. If I have no claim to this farm, if there's no boat and therefore no business, if the Main Street buildings are going to be tied up waiting on a couple of court rulings, what recourse do I have?"

"If by recourse you mean cash, this is exactly what I wished to talk to you about."

"Meaning there is none."

"Meaning there appears to be very little."

Ida thought. "It was my family money that bought the boat and buildings. I knew nothing of either purchase until after the fact. He claimed at the time he was temporarily cash-strapped, but that the job in Maine would put it right."

"What do you know about this job in Maine?"

Again, Ida had to think. What *did* she know about it? Not enough. In truth, she was beginning to see she hadn't known enough about anything. "A salvage job. A cargo of tin, I think. Or zinc. In Passamaquoddy Bay." At least these were a few of the words she'd gleaned in passing. "Didn't Mose ever speak of it?"

A pause, steeped in regret. "Mose and I hadn't spoken much of late."

Ida went to the desk and pulled out Ezra's letter with its mention of the Maine job. It should have taken Barstow a few seconds to digest it, but he seemed unable to remove his eyes from the page. Then again, it was probably the last mention of a living brother that he would ever see.

Ida took a good sip of whiskey and filled their glasses again. She'd felt the first glass as a looseness in her limbs; she felt the second as an expansion, a warming, an illumination inside her head. While she was up she went to the kitchen to check on the stew—it had taken on enough character to be presentable. "I don't know what you've been doing for meals," she called, "but if you'd like to share this—"

"It smells wonderful. Thank you, yes."

"Bring the whiskey."

Barstow brought the whiskey. Ida set it on the kitchen table, laid out two bowls, the bread board, the crock of butter. She motioned to Barstow to sit but with a half bow he indicated that she should do so first; the gesture was one Mose had often used, but in Mose it had always read as jest. Mose. At the salvage company Henry Barstow had offered his sympathies—twice—but what had Ida said? Nothing. She set down her spoon. "I'm sorry I didn't say it before. How sad I am about your brother."

Barstow looked up from his stew and nodded once, a short, businesslike nod, the kind her father and brothers would have used before moving the talk along, as if in danger of being pushed over a precipice.

"I liked him," Ida said. "And that means more than you might think, since I didn't like my own husband much." She could hear the whiskey in her voice. Her words. She attempted a laugh that came out like something torn. "I wonder how many widows say *that*."

"Perhaps not many, but I'd guess a few think it."

Ida said, "Did your wife ever get her portrait?"

Barstow's eyes widened. "You remember that? As it happens, she didn't." But there Barstow changed the subject, asking about the leased office in Boston, of which Ida knew little beyond its existence; about where to get some roof shingles, of which Ida knew a lot, having had to arrange for repair of the barn roof the previous winter; about what had happened to the Mayhew boy who fell overboard Monday, of which Ida knew nothing. He asked, and she told, of her old home on Beacon Hill in Boston, but her words felt cold, detached, the things that had once warmed the place now dead. She asked and discovered that he'd left the island years before to open a carriage shop in New Bedford, but something about that topic seemed to trouble him; again, the double lines between his brows; again, he found another topic. He waved at the empty walls. "I see nothing of your work."

"The sheep consume my time these days. Singly and in the aggregate."

Barstow smiled, and sure enough, Ida felt the corners of her mouth lift in answer. She took a breath, allowing her smile to widen. It felt so good, so comfortable. What was it in this man that made her feel that she could be herself? But in the next minute Ida was shocked to feel the first burn of tears since Ezra's death. *Why?* Because she couldn't remember when she'd last felt comfortable with Ezra. Because an old and searing loneliness had just blasted through her. Because she'd finally said the words out loud and to a near stranger: *I didn't like my own husband much.*

5

IDA GAVE THE EWE ANOTHER DRENCH. Others—Ezra surely, Lem probably—wouldn't have bothered, but Ida found herself reluctant to give up. She wasn't sentimental about the flock—she was already too much the farmer's wife for that—but she'd had enough of death. The animal lay in the straw without struggle, not a good sign, and after Ida emptied the horn she walked out into the hay field to gaze out at the Sound and think. She'd gotten as far as acknowledging that Ezra had probably intentionally deceived her about the farm, when she spied movement along the track and heard a distant song. *Oh, Shenandoah, I love your daughter, Way—aye, you rolling river . . .* The song stopped just as Ida was able to recognize Henry Barstow's long, effortless gait, but as he drew close she knew by looking at him. "The farm is Ruth's," she preempted.

"The title was transferred to Ruth Pease on January the seventeenth 1896."

And when had Ezra pledged his troth? How odd that Ida couldn't remember either the proposal itself or the date of it. It had been after the New Year and before the second of February, because Ezra had blown into the Boston town house declaring an ancient Candlemas tradition of betrothed couples always sharing a bed on that day. There had been a storm outside and a fire inside, and Ezra had entered so confident, so sure of his success, that Ida couldn't summon enough energy to resist. Oh, she'd made a feeble attempt. If her parents had been alive, of course, he'd have been summarily ejected, but she was alone in the house with no one but the maid, and the maid had wandered off somewhere as soon as Ezra entered.

"Hold, now," he'd said to Ida when she stepped back, raised her hands to fend him off. "You can't be thinking of turning me out into *that*?" He pointed at the window, where wind and rain assaulted the glass hard enough to make it rattle. He took off his coat. Ida remembered that—he took off his coat—and then she remembered nothing until she was standing in front of the fire in her corset and Ezra was lifting the corset cover over her head even as Ida was protesting that they weren't yet wed and Ezra laughed and said *If you think I'm waiting on that now* and Ida distinctly recalled thinking that if they made a child before the wedding her parents would surely eject her from the house and where would she ever go and then she remembered that her parents were dead and by that time Ezra had unhooked her corset and was kissing her naked breast . . .

As if reading her thoughts Henry Barstow said, "You weren't Ezra's wife at that date."

Ida flushed so violently Barstow peered at her in concern. "Are you all right, Mrs. Pease?"

"Yes, of course."

"I only mean to say if you'd been married on the seventeenth of January you'd have had to sign the deed too."

"I see. Yes. But it doesn't matter. I've decided to go back to Boston as soon as I get packed." Of course it wasn't so much a decision as an acknowledgment of the facts. Without a home or an inclination or an attachment, with the hinges on her paint box about to rust shut, what on earth could keep her where she was?

"How?" Barstow asked.

"How?"

"I mean to say, with what? Until the property issue is settled—"

"Are you telling me I don't even have enough money for the boat?"

"The boat, yes, but then what? Looking at the records, it appears your Beacon Hill property was sold soon after your marriage. Where would you live? How would you pay for food and clothing?" He locked, it appeared, at her waist, where she'd cinched her skirt with an old, frayed, purple belt, the only one with enough holes to accommodate her shrinking waistline; since Ezra's death she'd hardly bothered about food. Ida pulled her jacket closed over the gap.

"I'll do my best to settle the estate as soon as possible," Henry continued, "but realistically—"

Ida raised a hand to stop him. She turned around and set off for the house, Ruth's house, where it appeared she was now trapped.

FOOL. TO HAVE MARRIED A MAN she knew so little. To have lived with him for over two years and learned even less. Ida climbed the stairs to the room she'd shared with him and opened the closet. At least she knew his clothes: the suit she'd once admired, the oiled jacket she'd once worn, the nightshirt with which she'd been intimate. She began to pull clothes off the shelf and toss them onto the floor. She might be trapped here but she wasn't trapped forever; when she was able to leave she wanted to be ready, not to waste a night or a day or an hour attempting to sort through Ezra's mess. She pulled her trunk from the closet and faced the rows of pegs, too many of them filled with Ezra's things; she plucked up the vest she'd last seen him wear standing on the deck of the *Cormorant* waving good-bye . . . to Chester Luce. Only now, gazing backward at that misty image, did she realize she'd never been centrally positioned in his focus.

Focus. That's what she should be doing, focusing on her life, not on Ezra's death. She whirled and stormed across the hall to her studio, established with some mild objection from Ezra in the northeast corner chamber, but as a year and then two went by without children, he'd ceased to grumble over the wasted space. She pulled her paint box off the shelf, determined to reclaim something of the day, to recall something of who she was before her life became as peripheral to the dead Ezra as it had to the living one. A bowl of apples, a pair of brass candlesticks, and three worn-out old books piled irregularly one atop the other sat in the middle of the table; she'd sketched in the objects but recalled deciding to wait for stronger light before attempting to introduce paint and had never gone back. Now the late-day light burnished the candlesticks and highlighted the apples, picked up the gold letters on the spines of the books. She could do this now. She should do this now. She thought of the bowl of lilies her mother had placed on the card table in the foyer, and how pleased she'd been that Ida seemed to have captured their exact purpose, which was to stop visitors with the beauty of the lilies, then draw the eye from the golden bowl to the gold inlay on the table. But what was the purpose of this mishmash of objects sitting idly in the center of an old, scarred table, the apples already shriveled, wasted, sacrificed to Ida's pretentions to paint? She returned her paint box to the shelf.

WHEN IDA CHECKED on the ewe the next morning, it was dead. She called Lem to do the butchering—a chicken was one thing, a sheep was another—and by the time Lem arrived

Ida was deep in preparation to paint the pie cupboard. She'd donned one of Ezra's shirts, wrestled the cupboard onto an old sheet, scraped it free of its chips and flakes, and pried the cover off a tin of brick-red paint she'd found in the barn. Lem peered into the can with her.

"Not exactly what I thought you'd be painting."

Ida made no answer. She dipped her brush and drew it over the vertical face of the cupboard; as the fumes reached her she crossed the room and opened the window. The sharp December air whipped into the kitchen, carrying with it the sound of wind and sea and sheep—not the high-pitched sound of fear or pain or panic, but the mid-range sound of normal sheep-to-sheep conversation. Yes, in her two years on the farm she'd learned something about how sheep talked.

"Has Ruth ever spoken to you about the farm?" Ida asked Lem.

"Now and then."

"And did you know it's her farm? That she wants me out and you in to manage it?"

"Not all of that."

Ida slapped her brush down, wiped her hands on Ezra's shirt, and stepped up closer to Lem so he'd be sure to see the churning black in her pupils. "How much of it?"

"I knew Ezra'd deeded the farm to Ruth in exchange for a loan. She wouldn't lend the money otherwise. Figured he'd buy it back when he could."

"And you never saw fit to tell me this?"

"Not my business, Ida."

"Even after Ezra drowned."

"Assumed you knew." He paused. "My wife, I'd have told her."

Lem had been widowed for twenty years; once in Ida's presence Ezra had teased him about marrying again, but Lem had cut him short. "If you can't match what was, why go backward?" Yes, he would have told that shadowy, matchless woman the exact state of his affairs up front.

Ida opened the turpentine jar and dropped the paintbrush in it. She put the top on the paint can and hammered it closed. Spots of brick red flew onto her shirt and onto the wall behind the cupboard. Lem picked up the rag, dipped it in the jar of turpentine, and wiped off the wall. He handed it back. "Put the rag on top of the can before you hammer it next time." He headed for the door but paused. "If I knew you didn't know—" He stopped.

"What, Lem? What would you have done?"

"I don't know, Ida, and that's the truth of it. I just don't."

6

IDA HAD LONG GROWN SICK of mutton by the time Henry Barstow returned. She'd walked into town, heading for Bradley's harness shop to get a halter repaired, but was diverted by a group gathered on the shoreline. A crisp breeze chilled her west-facing nose but the sun in the east warmed the back of her neck; Ida decided to linger. Numerous vessels still lay scattered along the shore but fewer than at first; even now a crew was at work digging out around a schooner, no doubt in hope of her lifting with the next good tide. Another group stood with their eyes fixed on the middle of the harbor where a salvage lighter sat parked. Ida picked out Chester Luce at the fringe of the group and walked up. She pointed to the lighter.

"They're refloating the *Addie Todd,*" Luce said. "They salvaged the cargo of lumber, and the divers are down there patching the hull now. They'll start pumping her out soon." He didn't seem to have much more to say to Ida, and as no one else did either, she walked on to the harness shop and left the halter, too distracted to remember to ask when it might be done. She was thinking instead of the windfall that would have come to Ezra and Mose if they'd stayed put in Vineyard Haven. After they bought the *Cormorant* they'd shelled out three hundred and fifty dollars for pump, compressor, pipes, and a diving suit for Mose, but not three days later they'd raised a large coasting vessel and made back the whole sum plus a fifty-dollar profit. Soon after that they'd salvaged a cargo of tar and been paid 60 percent of its value. A bronze bell got them twenty-five dollars, an anchor and chain another hundred. In the slow times Mose had worked as diver-for-hire at five dollars a day and added that to the coffers, and those were just the sums Ida had heard about. How could all of that have been lost at cards? Ida considered the long evenings she'd spent alone. Easy enough.

Ida headed home by the main road. As she passed the salvage office she could hear singing, muffled through door and walls but clearly Henry. She paused outside until she'd identified the tune:

> Well, I had an old hen and she had a wooden leg,
> Just the best old hen that ever laid an egg,
> She laid more eggs than any hen on the farm,
> But another little drink wouldn't do her any harm . . .

"Turkey in the Straw." Ida smiled; she pushed open the door. Henry had managed to get the stove to stop smoking and had dried out what needed drying, returning it to the shelves, but the junk still sat in a pile although it looked to be a neater pile. Beyond the pile, a bicycle leaned against the wall.

A *bicycle*?

Henry followed Ida's gaze. "It's a beauty, isn't it?"

"I . . . yes."

"Do you ride?"

"Yes . . . no . . . that is . . . I want—" She wanted to ride a bicycle. She was suddenly, desperately determined to learn to ride a bicycle. Once Ida had been on the dock when a group of women with bicycles had wheeled off the boat and spun down the road; they were dressed alike in flat straw hats, close-fitting jackets with leg-o-mutton-sleeves, skirts that fell just above the ankle, and gaiters. She'd gazed after them until they'd turned the corner, not one faltering or falling, and she could still summon the image of them sweeping away from her—upright, confident, smiling. *Free.*

Ida pulled her eyes from the gleaming machine and whirled on Henry Barstow. "I want to learn to do it."

Barstow gave Ida a thoughtful look. He pulled the bicycle out from the wall and pointed out its features: leather seat, curved handlebars, and the latest innovation—coaster brakes. "You see?" He used his hand to roll the pedals forward—go—and backward—brake. He leaned the bicycle back again the wall, went to the stove and poured out a coffee that came thick and black from a pot, as if it had been sitting on the stove for days. He offered it to Ida. He began to talk, more than Ida had heard him talk yet—of his carriage shop in New Bedford, of how the automobile would soon put a crimp in his business, of how he'd begun to add bicycles to his inventory, of which bicycles were best, of the various features of each. Some of it Ida bothered to follow and some of it she didn't, but she liked the sound of his voice—that deep, male richness that she'd come to miss. Or perhaps it wasn't the maleness that she liked—it wasn't often of late that she'd enjoyed the sound of Ezra's voice—but the calmness in it. It told Ida she could relax and be herself in its presence. But of course there was also the heat of the stove and the coffee burning seductively down her throat . . .

Henry switched to talk of their mutual affairs. He still needed to inventory the warehouse but he'd received the valuation on the property itself; he began to sift through the papers on the desk looking for it, the golden hairs on the backs of his hands glinting in the light, but as Ida watched him deftly peel back sheet after sheet she remembered another encounter she'd once had with Henry Barstow.

*   *   *

IDA AND EZRA had walked into town for a rare dinner out at the Bayside and it had been a lovely evening, one of those times when Ezra had seemed like the Ezra of their courtship. He'd reached across the table to feed her an oyster, made a fuss of wiping her lips with his napkin, even rested his hand over hers, right out in the open, right on the tabletop. She remembered looking down at their joined hands on the starched white cloth and thinking that maybe it *would* be all right.

And then. Tracking backward, Ida could now see that her marriage hadn't gone wrong in one great avalanche—it had been more like the steady drip of snowmelt off a spring roof. That evening, that particular drip, had as its catalyst Tully Mayhew, just back from California and hailing Ezra through the restaurant window; with him were Mose and Henry Barstow. Ezra leaped up, ran into the street, slapped and laughed with Tully, and then returned to the table. "Tully Mayhew's back!" he told Ida, as if this was news she'd been waiting on for weeks. "They're headed for Duffy's. You don't mind, do you?"

"Mind what?"

"My going to Duffy's, Ida," Ezra said, as if speaking to a child. "We've finished dinner." Ezra peeled off bills and laid them on the table. He lifted his eyes and caught Ida's look. "What is it? The city girl wants me to walk her home? All right, let's get along."

"Go," Ida said. She pulled another bill out of Ezra's hand. "I'm going to have coffee. And dessert."

"You've got coffee and pie at the house."

"Yes, I do, but right now I'm in the mood for someone else's coffee. And cake."

Ida turned to signal the waitress and by the time she'd turned again, Ezra had left.

*   *   *

IDA ORDERED a piece of yellow cake with butter frosting and a cup of coffee and another cup after that. She watched the few other diners—a table of six men, strangers to Ida, likely off one of the ships in the harbor, and a husband and wife she recognized who lived cut along the county road but whose names, if she'd ever known them, had long escaped her. She gazed at the lanterns on the anchored boats, fighting the jangle of the coffee, attempting to stay unruffled. Calm. Ezra was right—they *had* finished dinner, and they would never stay to order dessert when Ida had an apple pie in the pie cupboard at home; neither did it made sense for Ezra to walk up the hill only to walk back down again a minute later. Even so, it rankled a special night turned into a contentious one.

Ida must have been sitting there longer than she'd thought because Henry Barstow passed the window, looked in, saw her still sitting there, and stopped dead. He came in.

"I'm surprised to see you here. Ezra said you'd gone home. Is everything all right?"

"I've been enjoying the view."

"Ah." He turned to look out with her.

"You weren't long at Duffy's," Ida said.

"I try to exit with my dignity intact." He smiled. "And my pocketbook."

"Ah. Ezra never minds leaving those things behind."

"Or his wife?" Barstow looked away, looked back. "I'm sorry. It's not my place to—"

"He wanted to walk me home. I told him I wished to stay on a bit, watch the lights come up on the ships. But now I'm ready to go." Ida pushed back her chair and stood at the exact minute Barstow reached to help and Ida knocked into his arm, scattering some papers he'd been carrying. She leaned over to help collect the pages but by the time she'd gotten there he'd already deftly sorted them into a neat sheaf.

He straightened. "May I walk you home?"

The little dance with the papers had left them standing so close Ida imagined she could feel the heat from the lantern light reflected in his eyes. *Extraordinary,* he'd said in Boston, referring to her painting of Mrs. McKinley. On a few occasions, usually late and in the dark, Ida had wondered what he'd found so extraordinary about that work. Now she imagined them discussing it as they climbed the hill side by side, one of those deft hands under her elbow as they walked . . .

"No," Ida said. "No thank you."

"Please. I'm not just playing the gentleman. I've been hoping for a chance to talk to you about commissioning a painting."

Ida felt her shoulders ease. A commission. No one could fault her for accepting a walk and a talk over a commission. And besides, who was there to fault her—the six strangers off the ships? The couple from out along the county road had long gone. Ida and Barstow set off down the street, side by side, step synced to step.

IDA HAD ALREADY LEARNED that October on the Vineyard was never one thing—the sun could bake them one day and the wind could frost the grass the next. It was true the sun had already sunk, leaving nothing behind but a diffuse gold band at the very rim of the earth that flickered and dimmed with each step they took, but the wind was still soft and halfhearted, tipping the occasional leaf and then retreating to the treetops. Neither spoke, but neither seemed to mind; when Ida slowed to look at an early star, Henry stopped and looked with her. Without the forward motion Ida grew aware again of how close together they stood; she resumed walking at a quicker pace.

"You wanted to speak to me about a commission," she said.

Henry didn't speak for so long, she began to think she'd misunderstood him at the restaurant. "Mose and I grew up on a farm in Chilmark," he said at last. "We had a good time on that farm when we were boys. But once we began to grow into ourselves we couldn't wait to get out, get off, get on that boat. And before I managed to book a return trip, my father died." Barstow cleared his throat. "Before he died, a photographer came to the farm and took a picture of my father working in the orchard. The photograph is fading out and there are other folks in it I don't care about. I wonder—could you paint my father in his orchard?"

"I do studio portraits," Ida said. "I don't know about an orchard."

"It's mostly my father I want. Will you look at the photograph, at least?"

"Of course."

They'd reached the track. The growing dark had brought out more stars but concealed the ground—not that the second part mattered since Ida was looking up at the stars anyway—but of course she would trip, and there it was, the hand under her elbow, light but firm, warm even through her sleeve.

"Whoa! Mind your feet."

Ida fixed her eyes on the ground and picked up her pace once more, which separated elbow from hand. "Do you miss the Vineyard?" she asked.

"On nights like this," Barstow said. He looked up at the sky as if to demonstrate the parts he missed and *he* tripped, but with no steadying hand at his elbow he went all the way down, measuring his whole long length in the dirt.

Ida bent over him. "Are you hurt?"

Henry didn't answer, mostly, it would appear, because he was laughing. *Laughing.* If that had been Ezra he'd have bolted upright cursing the invisible root that had tripped him, the loose boot heel the cobbler hadn't fixed properly, or Ida for whatever she'd said that had distracted him from minding his step or for tripping him up in the first place or just for bearing witness.

But when Henry stopped laughing and still didn't move, Ida grew concerned. "Do you need help?"

"All kinds, no doubt, but I believe I see the Big Dipper emerging. God's breath! Was that a shooting star or am I suffering from concussion? But as the odds are slim that you're going to join me down here in the dirt I'd best get up." He jackknifed upright, reclaimed her arm, pulled it through his, and locked it there with the opposite hand. "Now if I fall you go with me," he said.

Ida laughed, and she laughed again, all alone, after he'd left her at her door, thinking of that ridiculously long shape lying in the dirt and grinning up at the stars, regretting not lying down in the dirt with him.

NOW, AT THE SALVAGE OFFICE, watching Henry Barstow's hands a second time, remembering that other night and the feel of those hands, Ida flushed and stood up.

Henry stopped shuffling his papers. "Must you go? I'd hoped to repay you for that dinner."

"No," Ida said. "No thank you."

SHE WAS LONELY, that was all it was. But how dangerous, this loneliness! The last time she'd felt this lonely she'd run off and married a sheep farmer, and not a month ago she'd said to him, with as much feeling as she'd ever said anything to anyone: *Go. Stay there forever.* Now he *was* gone forever. Ida had seldom been lonely when Ezra was gone for a week at a time, the peace overriding any other emotion, but now the permanence of this new state left her feeling hollow, unstable, vulnerable, as if she'd never weathered a storm or chased off a fox or corralled an ornery sheep. She lay in bed remembering how Ezra used to rest his hand on her hip as they slept, remembering the hot weight of that hand and how content, how anchored she'd felt lying under it. She remembered how he'd smelled of what he'd eaten and drunk and worn and done and smoked, the smell of his life and parts of hers. She missed that smell. Certainly if she could miss a man's smell, she must have loved him once? Must have been able to forgive him once? But to deceive her about a late night at Duffy's was one thing; to deceive her about the farm, to deceive her with *Ruth* . . .

Ida got up and went downstairs, as restless as a ewe about to lamb. What had Lem said? Ezra had signed over the deed to Ruth, yes, but he'd planned to buy it back. With Ida's money, no doubt. So why hadn't he? On their marriage, Ezra had been disgusted to find the Beacon Hill house heavily mortgaged; perhaps its sale and Ida's family money hadn't been enough for the farm and the boat and the business on Main Street, and he'd chosen to leave her homeless in the event of his death versus sacrificing his dream. In fairness, Ezra hadn't chosen to die on the *Portland,* hadn't chosen to leave Ida dependent on Ruth for her shelter, and yet Ida had to wonder now if she'd ever been anything but money to her husband. She thought back to the day they'd met, to Ezra's eyes fixing on hers from all the way across the room, and again wondered—had they fixed on her heart or on her locket?

Ida circled to the desk, sat down, and rolled back the lid. She began to paw through the cubbyholes, looking for the only letters Ezra had ever written her, composed during that brief spell after their meeting when she was in Boston and he had returned to the island. There weren't many letters, the meager number exhibiting how precipitous the courtship had been, the contents exhibiting that she'd been an easy enough mark. *I wish you were here,* he wrote in one. *I see your eyes whenever I close mine,* he wrote in another. *Come,* he wrote finally, as if he were commanding Bett, and she'd come, left home and career and what few friends she'd managed to keep after sinking into the solitude of her grief.

Ida combed through the rest of the papers in the desk: the farm book; a collection of business cards; the papers for the ram; some marine outfitter's catalogs; bills and receipts; a sheet of letter paper, blank except for a *Dear Sirs* written across the top in Ezra's hand before, presumably, he'd been interrupted. This was why she felt suspended, she realized; Ezra's old world was still here, still intact, still waiting for him to return and finish his letter. What Ida needed was a good clear-out, a nice, deep line in the sand marking where she would leave the past and move into the future, whatever her future was.

Ida stuffed the business cards back in their cubbyhole in case she might find need of them. She saved the papers on the ram, the farm book, and the bills and receipts, but she took the letters and the catalogs and threw them on the floor next to the stove to use when lighting the next fire. She climbed the stairs and approached the closet again, ready now to face it. When her father and brothers died she'd given their clothes to a neighbor; when her mother died she'd kept her clothes and jewelry for herself, even the things that didn't fit, even those she'd ruined with failed alterations. She wanted nothing of Ezra's; she would ask Lem if he wanted anything, and if he didn't, she'd take them to the Seamen's Bethel to be donated to the shipwrecked sailors.

Ida opened the trunk that still sat in the middle of the room and spread her town clothes out on the bed. She began to fill it with Ezra's clothing, shoes first, soles facing, as her mother had taught her, but when she got to the oiled jacket and wool sweater she rethought her decision to keep nothing—she'd already put those items to good use and might do so again. She folded the sweater on the shelf and hung the jacket back on its peg along with the best of her town clothes; she would spend her free time cleaning and mending them, getting them ready for Boston. She attempted to shove the trunk back into the closet until she could engage Lem and his wagon, but the trunk was heavier now that it was full of Ezra's things, and she shoved it so hard it slammed into the rear wall, popping loose a piece of paneling. Ida pulled off her shoe, intending to bang the panel back into place, but as she bent low she saw that a piece of newspaper had been stuffed in behind the paneling. Ida lifted it out and felt something heavy inside. Lumpy. She unfolded it and a half dozen pebbles rolled out into her hand—rough, heavy, glittering. Too heavy. Too glittering. Too . . . *gold.*

know you'll find gold. You don't know you'll even live to get there."

"Lord, I never knew a woman to argue so hard against being rich. Well, you can thank me when I get back from the Yukon."

Ida tried again over dinner. In bed. In the morning. She talked about the farm—Ezra's family farm—with a warmth she didn't feel, with a panic she did feel. She questioned the man who had asked Ezra and Mose along. *Who is he? How well do you know him? What if he takes your money and disappears?*

Looking back, Ida could barely believe she'd pushed on for so long, but at some point—Ida could no longer remember exactly what point—she'd stopped arguing, which allowed Ezra to stop arguing and proceed with his plans unimpeded, until one day Ida had overheard Mose and Ezra in their own argument, Mose questioning the dangers and expense of the journey, the character of the man from Duffy's, the probability of actually finding gold. Ezra responded as if he'd never heard such concerns before, first incredulously, then angrily, but the subject of the Klondike disappeared from his conversation.

NOW IDA STOOD half in and half out of the closet, fingering the nuggets. Ezra and Mose had not gone to the Yukon; where then had this gold come from? And why did Ezra feel the need to hide it behind a wood panel in the closet? Not to hide it from thieves, since Ezra left his pocketbook on the bedside table and the door unbolted at night. Was he hiding it from Mose, the gold come out of some salvage job and Ezra didn't want to fork over his partner's share? Or perhaps he was hiding it from creditors—Henry Barstow had said there wasn't as much money as there should be, and maybe here was some of that money.

Or maybe he was just hiding it from Ida.

Ida's thoughts had stalled there when a violent knocking erupted below. She peered out the window: Ruth, beating on her door with her stick. Ida hurried down and got there before the wood splintered; Ruth fell into the house red-faced from exertion. Or ire.

"I'd like to know when you started locking doors!"

"The day I realized I didn't have to leave it open for Ezra anymore." In fact, Ida had started locking the door the day she'd watched from the oxcart as Ruth opened it and walked in.

"Yes. Well. That's just about the very subject I've come to talk about." She pushed through to the parlor stove and sat down. Ida gave some thought to not following, but she did discover a stirring of something that was half curiosity and half alarm. What was Ruth cooking up now? She joined Ruth at the stove.

"It's almost a month and we still haven't marked my nephew's passing. Even those Barstows who never ever did a proper funeral for their parents, even that Barstow fellow put a nice notice in the paper for his brother."

"What notice?"

"'Moses Judah Barstow, late of Vineyard Haven, always with us.' I've waited on you this long but no more. I talked to the Reverend Beetle and the service is set for Friday at one o'clock. I'm here as a courtesy, asking your preference on hymns and any words you'd like spoken. You have no folk and not much I can see in the way of friends, but there are people on this island who want to pay their respects to a good man gone and they'll have their chance Friday at one." She threw it out as a challenge, as if Ida planned to argue some part of that sentence, but Ida didn't. She could listen to Ruth's plans as if from a distance, as if it had nothing to do with her.

"I have no preference on hymns. Or words." She stood up. "Thank you for stopping by."

Ruth blinked. "We'll take the carriage. We'll pick you up at quarter to."

"I'd prefer to walk, thank you." Ida could feel the stillness inside herself, the kind of stillness that felt like a solid wall, but apparently Ruth felt no wall.

"The carriage will stop here at quarter to," she repeated.

IDA SAT ON THE BED, upright, clothed in black, two hands behind her propping her up. After a time it occurred to her that her hands touched the very spot where Ezra used to lie; she swiveled sideways and smoothed the coverlet over what might have been Ezra. Had been Ezra. She let her hand lie there, attempting to feel some remnant of him, attempting to feel some remnant of anything. She heard the carriage come and go, pictured Ruth's face set in an anger that turned to humiliation as she sat in church waiting for Ida to appear.

No. Ida didn't want to humiliate anyone, especially an old woman who wanted only to mourn her nephew in the company of her friends. Ida pushed herself off the bed, collected her cloak and a purse stuffed with a handkerchief useful both for wiping tears and hiding their absence, and set off.

The pews were full. Ida considered sitting quietly at the back, but the point was that Ruth see her there, that everyone else see her there with Ruth and Hattie: the widow. And besides, she'd seen Henry Barstow seated at the back, near the door, as if reserving for himself the option of exiting before the end of the service. Ida walked along the length of the aisle, eyes straight ahead, collecting whispers in her wake like the rustle of a silk gown. Hattie slid over to allow Ida room, but not enough room; each time Hattie inhaled and exhaled Ida felt the ebb and flow of it in her own shoulder and hip. She unclasped her bag, removed her handkerchief, and touched it to dry eyes.

The organ erupted into a hymn Ida didn't know. As it gasped its last the reverend stood and began a prayer Ida also didn't know, spoke words that described an Ezra she didn't know. The boy so full of life and laughter. The man so upright and strong and devoted to his family. The community leader responsible for a much-needed dredging of the harbor (for which he got well paid), the repair of the West Chop lighthouse (which guided him home), and the expansion of the Seamen's Bethel (for which he provided the lumber at well over cost). By the time the reverend had reached the part about the Bethel, Hattie's handkerchief was a wet, pulpy mass and her sniffing audible to the rafters. Ida opened her bag, jammed her handkerchief in and snapped it shut, the sound following Hattie's sniffs skyward.

Ida had always thought of grief as love cast adrift, something that haunted the living heart once it lost its object; she was therefore unsurprised when she could feel none of it sitting in that church. She did feel a hollowness that might be called sadness, but it was a sadness over what she'd let slip away of herself in her years of grief, in her years with Ezra, and she didn't know what to do with that.

Ida was brought out of her reverie as the service closed, as all island services closed, with a reading of Tennyson—*May there be no moaning of the bar when I put out to sea*—which could not by any stretch be said to apply to a man whose last breath had been choked out of him by frigid November sea water.

THEY STOOD OR SAT around Ruth's parlor, the guests on their arrival stopping in front of Ida where she sat in the chair nearest the door, but it was as if she sat above her chair and looked down on them all.

"That he should have been on that steamer," said Chester Luce, shaking his head at fate and moving on to Hattie, with whom it appeared he had a lot more to share.

"Condolences for your loss," said George Amaral, who ran a lobster boat out of Creekville. His wife, Rose, who managed the Seamen's Bethel, said, "Come by for a cup and a chat," before she seemed to catch something in Ida's face. "But only if you want to."

"Come along, Rose," her husband said.

Rose ignored him. "In fact, I'm trying to speak to all the island women about—"

"God's breath, Rose, you're not starting in with that voting rubbish at Ezra Pease's funeral."

"It's important that we women unite," Rose said, again ignoring him, but when her husband grabbed her arm she trailed away after him. "Do stop by," Rose said, and gave Ida's hand a squeeze, for which Ida felt briefly, unreasonably, grateful.

A plate of cake arrived; a cup of tea that Ida was forced to take up in her off hand, which caused her to spill it; she set both down and snatched up her purse, looking for that pristine handkerchief. When she finished dabbing at her skirt, she lifted her eyes and found Henry Barstow leaning against the doorjamb that led to the back porch. He knew. He alone of everyone in the room knew that her widow's weeds were a sham, that she was playing a stage part and poorly.

Ida fanned her face and pressed a palm to her forehead, signaling to anyone watching her need of air; she stepped onto the porch, feeling the eyes at her back as Henry followed her through.

"Did Mose or Ezra ever talk to you about going to the Klondike after gold?"

A look of confusion washed across Henry's face; not the subject he'd been expecting. "Ezra talked to me of the scheme," Ida continued. "I tried to talk him out of it. Later I heard Mose doing the same, but Ezra wasn't one to give up on an idea, especially a bad one. I got to wondering if they'd talked of it with you. Or better yet, if you'd found mention in those account books of a secret stash of gold." She smiled as if indicating a jest, but Henry didn't seem to follow. His smile went only halfway. But then again, they were at a funeral.

"No one talked to me of the Klondike. I found no mention of gold."

"Everything all right out here?" Lem spoke from behind Ida.

"Everything's all right," Ida said. "I grew overheated and now I'm overtired. If you would make my apologies, I believe I'll just slip quietly home."

"Let me—" Henry began.

"I'll take you home," Lem interjected.

Ida held up a hand to each. "Please. I only need air and quiet. Say nothing unless asked; most won't notice I'm gone."

She plunged down the steps and over the lawn. She could never have dared such a thing in Boston, she thought, and then amended; she *would* never have dared. Why? Because there she'd cared about everyone and what they thought; here, no one.

8

AFTER THE FUNERAL Ida began to have some trouble attending to things. She would be engaged in a task and something about it would draw off her thoughts; for example, one morning while scattering corn for the chickens and collecting the dwindling eggs she found her thoughts drifting to the ship that had perched on the beach like a setting hen; she began to wonder what was happening with the *Addie Todd*. She set off for the beach.

It was a bright but raw day, the wind shoving Ida from behind, the sunlight signaling her from the waves; the *Addie Todd* had still not appeared above the surface, but fewer people stood watching. Ida strolled near enough to collect the day's report without having to engage directly with anyone and learned that equipment trouble had delayed the operation.

"She'll be up by Christmas," one of the watchers predicted, and off Ida's mind went: Christmas.

Traditionally Ezra and Ida went to Ruth's for Christmas dinner, and Ida had learned early in her marriage that this invitation was not one to be negotiated, but surely if there were ever a year when Ida might be excused, this was it. So when Ruth presented her invitation Ida said, "Thank you, Ruth, but I've decided it would be best for me to stay at home this year."

"Very well," Ruth said. "But I hope you're not serving us mutton."

* * *

CHRISTMAS ALSO MEANT it was time to separate the ram from the ewes, a task Ida had never attempted before and didn't wish to now, for the simple reason that the beast always looked at her with a look of . . . well, hatred. She stared at him standing on a rise in the field, looking down his arrogant Grecian nose at Ida. He *was* handsome, she would admit—gorgeous, in fact— sturdy leg bones, strong shoulders, nice tight wool, bold, bright eyes well spaced on either side of a strong brow. All right, so she'd given the beast his due, and here he was already stamping the dirt at the sight of her. She collected Bett, opened the gate, pointed at the ram with her crook, and gave the dog the command to *shed;* Bett isolated the ram and drove him into the smaller paddock without trouble, but once in the paddock Ida noticed that the beast held one foot off the ground. Ida braced herself, slid through the paddock gate crook at the ready, and called to Bett to keep the ram cornered. The next thing she saw was sky. She scrambled to her feet and fled the paddock.

Lem came, looked without comment at Ida's muddy backside, removed a stone from between the ram's toes, and somehow managed to stay upright. Once safely out of the pen, they stood side by side admiring the ram, or rather Lem admired it and Ida glared at it.

"For an animal with such a pleasant job, you'd think he'd be better natured," Ida said.

That shocked the kind of full-bellied laugh out of Lem that Ida rarely heard, and hearing it now cheered her unreasonably. Her mind floated again. "Would you like to eat Christmas dinner with us?"

Lem twisted to look at Ida. "Well, yes, I guess I would. I'll bring punch."

Ruth had never served punch. Ida felt better at once.

* * *

HATTIE ARRIVED at seven A.M. in a ruffled flannel tea dress, her apron neatly folded under her arm, vegetable parer in hand. "Mother sent me to help." She stopped short just inside the kitchen door to drop her cloak onto the peg, and when she turned around her face was shimmering with tears. "I can't bear not having him here today. Do you remember last year? That song he made up about Hattie's hat? Sometimes it feels like I haven't laughed since."

Ida remembered no song about a hat. She remembered no laughing. But one thing was sure—there would be no laughing this year. Hattie began to attack the turnips, recalling other Ezra moments as she peeled, most of which predated Ida's marriage: Ezra teaching Hattie to play poker; Ezra taking her to catch herring at the creek; Ezra rowing her across Lagoon Pond; Ezra taking her aboard the *Cormorant* and allowing her to parade around in Mose's dive suit. That was when Ida knew that Hattie was in some Ezra world of her own devising—Mose had once told her the full dive kit weighed 150 pounds.

But in amongst her verbal creations Hattie managed to peel the turnips and apples, boil and mash the potatoes, and roll out the pastry for the pie, while Ida washed the turkey, chopped oysters and onions for the stuffing, set the cranberries to boil, soaked the soda crackers in milk for the pudding, set up another pan for the accompanying sauce of sugar and wine and nutmeg and raisins, and strained the stock for the clear soup that had been simmering since dawn.

Ruth was bringing the nuts.

WHEN LEM ARRIVED he claimed a spot on the stove for his punch, but even before it got poured into the cups, something went awry. Hattie had returned with Ruth, the former dressed in black satin and the latter in black silk. Ida had dressed in a crisp white shirtwaist and black brocade skirt, which she'd cinched with the same purple belt that had once attracted Henry Barstow's notice—the belt drew all four eyes and pinched both mouths, but this she'd expected. The part she hadn't expected was the fact that Lem's entrance seemed to cause Hattie to temporarily lose her speech. Granted, Lem barely looked like himself, clad in wool suit and tie, his hair neatly damped and parted.

"Well, I'd no idea," Hattie said at last.

"No idea of what?" Ida asked.

"That you'd invited Mr. Daggett."

"Who wants punch?" Lem asked.

Ruth did not. Hattie did. Ida did. She held out the cups as Lem poured; before she even tasted it she could smell the fermented cider and the cinnamon and nutmeg and cloves; perhaps something citrusy besides. Lem lifted his glass. "To Ezra," he said. "May he rest in peace."

"Well, in that case I should not refuse a small cup," Ruth said.

Even with the punch the meal was a quiet one, and Ida couldn't blame it all on Ezra; where she'd hoped Lem's presence would have eliminated a few conversation gaps, it only seemed to cause a bigger one. After Ida and Hattie retreated to the kitchen to clean up, the talk seemed to flow better in the parlor, Ruth's chirps and Lem's rumbles drifting over the exhausted silence in the kitchen. When Ida and Hattie returned to the parlor, Ruth stood up.

"Time to wander."

"I'll drive you," Lem said.

"There's no need of anyone driving me," Ruth retorted just as Hattie said, "Thank you."

Ida's three guests left, and sooner than she'd expected, Ida was alone. She sat herself in the chair Lem had recently occupied and breathed in the relief of an empty house, but after a time the relief wore off. The tick of the clock grew loud, echoing around the room. Ida had just decided to give the day over to her bed when someone knocked on the door.

Thrusting her way through ghosts of Christmases past, Ida opened the door on Lem.

"Forgot my kettle."

Ida stepped aside. Lem stepped in, picked the kettle off the stove, swished it. "According to the rules of hospitality as I know them, the kettle's mine but the contents are yours."

Ida set out two fresh cups. Lem poured. They returned to the chairs by the fire. The stillness of the scene, Lem's total concentration on the cup in his hand, reminded Ida of several of her early portrait sessions, the subjects intent on looking anywhere but at the artist, afraid to speak lest they creased their brow. But Lem's face couldn't disguise the years or the weather or the care, even in stillness. Ida leaned forward. "Lem. Let me sketch you."

"Thank you, no."

"It won't take long. I haven't tried a portrait in months. If I don't start again soon—"

Lem drained his cup and stood up. "Some other time."

"Why not now? You're all spruced up. You're warm. You're fed. You're full of punch."

They eyed each other, Ida attempting to gauge the degree of Lem's resistance, Lem no doubt attempting to gauge the degree of Ida's desperation. She said nothing else; he would or he wouldn't as he decided; that much she could see. At the end of it Lem made a half circle and perched on the edge of his chair, holding out his cup for more. Ida filled his cup in the kitchen and collected her pad and pencil.

But whatever stillness Ida had observed in Lem disappeared the minute she picked up her pencil. He crossed and uncrossed his legs. He ran his fingers through his hair. He tugged his collar. He leaned forward. Back. Forward again. Ida gave out no criticism or correction, but she realized she needed to distract him or she'd never get a single line drawn.

"So tell me, how many lambs might we get this spring?"

Lem's mouth twitched, a twitch that said, *I know what you're up to,* but he answered. "I count twenty ewes carrying, best I can tell."

"You like the new ram?"

"I've never seen a finer. I told Ezra, he did well there."

Lem went on. A big-headed ram had once created so many big-headed lambs that they'd lost nearly a dozen; a pushy one had tried to jump the fence into the ewes' pasture and broke his leg; another stood calmly in the corner no matter how many ewes squatted in front of him. Lem never grew easy, but by the time Ida set down her pencil he'd stopped tugging at his cuffs and resetting his shoulders, and the damp of perspiration had dried on his brow.

Ida walked him to the door. "Tell me this, Lem. Do you want to manage the farm?"

"No. And that's what I told Ruth."

"When? When did you tell her that?"

"The day after you told me what she said to you. I also told her you'd been managing pretty well whenever Ezra was gone, and I'd help where needed." He paused but stood there so long that another thought occurred to Ida.

"Why did you come back here tonight? Really?"

Lem gazed over Ida's shoulder as if at Ezra's ghost. "I don't recall that first Christmas alone being the best day of my life." He paused again. "I'm not going to say Merry Christmas to you,

Ida, but I will say thank you for a nice night and may peace settle on you soon."

He was out the door before Ida could think what she might
wish for Lem in return. She watched him climb into the wagon,
watched him snap the reins and move forward, watched the
wagon stop, watched Lem lean forward, fumble in his coat. Ida
couldn't see what he was doing, but she stood and watched until
he rose from his hunched position and the wagon had moved off
again. Odd, she thought, that this man was the one person who
seemed to genuinely care what happened to her, care what she
thought. Felt. As she cared what happened to him. The wagon
paused again. Ida took a step after it, but before she could take a
second step it bolted ahead and down the track.

9

IDA WOKE TO A SOUND FROM BETT, that unearthly, I-mean-this growl that carried right through the window glass. She went to the window and looked out but saw nothing. She threw on Ezra's boots and jacket, went downstairs, lit the lantern, picked Ezra's Springfield rifle off the hooks over the mantel, and stepped out, but by the time she got there Bett had opened her throat wide and whatever it was had already crashed off through the woods.

Ida called the dog back and returned to the house but didn't send Bett to her kennel. "Come," she said, and Bett followed her inside, all the way up the stairs to Ida's bedroom. Ida settled her on the rug next to the bed, but in the night she woke to feel the dog's hard back pressed against hers, the dog's nose an inch from Ida's pillow. Well, she wasn't about to get up just to put the dog out. And truth to tell, she liked that warm body against her own.

NEXT MORNING Ida and Bett made a brief foray into the woods, but Ida didn't have the tracking skills to decipher anything she saw, and Bett soon lost interest in the nothing they were tracking in favor of the squirrel that they weren't. They returned to the yard and stood staring out at the sheep, huddled in a single bunch around the hayrack. It seemed impossible that the hayrack could need filling again so soon, and the thought of it exhausted Ida. But of course she hadn't slept, listening for every odd noise.

Ida yawned and set to pitching hay, daydreaming of storming up the hill to Ruth, handing her the farmhouse key, getting a room in town, and signing on as a waitress at the Bayside. With Lem now out of the picture, Ruth would be forced to hire a new manager, and thinking what that might set Ruth back, and how much a strange face around the farm would irritate her, added considerably to Ida's fantasy. But how much *would* a new manager set Ruth back? Ezra had worked for a percentage of the profits, but Ida had no idea what that percentage was. And why was that? Why was it Ezra had worked for a percentage of the profits while Ida was expected to work for nothing beyond the roof over her head?

Ida went inside and sat down at the desk. She pulled out the farm book and flipped through it page by page, noting the money received for last season's wool and for the lambs sold in October, marking the notations for Lem's wages, the hayers, the bills from Luce and Tilton and everyone else. At last Ida came to a line marked *EP* with a sum attached that Ida worked out to be 50 percent of the profits.

Ida hunted for a fresh sheet of paper in the desk, but if there had been any, she'd burned it along with the catalogs. She retrieved her sketch pad and pencil from her studio, flipped it to the back page and began a neat record of her numbers. When she finished she flipped through the sketchbook till she came to the page with the drawing of Lem; she'd done nothing more with it, and now she saw why. It wasn't the Lem she knew. She put on her coat and hat, tucked the sketch pad under her arm, and headed uphill to Ruth's.

* * *

FOR A BEACON HILL GIRL it wasn't much of a hill, but the wind managed to come over and down with fresh force straight at Ida; she hung tight to the sketch pad that held her numbers, tucked her chin and forged ahead. She was mulling over the words she planned to use on Ruth when she looked up and saw a boy squatting in the dirt of Hattie's winter-blasted garden, digging a hole with a stick. He looked to be about five years old, still with a too-big head and too-big ears on top of a skinny neck, fine hair the color of wet sand protruding from under a green wool cap. "What are you doing?"

"Digging a hole."

"What for?"

"See what's in it."

Ida peered in. "Find anything?"

"Not through digging it yet."

"Ah."

Ida stepped up to the door and rapped. Hattie opened it, looking around Ida at the boy.

"Who's that?" Ida asked.

Ruth came into the room. "Somebody's mistake."

"My cousin Mary Nye's boy," Hattie said.

"Second cousin once removed," Ruth amended.

"His mother's dead," Hattie continued.

"And Lord knows who his father is," Ruth said.

"His grandparents are raising him up. But his grandmother's in hospital and his grandfather—"

"Is useless," Ruth said.

"So I offered to take him for a bit."

"Forty-five-year-old spinster decides to be a mama. What's it your business?" Or that's what Ida thought Ruth said, assuming she was still talking to Hattie. Ruth rapped the table in front of Ida. "I said, what's your business?"

"I've come to talk to you about the farm."

Ruth peered at her. "Well then, sit."

Ida set her pad on the table and shrugged out of her jacket. Either Ruth's house was plenty warm, or Ida really was as nervous as she felt. Without asking, Hattie opened Ida's sketch pad and flipped through till she came to the picture of Lem. "When did you do this?"

"Christmas night."

Hattie looked at Ida. "I saw no sketching going on."

"Later, when he came back to collect his kettle."

Hattie studied it some more. "It's nothing like."

Ruth looked too. "No, it isn't." Ida wasn't surprised by Ruth's remark—she'd never complimented a work of Ida's—but Hattie was always so effusive it rendered her opinion worthless. The sketch of Lem wasn't good, Ida knew that, but *nothing* like? It was one thing for Ida to say it, but for Hattie . . .

The boy came into the kitchen, skirting Ida like a cat.

"Say hello to Mrs. Pease," Hattie said.

"Hello."

"Put those boots outside!" Ruth ordered. She turned to Ida. "I can't think what their floors looked like in New York. Come into the parlor. We can't talk in this mess."

THEY SAT IN THE PARLOR by the stove. Ida began. "Lem tells me he isn't interested in managing the farm. I need a place to live and some income until I get myself set up to move back to Boston. It occurs to me we might work something out."

"Lem will come around."

"Lem won't. He told me flat out. He wants his fair wage for shearing and emergency calls at lambing and that's it. I can do this, with Lem's help." Ida elaborated, listing all the things Lem had taught her: how to watch for the restless, circling ewe who was about to lamb; how to tell a normal presentation from one that needed human help; how to watch the weather in order to call just the right time for shearing and haying as neither could be done wet; how to cull the sheep that would go to fall market. She mentioned a feisty ewe they should ship out, another who had aborted twice and even if it carried to term this time would only weaken the strain going forward. She talked of a couple of ewes too old to breed that should be sold while they still carried decent fleece. She watched Ruth as she talked and saw that this was talk the old woman understood. Ida finished by saying that until Henry Barstow settled the estate and Ida had recouped enough in funds to house and clothe and feed herself in Boston, she needed to house and clothe and feed herself on Martha's Vineyard.

There Ida held out her pad and pointed to the number she'd come up with—35 percent of the profits. Ruth waved the pad away. Behind Ida, Hattie said, "That's not half what Ezra got. You don't take Ida you'll be paying a stranger twice that much."

"Ida's not Ezra. She'll call Lem at the drop of every hat, adding to my expense."

"That's why I don't ask for Ezra's fifty percent. I know I'll have to rely on Lem more than Ezra did." There Ida recalled something another female art student had said while complaining of the difficulty in finding time to paint. *What I need is a wife.* "And I don't have a wife who works for nothing the way Ezra did."

Hattie chirped out a laugh. "So she gets her thirty-five percent and you still save, Mother. And Lem said you can trust her."

"Trust her! Didn't she just say? As soon as she gets enough money she's away to Boston."

Which was it? Ruth wanted her here or wanted her gone? Ida guessed she now wanted her here if she could get her farm work done on the cheap. But there would be no money till the summer wool sale; she'd be foolish to leave before that. "I'll sign a contract," Ida said. "I'll stay through getting the wool to market."

Ruth looked at Hattie.

"That will give you plenty of time to find a new man before fall," Hattie said.

Ruth stared at Hattie. "Get me some paper," she said. She turned to Ida. "I'll have a contract for you to sign tomorrow."

"Thank you, Ruth."

"Well, you ought to thank me," Ruth said.

Ida left. Hattie followed her out. "That's more than half what Ezra got," Ida said.

"I know, but she doesn't. I do the books."

"But why—?"

"She's called me a forty-five-year-old spinster one time too much."

As Ida struggled to adapt to this new idea of Ezra's cousin, Hattie added, "I'm forty-*two*. In March."

OLIVER NYE WAS BACK in the yard, digging another hole. This time he didn't look up; he'd met Ida now; clearly she wasn't worth the trouble of lifting his head twice. But Ida had met Oliver now too, and she knew something of being orphaned; she pulled her skirt tight and squatted beside him.

"A new hole?"

"T'other didn't have anything in it."

"Ah. Well, it looks to me like you're a pretty good digger."

She stood up and started to walk away. Behind her she heard that high, tight little voice: "My father's a *really* good digger."

Ida turned. "Is he, now? And what does he dig?"

The boy paused in his digging, presumably the better to think. "Rivers," he said.

HENRY BARSTOW DIDN'T RETURN to the island until the end of January. It was true that it seemed to either rain or snow in turn every third day, and the sea added its usual complications for the crossing, the steamer canceling its run just when everyone seemed to need it most, but nevertheless, a month seemed a long time. For one thing, Ida had begun to fret over the gold in her closet. By rights Henry, the executor of the estate, should know about the gold, but if she told him, would he confiscate it as part of the estate and send it into the same limbo as the real property, waiting on the courts to declare Ezra dead? Ida had already come to think of the gold as hers alone; Henry had found no record of it, which meant it had nothing to do with the salvage company and needn't be shared. Or did it? What if Ezra had reclaimed it from some wreck and then hidden it from Mose? The longer Ida thought on the thing, the more it seemed that this was the only logical explanation. Ida held no delusions about Ezra's honesty; the question now was what delusions she might hold about her own.

But Ida had no doubts of Henry Barstow's honesty; he'd proved himself early on by sending her after her own attorney to protect her rights in the estate settlement. She would tell him about the gold next time they met.

HATTIE KNOCKED ON IDA'S DOOR on her way back from the exchange. "He's back," she said.

"Who?"

Hattie looked at her. "Henry Barstow. The one you've been asking me to ring every week."

"Twice. I asked you to ring twice."

"Three times."

"So he's back. Thanks."

Ida waited for Hattie to top the hill before she headed down it.

THERE WAS SOME SMALL COMMOTION going on in front of Luce's; two women and a man were standing in a tight circle with raised voices—or rather, one raised voice—and one raised hand.

The voice belonged to the man. The hand belonged to Rose.

"You shove that thing at me one more time, young lady, and I won't be responsible for what happens next."

"I only ask you to read it, Mr. Stone. It just says—"

"If I don't want to read it, I don't want to hear it. How much clearer does that get? Come along, Ella."

Rose Amaral made one last attempt to hand the pamphlet to Ella Stone; Ella took it, ripped it in two, and dropped it in the street. Rose turned away in the direction of the Bethel. The Stones entered Luce's. Ida walked up and retrieved the torn pamphlet. She held the two halves of the cover together and read. "WHAT WE WANT: A World regenerated by the combined labor and love of Men and Women standing side by side, shoulder to shoulder, a calm, lofty, indomitable purpose lighting every face.—Julia Ward Howe."

Ida tucked the pamphlet into her pocket to read later and walked into the salvage company with a single purpose—to tell Henry about the gold—but leaning against the wall was a bicycle, a different bicycle, a smaller one, with an oddly angled crossbar. Henry leaped up, grinning. "Come!" He rolled the bicycle out the door. When Ida didn't move at once he said, "You wanted to learn, yes?" He was still grinning, the kind of grin that demanded company—Ida's cheeks were stretched wide by the time he'd led her out the door and off the main street into the alley.

"Whose bicycle is it?"

"My wife's, but she's gone off it. Now stand here and let me check the seat." He eyed Ida's legs, pulled a wrench from his pocket, and adjusted the seat.

"Now remember, it's nothing but balance." He knelt at Ida's knee and rotated the left pedal with his hand until the right rose up on the other side. "This is your start position: just after the right pedal starts its descent." He rotated the pedal backward. "You remember I showed you the coaster brakes? This is how you stop. Now here, step through and arrange your skirt. No, like this." He knelt again and settled her skirt to fall evenly on each side; Ida flushed. "Take care not to get the cloth tangled in the chain. You want to keep a light hand on the handlebars; this is where your balance comes from. You steer with your body, not the handlebars. Now put your right foot on the pedal, push off the ground with your left, find the seat, push down on the right."

Ida did as he said and kilted sideways so fast she would have landed in the dirt if Henry hadn't caught her at the hips. She could feel her heart beating in her throat, not—surely not—because of those hands on her hips. She pushed off again, so fast Henry wasn't ready, so when she wobbled this time she really did hit dirt. Henry helped her up, brushed her off. "Are you—"

"Of course I am. I can do it."

"Of course you can." He was grinning again. This time he didn't let go but ran alongside, clutching her waist, calling instructions, a single meaningless phrase he repeated over and over: *Find your balance.* It meant nothing. Once, she got going fast enough to outpace Henry and keeled over again. She grew hot in the January chill.

"Are you quite sure you're all right?" Henry asked, but Ida only clambered back up. This time Henry managed to keep her upright by grasping tight to her waist and not letting go, but the concept of balance eluded Ida and appeared to frustrate Henry.

"Don't you feel it?" he kept asking. "Don't you feel your balance?"

Ida had to shake her head every time in the same mortification she'd felt when her brothers sailed away from the wharf on their first coastal trip without her. Oh, she'd wanted to learn to sail! She wanted to learn to ride that bicycle! But this balance. She felt nothing but Henry's hands on her.

Finally, knees quivering, Ida gave up.

"Come tomorrow and we'll try again," Henry said, but he didn't say it as if it were a thing he was looking forward to, and why should he? Those double lines were back between his brow and he was more red-faced and sweating than Ida, his hair now damp at the neck.

Ida had walked—or waddled—halfway home before she realized she'd forgotten to tell Henry about the gold; the bicycle had outshone it.

10

JULIA WARD HOWE'S MOTTO for the women of America was "Up to Date!" Her fee for a speaking engagement was two hundred dollars, and she was to appear in Boston on four different dates. Ida wrote the four dates in her almanac and pondered what might have to align in this new, skewed universe of hers to get her there at any one of those evenings. Too much.

IDA DIDN'T RETURN to the salvage company the next day, or the next, or indeed, the one after that. With the clear-eyed perspective only a new day could bring she confirmed in her own mind that Henry Barstow's invitation hadn't been a warm one. She needed to tell him of the gold—it was as if she could feel those nuggets festering in her closet—but she couldn't bring herself to face Henry after the mortification of the failed lesson. And besides, she had painting to do.

As Ida sat drinking her coffee that brick-red cupboard had begun to annoy her, standing out as a too-bold spot of color in an otherwise dark and drab kitchen; it needed some other color to balance it. Mr. Morris had taught her well about values, about composition, about light and dark. Thinking of Mr. Morris, of her beloved Museum School, Ida felt the ache as if she'd suffered an amputated limb, but she would not allow herself to indulge in self-pity. She'd made her choice to leave Boston, and now she must push all Boston thoughts away. She rinsed out her cup, swept away her breakfast crumbs, and attacked her chores, but once she'd finished and was satisfied all was well with her creatures she changed out of her now-fouled skirt and boots and set off.

Over the two years Ida had lived on the Vineyard she'd visited Tilton's Hardware a half dozen times, but old Mr. Tilton still gazed at her as if he couldn't quite place her. He fetched the can of ochre paint she requested, and she handed over her money, offsetting her guilt at the expense by thinking of the gold in her closet. Mr. Tilton admired the color and seemed to have contemplated saying something else to her before falling silent. Just as well, thought Ida; he'd say something inane and she'd say something inane back and to what purpose?

Once home, Ida set to work. She painted the splash board behind the tin sink and stood back, but the result only half pleased her: the ochre was a good complement to the brick-red pie cupboard but now she had two bright spots on opposite sides of the room. It wasn't enough. She painted the wooden stool she used to hang herbs off the beams, and that helped, but it still wasn't right. The shelves? Yes. But after Ida had completed the first shelf she stood back to assess and found she still wasn't happy; the golden glow certainly enlivened the kitchen, but three more shelves might be too much glow. She considered returning to Tilton's for more brick red but then thought of the money wasted on the ochre, and gold in a closet was not cash in the bank. How *did* gold in a closet become cash in a bank? She must ask Henry when she told him of it, which must be the next time they met.

She'd decided this without wavering when she looked out the window through the last of the day's light and saw Henry Barstow pedaling effortlessly over the rise on his bicycle. On his *wife's* bicycle. A scarf covered half his face and a wool cap covered most of the rest of it, but there was no mistaking the high cheekbones, the dark eyes, the long legs winging out on either side like a cricket's, his posture—leaning low over the handlebars with his elbows akimbo—contributing to the insect effect. He pulled up to Ida's door and leaped off, not as Ida leaped off, but with both legs at once so that for a moment Ida thought he was going to do a handstand on the handlebars. He bounded up the steps and knocked.

As soon as Ida opened the door he cried, "Come out! I've solved it. I know how to teach you. I was disgusted with myself the other day; how could I not manage to teach this simple thing? Come. Come out!" He stood, already half-turned away in his hurry, a child wanting to play, grinning at Ida as if life held nothing but joy, had never held anything but joy, would hold nothing but more joy ahead. Oh, what Ida wouldn't trade for a mind that could focus so completely on one joyful moment! But why was it so joyful for Henry Barstow? Why should he care a single pin whether Ida learned to ride a bicycle? But if Ida were truthful with herself, she didn't care a single pin why or what or how—she wanted to learn to ride that bicycle. She grabbed her jacket and hat and gloves and went out.

"All right, new rules," Henry said. "You won't pedal this time, you'll push." He wheeled the bicycle to the hard dirt at the top of the track and swung aboard, long legs kinked up on either side. He stamped the ground with one foot. "Nice and dry and hard. Perfect."

"Especially if I fall on it."

"No, no, no, there will be no falling!"

It was as if Mr. Morris had materialized out of the island mist. *No, no, no, don't stop!*

"Now watch me," Henry said. "This is how we begin. Not pedaling. Pushing." He pushed himself along the ground with his feet, then lifted his feet and coasted a few yards, letting the bicycle wobble as it would. He pushed again, lifted again, coasted again. He turned left and right. He got off and waved Ida on. The seat had been lowered even more, she noticed, which explained the extreme insect effect when Henry rode up, but the result of the lowered seat was that Ida's feet could now rest more securely on the ground when needed, and immediately her confidence rose. And yes, she could push with her feet and move the bicycle along as Henry had, but what was the point?

"This is how you find your balance," Henry said, as if she'd spoken her question aloud. "Push harder! Now lift those feet and coast. Yes! Do you feel it? Feel the balance?"

This time Henry didn't trot with her; he put no hand on her; he stood, tall and straight as a mast with arms folded and eyes alight with confidence. Ida took a breath, inhaled that confidence; pushed; lifted; coasted. She began to relax. The hard-packed area dropped off into the downhill track, forcing Ida to turn often to keep from rolling down the hill into town, and she discovered it was true what Henry said; her hands might direct the handlebars, but her body did the main job of turning. She wasn't actually riding a bicycle, but she was having fun; she turned to look at Henry and wobbled dramatically, but she righted herself with ease, and in the righting she felt it. Her balance.

HE LEFT THE BICYCLE WITH HER. Ida attempted to protest, but Henry insisted, and in truth Ida *wanted* that bicycle; she wanted it so badly she couldn't bring herself to object over an excess of delicacy about accepting a gift from a man, and, come to that, a gift that belonged to the man's wife.

"I'm going to New Bedford tomorrow," he said now. "I'll be back on Saturday for lesson two."

Saturday. Five days away. Ida's disappointment dragged on

her like a tub of wet sheets. But she said only, "That would be lesson three."

"*Your* lesson two. That first day was *my* lesson on how not to teach someone to ride a bicycle."

After Henry left, Ida stashed the bicycle in the barn to protect it from the weather, latched the barn door, and immediately unlatched it to look inside.

A *bicycle*. In her barn.

At least until Henry's wife wanted it back.

IDA WOKE THE NEXT DAY with the remains of the week's plans fully in place: do the farm chores, clean the house, make bread, call Lem about Ezra's clothes, paint the chairs and table with that brick red. Instead she pushed herself around on the bicycle, feeling that balance, coasting longer and longer, until she came to the right level spot at just the right speed and put her feet to the pedals. She was so elated to be flying along under her own power she forgot what Henry said about the coaster brakes and had to stop herself by steering onto the grass and falling over. She didn't care. She fell again because the coaster brakes worked better than she thought, but a little practice while clinging to the stone wall took care of that. She began to feel her muscles, to feel herself growing strong, and as she grew strong she grew confident. She fell again because her skirt got caught in her boot heel, and that night she rifled through her wardrobe, picked out a faded wool skirt with a full cut, and shortened it a foot.

The next day that long, sloping track called. Ida approached with clammy palms in the winter cold; she straddled the bicycle and pushed off. At first the grade helped her reach the proper speed and kept her from wobbling, but at the next drop her speed began to alarm her. She should brake. She *could* brake. And yet before she'd quite made up her mind to do it, the most remarkable feeling came over her. She was flying! Escaping! She was unstoppable, unbeatable, unsinkable, unafraid. She was *up to date.*

The feeling lasted until Lem's wagon rounded the curve. Ida backpedaled hard, which stopped the bicycle but didn't stop Ida; she went over the handlebars in one unlovely arc. The track was harder than the grass, but she'd come down on her shoulder and instinctively rolled with the blow. She sat up, struggling to cover her exposed limbs.

Lem bent over her. "Are you hurt?"

"No," she lied. Her shoulder. Her neck. Her hip.

"What the devil do you think you're doing?"

"I went too fast."

Lem picked up the bicycle and put it in the back of the wagon.

"I don't need you to—"

"Get in."

Ida got in.

"What kind of a fool thing—"

"Mr. Barstow is teaching me to ride a bicycle."

"He gave you that machine?"

"Loaned it."

"And you take it upon yourself to charge down the hill on it."

"I was planning to brake."

"And were you planning to land with your skirts around your neck?"

"I wasn't planning to *land* at all."

"Things happen you don't always plan on. You of all people should know that, Ida Pease."

"It was worth it."

"What was?"

That feeling of freedom. Of invincibility. Of *joy*. How long since Ida had felt joy? She looked sideways at Lem's stony profile and wondered when he'd last felt it, if he'd ever felt it. And there was Henry, so full of it. If he could teach Ida that too . . . But Ida could say none of this to that stone face. They rode the rest of the way in silence. When they reached the house Lem didn't get down from the wagon seat, either to help Ida down or to help her bike out She jumped to the ground nimbly enough and yanked the bicycle out of the wagon bed if not gracefully at least effectively, but as she wheeled the bicycle past Lem where he sat at the reins she peered sideways at him. This wasn't like him to hold himself so aloof, to begrudge her a possible—although debatable—error in judgment. Or maybe it was.

"Lem," she said.

He wouldn't look at her. His face looked as gray and rocklike as she'd ever seen it, and he kept his eyes on his boots, curled up like a man twice his age.

"Get out of my way," he said. "I've got work."

Ida watched him wheel the wagon around and retreat down the track, which was another odd thing, because until he'd almost run over Ida he'd been heading up.

BY THE TIME HENRY RETURNED, a spider had cast a web across Ida's broom closet door, but she'd managed to barrel safely down the track six times. She'd also removed the stays from her corset. For some reason Ida felt as shy about sharing her exploits on the track as she did about sharing the information about her corset, which she never would share, of course, but why not the track? Perhaps it was because Lem had been so appalled at her, and after all, it wasn't her bicycle. Perhaps she *had* been reckless. So they began the second lesson with Henry walking beside her, his hand on her thigh, demonstrating how pressure on one pedal gave rise to the other, how to balance the give and take between the two muscles. But after a few turns of the wheel Ida couldn't bear it; she shot out from under his hand, partly because she wanted to show off, but partly because . . . that hand. She rode to the top of the track and turned to see Henry grinning all the way to the edges of his face. She came to a not entirely graceful stop, and he laughed out loud, which made Ida laugh out loud, and that was what they were doing when Hattie and Oliver came down the hill.

Oliver looked at the bicycle. Hattie looked at Ida's shortened skirt.

Hattie said, "What on earth—"

"It's a bicycle," Ida said. "Want to try it?"

A light switched on somewhere behind Hattie's eyes. She looked down at Oliver. "Another day, perhaps?"

Ida nodded directly at that light in Hattie's eyes. A promise.

Henry spoke to Oliver. "I'm afraid this isn't the right size, or I'd have you try too."

"My father *already* got me one of those," Oliver said. "It's purple." He paused. "And gold."

Ida said, "Mr. Barstow, this is Master Nye, digger of holes."

"How do you do, Master Nye. I've dug myself into a few of those a time or two."

"My father's a ocean digger," Oliver said.

"I thought he was a river digger," Ida said.

"A *ocean* digger."

"Did he start out as a hole digger too?" Henry asked.

Oliver thought. "A hole digger *then* a river digger *then* a ocean digger."

"Come along," Hattie said. She caught Oliver by the hand, and they proceeded down the hill.

Henry looked after them. "Who *was* that?"

Ida told him—Hattie's cousin, something removed; she began to tell him the rest; the dead mother, the unknown father—but at the word *mother* her voice turned unreliable. She'd been about to ask Henry to stay for supper as a thank-you for the bicycle lesson, but now he looked at her too keenly. She cast about for a change of subject, but Henry found one for her.

"I never did commission that portrait of my father. Would you look at the photograph and consider the job?"

Ida nodded. As Henry moved away she called after him, "Thank you. For the bicycle. For the lesson." For the joy.

EZRA HAD ATTEMPTED to teach Ida something once. One evening, still in the hopeful period of her marriage, Mose had stayed to dine; after Ida had cleared the table the men pulled out the Nine Men's Morris board and the whiskey bottle while Ida retreated to the parlor to tackle her mending. It was late spring and Ida had opened the window, the welcoming breeze making her feel hopeful that she would come to be part of this new place, that the salt prickle in the air would become a friend she would welcome over many more springs. But that night she found herself distracted by the calls of "mill!" and "pounded!" and "break!" that filtered her way through the parlor door.

So, Ida asked Ezra for the lesson. Mose was in New Bedford visiting his brother and his family, and Ezra had pondered heading off to Duffy's. Conscious of a dangerous bifurcation creeping into her marriage, Ida had plucked from the shelf the Nine Men's Morris pegboard with its gleaming brass pegs and set it on the table. "Stay," she said. "Teach me to play this." But because she held out little hope that Ezra would agree, she also sent him a suggestive smile that contained a touch of challenge. "Winner gets to pick the next game."

But the game, which had appeared so simple, was not, and Ezra's patience ran dry ten minutes in. "Not there! You can't move there. What's wrong with you? You can't break up my mill."

"You broke up mine."

"But only when there were no other men to remove. How many times do I have to tell you?"

"Once would be nice." Ida replaced the illegally captured pin and moved again.

"*Now* what do you think you're doing?"

"Taking your man. A legal one. Which puts me up two."

Ezra pointed, counting, but seemed to come to the same total. He frowned, picked up one of his men, and leap-frogged it over Ida's.

"Wait, what are *you* doing? You said you can't jump over men."

"It's called flying. It's only allowed when one player is down to three men."

"And when was I to learn about this flying?"

"I told you about flying, Ida. Pay attention, for God's sake. It's your turn."

So Ida flew too, and by her calculation won the night, but Ezra cried foul on her particular method of taking flight and declared an end to the game.

LATER, IN THEIR BED, Ezra pushed into her so preemptively, so violently, that she gasped.

They never played Nine Men's Morris again. Thinking of that night and its aftermath, Ida would have to say that had been more than a gentle drip of snowmelt.

11

FEBRUARY ARRIVED with an unusual stillness to the air and warmth to the sun. To add to that rare gift, Ida looked out to see Henry coming up the track on his bicycle, singing. What was that song? Not "Arkansas Traveler." Not "Shenandoah." It blew across the still air with the tempo of a rollicking sea chanty, but just as Ida recognized the tune—*Buffalo Gals, won't you come out tonight, come out tonight, come out tonight* —the song broke off hard as Henry neared the door, and it occurred to Ida that there was something private about Henry's singing, something he held to himself that was not to be invaded. But he'd come on a mission. Or rather two missions. First he held out the photograph of his father.

Ida took the photo and studied it. Henry's father stood to the left of two others, one arm extended to lean against an old apple tree, one leg crossed over the other. She noted the fair hair, like Henry's, the dark eyes, like Henry's, the long nose balanced by the high cheekbones, also like Henry's. She took note of the same long torso, the same narrow hips, but something more workmanlike in the father's legs. Ida had never attempted a portrait from a photograph before, but she'd have help with this one; she need only look at Henry.

"I'll try," she said.

Henry exhaled happily.

"Now to my next question. West Chop Light. By bicycle. It's only a mile and a half, a flat shell road with few houses along it." He appeared ready to say more but Ida was already off for the stairs. She changed into her shortened skirt and warmest jacket, adding hat, mittens, scarf. Sun or no sun, it was still February.

They rode side by side, away from town, Henry keeping a wheel's distance back to allow Ida to set her pace. They passed sun-and-salt-bleached grass and farmhouses closed down tight against February, their chimneys puffing translucent smoke. They passed the occasional wagon or carriage, and Ida noted the bend in the necks as the occupants struggled to identify the odd pair out recreating in winter. Ida wobbled, of course, but grew steadier as she rode, feeling her muscles and her nerves and yes, her balance; feeling the sun and the air and the pure joy of it.

At the lighthouse they stopped to rest, leaning against the sun-warmed lee side. They didn't speak, Ida content in the silence—so oddly content in the presence of this little-known man who felt so known. That contentment lasted until she looked at Henry's profile.

"What do you think of so intently?" she asked.

Henry shook out a smile. "How nice it is."

"I don't think so."

"You don't think it nice?"

"I don't think that's what you're thinking."

Henry said nothing for a time. "The lawyer handling the estate is compiling papers," he tried. "But I must urge patience. It may take some time."

"Mr. Littlefield warned me. But you don't mean to pretend that pondering estate lawyers' papers has turned you so glum."

"I'm married," Henry burst out.

"I know that. And I can't think why you feel it necessary—"

"My wife's in Newport with another man."

Well, Ida didn't know that.

"I'm to go there and discover them so she can get a divorce. Apparently Newport is the place one goes for that."

"But you don't want to go?"

Henry paused. "I confess I didn't want a divorce. I don't know why. It hasn't been . . . happy. It just seems to me people should keep their promises. But I suppose when there are no promises left to keep—" He fell silent.

Ida thought of the woman who'd wanted her portrait painted in the "Sargent style," who attributed Ida's artistic accomplishments to nothing more than an abundance of free time. She'd taken no liking to her, but she couldn't say that now, didn't dare say that now, especially not while the sight of Henry's anguished face, of his careful hands retying his scarf, caused a physical pain somewhere just above her breastbone.

"Sometimes it's hard to give up what one knows for something one doesn't," she said.

Henry swung around to face her. "Like Boston? You're thinking of Boston. Or . . . of course. You're speaking of Ezra."

"I'm speaking of your *wife*." All right, yes, her tone was . . . well, a *tone*. Ezra was right about that. She pondered this, then added, "I wonder if I'd ever have found the nerve to leave Ezra."

"Divorce isn't an easy thing to accomplish."

"Leaving is."

Henry swiveled to stare at her.

"I only mean to say, thinking to myself that is, thinking *of* myself, that at the basest level, what could be easier? You open the door and walk through it. But of course I've already admitted to the thing I lacked in order to open that door. Nerve."

"And then there's the question of what you would do for food and clothing and shelter. Thinking of yourself, that is."

"Well, yes. That. It turns out I was better positioned in that regard *before* my marriage."

"And if there are children—"

Well, of course. How foolish of Ida not to guess that. "How many?" she asked.

"Two girls." Henry looked out at the February sea and could not have been warmed by the sight. Ida shivered. Beside her, Henry felt it and jackknifed away from the lighthouse wall.

"You're cold." He began to remove his coat, but Ida waved him still. She didn't want his coat. She didn't want Henry.

THAT NIGHT Ida felt parts of her legs she didn't know she owned; she woke to the throb and stayed awake to the rest of it—Henry, married Henry, with a wife he was reluctant to divorce, a wife Ida doubted he *would* divorce. And two children. But what did it matter to Ida? She was a new widow still attempting to grieve for her husband; she had no business riding around the island with a married man. She had no business accepting the loan of his wife's bicycle.

So Ida decided the thing in the middle of the night—neatly, painlessly—and woke in the morning again thinking of Henry. She didn't understand all that it was that drew her, what it was that had drawn her to him that first day when he'd arrived at the gallery with his wife. *With his wife.* Did she hear herself? But why shouldn't her mind return again and again to that day, that day of her first exhibit at the Guild, that day Mr. Morris had told her she'd gotten it just right, that day a stranger had called her work extraordinary . . .

Yes, there was that. But in truth he might have finished that sentence in any number of ways: *Extraordinary the way that*

painting says nothing. Extraordinary the way a prominent subject
can get a third-rate work into a prestigious gallery. Extraordinary
the way the ground overtakes the whole, no matter that Mr. Morris had decreed it just right. Ida knew nothing of Henry's views
on art. She knew nothing of Henry. But even so, she couldn't
picture any of those words escaping his mouth. Even so, he'd
told her to paint the next Russell, which told Ida that even if he
knew nothing about art, he knew something about artists. He
knew something about *her.*

And he was married. And Ida was newly widowed. Enough
of it.

IDA GOT OUT THE BICYCLE the next morning and rode it into
town to return it to Henry, return it to his wife, but she couldn't
help relishing that last moment of freedom. Before their marriage Ezra had spoken, not only of "his" farm, but of "his" horse
and carriage. In truth it was Ruth's horse and carriage, and Ruth
had not proved amenable to lending it; if Ida wanted to go anywhere she walked, another strong contribution to her sense of
feeling trapped. The freedom Ida felt now, with the two simple
wheels under her, drew her to ride past the salvage company
and out along the beach road, feeling everything ease in her as
she felt the pull in her muscles, the wind against her face. She
hadn't realized *how* trapped, how strangled she'd felt until these
few moments when she was free of it. Until she was about to
lose the bicycle.

Ida turned around. Back in town she saw that the *Addie Todd*
had still not risen from the sea, and a group of workmen who
should have been on the salvage lighter now stood idly on shore.
She pulled up alongside the beach and wandered over; again,

Chester Luce was among the crowd and she approached him as she had before; she imagined (or did she?) that he looked at her differently this time, but she refused to let it divert her.

"A dispute with the owners over funds," Luce explained. "They don't want to leave in case word comes that it's been re-solved, but they don't want to work if they won't get paid."

Ida turned around to head back to her bicycle but behind her she heard a shout. She turned again and saw John Cottle stride up to George Amaral where he stood at the edge of the group, clamp a hand on his shoulder, and haul him around.

"I told you, Amaral, you keep your wife out of my kitchen."

"And I told you, Cottle, my wife can go where she wants."

"And say what she wants?"

"And damn well say what she wants." Ida edged closer. This was George Amaral, the man who'd tried to shush his wife at Ezra's funeral?

"You want them voting, is that what you're telling me?"

Amaral laughed. "Never happen."

"Oh, you think not, do you? Have you heard your wife?"

"I've heard her. And it looks like you think more of her talents than I do."

"I think plenty about her talents. She's got my wife yapping at me across the dinner table, enough to curdle my chowder. This from a woman who never dared a cross word to me in all our marriage. What are you thinking, man? Letting your wife's mouth run like that? You put a stop to it, or I will."

George Amaral took a step closer to Cottle. "Are you threat-ening my wife?"

"I'm protecting my home! My peace! My—" Cottle lifted his head and saw Ida. "And what are you glaring at? Are you one of those too? One of those sufferages?"

"I'm one of those who believes a wife should be free to speak

without her husband's permission," Ida said. "Just as you should
be free to speak without hers."

George Amaral pivoted to face Ida. He didn't look all that
thrilled with her defense, if that's what it was, and after that one
quick look to put the face to the voice he turned back to Cottle.
"You leave my wife alone." He strode off.

Cottle hollered after him. "That's what *I'm* saying! You leave
my wife alone!'

That's done it, thought Ida, as every head in the group behind
them swung around—Mrs. Cottle's reputation ruined, and Rose
Amaral about to become the victim of those patronizing whispers that always drift after a woman but never before her. She
would have tea with Rose, she decided. Soon.

But Cottle wasn't yet through. As he turned back to the group
of men on the beach it appeared that not a few were laughing
at him, picking up on Amaral's theme of women's suffrage as a
doomed cause. It took less than a minute for Cottle's hackles to
rise once more. He poked the nearest sniggering gentleman in
the back. "Can you count, Chidwell?"

"Can I count!"

"Utah. Idaho. Colorado. Wyoming. Women vote in all those
states already. If we don't watch out, we'll be peeling the potatoes while our wives are out running the country." He whirled
on Ida. 'What are you smiling about? You think any bunch of
fools can run the United States government?"

"They've done it before." More shouts, more laughs, again at
Cottle's expense.

So Ida had made no friend that day.

IDA RETURNED TO HER BICYCLE, thoughts back on salvage
now. Henry wasn't in the office but his bicycle was; she recalled

he'd mentioned inventorying the warehouse and tried there next, but still no Henry. She stood in the door and looked around; some order had risen from disorder, items now grouped into categories, unclaimed salvaged items separated from salvage equipment. Ida went over to the salvage equipment and poked around, wondering if the salvage company on the beach might want to purchase it, but she didn't see much of anything that could possibly be worth anything. She was about to leave when she paused; *why* didn't she see much of anything worth anything? For example, where was Mose's dive suit? Ida rolled her eyes toward the ceiling; the salvage equipment was on the *Cormorant*, of course.

Ida left the warehouse, returned to the office, and climbed the stairs to the apartment. From outside the door she could hear singing:

> *Hot is the lava tide that pours*
> *Adown Vesuvius' mountain*
> *And hot the stream that bubbles out*
> *From Iceland's gushing fountain.*
> *And hot the boy's ears boxed for doing*
> *That which he hadn't oughter,*
> *But hotter still the love I feel*
> *For Squire Jones's daughter.*

Ida rested her forehead against the door and listened until the song ended before knocking. When Henry opened the door her face inexplicably heated; being inside a single man's apartment sat high on her mother's *things one never does* list. Soon enough though she was distracted by how much the apartment had changed; or more precisely, how much it had been cleaned: no dust and dirt and mouse droppings, no clothes festooning the chairs, no stray boots on the kitchen table; a kettle actually simmered on the tiny stove and an attenuated gray tiger cat skirted the perimeter of the room. Curiously, a newspaper image of the *Newburgh* impaling the Union Wharf had been tacked to the wall.

Henry pointed to the cat. "I lured her in with a piece of bacon. I'm now down four mice." He pointed again. The lower right-hand light on the pane of windows nearest the door had been knocked out and a thick piece of canvas hung over it. "So she can come and go as she pleases."

"You're really settling in."

Henry peered at her. "This makes for a difficulty?"

"No. *No.* I saw you'd sorted the warehouse and thought you might be finishing up, moving on."

"I've barely begun to sort the warehouse."

"I didn't see Mose's dive gear. It would be on the *Cormorant*?"

"I'm sure."

"That burned boat may not be worth the expense of raising, but what of the gear?" Ida explained about the lull in the *Addie Todd* project. "Maybe they could use another job to fill in the time. We could give them a percentage of the salvage." She *had* learned something from Ezra, after all.

HENRY INSISTED THEY TAKE their bicycles to cross the street and coast down the single block to the shore, but since it was likely Ida's last ride, she didn't argue. They transacted the deal in fifteen minutes, a half-and-half split, settled on a handshake between Henry and Morgan, while Ida, the one whose idea it was, stood aside and watched with her hands hanging limp. When they returned to the bicycles, Henry pointed the other way, toward the beach road, and again Ida didn't argue.

They rode all the way to Cottage City, the smooth concrete roads a treat after the rougher going in Vineyard Haven. On the way back they stopped to rest on the lee side of a dune, against a piece of a wrecked dory no doubt washed up there during the gale.

"Oliver on your mind?" Henry asked, pointing to Ida's boot, which had begun to dig its own hole in the sand.

"You're the big expert, digging yourself all those holes. Or so you said."

Henry began to dig his own hole in silence. It was that silence that drew Ida to persist.

"What holes have you dug yourself into, Mr. Barstow?"

Without looking up, Henry spewed out one long string: a certain night at Duffy's with Mose; another night at Duffy's with Mose; a trip on the *Cormorant* in a storm; the carriage shop; the job of executor; he supposed he should now include his marriage . . . He stopped digging and looked hard at Ida. "But no, I can't consider the job of executor as a hole." He stood up and held out a hand for Ida.

They rode back, Henry leading the way, continuing past the shop and up the hill to Ida's, which meant that she couldn't return the bicycle unless they rode back to the shop and Ida walked home. Ida pictured the scene: her pushing the bike at Henry, Henry pushing it back, an argument igniting; Ida had enjoyed the afternoon too much to end it in argument. If life with Ezra had taught her one thing it was that another day for arguing was always around the corner.

12

IDA WOKE AGAIN IN THE NIGHT, imagining sounds. Footsteps. Knocking. She and Bett and the gun made another circuit that revealed nothing, and Ida finally had to face up to a new groundless edginess in her, caused by . . . what? She'd never been so edgy when Ezra had gone off and she'd been alone. What had changed? The gold. It came to her as she returned to her bedroom and crossed by the closet to her bed. Ezra had been hiding that gold from someone, and now she'd decided that someone had come looking. But no one had. There were no footsteps, no knocking, no anything. Ida snuggled in with Bett and fell asleep only to wake an hour later to another sound that proved to be a branch ticking against a downstairs window.

DESPITE HER FATIGUE the next morning, Ida would have returned the bicycle right then if Hattie hadn't called to say that Ruth was waiting with a contract for her to sign. This time there was no one digging holes in the yard; she asked Ruth as soon as they'd settled at the table, "Where's Oliver?"

"At the exchange with Hattie. I told her, 'I've raised my child.'"

Ida only hoped she hadn't said it in front of the boy, but it was a thin hope. Ruth pushed the paper across the table to Ida. Ruth had kept to Ida's figure regarding the percentage on the wool profits but declared it forfeit if Ida lost more than two sheep at lambing time.

"Six," Ida said.

"Three."

"Five."

They went back and forth, Ruth growing heated, Ida staying calm, until the calmness wore Ruth down. They settled on no more than four lambs lost, but no matter the loss, 20 percent of the profits at the livestock sale. Ida made sure to include the provision that her presence at the farm was not required beyond the wool sale.

As Ida rose to leave, Ruth said, "You were seen."

"Seen?"

"You and that Barstow. Out riding around on bicycles."

"He's teaching me."

"The bicycle is bad enough. Displaying your posterior like that. Skirts flying every which way. And then the matter of you barely widowed and him a married man."

"So. No need to worry, then."

Ruth stood up out of her chair and pointed at Ida. The storm that roiled her features took Ida aback. "I should like to know what your mother was thinking when she raised you up. Have you never heard the word *manners*? Or are you too ignorant to know what the word means? I won't have you dishonoring his memory by getting called harlot all over town. Do you hear?"

If there was one word Ida knew growing up it was the word *manners*, and in particular, manners when applied to one's elders. And it was true, there was a time when Ida would never have spoken to someone like Ruth the way Ida now spoke to her. But somewhere along the way, after Ida's parents had died, after she'd married Ezra, after she'd been snapped at by Ruth too many times to count, it had occurred to Ida that *manners* traveled in both directions. If Ruth wished to ignore the rules when she spoke to Ida, Ida could bloody well ignore them when she answered back. But what was the point—or better put, the

gain—in jousting with Ruth? There was no need for another re-
tort. There was only need for feet on the ground. Ida left.

ON WEDNESDAY one of the ewes aborted. Ida knew because
of the bloody tail, but she called Lem anyway to be sure. He
cleaned up the animal and came in to wash; he looked at her
shelves—all three painted now, and the splashboard and the
stool—but said nothing. Ida wished he had—she was still trying
to decide if she wanted to paint the table and chairs.

"I hear you're signing on with Ruth," Lem said. He paused. "I
hear other things too."

"If from Ruth, I hope you know enough—"

"He has a wife, Ida."

"Who does?"

"Are you getting cute with me now?"

"I've already had this talk with Ruth, Lem. First it's bicycling
isn't ladylike—"

"It isn't. Coming up that track to see you sprawled in the
dirt—"

"I must say I'd expected better of you, Lem."

"I might say the same of you, Ida."

Ida went to the door and opened it. "Thank you for stopping by."

"ONLY BECAUSE there's nothing for him to do while I'm working," Hattie said. "And you seem to have free time on your
hands." She looked without looking at the bicycle leaning against
the barn. Ida had never seen anyone master the look-without-
looking as well as Hattie; the eyes didn't shift directly left but
rotated upward as if looking for rain, only sliding sideways on

the way back down. But she wanted to ride that bicycle as much as Ida had; Ida could feel it. Since the day of the contract Ida had come to think something better of Hattie; she'd also come to think something worse of Hattie's life, stuck there with Ruth except for those few days of freedom at the telephone exchange. "I'll give you a lesson on your way home," Ida said.

"Would you?"

"I must warn you, your mother won't like it. Or Lem Daggett, for that matter, but he doesn't count."

Hattie's gaze drifted from Ida to Oliver, who had run from the dog pen to the sheep pasture, scattering the sheep to the far end. He wandered next to Ida's herb garden and started digging up the dirt with his boot.

"You'll mind him?" Hattie asked.

"Don't they have dirt at the telephone exchange?" But just then Ida noticed the perfect curve of Oliver's neck as he bent over the ground, and the way the sun backlit his ear, turning it into a translucent shell. Perhaps she could sketch Oliver, paint Oliver, while he was distracted with his digging. "I'll mind him," Ida said.

IDA HANDED OLIVER the bucket of corn and led him to the chicken house. She showed him how to scatter the corn on the ground and to watch his feet as he did it. When the chickens were all busy pecking up corn kernels she walked Oliver into the coop and showed him how to feel in the nests for the eggs; winter production was slow, but Oliver located three eggs and set them meticulously in the basket. Next she took him to the pasture fence to look over the sheep.

"We do this every day," she said. "Even if it's cold, or raining, or snowing, or—"

"Hailing?"

"Hailing," Ida said. "We look over the flock to see if any are limping or sluggish—"

"What's sluggish?"

"Moving slowly. Head hanging. Not eating. Lying down."

"That one's lying down." Oliver ran along the fence to get closer to the resting sheep and spooked it into rising and trotting off. He raced back to Ida. "Not sluggish?"

"No."

He wanted to know the mother and father of the sheep who ran off, and when Ida realized she knew who the mother was, she felt proud. She pointed to the ram in his paddock. "He's not the father of any of these sheep but he'll be the father of all the lambs born this year."

"Where's these sheep's father?"

"Sold. You can't keep the same father year after year."

"Why not?"

Ida wasn't up to explaining about inbreeding. "It's the rule," she said, which for some odd reason seemed to satisfy the boy. He went back to his hole and Ida went inside to finish her wash, but when she looked out and saw the same intense pose she'd noticed earlier she picked up her pad and charcoal and positioned herself at the window. The curve of his head and neck were easy enough, the shell-like shape of the ear, but she couldn't get the desperate clench of the fingers around the stick because they kept shifting, and although she knew just what she wanted to do with the light, the charcoal wouldn't capture it. It would serve as a study for a watercolor, though, or even a pastel . . . Ida was making notes along the edge of the pad when the telephone rang.

"Morgan's brought up a load," Henry said.

*   *   *

THEY STOOD in front of a mountain of blackened junk now piled on the warehouse floor. "Morgan said he'd take the capstan, winch, anchor, and chain as his share. The rest is ours."

"The rest of *what*?" Ida kicked aside what looked like part of a galley stove, extracted a bulbous, black orb with a hole where the face plate had been. Mose's dive helmet. She fished again and found the lead sole of one of the weighted shoes, and a piece of copper shaped like half an ox yoke that she recognized as the corselet to the dive suit. Ida picked up the helmet and rubbed at the black until a gleam of copper showed. Henry pushed aside a few other bits of black. "Compressor." Ida bent to look and when she turned around Oliver was halfway into the pile.

"Oliver! Get out of there!"

Henry, at least, heard her. He waded into the pile, gripped Oliver by the back of the coat and hoisted him free.

They resurrected a blackened ship's lantern; a dented coffeepot; the ship's bell; and an odd, large, flat-bottomed copper kettle lined with some kind of gray matter. Henry scraped at the gray. "Tin? Zinc?"

"Why would someone line a copper kettle with tin or zinc?"

Henry didn't answer.

Before they finished they'd found three more identical kettles and piled them together on one side of the floor. Henry picked them up one by one and turned them over, brow knitted, as Ida looked on.

"What *are* they?"

"I can't figure it. Copper would heat better than zinc or tin. It's more durable. And then this odd hole just below the lip."

"And four of them."

They stood side by side and studied the kettles, Oliver anchored between them by Henry's hand on his shoulder.

Ida gave up first. She bent down to Oliver and attempted **to** erase some of the black by brushing it with her fingers, but it only smeared. "Hattie will kill me."

"Come," Henry said. He took Oliver by the hand and led the way up the stairs to his apartment.

Ida stripped off Oliver's outer garments and Henry stood him at the sink to scrub his hands and face with a gritty brown soap that Ida hoped never to encounter herself, while she took a wet cloth to the jacket and trousers. She could hear Oliver chattering away at the sink—something about a red ship with blue sails—interspersed with Henry's responses: *Indeed. Curious. You don't say.* By the time Oliver's clothes had gone from black to gray, Oliver had gone from black to spotless.

"All right," Henry declared. "Safe to take him back."

IDA HAD PLANNED to walk Oliver to the exchange alone, but Henry declared his own business with Chester Luce and fell in alongside. At the exchange Ida reminded Hattie of the bicycle lesson.

"Oh," Hattie said, "I think not today."

"Oliver can help. He says he has a bicycle."

Hattie laughed. "That his father bought him."

Oh, thought Ida. So not.

Ida continued on up the hill. Henry came with her. Ida didn't remind him of his business with Chester Luce—it wasn't up to her to keep his affairs straight—and besides, he'd launched into another topic of some interest.

"I wanted to tell you I'm going to Newport next week," Henry said.

Ida, thinking of the way Henry had captured Oliver off the junk pile, how he'd stood guard over him at the sink as if he'd done it before, said, "Are your girls in Newport too?"

"Good Lord, I would hope not. They're with my wife's parents." Henry paused. "Often, it seems."

As Ida had nothing to say to that, they walked on in silence. The low winter light had dropped below the hill by the time they reached Ida's house, and for no sensible reason other than to defy Ruth and Lem, Ida said, "Would you come in?"

IDA ROUSED THE FIRE and lit the lamps. She made roasted cheese and put it out with a leftover onion soup and the whiskey bottle, all of which seemed to please Henry. When he finished eating he stretched his legs to the fire and crossed his arms over his chest. Long before he spoke Ida knew he had something to say that would carry some weight.

"You told me you didn't like Ezra much," he said. "Even at the beginning?"

"Do you think I'd marry someone I didn't like?" And there it was again—the tone. Was Ruth right? *Had* she no manners?

"I don't know," Henry said. "I don't know how independent of each other the two things are—liking and loving. I know I wanted my wife more than anything on earth, but when I saw that portrait of yours at the Boston Art Guild—"

Ida swiveled toward Henry in surprise. "Of Mrs. McKinley?"

"I saw that woman's face and couldn't imagine it with either a laugh or a tear. Then I looked at Perry standing beside her, the same face, only younger, and I realized why the woman in the portrait looked so familiar. I'd never seen Perry with either a laugh or a tear. Or not an honest one, at least."

"Don't tell me that looking at my portrait made you decide to divorce her."

Henry stood up, walked to the window, looked out at that

darkness, walked back, looked down at Ida. "Perhaps I didn't explain my situation clearly enough," he said, his voice tight. "It was my wife who decided to divorce me."

"And you who decided to go to Newport."

"If you have a point to make, please do."

Oh, she'd heard that before. From Ezra. *Is there a point here?* As a rule, when they reached the *point* in a conversation Ida walked away, understanding that they'd gone beyond any hope of useful communication.

But Ida *did* have a point to make. "You do understand whether or not you divorce is not my business?"

"Excuse me. I thought we knew each other well enough to share our dilemmas. *I didn't like my husband much. My wife and I are divorcing.*" He moved toward the door. "Thank you for the lovely meal. I'm now two in your debt."

"Henry."

He turned.

"It only seemed to me you were testing your decision, seeking my opinion as to whether it was right. Which I can't give. You do see that?"

He studied her. "Yes, I suppose. Of course."

"But I must say, if you're testing your decision, it seems to me that it would imply some doubt."

Henry returned to the fire, dropped into the chair, and leaned forward, elbows on knees. "You and Ezra. What *was* it like in the beginning?"

ONE CLEAR, WARM SUMMER NIGHT, not long after they'd met at the wedding, Ida had opened the door of her empty brownstone to find Ezra Pease on the stoop. He wore a shirt with the sleeves rolled up, no tie, his coat slung over one shoulder; the light from the open door put a shine in his eyes and when he spoke his teeth gleamed.

"I've come to take you walking."

Without going back inside, without a covering of any kind, Ida had pulled the door closed behind her, and they'd walked up the hill side by side. Ezra talked of the fine night, of the crime of wasting it indoors; he inquired of her health and spirits; were things getting better?

"Not better," Ida answered. "Easier."

"Tell me about your family." Ezra's voice was low and intimate, as if only he would care to know, and Ida told him, at much more length than she'd supposed possible: how she'd idolized both her brothers far beyond any hope of them living up to her construction; how her mother had been warm and enveloping but her father had been distant, forcing her to strive to gain a look or a word. That striving made those looks, those words, far more valuable in Ida's eyes than her mother's warmth; Ida said this for the first time to Ezra Pease, and said it with such pain she'd been unable to say anything else for a time. But they'd reached the top of the hill, and Ezra took her by the shoulders and turned her, pointing, his head so close to hers she could feel his breath: the Big and Little Dipper. The Seven Sisters. The Summer Triangle. Ida pretended she hadn't known perfectly well where they were, and on the way down she'd recovered herself enough to ask of his family. The situation was similar but vastly different: father, mother, and three sisters all dead, but slowly, one at a time, over a span of twenty years.

"I have one aunt left," he said. "And a cousin. I'd like to take you to meet them, to see my farm." *His* farm.

* * *

IDA TOLD HENRY SOME, but not all of this. Her intention had been to show that her decision to marry Ezra had not been irrational, that she could reasonably have done so with the expectation of perfect happiness. But what had seemed so dazzling on that night, so star-filled above and below, now seemed contrived, even manipulative, in the retelling. Granted she was younger and freshly bruised, but why hadn't she seen then what she saw now? For one, the way Ezra had assumed Ida's willingness to go out walking alone. For another, the ways he found to put his hands on her in a context she would be unable—or at least unlikely—to oppose.

But when Ida finished telling Henry her tale he said only, "Yes."

"At the beginning, I forgave Ezra everything," Ida said. "At the end, nothing. Perhaps I'm in part to blame."

Henry leaned over, gripped the arm of Ida's chair. "There are some things that are unforgivable," he said. "There are some people . . . There are times when one must stop striving to forgive or understand or explain and simply move on. To open that door and step through it." He looked down at his hand, still gripping the arm of Ida's chair, as if unsure as to how it got there. He drew it away; stood up. "I must go," he said.

He opened Ida's door and stepped through it. After he'd gone some way down the track his voice wafted back up the hill through the night: *Oh Shenandoah, I love your daughter . . .*

Again, Ida had neglected to tell Henry about the gold. By now, it seemed, she should be wondering why that was.

13

IT BECAME A ROUTINE; on the days that Hattie worked she dropped Oliver with Ida on her way to the exchange and picked him up on her way home. Ida tried twice more to give Hattie a bicycling lesson, but each time she refused. "I have Oliver," she said the first time, even though Oliver was deep in the barn attempting to get the ox to smile, and "I'm tired to the bone," she said the second time, but then ran up the hill after Oliver.

Ida didn't mind caring for Oliver, but she did find the boy troubling, in part because of her lack of experience with children; neither brother had lived long enough to provide Ida with nephews or nieces and there had been no child during her marriage to Ezra. Ezra had been convinced the fault lay with Ida and Ida had been too unsure of her scientific ground to counter his claim, but she hadn't minded her childless state; Ezra, the sheep, the chickens, these had been enough to tax her, and she was quite sure if she did have children it would put an end to her ever getting out her paints.

The second reason Ida struggled with Oliver was the boy himself. Why was his head always down? Why did he eat as if it were a punishment? Why did he speak so little? Why did he *dig* all the time? Ida did find ways to lure him out of the ground: he was fascinated by Bett and the ox and the sheep, and she'd managed to interest him in the chickens to the point that he would scatter their corn and hunt for eggs, but if the schedule held any gaps, he filled them with holes.

The days of icy winter rain were hardest. One such day when

Oliver had returned from the window for the eighth time to declare on the basis of nothing that it was stopping now, Ida took out her sketch pad and pencils and attempted to teach him his letters. Oliver had just announced that he hated letters and supposedly accidentally snapped off the point of his pencil when the telephone rang: Henry Barstow, with a question about a notation in one of the ledgers.

"What does EMS mean followed by various numbers?"

"I haven't the first idea. Oliver, stop digging at that plant!"

"Sounds busy there."

"I'm teaching Oliver the alphabet. We've mastered *O*."

"You've gotten all the way to *O*? Impressive."

"We haven't gotten all the way to *O*, we began with *O*. I'm teaching him his name."

"Oh."

Ida laughed, ridiculously cheered. "And now he's lost his pencil. Oliver, leave that plant alone! What time is it?"

"Ten to two."

Ida sighed. "Two hours and ten minutes to go. Ah well, the odds were good I'd have killed that plant anyway. Is it still miserable out?"

"Extremely."

"Ah, well. Stay warm."

"And you."

THE KNOCK CAME at five after two, startling Oliver and Ida both. Ida opened the door and Henry whooshed in shaking off the rain as Bett would do. "The perfect rainy day to visit friends indoors."

"I *hate* rain," Oliver said.

"I wonder how you feel about chess."

"I *hate* chess."

"Ah, that's too bad, as I was in the mood for a game. Ida, what about you?"

"If you'd teach me."

"That's one of my favorite things to do." Henry reached into his pocket, pulled out a small case, flipped it open, and tipped out what looked like dozens of tiny pieces made up of bits of horses, people in odd hats, and broken turrets. Or bedposts. He arranged the pieces on the table in front of Ida, demonstrating how each one moved. "The queen has all the talent but only the king matters. Unfair, I know—"

Ida sneaked a look at Oliver at the window; no child could have resisted the miniature kingdom that Henry had produced, and sure enough, Oliver had turned around and fixed his eyes on the board. When Henry finished demonstrating how the pieces moved and a bare minimum of rules he pointed to one of the pawns. "All right, Mrs. Pease. Which way does he move?"

"Straight!" Oliver shouted, plopping down at the table.

WHEN HATTIE ARRIVED to collect her charge, a slightly frayed Henry and an obstreperous Oliver were sprawled on the rug in heated argument over why a knight couldn't carry a pawn on its back when it jumped, and Ida sat perched on the sofa, attempting to sketch Oliver. She hadn't been pleased with the efforts thus far—her usual subjects didn't go from kneel to crouch to belly flop in rapid succession, and parts of him were a blur. As Hattie approached, Ida closed her sketchbook.

"Mayn't I look?"

"No," Henry said from the floor. "Or so she told me. I attempted one peek and that's when she exiled us to the floor."

"Too soon for showing," Ida said, but in truth her pencil

had slid from Oliver to Henry as if of its own volition and she was afraid of what that meant, afraid of the echoing sadness she kept mining in his features. Was he recalling playing chess with his daughters? Or with his brother? Or had he been one of those lonely boys who'd played by himself? Even more troubling was the fact that she'd dared take out her sketch pad in front of Henry in the first place.

"Come along, Oliver," Hattie said.

"It's my *turn*."

"Game over," Henry said. "I have to play with Mrs. Pease now."

Hattie opened her mouth but closed it without speaking. She collected Oliver and left.

Henry packed up his game and stood. "Did I cause trouble for you just now?"

"How?"

"If Hattie tells her mother I was playing with Mrs. Pease—"

"Too late. Ruth's already told me to stop riding around with you. So did Lem Daggett."

Henry studied her. "And are you?"

"I was until they said that. Tea?"

"Tea," Henry said.

Tea led to Ida's offering Henry a bowl of chowder. The chowder led to Ida thinking—and talking—of Mose. "He used to bring us clams," she said. "In exchange for a bowl of chowder. He approved of my chowder. He approved of anything I put in front of him, come to that. He said he could smell my chowder at the bottom of the hill."

Abruptly, Henry stood up and carried his bowl to the sink. "It's grown late. I'd best go."

So Henry didn't wish to talk of Mose. Although Ida had had no desire to talk of Ezra, she'd imagined Henry would have a different feeling about his brother, that he might like to remember and talk of him with someone who had cared for him too. How desperately she'd wanted to talk of her brothers, but after her mother drowned, Ida had had no one to talk to about them. Even so, if it proved too difficult for Henry, Ida would respect that and move on. If he ever happened to stop by again.

HE STOPPED BY TWO DAYS LATER. The rain had dissipated but the clouds hadn't; they hovered, pressing the sky low. Ida had been standing at the window making a study of the clouds, attempting to learn what they predicted, but she'd managed to draw few consistent conclusions when Henry wheeled into view. He approached the house carrying an odd, deep, flat-sided basket trailing two leather straps. "A basket for your bicycle," he explained. "So you can carry your sketchbook."

Ida took the basket and looked at it. She looked at Henry. She thought of piling her paint box and paper into the basket and riding . . . where?

Anywhere. That was the joy of it. "Thank you," she said.

SHE WENT AFTER THE CLOUDS. They rolled over her as she checked the sheep, danced above the trees as she untethered the ox from the wood and led him back into the barn, followed her as she wheeled the bicycle into the yard. Her charcoal and paper fit so neatly in the basket it was as if Henry had measured, and she flushed with purpose; she was an *artist*, not a sheep farmer, not a scandal. Ida kept an eye on the clouds as best she could between watching out for ruts and stones, plotting the shapes and values that would best define the mood of the day.

When Ida reached the lighthouse, she was blissfully tired and fully warmed. She sat, happy to wait for the right combination of clouds and lighthouse, shadow and light, gentle and hard, soft and stark—the redbrick column had recently been painted white and it should have taken well to her black and white charcoal on the toned paper but her fingers felt stiff. Awkward. She felt she'd gotten the lights and darks of the clouds just right, but she'd somehow missed on the shapes; for one thing they didn't stay still, as Oliver didn't stay still. But just as a familiar tightness gripped her brow she remembered another one of Mr. Morris's classes. He'd stopped at her easel to study a drawing that had already turned Ida hot and impatient and out of sorts.

"There's nothing right about it," she said. "It can't be saved. It doesn't belong in this room with the others."

But Mr. Morris only reached down into the pit where Ida wallowed and fished her out. "Never attack one's own drawings. Acknowledge only and move on."

Ida looked and acknowledged that the problem wasn't so much the lack of stillness in the clouds but that in her rendition they looked too solid, too stuck. She flipped over the paper and tried again, refusing to pack up until she'd created the looseness, the soft edges she was after. She rode home half pleased.

IDA TOPPED THE HILL to find Lem standing at the fence looking out over the sheep. The sight of him caused her to wobble, but she managed to leap free and land upright.

"Pretty late to be out riding alone," he said.

"If that's your way of asking if I *was* riding alone—"

"It's my way of telling you it's near dark. If you can't see the road—"

"You're right," Ida said. "I struck a stone just there, did you notice? Come inside. I'm freezing."

Once inside, Ida pondered and discarded the idea of asking Lem if he'd like a whiskey, fairly sure that even if *he'd* like one he wouldn't like the idea of *Ida* liking one. Christmas punch was one thing; straight whiskey in the middle of the week was something else. And she was damned if she was going to sit there and watch Lem drink it. "Tea?" she asked.

Lem nodded. Ida fed wood into the range and pumped up water for the kettle. She kindled a blaze in the open fireplace and tapped the back of the chair most recently occupied by Henry. Lem sat down. The wrong kind of silence fell, as if someone were awaiting an apology. Ida could think of no reason why she owed one but could think of a reason why Lem did; such thinking did nothing to soften the silence.

"His wife's divorcing him," she said finally.

"So you go riding when she does. If she does."

"I don't care what people say."

"Your aunt cares."

"She's not my aunt."

"Ezra was her nephew, one of her two remaining kin. She thought the world of him. She thinks you disrespect his memory."

"The two of you talk about this?"

"There's another rumor that Barstow gave you that bicycle."

Ida could feel an old rage building, her mother's voice ringing. *No, you can't drive the carriage. No, you can't go hunting with your brothers. No, you may not ever accept a gift from a man . . .* Even when the gift in question was a box of fudge. With nuts.

Ida went to the pantry for the whiskey bottle and poured a good dollop into her teacup. She held up the bottle to Lem, ignoring the stiff neck that greeted her. "I'm chilled straight to the bone. You?" Without waiting for him to answer she poured an equal dollop into Lem's cup. "I wanted to learn to ride a bicycle," she said carefully Calmly. "Henry Barstow loaned me this one. He felt—and I must say I agreed—it's difficult to learn to ride without one."

Lem didn't smile.

"But the basket might be considered a gift, although since I'll have no use for it once I return the bicycle, I'll probably give that back too. I love that gift—I can carry my art supplies now. I rode to the lighthouse and worked on clouds. Come to think of it, I might keep the basket. When I get to Boston I plan to buy a bicycle of my own."

Lem stood up. "I'd best go."

"Go, then."

After he left, Ida sat where she was, drinking her tea, alternately flushing and paling as the conversation with Lem ran through her mind. She didn't know what she'd expected; Lem had been one of the few people on the island who'd seemed to accept her, welcome her, but maybe he was just like the rest, closing themselves up like daylilies whenever a stranger appeared. Ida finished her tea, reached for Lem's, and drank it down. If only she had money. She needed to leave the place before it was too late, before she turned into a whiskey-drinking recluse who could paint nothing but clouds. If *only* she had money. Ida peered into the teacup, but nothing was left beyond a pale gold wash. A pale *gold* wash.

Ida got to her feet and took to the stairs. She fumbled the trunk away from the wall, pulled out the newspaper, and dropped the golden nuggets onto the bed. A case could be made that perhaps Ezra had come by this gold honestly, using some means Ida couldn't fathom just yet, that he had hidden it in the closet for nothing but safekeeping, and if that were the case Ida did have money. But how much money? Not knowing for certain how Ezra had come by it, Ida was reluctant to flash it around the island.

Ida returned to the parlor, yanked open the desk, and hauled out the business cards she'd stuffed into one of the cubbyholes. She flipped through the sheep shearer and the dentist and the wheelwright and any number of illegible dirtied cards until she came to it: *Samuel A. Greave, Assayer of Fine Metals, 271 Bowdoin Street, Boston.* Boston. The homesickness hit her like a northeast blow. And no matter the provenance of the gold, the first step—certainly the first step—was to find out its value. And Ida had memorized four dates on her almanac, the four dates Julia Ward Howe would be speaking at the Horticultural Hall in Boston; the first was March the second, which was Thursday next. The lambs shouldn't have started yet. Could it be that it would all work?

14

IDA CALLED LEM. "I'm going to Boston on business Thursday next," she said. "Will you check the farm while I'm gone?"

"Business."

"Personal business. I'll be back the Friday."

Ida didn't trouble to read the silence.

"All right," Lem said, and they were done.

She called Henry next. Ida was no wheedler; she hated games; she began hard and clean, right where she needed to end.

"I'm going to Boston on Thursday next and I need to pay for the boat and train and room and meals. I know an inexpensive boardinghouse on Tremont."

"Boston?"

"On business. Personal business." It had worked well enough the first time.

This silence Ida did try to read but failed. "Very well," he said in time. "I'll bring the funds by."

Ida waited till Wednesday to call Ruth and was relieved when Hattie answered. "I'm going to Boston on business, so I'm sorry, I can't keep Oliver tomorrow."

"What business?"

"Personal."

"Personal!"

"I'll talk to you about it another time."

"Ida, are you all right? Is anything wrong?"

"I'm fine."

"Is it your health?"

"No. I'm fine."

"What *personal*—"

"Financial, Hattie. I'm pursuing all avenues. But I'd rather not have it spread all over town." Ida paused. "Or all over the house."

Silence.

"You understand?"

"Yes."

"Thank you," Ida said. "We'll chat when I return." She was fairly sure she meant it.

IDA PULLED her town clothes off the pegs where they'd hung since she'd unpacked them to make room for Ezra's clothes in the trunk, which still sat in the middle of the room. At first she'd forgotten all about the plan to ask Lem to take the trunk to the Bethel, and then she'd been so annoyed with him she was disinclined to ask him for a favor. Now she pulled her carpet bag off the shelf, folded in extra drawers and stockings, adding her nightdress and one extra skirt to avoid going down to dine in a mud-spattered travel outfit. The boardinghouse she had in mind was run by a Mrs. Clarke, the widowed mother of one of Mr. Morris's art students, which would allow her to find out if he was still teaching and perhaps arrange a brief visit.

Next Ida went out to return the ox to the barn, and just as she was exiting the wood with the animal she saw Ruth, Hattie, and Oliver coming down the track.

Oliver raced up to examine the ox; Hattie came on fast behind him. "She's come to find out what this personal business is," she whispered. "I thought I'd come along in case you needed extra troops." And to find out for herself what Ida's personal business was.

Ida led the ox into the barn, Oliver trailing them. "My father has oxes," he said.

"Oxen."

"Ten oxens."

"Ten oxen. That's a lot."

"Oxen," Oliver repeated. "What's his name?"

Ezra had called the ox Stub, short for stubborn, but now Ida had another idea. "He doesn't have a name. Can you think of one?"

Oliver dropped into his thoughtful look. "Ollie," he said.

"You don't think I'll confuse him with you?"

"It's Oll-*ee*," Oliver said.

So that was that. Ida moved on. "Oliver, I wanted to tell you that I'll be away for a couple of days." It was important to Ida that Oliver hear it from her, that he understood she would be back, but it turned out it wasn't important to Oliver. Without a blink he gave Ollie a pat and ran back outside. Ida should have followed but instead she lingered in the barn, breathing in the animal steam, wondering how it was that she, a rising artist from Boston, was hiding out in a barn on Martha's Vineyard in the company of an ox. She jumped when Ruth spoke from behind her.

"I don't think it unreasonable to expect my manager to inform me when she's leaving town."

"It's entirely reasonable." Ida removed the ox's harness and circled Ruth to hang it on its peg. "I assumed when I called your house and spoke to Hattie she'd alert you, which it appears she did, but next time I'll be sure to speak with you in person. I've arranged for Lem to come by. Is there anything else?"

"Funny time to be charging off."

"It's the only time. I have to be here for the lambing."

"It must be pressing business."

"Pressing enough."

"I'd like to know what's so pressing."

I'm sure you would, Ida thought. But next she thought, *why not?* "It appears all of my family's assets aren't yet accounted for. I'm off to sort it out." Which was true. At least for a short time, Ezra had been her family, no matter the opinion of this woman still blocking the door.

THE ENVELOPE HENRY DROPPED on the table was thicker than the last. "I see no reason for you to stay in . . . how did you describe it? An inexpensive boardinghouse? In fact I took the liberty of reserving you a room at Parker's."

Ida looked from the envelope to Henry.

"I'll cancel it if you don't want it, but I didn't want to suggest it if it turned out they were full up. I've had another thought, which means it can all go down as estate expense; I could accompany you on this trip. That way we could visit the salvage office and close it up. What do you think?"

Ruth. That was what Ida thought. And Lem. And even that look she'd collected from Chester Luce. What would they say when they heard that Ida and Henry Barstow had boarded the ferry together for Boston and not returned till the following night? But then she thought: the Parker House was next to the Horticultural Hall. Could it be that this would all work out? But she needed Henry to understand a few things first.

"I have personal—"

"As do I. But it would cut the tedium of travel and allow me to repay one of the two dinners I now owe you; Parker's dining room is unsurpassed, and I never do enjoy a solitary meal out."

Everything he said made sense. Of course he made sense.

And Ruth had already declared Ida a disgrace—what to lose from that quarter, other than her employment and the roof over her head?

"If appearances are a concern," Henry added, "we can board the ferry separately. No one could blame you if an acquaintance just happened to take the same boat."

No one except Ruth. Lem. Chester Luce. But staying at Parker's. Dinner at Parker's. A lightness filled Ida just thinking of it—the expanses of marble, the soft glow of the parlor furniture, the glittering dining room, the absence of sheep.

"I'll be boarding early in the morning. You're a grown man—where and when you go isn't my business."

Contrary to where and when Ida went, which appeared to be everyone's business.

IDA WENT TO BED EARLY, taking that last minute before sleep to do what she'd been doing most evenings of late, pulling the photograph of Henry's father out of its folio and examining it under the light of the lamp. The man was and wasn't Henry; the physical self, yes, but there was a blandness in that face that Henry's lacked. She supposed that when your wife left you for another and your brother went down at sea some of the blandness would be erased, but some of what Ida kept seeing in Henry didn't look like it belonged to either the wife or brother.

Ida hadn't yet begun the painting; she'd been unable to decide whether to remove Henry's father from the orchard or not. A simple portrait was what she was used to, but the way the man leaned against the tree fascinated Ida, as if he were laying claim to it, as if he were physically part of it, and it had begun to seem like an amputation to cut that tree out. And what of the man's coloring? Before she began she should ask Henry if his father possessed his same complexion or if he was paler or darker, if that light hair was the exact dried-beach-grass color as Henry's, if the eyes were the same burnt sienna as Henry's . . .

It wasn't the kind of rumination that was apt to lead to sleep, but when Ida's eyes finally lost their focus and her mind began to go blank it only left space for something else. She bolted up, went to the closet, and opened the panel in the wall. How could she forget to pack that? She removed the gold from the paper, stuffed the nuggets into her reticule, pulled the drawstring tight and knotted it. She looked at the carpet bag. *Parker House.* She opened the bag, removed the extra skirt, and selected in its place a favorite old ensemble: a heliotrope and mauve dress with trumpet skirt, embroidered décolletage, and fitted bolero jacket.

Next morning Ida rose before light and did her chores. She went inside to wash and dress, fussed idiotically over her hat, and still arrived early at the dock. She cast a brief look at the shore, noting that the *Addie Todd* had been refloated and anchored at the mouth of the harbor, the *Newburgh* had been towed off, but the wharf still contained its kink, and battered hulls and other debris still littered the beach. She boarded and took a seat as far back from the gangway as she could, and when Henry Barstow arrived he ignored her so effectively she believed he hadn't seen her. Ida watched him select a forward seat and strike up a conversation with one of the Mayhew brothers, never once looking back.

But on the train to Boston Henry took another tack. He entered her car, began to pass her seat, and did a double take as graceful as a pirouette. "Mrs. Pease! How extraordinary to find you on this train." He pointed at the empty seat beside her. "Would I be intruding?"

Ida shook her head, too afraid she'd laugh if she spoke. He

stowed his case, took out his handkerchief, wiped the cinders from the seat beside her, and sat.

"Are you staying the night in Boston or making a day trip?"

"I stay the night."

"And where—"

"The Parker House."

"Ah! Of course. As am I. Where else? I wonder if I might invite you to dine there this evening or do you have other plans?"

"I have no plans until eight this evening."

"There, we have that settled. Now we can sit back and enjoy the trip."

And to her surprise, Ida did. As a rule she found train travel dirty, smelly, and tedious, but this time, with each mile that chugged by, she felt something in her unwind; she knew no one on the train but Henry, so that was the first good news; the next good news was that Henry was good train company. He was in high spirits, he talked some, he listened some, he didn't fight the occasional silence. He laughed just when Ida needed validation of her wit; he frowned when no other expression could be deemed appropriate; for example, when he asked if she had folk to visit in Boston and Ida told him they'd been lost at sea, a true if insufficient statement. But Ida had learned from Ezra that sympathy could be meaningless as well as cheap, that sometimes its purpose was to acquire something for the sympathizer. Ezra's sympathy had demanded certain personal returns; if Ida read Henry's eyes right they asked for something much more difficult to give: that she let him know her. Ida wasn't ready to do that. She might have managed to describe her brothers and her father being sucked into the sea without a trace, but of her mother's unforgivable act? She could not.

But that too was all right. Ida saw at once that her refusal to elaborate was all right. When a man came through the cars selling magazines, newspapers, and candy, Henry bought one of everything, and it helped to move past the gap. They sat in silence reading, Ida sucking on sassafras and Henry on cinnamon, as the miles flowed under Ida like silk.

The sight of the brand-new South-Central Station jolted her awake. How could such a grand thing, all eagles and columns, a modern-day colosseum, spring up in her absence? She walked along looking up until Henry finally took her arm to guide her to the next shock—the entrance to the underground tunnel through which the trains now ran. Two nickels bought them entry; Ida peered down the brightly lit, gleaming white tunnel and for the first time in her life Ida felt a stranger in town, as if Boston had left her behind and gone on without her to become something else.

15

HENRY MADE A MOTION toward engaging a hack to take them from the Park Street station to the Parker House, but as they each carried nothing but a small carpet bag, and Ida could already see the familiar sites ahead of her, she wanted to walk. Henry took her bag from her and they set out. The bare, gray winter Common didn't lure Ida, but she'd always thought of the white arrow of the Park Street Church steeple as a kind of beacon: Parker House tea and cake ahead. Her pace freshened. At the Granary Burial Ground she slowed to glance at the gravestone of James Otis.

"Did you know," she asked Henry, "that well over one hundred years ago he agitated for the woman's vote? First admitting them to the educational avenues reserved for men and then giving them the vote?"

Henry gave Ida a thoughtful look. "And yet here we are."

Yes. There they were, Ida thought, thinking of Rose Amaral. Tea with Rose Amaral. Soon. But there, now, was the Parker House, a fairy castle of a thing encased in marble, bedecked with turrets and bay windows, with the single word engraved over the door as if everyone who mattered would already know what it was: Parker's.

Ida allowed the bellman to take her bag and walked up the marble steps and over the plush carpet. How far away the farm seemed to Ida at that moment! She looked around for Henry but found he'd disappeared; a wash of alarm swept through her until it occurred to her he'd no doubt wanted to allow her to engage her room without him lingering nearby. Ida completed her registration and was just stepping into the elevator as Henry appeared at the front desk; she blushed because she felt silly, and heated again because she felt dangerous. And yet, oddly, safe.

IDA'S FIFTH-FLOOR ROOM faced west, giving her a near view of the Common and a far view of the Charles River. She'd thought to soak in the tub first and then venture out to the assayer's office, then if time remained, to visit Mr. Morris at his studio, but she couldn't stop looking out. When she got through looking she started touching—the buttery dresser, the velvet loveseat, the feather bed—and then circled back to the window; by the time she drew herself away it had gotten too late for the tub. She fixed her hair, repositioned her hat, put on her coat, and jumped when the phone rang.

"A Mr. Barstow for you, ma'am."

"Please connect."

"Hello." He sounded close. Intimate.

"Hello," Ida said.

"If you need anything I'm in room 508. How is your accommodation?"

"I don't see how our shabby little estate can afford two rooms at the Parker House."

"I hope you aren't suggesting something shocking," he said, in such a perfect imitation of Aunt Ruth that she burst out laughing. Oh, how good it felt!

"I'm going out," she said, collecting herself.

No argument. None of Lem's *You're going out* alone? None of

Ruth's and Hattie's *Where are you going? What time will you be back?* "Very well. Meet at the dining room at six?"

"Six. Yes."

ALL THE WAY to the lobby Ida felt the weight of her reticule, as heavy as her guilt. She should have told Henry. She should have taken him with her. But once on the street she took a deep breath and realigned her shoulders; what she hadn't done was done—only what she would do lay ahead.

Again, Ida chose to walk. Winter in Boston could be many things—damp and gloomy, dry and crisp—but it always came with a wind that could discourage the most determined walker in venturing beyond a single block. This day's wind blew with her, though, propelling her past Horticultural Hall so fast Ida almost missed a placard announcing the eight P.M. lecture.

Ida continued along School to Somerset and onto Bowdoin Street, where a pasteboard sign in a second-story window declared it the offices of Samuel A. Greave. The stairwell smelled of mice, living and dead. Ida gripped her reticule around the neck, reached the top of the stairs, and through the glass-paned door spied a man behind a counter hunched over a tray of what looked to be jewelry.

Ida stepped in. "I wonder if I'm where I belong. I'm looking for—"

The man's eyes lifted, widened. Damp, flaccid lips parted. "Whoever it is, I'm it. Samuel Greave."

"Yes. Mr. Greave. I wonder if you'd be able to evaluate the worth of what appears to be a gold nugget."

The lips snapped shut. The eyes narrowed. "Hand her here."

Ida didn't want to. She didn't like those lips, those eyes, the general air of the man. But it didn't matter if she liked the man, did it? She'd come here for a purpose. She opened her reticule and extracted a single nugget. She set it down on the counter and almost before it had touched wood the man's rakelike fingers clawed it up. His other hand fumbled in a drawer for a jeweler's loupe, which he fixed to his eye.

"What's the name again?"

"I didn't say, but it's Mrs. Pease."

The loupe came down. The man squinted at her again. "From—?"

"Boston. If you don't mind, I'm in a bit of a hurry."

Greave stared at her a few more seconds, pulled out a small scale, and plopped the nugget onto it. "Just over half an ounce. Ten dollars. You got any more in there?"

"It's gold, then?"

"It is that. Where'd you get it?"

"It was in the family." Ida held out her hand for the nugget. "Thank you, you've been most helpful."

Again, Greave squinted at Ida. "Pease, you say. And where'd you say you were from?"

"Boston. I *am* in a hurry."

Greave replaced his loupe and looked at the nugget again. He removed the loupe and pointed at Ida's bag. "Looks like you've still got some weight in there."

Ida plucked the nugget from the man's fingers, returned it to her bag, and swung for the door.

"Hold on there, missy. You show me what's in that bag and I might do better on my number. I might just take the whole lot off you."

"Not today, thank you."

As Ida pushed through the door she felt movement behind her; Greave, rising from his chair, coming around the desk. She hurried down the stairs into the street, uneasy in a way she'd never been in Boston; an irrational fear that Greave intended to follow her assailed her. She walked fast to the corner and turned; a man stood on the street in front of Greave's building, but Ida couldn't tell if it was Greave or not. To be safe, Ida turned left instead of her intended right and added a few more unnecessary turns. When she looked behind her again she saw no Greave. Bloody gold. It caused her to hear things on the island and see things in Boston. *Enough.*

Ida corrected her route, pondering what she'd just done. She could have used that ten—she could have used whatever Greave planned to give her for the lot of them—but something wasn't right about the man, the offer. If Ida were a cat, the fur on her back would have risen the minute Greave seemed to start at the name Pease, at the way he seemed to doubt her when she said she was from Boston, at the way he whisked the nugget off the scale when Ida leaned in to look. There were men who looked and acted and smelled dishonest, and Greave was one of them.

And then there were men like Ezra. What was the truth of Ezra?

Ida paused to look around her and was startled to see that she wasn't far from her old home, that if she simply climbed Mount Vernon Street she'd be standing in front of their old, blue door. *Blue,* her mother had said. *Absolutely not, the Wymans' door is blue,* her father had countered. *Green, then,* her mother had said, a nice *peacock green* which Ida could have told her father was actually blue but didn't. A longing to see if that old blue door was still there battered Ida; she started to walk past the turn but stopped in the middle of it.

Ida climbed the hill and there it was, perched above the same sloping lawn, centered on the brick facade of the same old town house: the blue door. And there was the sagging railing her brother had hit with the carriage. And if she walked around back, no doubt Ida would see the mismatched carriage house doors, still waiting for replacement, and the brown stubble of the rose garden. And the marble birdbath. And the cherry tree.

Ida stayed where she was, in the street. For the most part they had been a happy family, able to laugh over the blue door even if her father swore every year that he was going to have it repainted, a ritual Ida suspected he kept up only to give the others their annual burst of amusement. If Ida closed her eyes she could see their faces and forms so clearly she might believe they lived there still, without her, perhaps inquiring over breakfast every third day or so where Ida had gone, but she'd never contributed that much to the family conversation anyway, preferring to keep to her corner. Her paints. Her dreams. What she remembered most about her father were those rare moments when the stiffness cracked and he bellowed out a great laugh. What she remembered most of her mother was the way she always seemed to be hurrying out of the room. Her brothers she remembered as alternately looking out for her or tormenting her, which left her hovering in perpetual thrall to them, never knowing which side of which brother would appear next.

For the first time, standing there in the street, Ida reflected on what had gone on in her father's and brothers' heads as their ship went down. Did *they* have time to reflect? Did they regret something they'd done or not done with their lives? Ida guessed not; all three men had a way of taking what came and moving on without dissecting it; Ida suspected her mother had simply dissected it once too often and then couldn't put the pieces together again.

But what of Ida? What would she have done differently if she'd known she'd be standing on the street outside her former home, alone? Married the neighbor's son as her mother had urged? Taken her father's advice to give up art school and spend her time perfecting her domestic skills? Talked more at breakfast? No. No. Again, no. But she might have listened harder to the silence and remembered it when Ezra came to call.

ON HER RETURN TRIP Ida continued to look back at each turn, occasionally spying a Mr. Greave scurrying in and out of shadows but always he turned out to be nothing but more shadow. She shook off her silliness and took the wide loop that would bring her past the museum in Copley Square, but she stood in front of it a long time before braving the marble steps and granite columns. Once inside she ignored the Flemish tapestries, the armor, the Egyptians and Greeks, and headed straight for the school, stopping in front of Mr. Morris's old door to listen. The voice inside was a woman's, but the words were Mr. Morris's—*define the whole . . . respect your spaces . . . make your strokes bold, cheerful . . .* She twisted the knob and cracked the door open. Inside the narrow frame she saw one of Mr. Morris's former students, a woman named Helen Ballou, whom Ida knew well and wasn't surprised to see in this new roll; when Ida informed Mr. Morris she was leaving Boston to marry a Martha's Vineyard sheep farmer his attention had taken an abrupt turn toward Helen, and there it had stayed. Ida had never been asked to assist with a class again. As Helen expounded she circled the room with Mr. Morris's same purposeful stride, his same confident air. *No no no. Yes yes yes.* Ida might have—no, would certainly have—been the one circling that room if she'd stayed in Boston.

Ida turned her attention from Helen and fixed her gaze behind her to the nude man reclining against a length of blue cloth on a white dais. Every woman in the room studied the man with intense concentration, working charcoal over paper just as if they stared at . . . well, a stuffed owl. But now Helen spied Ida and moved to the back of the room, pointing to the hall. They stepped outside, and Helen immediately engulfed Ida in a hug much warmer than Ida had expected. She held Ida away and took her in.

"Ida Russell!"

It felt so good to hear her old name that Ida didn't correct her. "It's good to see you, Helen. You've taken over his class? Does he not teach at all anymore?"

Helen peered at Ida. "You don't know?"

Oh, Ida hated it when a sentence began that way. "Tell me and I'll be able to answer that question, Helen."

"William drowned eight months ago. He was vacationing in New York. He walked into a pond and didn't come out. Some thought it was deliberate; a large mural he'd devoted himself to was destroyed by damp, and he'd been . . . despondent."

Ida stood stunned. Silent.

Helen laid a hand on Ida's arm. "I know, Ida. I know. I'm sorry to have to tell you all this standing in a hall, but I'd best go in. How long are you in town? I'd love to sit with you and catch up, to hear what you've been working on. Or come join the class! I actually have some sway here now; I could say you'd come to help teach—one swing around the easels and then you sit and paint as long as you like, no charge."

"I'm here but a single day," Ida answered, and the relief she found in the honest excuse dismayed her.

"Next time, then. Or write me here. I must go." Helen hugged her again and disappeared through the door.

Ida stood where she was. After a time she laid her hand against the closed door and closed her eyes. She could not, she would not, credit it—that Mr. Morris, her Mr. Morris, had done as her mother had done. Ida had never told Mr. Morris of her family, but she'd once heard some students in the class whispering about her, about her mother, about her father and brothers, behind barely compressed lips. If students knew, surely Mr. Morris knew, but he would never take her mother's painful tale and use it as a pattern, a guide. He wouldn't do that to her. But of course it was nothing to do with her.

Ida made a sharp pivot and strode down the hall toward the door. She could not mourn one more time. Not for Mr. Morris, not even for her past life. Or were they so entwined that there was no sense in attempting to separate the two? The man, the school, had been everything to her while she lived here, but now that man and that old Ida were both gone. Ida dashed at her tears and pushed out into Boylston Street, her beloved Boylston Street, for the first time in her life feeling the trespasser, whatever had made this place her own now gone.

IDA WALKED. It was all she could think to do. Scenes washed over her like haphazard waves on a rock-strewn beach, diverted left and right as they hit the boulders, at times running backward to confront themselves on the way in. Her earliest impression of Mr. Morris had been the right one; he'd picked her out, cultivated her, seen something in her work that deserved greater nurturing. It had all been borne out the day he'd tapped her on the shoulder as she'd been packing up her easel.

"Hold a minute, Miss Russell, if you'd be so kind."

The day had already been a rewarding one; the model, a young woman clad in a lilac dress and holding a white parasol, had presented certain challenges: how to keep the parasol from dominating the scene, how to do justice to a face half in shadow, how to capture the expression of boredom and yet translate it from a bored young model to a young woman bored by . . . what? Was she waiting for a friend? Tiring of a beau? Tiring of her life as a young woman of privilege, gravitating from one senseless social gathering to another, just as Ida had tired of it? Yes, that was the note. And Ida had gotten it just right, she thought, or nearly so, and she'd stopped at a place where she knew what came next, which solved half the next day's struggle.

Ida lingered as the other students packed away their paints and easels and funneled out the door. Mr. Morris fussed about with some papers until the last student was out, and then lifted his eyes to Ida.

"I've an appointment in New York regarding a large commission. I'll be gone for the next two classes. I wonder if you'd take my place here."

Nothing, Ida thought now, nothing had ever astounded her more, thrilled her more. There had been a second's hesitation; how not to hesitate when she was being asked to teach before she'd even finished being a student? But quite soon after— surprisingly soon after—Ida remembered one of Mr. Morris's favorite maxims: *An artist never stops learning.* It was fair, then, to keep learning as she taught. And she remembered a second Morris maxim: *Be bold.*

And so she was bold.

And yet somehow Mr. Morris had lost all his boldness.

Ida walked and walked, Mr. Morris keeping company inside her head, until she remembered Henry. She would be late to dine.

IDA'S RECENT WEIGHT LOSS meant the old heliotrope and mauve dress didn't fit as glovelike as it once had, but it allowed for the gentler lacing of the corset from which Ida had so long ago removed the stays. Now when Ida walked she enjoyed the luxurious sensation of actual movement inside her dress. As she entered the dining room Henry stood, bowed, grinned, and again, even despite Mr. Morris, or perhaps because of it, Ida found it impossible not to grin back. She needed that look in his eyes, needed this single night of distraction; she would not waste it wallowing in Mr. Morris's despair. Anger washed through her, the same old anger, at Ezra, at her mother, and now, at Mr. Morris. They had had enough of her nights or, in the case of Mr. Morris, were bound to have more of them, but they would not have this one night too. Ida forced her mind to the way the chandeliers turned Henry's hair to gold while dulling everyone else, the way her own locket seemed to glow brighter than any other jewel in the room, as if Ida and Henry were the subject of a painting and everyone else was just the background. Yes, she would stay in that painting—for this one night alone.

Ida ordered all her old favorite Parker specialties: the scrod, the rolls, the Boston cream pie. Henry followed suit and added a bottle of wine. Ida was glad when he bypassed any business talk and asked instead, "How does the city look to you?"

If he'd asked her earlier that afternoon Ida would have answered, "Wonderful." She might have talked of that ease she felt seeing houses and shops in orderly rows, not darting about over every hill and cartway. Now she could only think of that mournful walk home from the museum. She pushed—again—to bury the day's sorrow.

"Wonderful," she tried anyway.

"And what of the traffic?"

"Oh come, there's hardly any left, what with these underground trains. And I do love the electric trolleys—no manure to step around. I walked all the way to Beacon Hill and didn't stop once to clean my shoes. But what of you? Did you succeed in your errand?"

"I did, to the extent that I would call it success. I've retained an attorney who specializes in divorce. He's prepared me for the road ahead. I'm ready now."

"Good." Ida held up her hands. "I don't mean to say—"

Henry ignored the backpedal. "And you?"

And there was Mr. Morris, again. But if she spoke his name she would lose herself, lose the night, lose it all. Ida gripped the edge of the table. "I stopped at the museum today and got reminded of how far we've traveled, what distance remains."

Henry looked at her blankly. Ida thought of attempting to explain about the life class but hesitated. She might not flinch at sketching a nude man, but how to explain that burning desire to another man, so close across the table, even a fully clothed one?

"Have you heard of the sculptor Anne Whitney?"

Henry shook his head.

"She entered a blind contest to design a sculpture of Charles Sumner. She won the contest, but when the committee discovered she was a woman they refused to give her the commission. It was inappropriate, they said, for a woman to sculpt a man's legs."

Henry cocked his head. "Through his clothes?"

"Through his clothes." Encouraged that Henry hadn't blinked there, Ida pushed on. "And today I saw a class full of women sketching a male model from the nude. You see, don't you, that if I wish to advance in my art I must be here, in this city?"

"If you wish to paint nude men."

"Michelangelo dissected corpses to teach himself how to sculpt the human form. If I want to be the best, if I want to earn those commissions from the society men and women who have the money to buy my portraits, I need to keep studying the human form. I need to keep learning."

Henry nodded. It was a nod, a look, of such new understanding that Ida kept on. And after all, there was only one subject to go on with now.

"I found out today my teacher killed himself in despair over a destroyed work. He worked so hard to teach me. He encouraged me. He—" Ida broke off. "I must become the best painter I can to honor him."

"I didn't know your teacher," Henry said. "But I imagine he might say to you now, if he could, better you paint to honor yourself."

And yes, of course, that was just what Mr. Morris would say. Who was this man who seemed to know Ida far better than she knew herself? Ida pressed the heels of her hands to her eyes. She straightened her shoulders. She leaned forward. "I want to show you something. In my room."

16

IDA SET THE RETICULE ON THE BED and sat beside it, in wait for the knock on the door. Henry hadn't walked with her to the elevator; she imagined him sitting at the table and pondering the proper amount of time before he followed her, and she was surprised by how long he chose to wait. He would not compromise her. And yet when she opened the door to him she saw at once that he felt the raw possibility of her invitation, their location; they stood several feet apart but she knew—oh, she knew—that if she took a single step closer there would be no one that night in the room down the hall.

Ida turned away with effort; she walked to the bed and up-ended the reticule, letting the gold nuggets spill out in whatever direction they chose. "I found these hidden behind a closet wall."

And there it all went. Just as Ida had watched it come into his face, now she watched it go, watched the face close and heat and cool until it ended tight-lipped and pale. He crossed to the bed; Ida picked up the nugget she'd shown Greave and handed it to Henry.

"I found an assayer's card in Ezra's desk and came here to ask him what it was worth. Not knowing where it came from—or how—I didn't feel easy showing it around the island. The assayer offered ten dollars for that one in your hand, but I didn't take it; I didn't trust—"

"And this was your personal business."

"I should have told you of the discovery, I know. I just didn't—" Ida waved her hand over the scattering of stones. "I just didn't. I'm sorry."

Henry weighed the rock in his hand. "You were wise not to take his ten dollars—you could double that at least. And you were wise not to dance these rocks around the island." He tossed the nugget back on the bed.

"You think they were stolen?"

Henry said nothing.

"If you think to save my husband's reputation in my eyes, don't take the trouble. *I* think they were not his by right. He'd come home from Duffy's and empty the coins and bills onto the kitchen table where they'd sit all night, even all day, the door wide open, but this he hides behind a secret panel in the closet. I think they were either stolen or salvaged and hidden from Mose, which is the same as stealing, only worse, because Mose was his partner. His *friend*. And if that were the case, half of this belongs to you."

Henry held up his hands. "You don't know that, Ida. Maybe this was Ezra's half of a salvage job and he wanted to keep it separate, a nest egg for you should something happen to him."

"And not tell me it was there? I could have lived a hundred years and never found it; if I hadn't knocked the trunk into the wall—"

"Maybe he planned to tell you and never got the chance. You told me once you didn't like him much. I'll tell you now that I didn't like him much either, especially not of late. But that doesn't mean we can assume we're looking at ill-gotten gains."

"Then why did you tell me it was a good thing I hadn't flashed that gold around town?"

"I have no idea why I've said anything I've said tonight. You sprang this on me and I'm tired and we have to get to the salvage office early if we want to make our train. I'm going to bed. Meet me in the lobby at eight?"

Ida nodded, watched his stiff back as it went out the door. She sat motionless on the bed pondering her mistakes, one made, one not made; first, she'd concealed the gold from Henry, and once he saw she had done so he pulled away. That was the mistake she'd made. The second mistake, the one not made, had only been prevented by the first one; if she'd trusted Henry, if he *hadn't* pulled away, if he'd taken a single step toward her, she would have done the wrong thing. She, Ida Pease, freshly widowed, would have done any and every wrong thing, and not because she'd been pressured into it as she had been with Ezra, but because she wanted to. With a married man.

Ida got up and went to the window. Outside, a splash of light from the Horticultural Hall painted the sidewalk. Ida had forgotten the other reason she was here in Boston: Julia Ward Howe. She checked the time. The lecture would be nearly over, but if nothing else, the hundred-yard walk might still her mind.

THE CROWD HAD already begun to flood the streets when Ida arrived, Howe just collecting her papers and preparing to exit the stage; Ida looked at the shrunken form, the snow-white hair, and realized with shock that the woman who had spoken so eloquently and so long for abolition and suffrage was now old. And yet not old. Instead of the traditional black worn by women lecturers she was clad in white cashmere, and when she looked down at Ida from the stage her gray eyes were as keen as a heron's as it scanned the marsh for fish. Those eyes reminded Ida of the commotion when Howe chose to use the moniker Mrs. Julia Ward Howe over the usual Mrs. Samuel Gridley Howe, of the fuss again when she traveled to Europe alone, of the courage it took to tour the country lecturing to audiences that could not all be considered friendly.

"Good evening," Howe said. "What did you think of my little speech?"

"I missed it, I'm afraid. I came from an appointment." When Howe said nothing Ida blithered on. *In town this night only, settling my husband's estate . . . so sorry to miss . .*

Howe tucked her papers into her satchel and took the three steps from the stage down to Ida's level. "I worked long and hard on a bill guaranteeing a widow half her husband's estate. How did you fare in your settlement?"

"There should be a fair divide." If half of nothing was fair.

Howe studied Ida for a second. "I was looking through my old journals last week in preparation for this speech tonight. I came upon the single sentence I wrote the day after my husband's funeral. 'I begin my new life today.' You see some of what I've been doing with that life. Would you like to vote?"

"I would."

That same nod again. "Then read. Educate yourself. Prepare. Fight. It will come."

"I do read. The newspaper. Other—"

Howe didn't wait for what other things Ida read. "Women have been voting in Wyoming since 1869. Since that date there has never been an embezzlement of public funds, or a scandalous use of funds, or a single case of graft. Would you like to know why?" Again Howe didn't wait for Ida. "A Wyoming senator explained it to me. The politicians learned early on that if they wanted the woman's vote they could never put up a candidate that wasn't of sound moral character."

"If Wyoming can, why not—" Ida stopped.

"Massachusetts? Exactly. Miss Anthony was once given an

enamel pin of our nation's flag. Every year that a state adopts women's suffrage she changes one of the enamel stars to a diamond. I want Massachusetts to have a diamond in that flag. I'm an old woman. You're a young one. Will you help yourself to your own freedom?"

Ida wanted to explain that she'd been exiled to a small island in the Atlantic Ocean, that she now lived isolated and helpless, but she couldn't bring herself to say the words in front of the force that was Julia Ward Howe. "I will," she said.

Howe thrust a small square of pasteboard into Ida's hand. "My card." She was so tiny, and yet her presence dwarfed Ida, her royal air making Ida feel like a child. But Ida wasn't a child. She was an artist.

"May I ask . . . has anyone ever painted you?"

"Many times. I was even sculpted in Rome. Apparently I sit well."

Yes, she would sit well, Ida thought, but there was more to her than the sitting: the strength shining through the stillness, the enthusiasm for life and work radiating outward, the eyes suggesting a secret core that only a good artist might capture. Ida took the card the woman offered her and slipped it inside her glove against her racing pulse.

"I hope you get to vote," Ida said.

"I won't," Howe said. "But you will."

HE WAS LATE. Ida stood in the foyer feeling conspicuous and out of place, more than one pair of eyes cast her way in speculation; that annoyed her and also the fact that she'd slept poorly, then ended up oversleeping, and had rushed madly to make it to the lobby in time. So many ghosts had haunted her night: Mr. Morris, of course, but Ezra too, and then there was that something that had sprung to life and then died between her and Henry. Just as Ida was about to ask the desk to place a call to his room, he came barreling out of the elevator tweaking at his tie.

"Good Lord, I'm sorry. It was a bad night. I overslept. I do hope you weren't waiting long." He led them outside and into a hack, Ida making no objection although again she'd have preferred the walk, but there was something about the musty, creaky vehicle that brought Boston home to her even more than the walk might have done. The air lay heavy between them with unsaid words, no doubt reproach on Henry's side, but as Ida had no excuse for keeping the gold a secret, she in her turn had nothing to say.

They remained silent until Henry shot forward in his seat, pointing. "There! That car! A Stanley Steamer. It will be the end of my business."

"How? I see one car and dozens of carriages."

"It will be the other way around soon." He sat back and they returned to silence until they arrived at the address on Washington Street.

Henry fitted a hand under Ida's elbow to help her over the filthy gutter and onto the sidewalk, but it seemed to Ida he made a point of letting her go the second she landed safely on the other side. Ida looked around. Ezra's next-door neighbors had been a grocer and a print office, but Henry had already looked several doors past them and pointed. A bicycle shop. He walked toward it as if in a trance and Ida followed; the row of bicycles was dazzling, but Ida's eye locked on the far wall of the shop where the bicycling attire hung—men's *and* women's. She reached for what appeared to be a shortened skirt, but when Ida pulled at the skirt it revealed itself to be bifurcated, like wide-legged trousers. She took it from its peg and peered at it inside and out until Henry motioned to her from the door, tapped his watch, mouthed the word *train*.

Ezra and Mose's office turned out to be a box of a room littered with dust squalls, old newspapers, and a handful of books stacked on the corner of the single desk. Henry opened the file cabinet while Ida looked over the books, picking a small pocket atlas out of the stack. She tried to remember what Ezra had ever said about his Boston office—*terrible chair . . . half-blocked view . . . noisy neighbors . . .* He'd complained of heat in summer and chill in winter, but no wonder, since the tiny stove probably burned through coal faster than they could lug it up the stairs. Ida pulled her coat tight around her, thrust her hands in her pockets, and pondered how bare and forlorn the place seemed, but with its usual occupants dead, how else could it seem? She tried to imagine Mose at the desk and Ezra poking through files as Henry was doing now . . . or wasn't doing. He stood in front of the window staring out.

"Well?" Ida asked.

Henry turned around. "I see nothing worth saving." He swung his arm wide to encompass the office proper. "You?"

Ida wanted nothing but to leave the place and told Henry so.

17

WHAT A DIFFERENCE, the going from the coming! How easily they'd sat and talked—or not talked—on the way into town, how stiffly they sat and not talked now! Ida could source its root in her failure to tell Henry about the gold, and perhaps she should have apologized again, but she could also think Henry might be a bit more understanding. At one point he seemed to lift his eyes to her as if about to say something that would start them again, but his eyes skated away. Ida contemplated what she might say to start the talk, but she felt so weighed down, so dull. She blamed Mr. Morris for some of that weight, but not all.

They suffered a stilted parting at the dock; Ida trudged up the hill, feeling friendless, to find Lem just coming out of the barn and Bett leaping frantically against the wall of her pen. Ida opened the pen door and allowed Bett to press against her, to push her nose into Ida's hand, to race around her in circles. When Bett tore off, Ida turned her attention to Lem but saw that his attention hadn't yet left what he'd been doing when she arrived; even now he stood half-turned toward the barn.

"What's wrong?"

"First lamb."

Ida dropped her carpetbag and hurried into the barn. Lem had housed ewe and lamb in one of the empty stalls and the ewe stood happily munching as the lamb sucked. Ida heard Lem shuffle in behind her. "It was so small I thought there was another one stuck in there, but she was just early. I penned her so I could watch her a day or two."

"I'd planned to be here for this."

"It's early. Like I said. It's all right. Everything's all right."

But it wasn't. Ida felt it and didn't know why she felt it—that this creature had begun its existence while she was away was of no consequence to any of them; she'd arranged for Lem to be on hand and he had been, yet she felt so betrayed—so *betraying*—as if she'd violated some silent covenant she'd made with her flock. Ruth's flock. Ida stood and watched as mother and lamb settled into the hay to nap. She could see the rise and fall of the lamb's round, full belly; if she did indeed lose four lambs, she vowed this one would not be among them.

"How was Boston?" Lem asked. Ida looked over at him, thinking there was something more than casual interest in the tone, but his eyes were fixed on the sheep.

"Changing," Ida answered. "Electric trolleys. Underground trains. I even saw an automobile. And a lot more people."

"Tell them to stay there."

"Don't worry, I'll be joining them as soon as I'm able."

Lem looked at her then. "I hope not till we're through lambing."

Yes, there was something in his tone, some echo of Henry and bicycles and Boston or some other transgression he had yet to name. "Would I be so upset over missing this birth if I were going away before the rest of them came?"

"I'm sure I don't know what you'd be, Ida. If you're all set I'll be off now. A warning—they like to arrive near daylight. Look for the enlarged udder, a swayback once the lamb has dropped, restless circles, lying down, getting up—"

"It's not my first lambing season, you know."

"It is though, isn't it? The first one that's your responsibility. Call me when they start to go."

Ida pointed to the pair in the hay. "What do I owe you for this?"

"No charge."

"Why not?"

"You asked a neighbor to watch the farm. You didn't hire the farmhand to watch it."

"Lem—"

"Next time you call, the hand will be out, don't you worry."

And just how did one do that? Ida wondered.

IDA TOOK OFF HER TRAVEL SUIT and hung it up for brushing; she unpacked the heliotrope and mauve with a sigh. She could feel the grit of the train on her skin, but she would have to wash later; she had work to do. Outside again, she collected Bett and loosed her in the pasture with the ancient cry: *Away!* The dog swung wide to the left and got the sheep well grouped; Ida's *Bring 'em here* drove them to the gate and they poured through into the near, small pasture where Ida could keep a closer watch over the flock. She gave Bett a *That'll do,* and the dog stood down. They walked together inside—the nights that Bett spent in the yard were few now—but after a good run she usually settled calmly at Ida's feet and got to work shedding fur over everything Ida owned. It was a price she was willing to pay for the soft eyes on her whenever she moved, for the touch of warmth against her at night, for the shared sighs.

IDA ROSE BEFORE DAWN the next morning and made her own restless circle of the pasture, looking out for the signs Lem had mentioned, but all was calm. She checked the ewe and lamb in the pen and spent the rest of the day catching up on farm and house chores but made time at midafternoon to pack up her sketch pad and wheel out the bicycle. If she planned to return to the Boston art world, she needed art that would sell in Boston. But what?

The wind chased Ida down the track and she let it direct her; it buffeted her all the way to the shore and deposited her on the beach, where the remnants of last winter's gale still lingered in stray bits of wreckage, eroded dune, the distant, crooked wharf. It struck Ida that this was just the thing for her to sketch— the storm was well known in Boston and this would serve as a record of it. If she captured what she saw now, if she then went back and attempted to recall what she'd seen then . . . She propped her bicycle against a nearby stone wall, found a rock facing east, and began to sketch.

It began well. Surprisingly so. The scene took naturally to her charcoal; the black and white desolation flowed viscerally over the page, but when she went back in with a few destructive, hacking strokes symbolizing the storm's rage she overdid it, allowing her own anger to creep in. At Ezra. At Henry. At herself for marrying Ezra in the first place, for letting Henry's new distance upset her so. At the end of an hour, Ida was chilled, exhausted, and less and less happy with her efforts; she packed up and set off for home. Still distracted, still unhappy, she soon came up with another reason for her foul mood: forgetting her usual caution she tangled her skirt in her chain and toppled into the sedge, where she spent the last half hour of daylight picking out the cloth.

IDA ATE COLD MUTTON FOR DINNER, cleaned up the kitchen, and climbed the stairs, trailed by Bett; the hip she'd landed on when she fell had begun to ache, and she was looking forward to dousing the lamp and getting straight into bed, but when she saw the torn skirt she'd left lying on the bed she roused. She rifled the trunk for a pair of Ezra's pants in a similar tweed, thinking to lay in a patch, but instead found herself carrying the skirt, pants, and oil lamp into the empty studio where her sewing machine still sat. Ezra had bought her that machine, an unusually thoughtful gift, or it would have been, if it hadn't come on the heels of one or another caught-out lie, the exact lie now escaping her.

Ida found a roll of tracing paper and ripped off a large swath. She began to draw, everything she remembered from the bifurcated skirt she'd seen in Boston. She ripped apart both garments and pieced them back together, Ezra's pants adding the material for the needed gusset that would enclose the legs. When Ida had finished, the result looked more like a baggy pair of men's trousers than a fashionable bicycling skirt, but she walked the room delighted with the way each leg moved freely within its own casing, the way the hem fell only to the top of her boots and no farther.

Next morning, after Ida finished checking the sheep and tending to the other animals, she put on the skirt—or trousers—and went to the barn for her bicycle. She'd just mounted it for a test run when Ruth, Hattie, and Oliver came down the hill. Oliver scooted off to the pasture fence, but Ruth and Hattie came straight for Ida. She dismounted.

"What on earth are you wearing?" Ruth said.

"A bicycle skirt."

"Don't tell me that thing goes out in public."

"Only when it's on top of a bicycle." Ida spread her legs apart, displaying the clever gusset. "This will keep me from breaking my neck."

Ruth looked as if she preferred the option of the broken neck. She stalked off after Oliver. Hattie remained. She pointed to Oliver where he hung on the gate, calling in vain to the sheep that had scattered to the far side of the pasture at his approach.

"It's good for him to be here."

Ida looked at the boy. "Do you know, I like having him here."

"I'm glad. I thought you should know him."

Ida looked at Hattie. "Why? Why did you think I should know him?"

Hattie looked away.

Ida looked again at Oliver, at that blocky little body, the wide-set eyes, the brows that angled upward toward the nose as if always in question.

"Hattie. Why should I know him?"

Hattie made no answer.

"He's Ezra's, isn't he?"

Hattie's head snapped up.

"Isn't he?"

Hattie nodded.

"With his own cousin."

"Second cousin once removed. No one counts that."

Ida looked from the boy to Hattie; suddenly the woman appeared deeper, darker, stranger. Ida opened her mouth to ask the questions that roiled through her head: Why didn't you tell me? Does Ruth know? Does Oliver? Does *Ezra*?

Ida asked that last one first.

"Oh, he knew. He just didn't admit it."

"Did he provide for him?"

"I wouldn't know anything about that."

"You never asked him? You never once said, how's Oliver, or where's he living, or does he need clothes, or—"

Hattie raised her chin. "How could I ask any of that when Ezra never admitted it?"

"And Oliver? What's he been told?"

"That's the odd thing. Nothing. One day he just made up this father of his and when no one told him otherwise he stuck to it."

"And Ruth?"

"Suspects, I think. I see her looking at him sometimes, not in a happy way, and she snaps at him all the time. She wants him out of her sight. I'm just as glad to oblige her."

"This grandmother—"

"She's having some kind of operation next week. We'll see after that. I'd offer to keep him anyway, but with Ruth—"

Ruth. Ida was sick to death of Ruth. When the old woman left the fence to return to them, Ida swerved wide and joined Oliver.

The boy pointed to three sheep standing grouped around a tree stump, picking off the lichen. "The others don't like them."

"Of course they do," Ida said, "but they're their own family— the grandmother, the daughter, the granddaughter." Or at least Ida thought they were.

"My father has sheep," Oliver said.

"Come," Ida said, "I have something to show you."

THE BOY STOOD at the edge of the barn stall, looking from the lamb to Ida and back at the lamb again, beaming.

"Can I touch it?"

"No. His mother won't like it."

Oliver watched the lamb nurse in silence for a time. "My mother died," he said.

"So did mine."

Oliver looked up at Ida with new interest.

"Come along," she said.

They rejoined Ruth and Hattie. "You've got a ewe ready to drop," Ruth said.

"I'm aware."

"Well, I hope you know what you're doing."

Ida waved at the sheep. "I hope *they* do."

Ruth, Hattie, and Oliver prepared to start up the track, but with a skill Bett would have envied, Ida cut Hattie from the group and held her back. "You need to tell that boy who his father is and that he's dead."

"Why? It won't make him feel any better."

"Maybe it won't, but it will save him a lifetime of looking in the face of every stranger. A lifetime of lying."

"Boys lie. They outgrow it."

Hattie started to walk on, but Ida caught her arm. "I mean it. Now, while it's almost fresh news. Not a year from now when it's turned into another ugly secret. I'm warning you; if you don't do it, I will."

NOW, ONLY NOW, did Ida remember. She'd never met Oliver's mother, Ezra's cousin Mary Nye, but the first time Ida heard the name, Hattie had whispered it to Ezra—supposedly out of Ida's hearing—at their wedding.

"I was thinking of having Mary Nye's boy here for a visit come summer."

Ida distinctly recalled Ezra's answer because his tone had changed so abruptly, just as Ida's ears had perked up when Hattie had dropped her own tone to that whisper. But Ezra's voice had turned the other way, each word dropping, distinct and heavy as a stone—a warning. "He'll arrive when I'm gone."

"I'm not sure just when—"

"When I'm gone, Hattie."

But of course Ida never understood the warning at the time, although Hattie must have; Oliver never visited the island while Ezra was alive.

THE EWE READY TO DROP WAS QUEEN. Ida watched her move with faltering steps along the wall, head lowered, sides heaving. *Most do fine on their own,* Lem had told her, and Ida repeated it to herself as she stood her vigil. The ewe dropped down, got up, dropped again and stayed there, raising her head and throwing it back with each contraction. The water bag appeared, then the hoofs, then the nose, and then the rest of it; Queen's head whipped around to break the sac and lick the mucus from its nose. The lamb shuddered, took its first breath, and stumbled to its knees. Queen kept lapping, washing down every inch of the lamb until it was thoroughly cleaned before she nudged it toward her bulging udder. "Oh, you sweet, sweet thing," Ida said out loud. The ewe's head swung around to look at her.

"You too," Ida told her.

RUTH APPEARED FIRST, alone this time. Ida watched from the kitchen window as she went to the paddock, spied the new lamb, and stormed toward the house. Ida met her with the door open.

"I expect to be told when a lamb is birthed."

"Oh," Ida said sweetly. "I didn't know that. The count is two so far, alive and well."

"I'll be keeping my own count, thank you."

"Fine. What's your method? I like to start at one."

Ruth leaned in. "You think to amuse me? You don't, you know."

I think to amuse *me*, Ida thought, but of late it was getting harder to do.

LEM WAS NEXT, coming up the track unsummoned. He'd told Ida the lambing was now her responsibility, but he seemed as unwilling as Ruth to trust it to her; he admired the new lamb but questioned why the pair in the barn hadn't been returned to pasture, pointed out the ewes he felt were nearest to birthing, and reminded her—again—of the signs to watch for. But the difference between Lem and Ruth was considerable; Ida knew enough to listen when Lem spoke. She returned the barn animals to pasture and watched the pair of new lambs bounce off in a wild game of tag that soon turned into king-of-the-hill over a twelve-inch tuft of earth.

"Two down," Lem said.

She listened and heard nothing in Lem's words but the words, and they fell on her light as a cloud.

"Coffee," she said, not like a question.

They sat at the kitchen table talking sheep until Hattie arrived with Oliver. Ida looked her question at Hattie; Hattie responded with a shake of the head. Lem rose. "Would you like a lift to the exchange, Hattie?"

"Why, yes, thank you, Lem." Before she climbed into Lem's wagon, she drew close to Ida. "*You* tell him," she said.

18

IDA SAW AND HEARD NOTHING of Henry for a week. It worried her into fitful sleep, leaving her awake and pondering if Henry had been that angry by her lack of trust or if he was ill or if he'd gone back to New Bedford to his real life. In the night, every possibility seemed likely; in daylight only one did: Henry, angry.

But in daylight Ida was busy. The previous year Ida noted that the lambs came along on a bell curve, first a few and then a few more and then a whole rush of them until it trickled out at the end of April. During the next week Ida woke to find two new lambs, watched another drop, and called Lem over one that wouldn't.

"Give it two hours," Lem said, but at an hour and forty-five minutes Ida went back to the phone; it would take him fifteen more to get there, she reasoned.

Lem arrived in ten; in less than two he'd clambered out of the wagon, stripped off his shirt, and felt inside the ewe.

"One nose, one hoof."

So there was the trouble; nose and both hooves had to exit together. Lem slid around inside the ewe until he found the other tiny hoof and guided it out; he took hold of each leg and applied gentle traction as the ewe heaved, easing out the lamb. Ida was so elated she gave Lem a hug that bloodied her coat, the feel of his bare back reminding her belatedly that this was not a thing she should be doing, but Lem himself seemed unperturbed. "Good you called," he said.

After he left Ida made a final circle of the pasture, went inside to sponge off her coat, and still feeling the good outcome of one phone call, decided to make another.

He answered the phone full of business. "Henry Barstow."

"Come by the farm," Ida said. "I have something to show you. Six of them, in fact."

"I'm tied up just now." The words, the line, felt dead.

"That's all right. Tomorrow then. They won't grow up overnight."

"Lambs? Congratulations. But I did want to speak with you. I've sold the Boston office furniture and terminated the lease. Someone's coming to look over the warehouse goods next week."

"Well, then . . . well done."

"And you. Well done to you. I'll get up as soon as I can."

He hung up.

CONGRATULATIONS . . . TIED UP . . . *well done to you*. All right, then, something *was* wrong, and Ida doubted it had anything to do with ill health. She'd apologized for keeping the gold a secret in Boston, but if he was going to stay angry she was going to *get* angry. Now that Ida thought of it, she *was* angry. Having to guess at Ezra's moods had tired her straight through; she was done with it.

Ida changed into her bicycle skirt, collected her bicycle, and rode into town, pumping the bicycle and her anger with the same stroke. She opened the office door to Henry's bicycle but no Henry. She tried the warehouse, but no Henry. She climbed the stairs to the apartment and knocked; when a woman opened the door Ida stepped back.

"Yes?"

Ida well remembered Perry Barstow, but clearly Perry didn't

remember Ida. "I'm Mrs. Pease," Ida said. "I have business with Mr. Barstow."

"Ah! Mrs. Pease and the never-ending estate business. I told Henry, even dead we continue to wait on his brother." She turned around, skirt in a careless whirl around her long legs, just as Henry entered the room and fixed his eyes on Ida. What was that look? Beyond surprise. A warning, perhaps? Perry turned to face Ida again. "I'm sorry, dear. What did you say your name was?"

"Ida Pease," Henry said. "Hello, Ida. We can talk in the office."

He approached the door as if to walk through it, as if to walk Ida downstairs, as if to do what he'd just said he'd do—talk to her in the office—but Ida held up her hand. "You're busy," she said. "We'll talk another time."

Ida exited the building, turned left for home, about-faced, and turned right for Tilton's hardware. Tilton actually gave her a nod as she entered, so she must not have looked as dangerous as she felt.

"I need paint."

"More of the ochre?"

So he'd remembered. But ochre wasn't the color of rage. "Brick red," she said. 'My husband bought some from you two years ago or so. I can bring in the can—"

"No need." Tilton disappeared and returned with a new can. "Only one brick red."

But so many colors for rage; Ida saw them in a kaleidoscope before her eyes all the way home. She wasn't raging at Henry: he'd done nothing but cohabit with his lawful wife. She was raging at herself for forgetting about the wife. Oh, Lem, she thought, why don't I listen harder when you speak?

* * *

MOST EWES LIKED to deliver near daylight, but not all of them. Ida saw it as soon as she crested the hill: the distressed animal lying on its side, the swollen lamb's head protruding from her, the lamb's eyes slits, its tongue blue. Again, Ida at a loss. Again, the call to Lem.

He managed to get there in nine minutes this time. "This calls for a smaller hand than mine," Lem said.

Ida stripped off her jacket and rolled her sleeve over her shoulder. Lem coached her on how to slip her fingers into the hollow below the throat, feel her way past the shoulder, and push and pull until the head shrank back and the legs came forward.

"Gentle pressure," Lem said. "If you pull, she'll push. Let her do the work. Ease it. Ease it." Ida gripped the legs, applied steady pressure in concert with the heaving of the ewe, and the lamb slid out, as ugly a thing as Ida had ever beheld. The ewe barely lifted her head, but when Ida set the lamb at her nose she rallied. By now Ida knew that deep, guttural chatter with which a ewe greeted her offspring, knew that by the time the ewe had licked the lamb clean she'd have created a bond that would last for life. She watched to make sure the lamb was breathing normally and found its way to its mother's udder; she straightened, senselessly holding her bloody arm away from her already filthy skirt, turned around and saw Henry Barstow standing at the fence.

AFTER IDA WASHED and changed they sat in the kitchen, drinking coffee topped with rich, yellow cream and eating thick slices of buttered bread. Since Ida was famished she ate in silence, waiting for Henry to speak, something she was getting better at.

"You seem . . . elated," he said.

"I've got a seventh healthy lamb, one I was sure was dead an hour earlier."

"They mean something to you, then."

"They mean money. They mean me getting off this island."

Silence. Again, Ida waited.

"She got tired of waiting for me in Newport."

"She doesn't much like waiting, does she?"

"No."

"How long has she been here?"

"Three days. She leaves in the morning."

"And then?"

"We divorce. I told you."

Which wasn't exactly Ida's question. Or maybe it was. She pushed away from the sink. "Come." She led Henry up the stairs and into her bedroom. She watched him look around, at the bed, the trunk, the bed again, the travel suit that still hung unbrushed on the closet door. She opened the closet and showed Henry the cubbyhole where the gold was stashed. "The paper the gold was wrapped in was six months old. Ezra was in Boston all the time. Why didn't he just sell the gold to that Greave instead of hiding it?"

"I don't believe—"

"You believe it was stolen, don't you? That's why you didn't want me flashing it around the island. But I'll tell you what *I* think. I think he was hiding it from me."

Henry said nothing.

"And would you like to hear another little secret Ezra never shared? Oliver is his child."

Again, Henry said nothing.

"I'm so tired of secrets. I'm sorry I didn't tell you about the gold. I'm sorry I didn't trust you."

"There's no reason on earth why you should trust me." Henry strode across the room to the trunk. "You've packed already."

"No. That's Ezra."

Henry stepped back so fast Ida barked out a laugh. "Go ahead. Look."

Henry did. He actually did. He even lifted out several layers of shirts, trousers, nightshirts, woollies. He returned to stand in the middle of the room, to cast his eyes everywhere but at Ida. He spied the photograph of his father on the table next to the bed and crossed to pick it up.

"I haven't begun it," Ida said. "I need you to tell me more about him. Did he share your coloring? He looks like he loved being a farmer. Did he?"

Henry continued to gaze at the photo. "I've been told many times I was my father, but I wasn't. I was never as vigorous, as brazen, as unconcerned about things."

"What things?"

"Mose was more my father. I looked like him and it confused people, but Mose was the one. Carefree. Bold. You liked Mose, you'd have liked my father."

"You can't think me carefree and bold."

Henry set the photo down and for the first time looked straight at Ida. "At times I've thought you carefree and bold. On the bicycle. At Parker House. Now."

"*Now?*"

"I shouldn't be here in this room. You know this, and yet you don't care. Those curtains are wide open. My bicycle is parked at your door. Were Ruth or Lem or anyone—"

"You're right. I don't care."

Henry strode to the window and whirled on Ida. "I wonder if you know what this does to me, being invited to your room, twice now, you all business, and me standing here thinking 'I can't breathe unless I touch her,' and then I think of my circumstance. Your circumstance. And I know I can do nothing but tell you what I came to tell you; I leave for Newport in the morning."

"I should have gone to Newport two years ago," Ida said. It was a joke, something to allow a retreat from the dangerous place they'd landed, but Henry didn't seem to see the humor.

"We don't though, do we? We believe the words. We believe we have to try. Even Mose believed. Do you know what he told me of you and Ezra? That Ezra had gone mad over a Boston painter and if he married her she'd be the making of him."

"My money would be his making. That's what he meant."

Henry shook his head. "I don't think so, Ida. But sometimes it's harder to give up a false idea than a true one. I have to go."

Ida stood up and crossed the room to Henry. "It wasn't all business. Either time. Even that first time, at the gallery. You looked at my painting. You looked at *me*. You told me my painting was extraordinary. You told me to paint the next Ida Russell. I can't breathe either, not touching you. But I look at our circumstances differently. I see them negating each other. My husband is dead. Your wife might as well be. Why must Ruth and Lem and—"

Ida had stepped in so close she could have touched his arm; she *did* touch his arm; she leaned toward him, but Henry gripped her shoulders and stood her away. "Ida. No."

He left.

19

SHE FELT THE FOOL. It was true he'd spoken first, but it was also true she'd spoken second, and with such heat. And he'd stood her away from him. Ida paced the room in an effort to cool her cheeks, but it only inflamed them more. She spied her travel suit still hanging on the door and went after her clothes brush; she craved movement, distraction, a change of subject, mental and physical. She beat at the cloth with such ferocity she dislodged it from its hanger, and it tumbled to the floor, something sliding from its pocket: the tiny atlas she'd found in the Boston office. In an unconscious gesture she must have slipped it into her skirt.

Well, she'd been after distraction. She picked up the book, sat down on the bed, and opened it to the flyleaf; *E. A. Pease* had been written in thick, black ink inside. Ezra had a way of writing his name as if he were angry at it, the beginning of the *E* jabbed so fiercely into the page it left a blot, the cross-stroke on the *A* dragging all the way into the *P*, the final *e* looking incomplete, as if in his haste Ezra had lifted the pen too soon, or as if to say, *Ezra Pease is not yet done here.* Except that now he was.

Another memory, not even that old, but already so frayed and brittle Ida had refused to pull it out too often in case it caused an irreparable tear. It had begun as something of an occasion— albeit a rare one—Ezra coming home with both of them, Mose *and* Henry, in tow. Ida remembered the cold as the door banged open, the slap of Henry's toolbox as he'd dropped it to the floor, the sight of the brothers, one on either side of Ezra like a pair of mismatched bookends, the feeling of life entering the room and lifting her like the wind lifted a bird's wings.

"Henry's going to fix the clock," Ezra said. "It turns out carriage makers are good at that."

"But only after you feed them," Mose said.

"No feeding necessary," Henry said, but Ida had already unhooked the skillet from the beam.

As they ate she watched the brothers and the way their bodies communicated with each other: a shrug of the shoulder, a raised finger, the barest look, as if they were bouncing a separate conversation between them without a single word while still adhering to the larger thread that included Ezra and Ida. And *Ida*. After a time a few of the knots that Ida had learned to live with loosened their grip. She relaxed. She cleared the table; Ezra took down the clock and set it in front of Henry.

Henry asked, "Would you have a clean dish towel, Ida?"

Ida opened the drawer, removed a clean, crisp towel, and handed it to Henry. He opened it, spread it out on the table, and smiled at Ida. "The best way to keep track of the pieces. Thank you."

"You're welcome. Thank you for doing this. The clock was my mother's."

"I told him," Ezra said. "I told him this was going to keep me in good for the next two months."

"It's going to keep *Henry* in good," Mose said. "Watch out."

"Oh, I've got nothing to fear. Ida knows not to bite the hand that feeds her. Don't you, Ida?"

"Seeing as how I just fed *you*—"

Mose and Henry both laughed. Ezra did not. Of course Ezra did not.

"Get the whiskey and get gone," he said to Ida.

"Actually," Henry interjected, "I was hoping Ida could tell me something about this clock. The workings are somewhat unusual."

"My father got it in Nova Scotia on a coastal trading voyage."

"Whiskey," Ezra said.

Henry got up, went to the pantry, collected the whiskey, and set it on the table in front of Ida.

"Whoa!" Ezra said. "Don't go giving my wife my whiskey!" He snatched up the bottle and jerked his head at Ida first, the door second.

Ida didn't move.

"Are you deaf, dumb, or just plain old—"

Henry had raised his eyes from the intricacies of the clock to look at Ezra. That was all—one look—but there was something in it that reminded Ida of the way Bett looked at the sheep. Whatever else Ezra had planned to say died on his tongue.

Henry spoke into the unexpected void, to Ida. "Nova Scotia, you say. It fits. You see these kinds of workings in France."

Ezra snatched up the bottle and stormed out to the porch.

"He's just showing off," Mose said, but looking at his brother, not Ida. "Showing us how obedient his wife is. He doesn't talk like that when you're alone, does he, Ida?"

Now Henry looked at Ida.

"He grows brave when we're not alone," Ida said. "For some reason he thinks I won't embarrass him in public. But I don't need to let him embarrass *me* in public, either."

"Or in private?" Henry asked.

Ida nodded. *From now,* she thought. From now. Henry smiled at Ida, but not happily. She could tell the difference by now.

"Mose!" Ezra shouted from the porch. Mose got up, grinning. "So I'm the one who obeys." He left them.

"I'm sorry for that," Ida said.

"Has he ever struck you?"

"Lord, no."

"He's not that brave?"

Ida considered. "He's not that afraid."

Henry smiled again—a better one.

They sat in comfort, in quiet, Henry asking an occasional clock question, Ida giving an occasional answer, Henry concentrating on the tiny clock pieces, Ida concentrating on Henry's hands as he worked.

Yes, even then.

AS IF IN RESPECT to Ida's exhaustion, the sheep were quiet. No new lambs, no new pending lambs, no distressed ewes. But as soon as Ida breathed her sigh of relief she began to worry; *shouldn't* there be new lambs, pending lambs, restless ewes? She called Lem, using as her excuse the trunk of clothes.

"I have Ezra's clothes packed up. You're about the size. Would you like them? If not, I wanted to ask if you could take them to the Seamen's Bethel."

"I think a shipwrecked sailor has more need of a good warm suit of clothes than I do."

"Can you take them?"

"Can and will. Should do it soon too. Rose Amaral still hasn't fully restocked the Bethel's clothes locker since the storm."

That settled, Ida moved the talk around to the eerie quiet in the paddock and listened to a sheeplike chuckle on the other end of the line.

"Don't go looking for trouble, Ida. It'll come."

*   *   *

IT CAME.

The ewe was old, too old to have been bred, even Ida could see that now, and the effort to expel her lamb was too much for her; the lamb got a single drink before the ewe died. They were coming faster now and Ida didn't have long to wait for the next one; she tried the trick Lem had shown her the year before, rubbing the orphaned lamb with the birth fluids of the new mother in hope the mother would think she'd given birth to two and would take on the orphan along with her own. For a second Ida thought it had worked; the ewe nuzzled the orphan, sniffing her all over, before lifting a foot to kick it away. Now Ida was the orphan's mother, which meant six bottle feeds a day.

Next came one of those soggy, late March storms that weighed down everything it touched with a mix of snow, slush, and ice, bringing down the phone line and exhausting Ida as she attempted to slog through it. The sheep hunkered in the field shelter in a tight mass, making it impossible to identify one from the other, but making it easier to track them when they wandered off to drop their lambs in private. She found one in the lee of a cedar, huddled with her offspring on a bare patch of ground. The lamb had been licked clean, so Ida guessed it had been fed, but to be sure she lifted it and felt the belly. Full, but the lamb was shivering, and Ida feared hypothermia. This pair needed the barn. Bett could get the ewe there but it was a long walk for a tiny lamb through the snow. Ida picked up the lamb, keeping it low so the ewe could see it, hoping it would follow it to the barn. It did. Once there Ida rubbed the lamb dry with a burlap sack, watched it through its next feed, forked down some hay, and left them to get acquainted with the orphan already in residence.

Ida's next worry was the thick snow drift along the west stone wall. She collected Ezra's crook, pulled Ezra's wool cap down to meet her collar, and walked the wall, thumping through the snow with the crook. When she struck solid she scraped at the ice and snow until she'd uncovered a first-time ewe with a dead lamb; she picked up the lamb and again the ewe followed Ida all the way to the barn, where they found Lem unsaddling his horse and wiping it down.

Ida made no effort to keep the relief out of her voice. "How'd you get here?"

Lem pointed to the horse, never one to waste words on foolish questions. He collected the dead lamb from Ida. "It's probably too late, but let's try one more thing. Get me that orphan." He disappeared into the far stall and by the time Ida returned with the orphan in her arms Lem had already skinned the dead lamb, leaving holes at the head and legs. He fit the skin over the orphan's head, pulled each leg through, and fetched the childless ewe; she sniffed the strange lamb in the coat of her own lamb and snorted. She backed off, circled, sniffed again, and walked away.

"I've seen it work plenty of times," Lem said. "Guess this one's too old. So you're still mama. Here's the good news, though—you've got yourself a milker."

THE OTHER GOOD NEWS—the only other good news—was that like most March storms, this one melted away fast. Once the hill had shed its ice, Ida trudged up it to give Ruth the updated tally: nine healthy lambs, one dead lamb, one dead ewe. She found the two women and the boy in the parlor; Hattie and Oliver on the loveseat with a book open between them, Hattie reading aloud to Oliver as Ruth perched close to the stove with a piece of sewing.

Ida submitted her report.

"Dead ewes count," Ruth said.

Oliver scrambled off the loveseat and tugged at Hattie's skirt. "May we go see the lambs? Please?"

Hattie exchanged a look with Ida.

"I'll take you down," Ida said.

"I'll fetch him in a half hour," Hattie said.

"A five-year-old boy can walk up a hill alone," Ruth said.

Oliver raced off. Ruth got up and followed him, no doubt with some final instruction about muddy boots.

"You'll tell him?" Hattie asked Ida. "Really, you *should* tell him. He was your husband. You can talk to Oliver about him. I hadn't seen much of Ezra in recent years." Ida looked at Hattie in amazement, not because she hadn't seen Ezra—who had? But because this wasn't the story Hattie had been selling around town. What Ida actually knew about Hattie was shrinking by the minute.

"I'll tell him," Ida said, "if you tell Ruth in no uncertain terms that Oliver is Ezra's. Today."

"But what will you say to him?"

Ida saw no need to challenge Oliver's intricate network of father fables; she'd say what she had to say and let the boy sort it out for himself. But what exactly to say? "The truth," she told Hattie. "With an extra word added. That we *just* found out his father was on the *Portland* when it went down."

Hattie nodded. "I'll tell Mother."

IDA DECIDED TO START WITH THE FUN. Oliver raced along the pasture wall pointing at each new lamb until Ida said, "Want to feed one?" She led him into the barn, armed with a full bottle; by now the orphan had figured out where the goods were and hopped over to Ida to lip her boot. Ida handed the bottle to Oliver; the lamb took it without fuss.

"Its name is Bett," Oliver said.

"I don't know," Ida said. "I don't want to call a dog and have a lamb come."

Oliver thought. "Bett—*ee*."

For an imaginative child, he sure came up short in the name department, Ida thought. "Come back tomorrow and you can feed her again."

Ida lured Oliver away from the lamb with a promise of hot cocoa at the house, but he insisted on stopping at the dog yard along the way to say hello to the real Bett. Once inside Ida fussed around a little too long, but finally she had Oliver seated at the kitchen table with a cup of cocoa and a slice of bread and jam in front of him. Ida sat.

"Oliver, remember I told you my mother died?"

Oliver nodded but didn't look up.

"My father died too. The ship he was working on sank."

There Oliver looked up.

"We've heard some bad news about *your* father, Oliver. *He* was on a ship that sank."

Oliver peered at Ida.

"It was a big steamship and everyone on it died. Your father died too. In a bad storm."

Oliver pushed his cup away. "I want to go home."

"Okay, we'll go right now. But I wanted to tell you one more thing. Your father was also my husband. We got married after your mother died." At least Ida hoped they did. She considered telling Oliver that his father had talked of him often, that he'd planned numerous visits, that he loved him, and it might have helped for today, but what of later when Oliver grew older and understood that for five years his father hadn't *ever* visited him, that he hadn't bothered to give the boy his name or provide for him in any way? It would add Ida to the list of liars and still leave Ezra the villain, two people Oliver could never trust instead of just one.

"Come," Ida said. "I'll walk you home."

THEY WALKED UP THE HILL, or rather Ida walked and Oliver raced ahead as if trying to get as far away from Ida as fast as he could. They found Ruth and Hattie sitting in frozen silence in the kitchen, Ruth's arms crossed in a posture of denial, if Ida were apt to read into it; Hattie appeared to have been crying. Oliver ran past them, still in his boots, up the stairs, into his bedroom, and slammed the door. Ruth made to rise but Hattie snapped at her.

"You leave him alone." She turned to Ida. "How did it go?"

Ida shrugged. "I gave him an orphan lamb to feed. I was hoping it would help."

"Better hope it doesn't die," Ruth said.

20

THE LAMBS KEPT COMING. Two living. One dead. Four living. One missing, presumed dead: Lem arrived one morning to find Ida examining a bloody spot just outside the field shelter. "Hawk," he said, pointing to the wing marks in the dirt where the bird had touched down, snatched the newborn lamb, and lifted off.

But by April Ida could look out over twenty-two snow-white lambs bouncing among the oat-colored ewes, a pair of ram lambs roughhousing, and a hundred different shades of living green shoots poking through the winter dead. She'd made it through winter. She'd lost only four sheep. She would receive her full payment. She should be—she could be—she *would be* happy.

There was one ewe left to go. Ida watched it circling, pawing, circling; she stayed guard at the fence until the animal's water bag broke and she made her decision. The lamb would come soon now; Oliver had seen newborn lambs but not one coming, and here was his last chance. She raced up the hill to fetch him.

The three Peases or rather two Peases and one Nye, were sitting together eating breakfast, which Ida took as a good sign. That Oliver didn't run from the room when he saw her she took as another. "Who wants to see a lamb born?" Ida asked.

Oliver looked at Hattie. "You do," Hattie said.

Admittedly, there was a certain risk involved. If something went wrong it wouldn't be the joyful experience Ida was hoping for, but then again, it would be a shared experience, more shared than Ida had anticipated. Hattie and Ruth came too.

When they got back to the field the ewe was lying on its side and clearly paining. Ida left Hattie and Ruth at the fence but took Oliver by the hand and led him behind the sheep. She lifted the tail and saw two feet and one nose. She breathed easier.

"Grab hold of the feet," Ida told Oliver. "The ewe will try to push the lamb out and when she does you pull ever so gently. Really, you're just going to keep it going straight, that's all."

Oliver looked up at Ida. "Like reins?"

"Just like reins." Ida helped Oliver place his hands but kept hers lightly covering them. She could feel the push. "Feel it?" Oliver said nothing, but his hands drew back with the impetus of the lamb. "Now pause. Okay, here she goes again." Oliver and Ida pulled twice more, and the lamb slid to earth in front of Oliver's knees. Oliver looked up at Ida again, beaming now. The ewe licked away the sac, the lamb shuddered its first breath and struggled to its feet. It was going to be all right. By the time Ida and Oliver had stood up and brushed off the dead grass, the lamb was feeding, tail moving in ecstatic circles.

"Its name is Bett-*see*," Oliver said.

"It's a boy."

Oliver thought. "Ben-*jie*."

When they joined the others at the fence, Hattie gave Oliver a big hug of congratulations, but Ruth turned to Ida. "Lucky for you. Four dead already."

Ida smiled sweetly.

OLIVER FED BETTY and while he did so he chattered on with more words than Ida had heard from him since he'd arrived, none to do with his fairy-tale father, some of it mere padding, using the expedient of one particular word stated over and over. Betty was *really really* hungry. Betty had gotten *really really* big since he'd last seen her. Betty *really really really* wanted to meet her brother Benjie. Ida held Betty up by her forelegs so Oliver could feel the full belly, and when he was forced to admit Betty was *really really* full, he gave her a final pat and trailed after Ida up the hill.

At the door to the house Ida said, "I won't come in. But I did want to tell you one more thing. That farm belongs to your aunt Ruth now, but it was once your father's. He'd be proud of what you did today."

"I made a lamb."

"You helped it be born."

"I *made* it."

All right, Ida could let that one go. "One more thing, Oliver— I have some pretty good stories about your father. You just let me know if you ever want to hear one."

By now Ida was prepared for the first three parts of Oliver's standard response the look, the pause to think, the skittering away, in this case up the steps to the door. The fourth part was always the wild card: silence, or a follow-up question, or some other tall tale about his father. This time Ida got the silence, but it was followed by a second look over the shoulder that Ida took for a good sign.

WHEN IDA RETURNED to the house she found a letter waiting from Henry:

It appears the second party in question is not in town at present—I'm told he'll be returning at the weekend. In the meanwhile I'm making a dash to New Bedford to see my daughters but plan to be on-island again by Monday. I've been thinking a good deal and should very much like to speak with you then.—H.

Ida read Henry's letter through twice; it was perhaps the most unsatisfying letter she'd ever received, and the second reading didn't improve it. Was she supposed to hang suspended in air till Monday when Henry told her whatever he wanted to tell her? Well, she would not.

Ida looked out the window. Lambing was over. She could breathe now. She could *see* now. The colors of spring had begun to intensify, to saturate the view: a new, vibrant green pierced the ground in the pastures; a mauve wash in the trees hinted at young buds sucking up the revitalized sun; a new clarity had appeared in the sky. If Ida were going to hang suspended over anything, she decided, it would be the seat of her bicycle. She changed into the proper clothes, put her sketch pad in the basket, added her paint box and a jar of water, and set off.

But where to? Time to try a new direction. Ida turned off the main street onto the county road and kept on pedaling until her thighs began complaining, until she looked aside and saw a large pond alongside a greening meadow, a salad of greens and blues and silvers and golds with a dark strip of ocean beyond. Ida knew how to paint a woman's skin whether it be pale or blushing; she knew a man's bearded face or a razor-chafed clean one; she knew silk and linen and muslin and wool and what happened to those fabrics and shapes when a man's or woman's shoulders and thighs pushed against them. She knew everything there was to know about hands folded, hands clasped, hands at rest, hands gripping cloth in an attempt not to show their owner's nervousness. She knew brown and green and hazel and blue eyes and knew how many different colors went into each of them. She knew lamplight was warmer than window light; she knew the problems a strong, slanting window light could cause when it struck a subject. What didn't she know? Grass. Pond. Ocean.

Ida wheeled her bicycle into the meadow and lay it down on its handlebar. She removed her jacket and, using it as a blanket, sat and stretched her legs out straight, her paper laid out flat across her knees, her paint box and water jug at her elbow. A few quick lines gave her the suggestion of her composition; why, this was easier than a sitting or standing person, with four limbs and a neck and so much clothing to account for! Sky first, Ida decided; that soft but strengthening blue could cause few problems. She wet her brush and streaked it back and forth across the paper, wetted the brush again, picked up ultramarine and a dot of yellow ochre and cadmium red, and there it was. Or wasn't. Too much ochre. Too dark at the horizon. Ida hastened more wet onto the page, but an intrusive breeze had already dried out the paint and now her too-wet brush had caused an unwelcome bloom in her sky. Perhaps a cloud . . . Ida squinted off at the sky: no clouds. Ida didn't want her first plein air painting to be a dishonest one.

Ida did better with an egret that was poised on a rock nearby. "There is no such thing as white," Mr. Morris had lectured her. "You think that cloth white? Look! *Look!*" And Ida had looked and seen that indeed what she took for white cloth was in fact full of purples and golds and yellows, and so it was with the egret. Ida gave it a lavender cast in the cool shadows and sat back, pleased, until she noticed the rock it stood on floated over the page untethered; Mr. Morris had taught her better. She amended this with a wash of yellow green to suggest the spring marsh grass and felt happier, felt the truth of what Henry had said to her but now added a second level of understanding to it:

as she painted to honor herself she also honored Mr. Morris. The feeling lasted until she attempted the pond; the colors were the right dance of greens, yellows, golds, and silvers, but the water just sat there; it *didn't* dance, and all Ida's efforts to enliven it only turned it muddier. Perhaps she honored no one, after all.

But Ida kept at it till the rising cold and damp had worked through the double thicknesses of jacket and skirt deep into her flesh and bone; she pedaled home encumbered by an old frustration she'd have once blamed on Ezra. But in truth, didn't it still belong to Ezra? Ezra was the one who had spent all her money, sold the farm to Ruth. Ezra was the one who had trapped her here and cost what little time had remained with her mentor. But no. Ida was the one who had agreed to the marriage. Ida was the one who had agreed to the move. She'd been happy enough to leave her sorrow behind, and if in her befogged state she hadn't quite understood what else she was leaving behind, she could not, in that, blame Ezra. Oddly, to shoulder blame instead of shoving it off on Ezra felt freeing.

IDA PARKED THE BICYCLE IN THE BARN, fed Betty, and went to the paddock to check on the lamb. The lamb was fine, but there was something wrong with the ewe; she stood against the wall with head down, sides heaving; she walked in jerky circles, throwing her head back along her flank as her eyes jumped wildly. Ida let herself into the paddock and sidled closer; she stripped off her jacket, reached under the ewe for the far leg, pulled it forward and tipped her. She felt inside and sure enough, there it was: a second, retained lamb, the wrong end facing outward. Ida ran for the house, the phone, Lem, but no one answered; Ida returned to the sheep and found her still on her side, panting. Ida reached in and pulled a back leg forward; she pulled another;

the lamb caught at the hip and would come no farther. What would Lem do? The ewe was fading, her breathing gone shallow; which to save, ewe or lamb? By now Ida doubted the lamb was even alive. She took hold of both legs and threw the whole of her weight backward against the grip of the ewe; she fell flat on the ground, but the lamb came with her.

Dead.

Number five.

Ida sat, breathing hard, taking stock. This fifth dead lamb was the one that would cost her, unless . . . unless she said nothing about it. Ruth had no idea this particular ewe had carried twins; in fact, she'd witnessed a successful birth only a few hours earlier and had likely put the numbers out of her head till the next season of lambing. All Ida need do was put them out of *her* head. The Feases all had their secrets after all: Oliver, the farm, the gold. It was about time Ida carried a secret of her own.

21

AT LAST, LEM ARRIVED to carry Ezra's trunk of clothes to the Bethel.

"Care to come along?" he asked Ida, surprising her.

"Yes," she said, surprising herself. She'd been wanting to see Rose Amaral but had never found it in herself to make that effort, had in fact been a little fearful of what she might find in a meeting with the apparently fierce Rose Amaral. This would be a safe way to do it—a brief exchange with the excuse on the ready of Lem's wagon waiting to take her home again. Ida climbed into the wagon beside Lem.

They bumped along saying little, so little that Ida felt the weight of the silence. "My bicycle rides smoother than this wagon," she offered.

"This wagon won't dump you out on the ground spread-eagled," Lem said. The way he said the word *spread-eagled* made it sound like something Ida had done on purpose.

"You don't approve of my cycling, do you, Lem? At first I thought it was just my bicycling with Henry you disapproved of, out of respect for Ruth's view on the matter, although why you should care so much what Ruth thinks I don't know. But it isn't Henry, is it? Or maybe it is Henry, but even without Henry, you don't think women should exhibit themselves like that in public."

"It doesn't show you to advantage."

"Whose advantage?"

"Yours. You're not planning to stay a widow forever, are you? Someday you'll want to find a decent gentleman—"

"'Decent' meaning one not divorcing. 'Decent' meaning one who doesn't let his wife go off bicycling."

"In trousers. Knees flashing in the wind. Knees and whatever else turns wrong side up. I'm not going to tell you what I saw that day on the track."

"I was in a skirt that day. If I'd been in trousers you'd have seen a lot less."

Lem sat silent. He rattled onto the wharf and pulled up in front of the Bethel, coming around to help Ida out, but Ida didn't move.

"When I came here with Ezra, you were the first person I met. You stepped out of the barn as if you lived there, and you didn't even smile at me, but there was something in the way you looked at me, at the way you came up to me and took my bag, that told me I might find a friend in this godforsaken place after all. I knew—I already knew—that I was going to need one. Aren't we friends anymore?"

Lem blinked. "To my way of looking at things, I'm the best friend you've got."

"No matter the—"

"No matter anything, Ida. That's just how it works. I might get disappointed in you now and again same as you get disappointed in me, but that's also how it works. Now are you going to come in or you going to sit there?"

Lem went to the back of the wagon, hoisted the trunk, and carried it into the Bethel. He'd hoisted it all the way down the stairs at home without effort but now he paused halfway to the door, set it down, took a couple of breaths, hoisted it again. Ida scrambled out of the wagon and followed him in.

By the time Ida caught up, Rose Amaral had already opened

the trunk. When she saw Ida she came around and grasped both her hands.

"Mrs. Pease. I'm grateful for this. You can't know the need. I'm so sorry about your husband. Such an old story on this island, and yet each time I hear it, especially perhaps this time, since I don't know you . . . but here, we can fix that. I have a pot on; come and sit and we'll have that talk."

Sit and we'll have that talk; such a gentle suggestion and yet it caused Ida's chest to tighten. But what was she to do? Rose Amaral had already started across the room, assuming Ida would follow her.

Ida turned to Lem. "Thank you for the transport. I'll walk home."

"YOU'VE SUFFERED SUCH A LOSS," Rose began. "I've many times thought how ill-equipped I am to comfort anyone widowed—my fisherman husband has tempted his fate more times in that boat of his and every single trip—"

"Five," Ida said.

"I . . . five?"

She'd lost five. She could no longer hear the word *loss* without taking the full count; Ezra was the last and least, but the number was five. *Five.* The room began to recede; Rose began to recede. Ida needed to shift the subject, fast. She looked around the enormous kitchen and spied a poster tacked over the sink:

> For the work of a day
> For the price we pay
> For the laws we obey
> We want something to say.
> VOTES FOR WOMEN!

Ida pointed. "You've heard of Julia Ward Howe?"

Rose's eyes, already warm, grew warmer. "I've read of her."

Ida relayed her conversation with Howe in Boston and watched warm turn to flame. "I've wanted to get up a group here for the longest time. This is all I needed—someone like you to egg me on. We start by asking everyone we know. I have several who would do it; you must know some. We could meet at the library, write up a piece for the paper, maybe get Mrs. Howe to speak to us."

Ida doubted Mrs. Howe would use up her valuable time with a trip to such an outpost, but Rose's energy flowed over and through her like a stiff current, reviving Ida, putting the room back where it belonged. As she looked at the animated Rose an idea occurred to her. She would paint Rose's portrait; *this* she knew how to do. A lot of burnt sienna in the hair with a touch of purple, a hint of that burnt sienna in the skin, the eyes one of Ida's darker mixes of complementary colors. She would paint her right there, seated at the Bethel's stove, the warmth in the eyes reflecting the warmth of the stove . . .

"I'd like to paint you," Ida said.

"How kind of you to say so, Ida."

"May I?"

Rose smiled sweetly. "No."

After they'd talked awhile longer Ida tried again, but there was no shifting Rose. On the other hand, by the time Ida left, she'd not only promised Rose she'd compose a list of women likely to attend a suffrage meeting, but she'd agreed to volunteer at the Bethel.

"WHAT STORIES?" Oliver asked. He and Ida were standing at the fence watching the sheep; Ida could make a case for some warmth from the sun on her back, but her hands and face were knotted with chill. Oliver had already run in sharp zigzags over the ripening grass to see if Betty would follow him, which she did until he'd fed her, but now she careened after the other lambs with that burst of energy only the first sun and a full belly could provide. Ida knew right off which stories Oliver meant, but the fact of it was that although she'd made her offer in good faith, feeling obligated to replace a long string of fairy tales with at least a few true ones, she couldn't think of a single story about Ezra that Oliver should hear. Who *was* Ezra? A fortune hunter, in every sense of the word. An adventurer, she supposed, always ready to sail off in search of the next great treasure . . . Treasure.

"Did you know," Ida began, "that your father could raise up ships from the bottom of the sea?"

There came the Oliver look. "What ships?"

"Ships that sank in storms. Or hit a rock. Or collided with another one. Sometimes a ship would have an explosion—"

"An explosion?"

"If they carried fuel, like coal. That exploded a lot."

"How did he raise them up?"

"Different ways. Sometimes he plugged the hole and pumped it out. Sometimes he built a second bottom on top of the first. Sometimes he just emptied the cargo and it floated up to the surface by itself. If he couldn't raise the ship, he'd just salvage the cargo."

"What's salvage?"

"Save."

Oliver thought. "Was he the only one who knew how to raise up ships?"

"No, there were others."

"Did they raise up the ship my father was on when he drownded?"

"Drowned. No, they didn't."

"Why didn't they?"

"Well, they never found the ship."

"Then how did they know it sank?"

"Things washed ashore out on the back side of Cape Cod. A life preserver with the name of the ship on it. The ship's wheel. Furniture." *Bodies.*

Oliver watched the sheep in silence for some time. "Maybe something of my father's washed up. Maybe we should go look."

Too late, it occurred to Ida that she should have saved some article of Ezra's clothing to give to Oliver. She pondered what else of Ezra's she might have but could think of nothing but the whiskey bottle. Then she remembered. "Wait here."

Ida dashed inside and up the stairs, into her studio and past her unfinished sketches of Lem, Henry, Oliver, even Ruth and Hattie. She pulled Ezra's little atlas off the shelf and thumbed through it; a color image of every state and country graced its pages, along with minute notations of its square miles, its topography, its crops and manufacturing, its railroads, its harbors. Would a boy like Oliver find such things of interest? He would, Ida guessed, if it was all he had of his father's. But would Hattie—or Ruth—take the time to read it to him?

Ida returned to the pasture fence to find Oliver missing from it. She found him at the dog yard, reaching through the slats to allow Bett to lick his fingers. Ida released the dog but stayed close; when Bett ran off after some unseen animal Ida handed Oliver the atlas.

"This was your father's," she said. "He'd have wanted you to have it. I know you can't read the words—"

"I can too!" Oliver snatched the book, opened it. Frowned. "*Some* words." But he dropped to his knees and began turning pages. He looked up. "Did he go to all these places?"

"Not all of them."

"Just the ones with the mark?"

Ida knelt beside the boy and looked where he pointed, to a couple of pencil marks on the page marked Massachusetts, one on the Rhode Island page, others at New York, Connecticut, Maine. "Yes," Ida said, understanding as some others might not the value of such communication from the dead. "And here's where he signed his name."

Oliver stayed bent over the meager little book for so long that Ida contemplated buying a man's watch and claiming it was Ezra's just to have something more substantial to pass on to the boy, but she wouldn't—couldn't—add anything more to the pile of Ezra lies.

22

MAY CAME, THE TYPICAL ISLAND MAY, one day cold as winter and gray as dawn, the next day pierced straight through with rays of light that might not yet warm the skin but did brighten the spirits. With the lambing done, Ida could relax some; she still circled the pasture daily and found the occasional lamb caught up in the briars Ezra had neglected to clear or a ewe with a hard, hot bag—a sure sign of mastitis—but for the most part all was quiet. She had time to bicycle to the Seamen's Bethel to meet with Rose, where they sat and composed a list of women who might be interested in attending a suffrage meeting. What that actually meant was that Rose composed a list and Ida contributed one name: Hattie's. She mentioned it one day when Hattie delivered Oliver.

"I've been working with Rose Amaral on a campaign for women's suffrage."

"Here?" Hattie laughed. "Better change the name to *suffer-age*."

Hattie had a point; Ida couldn't, in fact, see women like Grace Luce, Emmeline Tilton, *Ruth* joining the discussion. And why start a thing Ida wouldn't be around to finish? But Hattie would be here.

"You'll join us?"

"I don't know. There's work. Oliver. My mother."

"We can—"

"I said I don't *know*, Ida. There are other matters to consider."

"What matters?"

"I said I don't know. Now let me get to my work. I'm not a woman of leisure like some others."

Did she mean Ida? Ida opened her mouth; closed it. Opened it again. "Rose wants to call a meeting at the library."

Hattie had already started down the track. She called something over her shoulder that Ida couldn't hear, but it didn't sound like *I'll be there.*

AND YET, when Ida mounted her bicycle it seemed all things were possible if she only did as she did on the bicycle: pumped the pedals hard, one at a time. She rode to Cottage City and felt the strength in her legs; felt her courage; reveled in the miles of smooth concrete from which to choose her direction. The late-day sky had been banded by a pinky-gold flourish at the horizon that Ida hadn't yet managed to capture; it wasn't the same gold as a woman's necklace, or a tawny fleck in an eye, or any silk or satin she'd encountered. It wasn't the color of any paints in her palette. But as Ida rode home she thought she was wrong in that. The colors were there; all the colors were there; she just hadn't mixed them right. Tomorrow she would try adding some magenta to that wash of orange.

On the way home Ida stopped at Luce's and collected another letter from Henry. *Delayed in New Bedford,* he wrote and went on to explain about a potential order for three new carriages and his frustrated attempts to arrange a meeting with the purchaser. The rest of the letter was about the seven automobiles he'd seen in Newport and the three in New Bedford.

TWO AND A HALF DAYS of rain kept Ida—and Oliver—indoors. Ida took out the Nine Men's Morris, but soon abandoned the rules and left Oliver to fly about the board willy-nilly, to declare himself the winner. Ida was just pondering how much easier her life might have been if she'd taken that tack with Ezra when the sun and Hattie arrived together.

"I'm late," Hattie said, and rushed Oliver out the door. So she didn't want to talk, which was fine with Ida; it allowed her to get back to her mission of the golden light. She gathered her supplies and set off along the pasture wall, heading for an old, gnarled pear tree that stood guard against the wind at the far corner. She'd decided she didn't want to remove Henry's father from the orchard, so she needed to practice her trees. She set her sketch pad on her knees, the picture of Henry's father propped up between the pages, and sat staring at the figure. Oh, she knew that man, the unique dark/light coloring, the long bones, that loose-jointed way of standing. She imagined the man in the photo would move as effortlessly as Henry did.

As he was doing now, propelling his bicycle up the track.

Henry let go of the bicycle and broke into a gentle jog along the pasture wall, scattering the sheep to the far side. Ida slid off the wall and moved toward him, her own pace too fast, too eager. She slowed. As Henry approached her he too slowed, the things they'd last said to each other now leaving an arm's length between them.

Ida turned, and they continued together toward the house. Recalling Henry's last letter but one—*I've been thinking a good deal and should very much like to speak with you*—Ida waited for him to start, but Henry seemed more intent on the sheep.

"You've got a fine flock there, Ida."

"Yes."

"You did well."

"Fairly."

Silence.

"I hadn't expected to see you," Ida tried.

"This time *I* got tired of waiting. I told her I'd be on the Vineyard and to send word when she'd corralled the party in question."

They reached the house. "Supper?" Ida asked. What else *could* she ask?

She made them eggs, potatoes, and sausage; she served up the two plates with the neutral subject of Oliver and his chess game, waiting, waiting, for Henry to turn the topic.

"How are your neighbors?"

"The same," Ida said, although she didn't think Hattie was, but she didn't want to linger on that topic.

"All's well with the farm?"

"All's well."

Henry pushed his plate back. "Thank you. Again."

He was going to leave. He should leave. Ida knew this. And yet she said, "I wonder what you think of women voting."

Henry settled back into his chair. "The same thing I think of men voting. Some will cast wisely, some will cast irresponsibly, some won't cast at all. But they should all be allowed to cast or not as they choose. And you?"

"I don't think men should be allowed to vote at all."

Henry burst into laughter.

"Ezra thought it wasn't worth his time discussing because it would never happen. No man would vote to let women in."

Henry pondered. "How impossible it is. A man must vote a woman permission to vote."

"But some men will. You will."

"Now we only need a few more."

We.

Ida tipped her head.

Henry stood. "I'd best go."

No. "Yes."

Henry moved to the door, turned. "Ride tomorrow?"

No. "Yes."

THEY RODE OUT along the county road, Ida's basket packed full with paper, pencils, paint, a jug of water, and two pieces of mince pie wrapped in napkins. Henry carried a pack on his back. He led the way, turning them onto Lambert's Cove Road, then off it onto a dirt road not unlike the one to the Pease farm, but this road was overgrown; some of the trees, like the beeches, had already leafed out, but others, like the oaks, stood bare-branched against the sun, making the ride one of dappled cool and warm in alternating layers. At length the trees turned to scrub and grass and Henry dismounted. He motioned for Ida to follow and set off through what looked like a deer path until it opened up into a gap in a dune topped with beach grass as spare as an old man's scalp. Ahead Ida heard, smelled, and at last saw a rollicking line of surf.

Henry took Ida's hand and they slid down through the space between the dunes until the beach came into view. Ida looked to her left along the pristine sand glistening in the sun, a flock of winded gulls resting at the edge of the surf the only sign of life. Ahead the Elizabeth Islands chain sat like a smudge on the horizon; to the right more empty, scoured beach until a large building and wharf cut the view short. *Well done, Henry,* she thought. She pointed to the building. "What's that place?"

"The Makonikey Hotel. Now abandoned."

Henry opened his pack, pulled out a blanket and spread it on the sand in the shelter between the dunes, added two bottles of beer and a loaf of bread.

"I have pie," Ida said, remembering, "back at the bicycle."

"I'll fetch it." Henry jogged off.

Ida stepped onto the beach and started walking toward the old hotel as if toward a mirage, but the shapes never wavered or shrank. By the time she got close enough to see the fancy turret she could also see the absent windows, the missing shingles gaping like lost teeth. She turned to face the sea and saw that the wharf too had the appearance of dereliction, several of its pilings askew, the boards splintered or buckling.

Her mother's wharf. Ida had stood many times on the Union Wharf and had never thought of her mother; that wharf was too much the busy thoroughfare, too crammed with people and horses and carriages and carts and all the boxes and barrels and trunks they carried. No one could have walked unseen off Union Wharf with pockets full of stones, but this wharf, with its air of desolation and despair, this wharf was different.

As if compelled by an invisible hand, Ida stepped onto the planks and walked out. A violent rage overwhelmed her. What had her mother been thinking? How could she not care? How was it that Ida wasn't enough to hold her? Would it be possible that someday Ida would look around and find nothing to hold *her*? Ida approached the edge of the wharf and looked down at the swirling sea, at the way it danced around the pilings, sucking everything into its maw. In that last minute before her mother stepped out into nothing, had she hesitated, doubted, thought of Ida even at all? If she had, had it caused her to reconsider or was it already too late? Had the clutches of gravity already captured her? Was she, in essence, already dead at that first step?

The whirling of the sea water had begun to make Ida dizzy; she wanted to step back from the edge, she *tried* to step back, but she'd lost her sense of which way was ahead and which way behind. She lifted a foot and swayed, tottered, toppled over the edge.

Cold. Salt. Something gripping at her clothes and pulling her downward. She began to thrash uselessly, just as she had so many times in her dreams, her mother either always just out of her reach or grabbing hold of her and keeping her from regaining the surface. She was unable to tell up from down, unable to identify the goal. She heard a muffled, tinny sound; saw a shape like a pale jellyfish above her; felt someone's hands on her, strong hands, pulling her. Ida lashed out at the hands; she was not her mother! She would not be pulled down! But those hands, how strong they were, how sure, how skillfully they pinned her arms and hoisted her out of the water, stood her on her feet! But they still held her, pinned her. She fought free of the hands, sloshed through the water toward the shore, felt herself being grabbed from behind, lifted. She clawed. Kicked. Tore free again. Ran up the beach. Heard the dense thunk of heavier footsteps hitting the sand behind her, felt those hands catch hold of her again, shake her.

"Ida! Ida! It's me. Henry."

HE'D BROUGHT THE BLANKET WITH HIM. He kicked open the rotting hotel door and helped her out of her skirt and coat and boots, the wet ties and buttons defeating her. He wrapped the blanket around her, went to the fireplace, looked up the chimney, found somewhere a tin of matches, lit the logs already lying behind the andirons. He draped her sopping clothes over the fire screen and positioned it to the side so it wouldn't block the heat from reaching Ida. He returned to where she sat on the banquette, dropped to his knees in front of her and began to rub her trembling arms and back and shoulders until the trembling eased.

"I'm sorry," she said. She wanted to explain that fierce drive to get herself out of that water, the conviction that it was up to her to get herself out, the certainty that the hands that reached for her could only pull her under, as they always did in her dream. "I don't know what happened," she said instead.

Henry sat back on his heels, his eyes black, burning. "You pitched off the bloody dock, that's what happened. Let loose with a god-awful howl and went right over the edge! And then practically clawed my eyes out when I tried to help you."

"I'm sorry," Ida said again. "It didn't occur to me that you were trying to help me."

"What the bloody hell did you think I was trying to do?" He was breathing hard, as hard as she was. Harder.

"Don't be angry."

"Angry! Scared to death, more like. Bloody hell, Ida." He got off his knees, slid around beside her on the banquette, opened an arm. Ida slid inside it, letting him hold her hard against him, wanting him to hold her hard.

"My mother drowned herself," Ida said. She began to tremble again. She now knew exactly what had happened to her mother, how she'd have been pulled down by the stones just as Ida had been pulled down by her clothes; even if Ida's mother had changed her mind, even if she'd clawed the stones from her pockets and fought to regain the surface she'd have been disoriented, unable to tell up from down. How insidious that pull was! If Henry hadn't been there . . . If only Ida had been there . . . If Ida's mother had only *talked* to her about her despair . . .

Ida's eyes began to stream, as if they were emptying the water from her mother's lungs. "She put stones in her pockets. *Stones.* She walked off the dock with *stones* in her pockets. My father and brothers drowned at sea and so she walked off the dock. But *I* was still here. Why didn't she remember me?" Ida spoke through ugly, gulping sobs, things that no one should attempt to speak through, and yet Ida kept on. *All three on the same boat . . . waited and waited . . . stopped waiting . . . Walked to the wharf with the stones . . . alone . . . Where was I? Where was I?*

Ida's tears, her gulping, slowed. She pulled away from Henry and dried her face on the blanket. "It was like she was pulling me down," she said. "It was like she had me by the ankles and was pulling me down. You can't know—"

Henry pushed Ida's wet hair from her face; kissed her brow. "I can't know what it was like. I can only know how desperately I want to erase it for you."

Yes, erase. Or if not erase, replace, with something besides pain. When Henry's mouth touched her temple again she lifted hers to intercept it, but again, she felt that resistance in him. That wall.

"Ida. Wait."

"Why? I don't care about your wife. I don't care about Ezra." She didn't care about Ruth or Lem or any of them. She pulled at Henry's coat. He resisted her some more, but somewhere along the way he stopped resisting, and somewhere after that he forged ahead of her, and somewhere after that Ida stopped thinking and started feeling, things she hadn't felt in a long time, or rather had never felt, and couldn't imagine never feeling again.

23

LATER IT STRUCK IDA that it was as if Perry Barstow had been watching them on that wet, sandy banquette at Makonikey; a telegraph arrived summoning Henry to Newport the next day. He walked up the hill and stood stiffly, somberly in her kitchen.

"I have under half an hour if I want to catch that boat, but I couldn't go without saying—" Whatever it was, he couldn't seem to say it. Ida took a step toward him but for a second time he gripped her arms and stood her away from him. "Don't, I beg you, or I'll never leave here." But as he spoke he pulled her to him and kissed her with a kiss that spoke as much of desperation as passion. After the door shut behind him Ida closed her eyes, attempting to recapture all the rest—the warmth of his body, the tenderness in his hands, the agony in his eyes—but in the usual perverse way her mind now worked, it called up Ezra's eyes instead, in particular the look in them she most remembered, as if he wanted to gut and flay her. But that was when he looked at her at all.

IDA HAD HELPED Oliver feed Betty and the chickens, water Ollie, and dig in the garden, but they still had two hours to go until Hattie collected the boy again. Ida looked out over Oliver's crop of hillocks and holes and recalled the date; well past frost and she hadn't yet put in her kitchen garden. It wasn't the best day for it—raw, gray, damp with the kind of damp that was bound to turn to actual wet before it ended; in Boston Ida would have stayed inside sketching. But if they could get some seed in the ground it would be just the weather the garden needed. Ida went out to the barn and collected the metal cans of seeds she'd harvested the previous fall. She grabbed a ball of twine, drove stakes at each end of the garden, and ran the twine between them while Oliver watched at first, then hopped up and followed, then began with the questions.

"What are you doing? Why are you putting that stick there? Why are you making those lines with the string?"

That Oliver saw the string as lines was a good sign. Ida handed him the can of radish seeds. She took the trowel and filled in a few of Oliver's holes. "They're too big," she said. "Watch me now." She poked a tiny hole in the earth with her finger, dropped the seed in, covered it with dirt, and gently tamped it down. "Pretty soon it will be a radish."

By the time Hattie arrived to collect Oliver a row of radish seeds and half a row of carrot seeds were in the ground, but a good deal of the ground was on Oliver. Fortunately, Hattie didn't seem to notice; her eyes were fixed on the bicycle leaning against the barn. "Hey, Oliver," Ida said. "Want to help me teach your cousin to ride that bicycle?"

"No," Hattie said. "He doesn't. Come along, now."

IDA WAS STANDING at the pasture gate looking out at the grass, trying to decide if it was time to move the sheep to a new pasture to protect the tender shoots, Bett lying at her feet awaiting direction, when the dog's ruff stood on end and she growled low. "What, girl? What is it?"

Bett crouched, taut on her haunches, ready to leap. Ida followed her gaze and saw a stranger on horseback coming up the track.

"*Down.*" Bett lowered herself imperceptibly, but Ida could feel her own hackles rise as the man drew up and dismounted.

"Mrs. Ezra Pease?"

"Who's inquiring?"

The man took out a leather wallet and removed a card. When he took a step forward to hand the card to Ida, Bett rose to her feet, the rumble growing louder. The man stepped back.

"Bett. Stay."

The man looked from the dog to Ida and back to the dog. "Does that dog do what you tell it?"

"Mostly."

The man stayed where he was. Ida stepped forward and took the card. DERMOTT HALE INVESTIGATIONS. Yes, that was what she could see in his posture, a man comfortable in situations where he wasn't invited. But he was in the wrong place.

"Aren't you supposed to be in Newport?" she asked.

"Not if you're Mrs. Ezra Pease. Are you?"

"I was. He's dead." It seemed important for her to establish that fact. *She* was not the adulterer.

The eyes flicked as if making a mental note: *Ezra Pease, dead.* "I'd like to ask you a few questions, if I may."

If I may allowed the option of Ida saying *no*, but Ida found she didn't want to. The sooner she redirected the man the better. "If you're looking for the Barstows—"

"Pease. I'm looking for Ezra Pease. But he's . . . dead, you say."

"Dead. Drowned. He went down on the *Portland*. You've heard of the *Portland*?"

Hale gave no indication whether he had or hadn't. He pulled out a notebook and pencil and made a few quick, slashing marks. For the most part he kept his eyes fixed on Ida's, just as Ida fixed hers on his, noting their blankness, the kind that came from either an honest lack of thought or long practice at keeping thoughts hidden.

She tried again. "You were sent by Mrs.—"

"Where was your husband headed, Mrs. Pease?"

"Portland."

"And from there?"

Passamaquoddy, she might have said. "I don't know," she said instead.

"And for what purpose?"

"I don't know."

"How long had he intended to be in Maine?"

"I don't know."

"You don't know what plans he made for his return?"

"No."

"Or his purpose in going to Maine?"

"No. As I said. What's this in aid of?"

"Some questions have been raised about your husband's activities."

"Who by?"

"The people who hired me."

"Not Mrs. Barstow?"

"I don't know a Mrs. Barstow."

"Who hired you, Mr. Hale?"

He made no answer. The questions went on: about Ezra's finances, his friends, his recent absences, detailed questions there about times, destinations, duration. Ida continued to answer *I don't know* to all, whether she did know or she didn't, and even though her equanimity—whatever there was left of it—had fled, she let the questions go on, thinking Hale would come to one that would explain himself and his purpose. Every so often Ida attempted to ask her own questions, but she might as well have questioned Oliver. *I can't say. I'm unable to answer that. I'm not party to that information.* Ida pictured a small wheel clicking around inside Hale's head, randomly pulling out one or another of those answers and dropping it into his mouth.

At length he pointed to the house. "Mind if I take a look around?"

But there Ida had had enough. "I would mind. Yes."

Hale took a step anyway, as if to circle around her, but Bett stood, the rumble in her throat boiling over. A single word, *wait,* would have settled her back on her haunches, but Ida chose not to give it. "If I were you, I'd back up," she said.

Hale backed up.

"You only force me to come back again with the constable."

"We'll be here," Ida said. "Both of us."

THE THREE OF THEM SAT at the kitchen table, hovered over the little atlas, Hattie reading out loud from it, Ruth chiming in with the occasional correction. Oliver looked up as Ida came in and beamed. "Massachusetts has manufactering! And deep sea and coast fishes."

"*Fisheries,*" Ruth said.

"It has more than half the fishing bustles in the United States!"

"*Vessels.*"

"It has *two million* people!"

"You like your father's little book?" Ida asked.

Oliver nodded. Paused. "What *other* stories?"

"About your father? Well, let's see. He never missed the ferry. It was like he had a clock ticking away inside his head."

"Never?"

"Never."

"*I* never missed the ferry."

"See, just like your dad."

"Just like?"

"No, not just like. But it's never a good idea to be just like."

"He'd be lucky to be just like," Ruth interrupted. "And if you want to hear stories—"

"Maybe you could tell him some," Ida said. She nodded toward the parlor, but Ruth didn't bite. She did, however, grasp Ida's intention.

"Oliver, go fill the kindling basket."

Once Oliver left, Ruth said, "What. Assuming you came traipsing up here for a reason."

Ida told them about the investigator. "I'm wondering if he came up here."

"No," Hattie said. "No one came here. You didn't see anyone, did you, Mother?"

Ruth shook her head.

Ida looked back and forth between the two women. It occurred to her that she trusted neither of them.

But Hattie asked, with what seemed to be genuine puzzlement, "What on earth did he want?"

"He asked about Ezra. His work. His finances. He wanted to search the house, but I declined the offer."

"How *dare* he invade—" Ruth started, but Hattie cut in.

"He didn't invade anyone, Mother. Ida saw to that."

"No one's talking to you, Harriet."

"*I'm* talking to Harriet," Ida said. "I'm talking to both of you. The man threatened to come back with a constable and a warrant; if there's something shady about Ezra's dealings, I'd like to be told. I've already found out he had a son that you, Hattie, seemed to know all about, and you, Ruth, no doubt suspected. What else? What else do you think is not my business or of no concern or too embarrassing to talk about? It's time you tell me of it."

"Ida, honestly, I don't know of anything," Hattie said. "This is as much a puzzle to me as it is to you. Do you think he'll come back? I wonder what he was after, really. Maybe he wanted to extort money from you or—"

"Yes, Ida," Ruth said. "That's the first thing you do. Ask that man about *his* business instead of answering questions about Ezra's."

"I didn't answer his questions. But neither did he answer mine. Whatever Ezra's done—"

The door banged open and Oliver tumbled in with an armful of twigs. He dumped them into the wood box and slid into a chair next to Ida. "What other stories?"

Ida gave up. She told Oliver a now-comic, then-terrifying tale of getting lost in the woods and Ezra sending his old dog Moe to herd her home. She resurrected another of Ezra blowing "Camptown Races" on a cider jug while Mose—and Henry—sang, Mose poorly, Henry . . . Ida pushed Henry away, or tried to push Henry away, but as she did so it occurred to her that it had been some time since she'd heard Henry singing. She returned to Ezra. She got Oliver to dissolve into the first she'd heard of real little boy giggles when she imitated Ezra's imitation of the ox: she stood motionless in the middle of the room and slowly, a half-inch at a time, swung her head left and right.

Ida looked at the boy's shining face. *Oh, Ezra,* she thought, *what a hero you could have been. What love you could have claimed. What joy you could have nurtured.*

24

BUT IDA DISCOVERED it wasn't that easy to push Henry away. He'd wakened her physical self and abruptly gone off, leaving behind an ache like a phantom limb. Add to that, she'd finally begun work on his father's portrait and was forced to spend a portion of each day staring at another kind of phantom. She'd set out her supplies and mapped out her canvas, the haze of apple trees in the distance, the single gnarled trunk in the foreground, the man leaning against the tree, so utterly comfortable in his skin. The hand hooked on his belt conveyed an air of knowing just what to do with it next; the arm propped against the tree looked both strong and relaxed; the eyes linked to an intimate half-smile aimed at the painter. Or, rather, the photographer. And yet the eyes Ida painted were the eyes that had gazed down on her at Makonikey.

Ida tried again to push Henry away but in his place marched the investigator. Why had he wanted to see the house? What did he think he'd find? The gold came first to Ida's mind. If it was stolen, and this investigator had somehow gotten wind of it . . . but why an investigator and not the law? Why was the constable held out as a threat only as a last resort? It made no sense to Ida, but sense or not, the man wanted *something*.

Ida began to look, searching all the hollow places she could access, but other than a dead mouse, an embarrassing array of cobwebs, and some whiskey bottles so frosted with dust they surely predated Ezra, she discovered nothing. She went through Ezra's desk again but found nothing that she could possibly imagine meant anything beyond that card from the assayer of gold. That, and the keys to the buildings on Main Street: office, warehouse, apartment. If the investigator had attempted to call at the office he'd have found no one there, but that didn't mean whatever he was looking for wasn't there. Ida pocketed the keys and mounted her bicycle.

The building in its emptiness felt desolate, cold. Henry had done some clearing out, and while it helped that the floor was no longer piled with pieces of old chain, lanterns, and spittoons, it did nothing to cut through the desolation. She began by unlocking the desk drawer but slammed it shut when someone came down the stairs.

"I thought I heard something," the woman said. "A rat, I presumed. What are you doing here?"

It took Ida a full five seconds. The person. The place. The person in the place. The person with Henry's keys jingling in her fingers. Either a trick of the light or a trick of the mind made Perry Barstow's hair seem more brilliant, her skin more luminous. Even her voice sounded more knifelike.

Ida took a final second to make sure her own voice came out strong. Cool. It was the voice she used to call up in the face of any verbal assault from Ezra. Not that there was any assault here. "Shouldn't that question more logically be directed at you?"

Perry walked over to where Ida had left the bicycle leaning against the wall. She ran her hand over the seat, lifted it, wiped it on her skirt. "Henry told me he lent you my bicycle."

"I understood you wouldn't miss it. I was told you'd . . . gone off it."

Perry Barstow laughed. "That does sound like Henry. Gone off. Like a bad piece of meat. No matter. I gave up riding the thing once I saw what it did to my calves."

"What *are* you doing here?"

Perry Barstow looked down at the desk and picked up the pens, one at a time. "Henry and I have come to something of an understanding. I'm here to collect a few of his things."

"He's not here?"

"Heavens, no. He's at home with our girls." The woman looked harder at Ida. Henry had labeled his wife's eyes emotionless, but Ida saw enough in them to burn a hole through the desk. She turned for the door.

"Wait!" Perry Barstow called after her. "I remember now, you're that artist. The one Henry admired."

Idiotically, Ida flushed, not over anything she'd done or said but over the fact that even this empty-eyed woman had noticed in her husband's eyes or heard in her husband's words his admiration for Ida. No, not Ida, she corrected herself. Ida's *painting*. She mustn't mistake the two. But at least that admiration had been real, then, had been visible to another besides Ida, or even more disconcerting, perhaps Henry had actually mentioned his admiration to his wife. But when? Then? Now?

"I am that artist," Ida said.

"I believe I spoke to you then about a portrait. Do you know, the more I think on it now, I think it a fine idea. I could sit for you while I'm here, a gift for my husband. He's always wanted my portrait done."

"I'm already working on a portrait for Mr. Barstow."

"Oh, how lovely! May I see it? What photo did he give you? What have you put me in? I hope not white. I so hate a white gown. Like a shroud. Green is impressive against my hair. Or rather, my hair is impressive against green." She laughed.

"I'm sorry," Ida said. "I should have explained. The portrait I'm working on is of Mr. Barstow's father."

They stood eye to eye in silence, Ida unwilling to turn her back until she'd given the woman a fair chance to reply, the woman apparently unable to form one.

"I'd best go," Ida said at last.

"Did you find what you were looking for? I wonder Henry hasn't locked this place up. Oh well, I'll do it for him before I go." She jingled the keys in her hand. Henry's keys.

"Thank you, then I won't need to," Ida said, holding up her own keys. Ezra's keys. She jingled them much as Perry Barstow had done and stepped through the door.

IDA SLEPT POORLY, her head full of the flinty shards of Perry Barstow's words. *Something of an understanding . . . Home with our girls . . . A gift for my husband.* In daylight Ida had managed to dismiss the words as those of a spiteful wife, one who would rip up her paper dolls rather than let another child play with them, but at night the words chimed in a different tone. Henry *could* have gone home, seen his girls, changed his mind, and come to "something of an understanding" with the girls' mother; Ida could only imagine the pain of leaving his children behind. But even if all of that had happened, would the Henry Ida thought she knew and trusted send his wife to collect his things and never explain, never even say good-bye? Or was that desperate kiss in her kitchen his version of good-bye? She didn't know.

But Ida knew Henry. Trusted Henry. Or did she? She tried to think back to the days when she'd felt she knew and trusted Ezra, but she could no longer remember what those days had felt like. And if she'd been fooled by Ezra, why not Henry? The same old mistake only played out with a different man. But was

it the same old mistake? Ida thought back to that night at the
Boston town house, at Ezra pushing his agenda for lying with
Ida before they married, at Ezra overriding her objections. She
thought of her bedroom the night she'd shown Henry the hiding
place for the gold, of Ida's pushing *her* agenda, of Henry standing her away. She thought of Makonikey and how again that
had been Ida's agenda, how Henry had even then been reluctant
until she'd carried him too far along for any going back . . . In
the dark, alone, Ida's face burned.

A LONG TIME LATER—or so it seemed—Ida had almost fallen
into sleep when beside her in the bed Bett went rigid, growled
low in her throat, leaped to the floor. Over time Ida had stopped
hearing noises but now she was instantly on guard again, although it took her a few seconds longer to hear what Bett
heard—a commotion among the sheep. Ida raced to the window
and through the moon dark saw what appeared to be the entire
flock stampeding toward the gate, a dark arrow behind them,
another in among them, bringing one of Ida's flock violently to
the ground.

Ida snatched up the canvas painter's duster she'd draped over
the door, barreled down the stairs, grabbed the rifle, and called
Lem. "Something's got into the sheep." She hung up, thrust her
feet into her boots, grabbed the lantern, and raced to the door.
Bett was ahead of her, waiting.

Once outside, the sounds crashed on Ida's ears: Bett's pri-
mal howl; a sheep's squeal of terror and pain. She opened the
gate and let Bett through; in quick succession three stray dogs
rounded on her, snarling, but Bett gave no ground, and Ida was
about to call her off—better a dead sheep than a dead dog—

when Lem pounded up the track on his horse and dropped to the ground, shotgun in hand.

"Dogs!" Ida cried.

Lem lifted the gun to his shoulder and fired; one of the dogs yelped and stumbled as he attempted to leap over the wall, but two others cleared it and made for the trees. Lem vaulted after them; Ida heard two more shots, then silence. She held the lantern high and inventoried the carnage at her feet. One lamb dead, two bloodied, a bloodied ewe.

Lem returned and between them they carried the injured lambs into the barn, the injured ewe trailing in stoic silence; Lem went back for the dead one, taking care to separate it from the living ones, but he needn't have bothered; by the time he knelt to examine the wounded lambs they'd died too.

THEY SAT IN THE KITCHEN, Lem stirring the fire, Ida putting on the kettle, setting out the cups. And the whiskey bottle.

Lem pointed. "This some kind of habit now?"

Ida ignored him. "Whose dogs were they?"

"Looked like Croft's. He's been told enough times not to let them run loose nights. I'll be paying him a call in the morning."

Ida fetched the kettle, but Lem had already filled his cup with whiskey; Ida poured herself some tea but left room. She pushed her cup toward Lem once, and when Lem hesitated, again. Lem dosed her.

"What I can't figure is why Bett didn't sound the alarm earlier, keep them off," he said.

"Because she was inside, asleep on my bed."

Lem gave Ida a long look. "Sheets too cold with him gone?"

Ida went to the sink, poured out her tea, picked up the whiskey bottle and filled her cup. She leaned across the table toward

Lem. "This is a bad night following a bad day and I don't need you at me about Henry Barstow."

Lem raised his cup. Point taken. Ida slumped into her seat. "They got three lambs. This puts me over on the count."

"I know."

"I wanted to do this. I wanted to climb that hill to Ruth and say I'd done it. They were my responsibility and now—"

"And now you learned something, Ida. That's how it works. Take the lesson, file it away, move on." It was something Mr. Morris would have said. "What happened today that made it a bad one?" Lem looked at the clock. "Yesterday."

Ida hesitated. She would admit to a smallness in her, a thing that hated to be wrong, that hated to admit when someone else was right. But there was another thing in her, growing stronger by the hour, that wanted everything out in the open and told straight, no hedging, no subterfuge, no deceit. Especially not with Lem. "I ran into Henry's wife in town. She'd come to pick up some things for him."

Lem drained his teacup and stood.

"Where are you going?"

"You'd rather I stay and tell you I told you so?"

"I'd rather you stay and—" What? What would she rather he do? Put his arms around her as she cried over those sheep much as she'd cried in Henry's arms over her mother? She already regretted that; she wouldn't want to regret the same thing twice.

But *did* she regret it? Ida flushed, thinking of Henry's hands on her, a thing she found little desire to regret, but thinking of Henry at home with his daughters, thinking of those hands on his wife . . .

His wife. The place where his hands belonged. Still.

As if he were reading her mind Lem said, "The rules were written a long time ago, Ida. They were written for a reason.

Don't go thinking outside them and you'll save yourself a lot of grief."

LEM CAME BY in the morning to check on the wounded ewe and offered Ida a ride up the hill to report to Ruth.

"I can walk up a hill."

"I'm going up anyway, but trot alongside if you like."

Ida got into the wagon. They rode the short distance in silence; Lem stopped at the side of the house by the back porch. "One word of advice. Ruth Pease was once a sheep farmer's wife. Don't tell her where that dog was."

Ida looked sideways and saw Lem grinning. "Go on and get out or I'll make you help me unload this wagon."

Ida looked behind her and saw what she might have seen before: a bed full of cordwood.

"I'll help."

"No you won't. Nothing gets easier for the waiting."

But Ida slid out of the wagon and grabbed an armful of wood. Lem shook his head at her, but didn't say anything else, so they worked side by side, crossing from the wagon to the back porch, stacking the wood outside the door. After the third trip Lem stopped and leaned against the porch rail, his breathing coming hard, or that was to say, harder than Ida's.

"Getting old," he said.

Ida leaned on the rail beside him. "Just how old is that, anyway?"

"Fifty-three come fall. If I live." He grinned; pushed off the rail. "You go on inside, now. Ruth gets nastier as the day grows older."

Ida rounded the corner and walked into Ruth's kitchen. Without sitting down she told the old woman about the dead sheep. She told her she was over the count. She didn't tell her about the dog.

"So, it will cost you," Ruth said.

"I know that, Ruth."

"Same as it will cost me."

"I know that too."

"So we share and share alike." The idea seemed to please Ruth. She nodded, almost smiled. "You'll stay till the livestock sale then, get me a good price, see if we can recoup. Now, are you going to sit down or are we done?"

"We're done."

Ruth peered at her. "Sit down. We're not done."

Ida sat, but on the edge of the chair. Ruth went to the stove and began to fuss with the teakettle; Ida saw no recourse but to wait on a cup of tea she didn't want and suspected Ruth didn't want to give, but what Ruth did want to give was a sundry collection of advice that kept Ida long past the time when Lem's wagon rattled off down the track.

Ida walked back down the hill, looking out over the Sound, noting how it stretched out pale and calm in front, but how a dark line marked the farthest reaches at the horizon. She'd seen that line before—often, in fact. Perhaps that was the problem with Ida's rendering of water—she'd forgotten about the dark line that always lurked in the distance.

25

"DID MY FATHER EVER TAKE YOU ON A PICNIC?" Oliver asked. "My grandfather takes us on picnics."

Ezra *had* taken her on a picnic. He'd commandeered Ruth's carriage and packed it himself with delectables he'd gleaned from Luce's store: a thick slab of salt ham, crusty bread, sharp cheese, gleaming apples, a paper bag full of hazelnuts, a pair of enormous pickles out of the pickle barrel. *Fudge.* He'd also packed a jug of hard cider and another of lemonade and a pair of old quilts.

He'd borrowed the carriage from Ruth and driven Ida out to Squibnocket; Ida had adored the endless sweep of dune peppered with the occasional green swath and grazing sheep. Yes, sheep—someone else's sheep were quite picturesque, she could admit it—even to the point of regretting her sketch pad, but only for a second. It was September and brisk; Ezra spread the quilt in the lee of a dune, the rumble of the ocean at Ida's elbow, the sun warming her cheeks. They'd been married how many months? Ida couldn't remember.

"Are you happy?" Ezra had asked her, and although by then Ida had begun to sense the full weight of the place, the full weight of her marriage, the hard edges had been dulled by the cider and the sun and the surf. And the fact that he'd ask the question further warmed her. She looked at him and believed she could see down through the sinew to a heart she could speak to. "Yes," she'd answered.

They ate and drank and walked the shoreline, facing straight into the wind; they turned and allowed the wind to blow them back, Ida tucked in against Ezra's sheltering side. They dozed in the sun between the quilts, Ida's head on Ezra's shoulder, Ezra's hand on Ida's breast, and then Ezra woke and inched her skirt up and his pants down and rolled onto her and really, what was the difference in that conclusion than the one on the banquette at Makonikey? What was the difference in one man gone to the bottom of the sea and one gone back to his wife?

"Yes," Ida answered Oliver. "Your father took me on a wonderful picnic."

SO SHE INVITED OLIVER ON A PICNIC. She asked Lem if she might borrow the wagon, but he said no. "I've seen you with wheels under you." Instead, he offered to drive them, which somehow turned into Hattie and Ruth coming along, which somehow turned into them all taking the carriage to the lagoon, to which Ida and Oliver could just as easily have walked. They couldn't have carried Ruth's folding table and chairs, however, or the huge jug of cold tea, or the basket of brown bread and boiled eggs, or Ruth's picnic china, which was Ruth's regular china but the pieces with the chips.

After an argumentative setup—the two camps being tablecloth-because-no-civilized-person-would-sit-down-to-eat-without-one and no-tablecloth-because-the-wind-will-send-it-to-the-treetops—Ruth dispersed them to find rocks to hold down the cloth. Getting a sense of where the party was going and that this might be her only chance to give Oliver the fun day she'd envisioned, Ida sent him off on a scavenger hunt after specific rocks in a specific order: white rock; black rock; striped rock. But by the time he returned flushed and happy and laden with rocks of every possible description, the tablecloth had already been anchored with a dull gray stone on each corner.

The tea and brown bread and eggs came out, to which Ida added her lemonade, muffins, and fudge, but for reasons known only to small boys, Oliver would touch none of it. Ruth began the conversation by relating the provenance of each chip in the china. Hattie getting blamed for most of it, she felt called upon to rebut, but when that got her no grace she switched the conversation to sheep.

Hattie? *Sheep?*

"When do we shear?" Hattie asked Lem.

"What's *shear*?" Oliver asked.

"We clip off the sheep's coat so we can spin their wool and make *our* coats," Ida said. "Then they grow another coat before winter."

"Do you shear Bett?"

"No, not Bett."

"Why don't you?"

"Because Bett sheds her coat."

"Why don't sheep shed their coats?"

Ida gave the nod to Lem on that one. "Because for thousands of years we've bred them not to. It's now our responsibility to remove the wool for them. If we didn't we'd have some pretty unhappy sheep."

"What's *bred*?"

Now Lem shot Ida the look, *back to you.* She was saved by a clap of Ruth's hands. "Time to pack up!"

Immediately another argument erupted between Hattie and Ruth over the proper packing of an already-peeled boiled egg.

"Here's how," Ida said, snatching the egg and biting off half, handing the other half to Oliver.

For the second time in their acquaintance, Oliver giggled. He also gobbled down the egg.

IN FACT, it was time to shear, or so Ida thought, but Lem seemed to think otherwise, and Ida, no longer trusting her judgment on anything, didn't argue. When Lem finally began to mobilize faster than Lem usually mobilized, Ida said nothing; for one thing, there wasn't time.

Shearing occupied them all—Ida, Lem, Hattie, Ruth, and Oliver—for a full day. Hattie's presence was a surprise; she'd never drawn near the event since Ida had been around, but perhaps she now welcomed the chance to focus on something besides Ezra. Lem and Ida set up the pens; Ida and Bett gathered the sheep into the near pasture where they were funneled into the larger of the two pens; Lem hauled them out one by one into the smaller.

As in the past, Ida was always amazed at how resigned the sheep became once Lem took them in hand; he rolled them onto their backs, holding them in a half-sitting position between his legs, anchoring them with feet clad in special moccasins designed for the purpose. He clipped the belly first, taking care to protect the ewe's udder with his free hand; next he rolled the sheep and worked the back side until he could pull off the fleece in one whole piece, spreading it out on the table as if it were the ewe's woolly shadow.

That was where Ida and Hattie came in. They clipped the tags and dirty edges off the fleece, folded in the corners, rolled and tied the fleece with the tail ends, and stuffed it into the bag. In the past Ida had struggled to keep up with Lem, but either Lem had slowed some or Hattie was making more of a difference than Ida had planned to give her credit for. And then, of course, there was Oliver, crawling into the long bag to jam the fleeces in tight. Through it all was the din: lambs, unable to recognize their unclothed mothers, called and called for them: *Where are you?* The ewes answered back, even louder: *Right here, silly.*

After the first fleece Hattie and Ida were elbow deep in the greasy lanolin, and after the first bag Oliver was too. All three of them were sweating through their clothes. Ida was used to it but Hattie wasn't; the look on her face was something to catch, but you had to look fast and then get out of its way. As for Oliver, the sweat, the grease, the noise—he loved it all.

Ruth too. This had been her life—the cycles of the sheep farm—and Ida only saw it now as she watched and listened. Ruth called out to Lem now and again, "Watch that one, she's trouble!" but Lem never slowed and never seemed to have any trouble that Ida could discern. Everyone chipped in to load the wagon, and Ruth counted the bags as they were piled on; Lem drove the wagon to the dock, Hattie riding beside Lem and Oliver perched atop the bags. Ida stayed behind to clean up the detritus and attempt to ignore Ruth.

"There, over there."

"I'll get to it."

"*There*, I said!"

"Why don't you sit down?" Ida suggested. Surprisingly, Ruth did, perching on a stump within vocal range so she could recount sheep-shearing tales, occasionally lifting her face to the sun as if it were the last warmth she'd ever feel.

AS IF TO REWARD IDA FOR HER LABOR, the next day broke as perfect as June days got; a bright sun gave off only the gentlest heat; a toothless salt breeze pushed the hair off Ida's forehead; a hawk looped effortlessly overhead; the bright white sails of the

schooners traced the Sound. Ida had planned to visit the salvage office in search of whatever it was the investigator thought
he'd find, but at the last minute she tossed her pad and pencils
into the bicycle basket; she didn't want to let that day escape.
When she passed Mr. Tilton cleaning the sidewalk in front of
his store, she called out to him, "Has summer finally come?" He
caused her a wobble when he called back, "For today, Miz Pease!
Fine day for riding, isn't it?"

She decided to go with the breeze and set off toward Cottage
City, pulling off the road at East Chop when she glimpsed the
sails of a schooner in the distance. She was sitting taking careful
measure of length of ship versus length of mast when a group of
women in large floppy hats, some fashionable, some not, came
walking along the shore and stopped within hailing distance of
Ida; they began to unpack: Easels. Paint boxes. Folding stools.
Thermoses. Blankets.

One who appeared to be in charge of the group surprised Ida
by coming toward her. Her hat was one of the less fashionable
ones, her chin the most prominent, her eyes deep, dark, acute.

"You're not from the Institute."

"Whatever it is, I'm not."

"The Summer Institute. A curriculum for teachers, where
they may refresh themselves, expand their knowledge, bring new
ideas back to the classroom. It's a fine idea and I like to support
it. I also like to get paid. I'm Cecily Matson, the art instructor."
She held out her hand.

"Ida Pease."

Cecily Matson waved to where the group had arranged themselves in a semicircle on the sand. "We'll be sitting over there
painting the schooners. They come by here regular as clock-
work. Feel free to join us if you like." She leaned over and examined Ida's painting, which for some reason Ida had neglected to

shield from view. "Ah, they called to you too. Have you tried the schooners before?"

Ida shook her head.

"Then allow me to be bold. You've got it right except for the foremast. On a schooner, the foremast is shorter than the aft one."

"Always?"

Matson smiled. "When is *always* ever always? But almost always."

Ida stood up, rinsed her brush, emptied the water pan, capped the water bottle.

"Oh dear, we've driven you out."

"No, I've sheep to tend." It wasn't as much of a lie as some others, yet it wasn't as true as some others either, such as *Yes, Miss Matson, you've driven me out*, but Miss Matson didn't look like she believed Ida anyway.

"Oh, stay, do." She pointed to Ida's pad. "The way you've worked the light on the water. I've been attempting to convey to the ladies—sometimes it's the absence, not the presence, of color that makes a thing spark. Here, may I show them?" And before Ida could object, the annoying woman picked up Ida's painting and held it high. "This is—"

"Ida Russell," Ida said.

26

IDA UNLOCKED THE OFFICE DOOR, side-stepped the ghost of Perry Barstow, and turned her attention to where she'd left it last—the desk drawer. If she expected to find something illicit or at least disagreeable she found only the banal: a worn glove; three pencil stubs; a crusty newspaper article about a New Jersey shipwreck; a receipt from Tilton's itemizing nails, lamp wicks, lamp oil; a toothpick; a dusty horehound drop; the key to the file cabinet.

Ida moved to the cabinet and found more paper than she'd expected; she'd assumed Henry would have culled it all. She pawed her way through copies of contracts for jobs she'd never heard of in Connecticut, Massachusetts, Rhode Island, and Maine; she fingered invoices for chain and rope and oil and gasoline; she found letters from an assortment of men inquiring about salvaging their wrecks and, also, an assortment of women. Mrs. Joseph Simpson wanted to know if Ezra could reclaim her husband's catboat from the Herring River; Hepsibah Cain asked if he had a ship's anchor for her west lawn that would match the anchor on her east lawn; Belle Santerre wanted to know when he would return and how long he might stay when he did. Ida dismissed it all, including Belle, with a single flick of the finger, but when she came to a grimy pamphlet titled *Gold from Sea Water at a Profit: The Facts,* her fingers stopped moving.

Ida plucked the pamphlet from the file and sat down. The document appeared to be a prospectus of sorts for an organization called The Electrolytic Marine Salts Company out of Boston. A teaser on page one declared: *At the proportion of half a grain to a ton, gold in a cubic mile of sea water is worth $65,000,000.* At first glance it appeared to be just the sort of crazy scheme a man who wanted to charge off mining in the Klondike would fall for except for one singular coincidence: the gold nuggets in Ida's closet. Was it possible those nuggets had somehow come out of sea water? Ida folded the pamphlet and put it in her pocket. She returned to the files, stopping a second time when she came upon some paper that felt too stiff to be anything but official. Again she plucked it from the file; again she sat down to read.

Know all men by these presents that I Edward Sprague of New Shoreham on the Island of Block Island in the County of Newport in the State of Rhode Island and Providence Plantations for and in consideration of the sum of twenty-eight dollars paid to me by Ezra Pease of the County of Dukes in the Commonwealth of Massachusetts absolutely give, grant, bargain, sell, release, convey and confirm unto him the said Ezra Pease his heirs and assigns forever a certain tract of land at the westerly shore of Block Island known as Grace's Point . . .

Heirs and assigns. Now, today, in the Commonwealth of Massachusetts, that meant *widows. Widows* meant Ida.

THERE WERE THREE KEYS on the key ring: one to the office, one to the warehouse, and one to Mose's apartment. It was possible although not probable, knowing Ezra, that whatever the investigator wanted had been stashed in Mose's apartment, but Ida could supplement that slim motive for entering the apartment with another one—if Perry had cleaned out the apartment with no expectation of her husband's return, Ida wanted to know it. She climbed the stairs.

THE APARTMENT LOOKED THE SAME. Or did it? A canvas coat hung on the hook, but maybe not the kind of coat a carriage maker would wear to cultivate the moneyed trade in New Bedford. A pair of rubber boots, ditto. Except for a few ancient boxes and tins, the kitchen shelves looked bare, but Ida couldn't recall seeing much on them in the first place. Then Ida saw the window; the canvas flap had been removed and a board nailed across it. And leaning against the wall, one of the copper kettles lined with zinc.

Ida headed for the bedroom, feeling it a violation but not enough of a violation for her to change direction. She sat down on Henry's bed, stretched out on Henry's bed, shifted so her nose touched his pillow, taking in the musky, smoky scent. She closed her eyes and imagined his long torso tight against hers, his knees tucked behind hers, his arm tossed over her so that his palm lay open and warm and alive against her center, making her feel open and warm and alive . . .

Ida shot off the bed, strode the few feet to the closet, and opened it: a row of half-filled pegs contained a pair of winter long johns, a stained chamois shirt, and a moth-eaten sweater that Ida may or may not have seen Mose wear. On the floor she found a single glove, possibly the match to the one in the desk downstairs.

Ida returned to the kitchen and rummaged among the boxes and tins, clueless as to what she was looking for, unable to name a single thing that would prove Henry would or would not be returning to the island; canisters partially full of tea, flour, and cornmeal told no tale. A newish-looking recipe box surprised her; she never thought of Mose—or Henry—cooking, but as she leafed through it she saw that most of the recipes were for simple things like stew and buckwheat cakes and cornbread, things someone like Mose—or Henry—might certainly have attempted. One sheaf of recipes at the back of the box looked more complex, but as Ida drew them out she saw they weren't recipes at all but letters to Mose. From Ezra.

Mose—Block Island parcel secured but Maine site looks better for EMS purposes I'll look over again before purchase Zinc arrived 10th Should have the accumulators lined by 18th—E

Mose—Include "At the proportion of half a grain to a ton, gold in a cubic mile of sea water is worth $65,000,000—" Fish are getting bigger—E

Mose—Need to melt more jewelry Have to salt three for next run investors Can you put your hands on any Should be able to add some when I get home Look for me on late boat Friday—E

Ida spread out the letters and pulled the *Gold from Sea Water* pamphlet from her pocket. With it came the deed to the parcel on Block Island that she'd also added to her pocket, but heirs and assigns notwithstanding, it was the *Gold from Sea Water* pamphlet that Ida wanted. Yes, there were the same words in the pamphlet that Ida had read in Ezra's letter: *At the proportion of half a grain to a ton, gold in a cubic mile of sea water is worth $65,000,000.* And as she read the details the pamphlet offered up she came on other words that had appeared in the letters: *Accumulators. Zinc.* And a description of a convoluted process where an electrical current passing through sea water, copper, and zinc in a specially constructed accumulator resulted in the separating of gold from said water.

Zinc. Copper. The odd, flat-bottomed copper kettles lined with zinc that Morgan had brought up from the *Cormorant*. The accumulators? And this salting process—jewelry melted into what? Well, of course. Those nuggets. Nuggets that would be used to salt the accumulators. And the *EMS* notations in the ledgers that Henry had inquired about so long ago—here it was again in the letter. *EMS. Electrolytic Marine Salts.* Ida pored over the documents again, but she hardly needed to; it was clear enough to her that Ezra hadn't fallen for someone else's scam; Ezra—and Mose—were the scammers.

IDA RODE HOME with the various papers she'd collected crackling in her pockets. The sheep were in the far pasture where the grass was full and fresh and green; her artist's eye regretted that now the fields looked their best the animals looked their worst, small and forlorn and long-necked without their fleece, but that was all the time Ida could spare for sheep. She carried her papers up the stairs and dug out the gold from the closet, spilling it onto the bed alongside the papers. She picked up and examined each nugget, imagining it the melted-down result of someone's jewelry.

Someone's. Ida bolted off the bed and opened her jewelry box. Her mother's gold locket was there, and her father's gold stickpin; Ezra wouldn't dare touch those. But Ida *had* lost a gold ear bob—or thought she had—Ezra claiming she'd worn them on a rare night traveling in style in Ruth's carriage to dine at the Wentworths' in Edgartown. He'd even made a great show of searching Ruth's carriage. Yes, that was Ezra's style—take

only one ear bob because one could be lost, but two would in-
dicate theft, which would lead to questions, precautions. What
else was missing? A pearl ring set in a gold band her father had
brought home for her when she was still a child and had long
outgrown but treasured all the same; she'd kept it wrapped in
one of her father's handkerchiefs in the box. The handkerchief
was still there; the ring wasn't.

IDA SPENT THE REST OF THE NIGHT alternately tossing between the sheets or pacing between the closet and her
dresser, piecing it together. Ezra and Mose had created a fable
of gold from sea water and written a pamphlet describing in
just enough incomprehensible detail the process to extract it.
Flashy "accumulators" lined with zinc. A sophisticated system
of electric currents that reacted chemically with the zinc and
turned the sea water into gold. Big-fish investors being brought
to Block Island or perhaps Maine where they went round-eyed
at the sight of actual gold nuggets materializing out of a kettle
of sea water—gold nuggets manufactured from melted-down
stolen jewelry hidden in Ezra's closet. Then what? Some investor somewhere had likely gotten wise and sent Dermott Hale to
track the men down, but there Mose and Ezra had gotten lucky.
They had gone down on the *Portland*.

At some point Ida dozed, but each time she woke a new
question arose. The investigator Dermott Hale hadn't seemed
ready to stop once he learned the men were dead; the men must
not have been the first object of his search. Perhaps the money
was. Perhaps he hoped or believed the funds were recoverable.
Which led Ida to the next question: if Ezra had secreted some
money somewhere, and Ida found it, what would she do with it?
Again, that troubling question: in the face of the newly revealed

scope of Ezra's d shonesty, where along the line from honest to Ezra lay Ida?

THE *GOLD FROM SEA WATER* SCHEME had accomplished what nothing else had; it had driven Henry from Ida's mind, so when the telegram finally arrived, delivered by Chester Luce's errand boy, Ida had some difficulty putting it in the proper context. *Complications send me back to New Bedford. Would my direction were other.* Well, Ida already knew he was in New Bedford, with his daughters, and most likely now with his wife too. Ida balled up the telegram, opened the door to the stove, and fired it inside. She was tired of waiting for news. She was tired of waiting for life to have its way with her. She'd taken apart her house, the office, even Mose's apartment; if there was a secret hoard of money Ezra and Mose had left behind, she'd have found it by now or she never would. But Ida did hold in her hand something as good as money: a deed to a piece of land on Block Island.

Ida set off up the hill in big, gulping strides, her fist barely knocking on the door before she thrust it open herself, her lesson learned from Ruth. Hattie came into the kitchen first, followed by Oliver, who was just the one Ida wanted, or rather, she wanted Oliver's atlas. It cost her precious minutes of listening to the boy spout off his new knowledge about various states until an idea struck her.

"I wonder if you know which is smallest."

"Rhode Island!"

Oliver pushed the pages with his thumbs until he found the map of Rhode Island. He told Ida about its manufacture of cotton goods, about its *two* capitals, Providence and Newport, that Newport had a fine harbor and was known as a watering place.

"For horses," he said. Ida didn't think so, but the good news was that at least one of the two women he currently lived with continued to read to him, although no one had troubled to explain what a watering place was. The even better news was that Ida could look around Oliver's thumbs at the map, and on the western shore of Block Island she spied it: Grace's Point, ticked with Ezra's pencil.

OF COURSE, LEM DIDN'T LIKE IT. "You're going out to Block Island. By yourself. And you want me to mind the place."

"You understand I can't ignore a single asset."

"I understand why you want to do it; I just don't think it's an errand that's wise for a woman alone."

"What errand do you think is wise for a woman alone, besides a trip to Luce's? I've already been to Wellfleet alone, Boston alone—"

"I'll mind the place."

"I'll leave tomorrow and be back the next day. If you could just check in—"

"I said I'd do it."

"And you won't tell Ruth?"

"I won't tell Ruth." He hoisted himself into his wagon and started for the track. He looked back, called to her over his shoulder: "I won't tell Ruth if you won't try to tell me you went to Boston alone."

Oh, this island.

IDA'S RECENT IMMERSION had done little to reconcile her to water, but it helped that the steamer scudded across a placid Sound as if absent all effort. By the time they bumped up to the dock at Woods Hole safe and secure, Ida could almost have said she'd enjoyed the trip; she was leaving the island behind, the farm behind, the sheep behind, Ruth, Hattie, Lem, Henry. All of it.

It was a different story with the steamer from Newport: more people, more carriages, more baggage, more elegance, and seas so rough they almost cost her her breakfast. At the Block Island dock Ida's head continued to reel over the huge hotels perched on the bluffs like a flock of vultures; runners and hackmen accosted the passengers before they'd gotten both feet on the ground: *Surf Hotel, ma'am! Best on island! Step right here, I'll run you up . . . Ocean View, headland view, right this way for the thrill of your life . . . Pequot House has a room for you, miss! Clean, safe . . .*

At least Ida wouldn't have trouble finding a room if she needed one. She dodged the horsecars and the fine gentlemen and ladies filing onto the dock like sheep to the shearing pen. She hadn't expected the small island to be so populated, so hectic, so . . . *fashionable.* She accosted the first hack driver she saw and engaged him to take her to Grace's Point, to wait for her to explore, and to return her to town.

"Grace's Point," the man said, as if to verify Ida's madness, but he hoisted her in without argument. In a very few minutes they'd left behind the commotion of the harbor as well as the sprinkling cart, which meant they were forced to cope with the dust churning up behind the horses, and soon Ida could spy nothing but stone walls and empty fields on either side of them. Clearly they were not headed in the most populated direction.

The dirt road ended. The driver stopped in the middle of it and pointed ahead to a rock-strewn gully that appeared to drop off over the edge of a bluff facing the sea. "There?" Ida asked. The driver nodded, lowered his hat, and settled in for a nap.

Ida set off in the direction of the water. Just when she'd concluded that walking muscles and biking muscles weren't the same muscles, she came upon a slight hollow on the hill and what appeared to be an abandoned shack, its door half off its hinge, its roof missing more shingles than it had kept, the glassless windows nailed over with what looked like salvaged hatches from shipwrecks. Ida set down her bag and walked to the edge of the bluff to examine the shoreline; a precipitous drop ending in more rocks, the surf making miniature rainbows as it struck the solid objects and reared back up. She returned to the stoop and opened her bag, pulled out the deed, read over the landmarks. Was that the "great boulder" that bound the tract on the north? Was that shack what was meant by "homestead"? The sea was obviously the sea, bounding the land on the west, but bounding what exactly? What could this bit of land possibly be worth if it contained no landing, no farmland, nothing but one rotting shack and enough cobbles to pave all of Boston?

Ida had brought lunch—a thick pair of bacon sandwiches; her father used to tell her that sea hunger was bigger than land hunger and he was right; she dropped to the stoop and demolished both sandwiches in minutes. She wiped her hands in sand that had been warmed by the sun and felt the comfort of it sliding through her fingers; she looked around, pondering Grace's Point and what she might make of it. Well, nothing. What on earth had Ezra seen in a place so remote and inhospitable . . . other than the fact that it was remote and inhospitable. On her return to the busy harbor she would make inquiries for an agent to handle a land sale for her; at the least she might hope to reclaim the twenty-eight dollars Ezra paid for it, which was something.

Ida sat on, deep in thought. Had Ezra ever even been here? she wondered. Had he perhaps sat on this very stoop, eating his own bacon sandwiches, a favorite of his? Why did this place

make her so sad? What was she meant to do with these feelings, this place, this life? She leaned back against the door of the
shack and closed her eyes.

Ida dozed. Dreamed. Ezra, leaning over her, shouting her
name. Angry, of course—Ida could never manage to dream of
a pleasant Ezra. So real the dream was! So vivid was Ida's sense
of him that when she opened her eyes she actually thought for a
minute that the man who loomed over her, dark-haired, heavily
bearded, broad-shouldered, was Ezra.

"Jesus God, Ida, what are you doing here?" Ezra said.

27

IDA LEAPED UP; the beard might have fooled her for that single instant of waking, but never the voice. That voice. As to the face above the beard, there seemed to be something wrong with it; it wavered before her, teeth exposed, gleaming. He couldn't possibly be *grinning*? He seemed to be talking, but now there was something wrong with Ida's ears too—she could hear nothing. Ezra had stopped grinning and Ida's vision—and hearing—cleared.

"Jesus God," Ezra was saying. "Ida. If you aren't the last person I expected to see when I came over that rise." He peered at her hard. "And I'm the last person *you* expected to see, am I right?"

Ida said nothing.

"You thought I was on the *Portland*?"

Still Ida could say nothing. She was aware of time passing but how much time she couldn't say before Ezra tried again.

"You thought I was on the *Portland* and I drowned. Well, I guess now you know. I wasn't. I didn't."

Ida turned for the path.

Ezra came after her, grabbed her arm.

Ida whirled. "Don't. Touch. Me."

Ezra dropped his hand. "Ida, listen to me. Don't you want to know what happened? It wasn't some big cooked-up plot—"

Ida kept walking. Ezra kept following, talking. "Mose and I were in Boston, we heard everyone shouting up and down the streets, the *Portland*'s gone down, no survivors, no one even sure who was on board because the only passenger list was on the ship. I swear it wasn't like I said, oh, I think I'll run off and play dead, confuse the hell out of Ida . . . Ida! Will you hold up?"

Ida stopped walking and turned so fast Ezra was forced to back up. He took what must have been his first good look at Ida's face. "All right, you're angry. Yes. Fair enough. I see that. I do. But I'm trying to explain to you. I told you, it wasn't like we planned it. We'd run into some trouble with the company—"

"Which company, Pease and Barstow Salvage or the Electrolytic Marine Salts Company?"

Yes, that stopped him. Briefly. "How'd you find out about that?"

Ida said nothing.

"All right, Ida, that makes it easier. Yes, it was Marine Salts. Someone was after us; we thought why not disappear for a while, try someplace new? I was going to send for you. I was going to send you money and a ticket. To Paris. You always wanted to go to Paris, right?"

Ida whirled again and continued up the gully.

Ezra kept going. "Oh, Ida, come on. I know, I know, you're not too happy with me right this minute, but I've got lots of money now. It'll be a whole different life. That horse and carriage you've always wanted, jewelry like you've never seen, jewelry to put that locket of yours to shame. Your own studio. In Paris!"

Ida stopped again and turned. "Where's Mose?"

"Oh, nice, Ida. The first civil thing you say to me. Where's Mose."

Ida waited.

"Mose went to Australia. He wanted to send back some of the investors' money; I said good luck to you, see you later, just don't get caught before I get to Paris."

"This would be the money you scammed from your investors in the gold from sea water scheme?"

Ezra peered harder at Ida, eyes narrowed. "All right. Go ahead. Make your point. You always have to make your point, don't you, Ida? But did you hear what I said? *Paris.* Or did you miss that part? The part where your dreams come true and I take you to Paris?"

Ida could only stare back. It was beyond credible that even Ezra could admit to such a lie—no, not a lie, an entire construction of deception in which Ida had gone through months and months believing herself a widow—and expect Ida could then listen and nod and climb on the boat beside him for Paris. But then again, Ezra had managed to talk Ida into a sheep farm on Martha's Vineyard; why shouldn't he believe he could talk her into Paris? But back then she'd been buried in that fog of grief. Now she wasn't.

"How did you work it?" Ida asked. "How did you get them to believe you were mining gold out of sea water?"

Ezra hesitated. He studied Ida some more, seemed to see nothing dangerous in her, and began talking. Or maybe it was even simpler than that: Ezra just loved a good brag. Again, Ida was aware of time passing, of the sun dropping, of many, many words flowing from Ezra's mouth, but only some of them landed in her brain. She snagged only enough from the air to confirm it was much as she'd speculated, with a few twists thrown in: a lot of foolish bells and whistles with zinc and electricity and accumulators designed to be unfathomable to all parties; the investors brought to a remote dock somewhere in Rhode Island— but not Grace's Point—to watch a demonstration; Mose in his dive suit already under the dock salting the accumulators with the gold nuggets.

"Of course it's the same old bunch of nuggets every time." Ezra looked at Ida proudly—*proudly*—but apparently he didn't see the expected admiration in Ida's eyes. His tone grew defensive, petulant. "I'll tell you right now, it took some clever foot-work, and a lot of time and aggravation. But it was worth it in the end."

"Which end is that, Ezra? The one where you exile yourself to a patch of useless ground on Block Island?"

"The one where I sit in Paris counting it! Or maybe I didn't say. We took $750,000 off those fools."

Which was, of course, their fault. Ida wished she could look at Ezra now and wonder at how he'd changed, at the moral depths to which he'd fallen, but all she saw as she looked was the same old Ezra who'd been there all along. And the same old fool Ida.

Ezra shifted his feet, impatient now. "So what's it going to be, Ida? I've got to stick it out here for a while; I've got some other money coming in and I can't leave the country till I get it, but in the meantime I've got to keep out of the way of that detective. Back in that shack, though—in there is a ticket for the *Umbria*, New York to Liverpool. Then on to Cherbourg and the train from Cherbourg to Paris. It's real, Ida. Paris is real. And as soon as I find a nice place for us—a place with a studio—I'll send you *your* ticket."

And because Ida still stood there, no longer trying to figure out who Ezra was so much as who he thought Ida was—Ezra kept talking. She'd have to get her own train to New York—he'd hired a lobsterman who was going to get him there for an un-godly sum—but just wait till Ida saw that ocean liner. Ezra had seen the pictures. Mahogany furniture. Velvet curtains. Refrig-eration! Four decks to stroll around, even a music room, sepa-rate dining for first-class passengers only. And of course she'd be going first class all the way. And just wait till she had her first champagne breakfast! Just wait till she saw *Paris*.

At length it seemed to occur to Ezra that Ida wasn't saying

the things that—again unbelievably—he'd expected her to say. He took a step closer, lifted a hand, saw her face, dropped it. "All right, Ida. I know it's strange seeing me here—"

"I thought you were *dead*. I got your letter and thought you were dead. So clever, dating it the day the *Portland* sailed—I never questioned the delayed delivery because of the storm. And Mose, his letter to Henry, what *he* went through. The both of us."

"Oh, don't try that on, Ida. You probably did a dance when you got that letter. Things weren't that rosy with us. Admit it."

"I went to the Lifesaving Station in Wellfleet, the place where they'd piled up the unclaimed bodies. I walked around the bodies looking for yours. Can you imagine what that was like, Ezra?"

There, finally, Ezra blinked. "All right. I'm sorry, Ida. I am. But what do you want from me? How many times do I have to say it? I'm going to make it up to you, I promise. All of it. Things will be different now. We'll start off right this time because we'll have money. No more throwing it in my face that I don't have a horse or a carriage or a whole crew of farmhands or the cash to drop on a Boston hotel once a week. Now I can buy you a castle if you want! A castle on the Seine. You'd like that, wouldn't you, a castle on the Seine? And your own studio in Paris. Come along, now. Paris!"

It was too ludicrous. Too monstrous. And there the ludicrous and the monstrous merged and Ida started to laugh. Once she started to laugh she had some trouble stopping, so it was a second or two before she noticed that Ezra's face had darkened. Warped. Twisted.

"In case you have another thought in mind, in case you're thinking to hop back home and talk things over with the friendly constable, there are things you did with your money, or so it will appear, that put you in this deep as me. I go down, you go down, Ida, and don't you think different for a minute. So if you don't play fair—"

Fair. Oh, that Ezra could look her in the eye and say that word! But Ida could look Ezra in the eye too, and finally, finally, she could see all the things she'd missed when they'd married. She saw that Ezra's eyes never looked out on her but always back on himself, that Ezra was all that mattered to Ezra, and it would always be all that mattered. And seeing this, Ida understood for the first time that there was actually something to fear here, that a man who would do anything to make himself come out right was not a man she should feel safe around. Ida was alone on a deserted point of land within fifty feet of a deadly sea that could carry her off long before any sleepy hack driver might decide to come looking.

The adrenaline that surged through Ida cleared her brain, drove out any remnants of the surreal laughter that had overcome her, brought into sharp, clear focus that above all she needed to get away from Ezra. And because she knew Ezra now, she knew how to do it; not run—never run—let him think just what he'd assumed in his arrogance that she would certainly think: Paris. She would forgive all, forget all, overlook all for Paris. Knowing that much of Ezra's mind, Ida still had to move with care here—an immediate capitulation might leave him doubting it later on. Better she demand an accounting and then let Ezra glimpse in her what he no doubt believed she owned in surplus already: greed.

But first she could let him see nothing of her fear. She stepped close and caught Ezra by the coat sleeves; shook him like an angry mother might shake her child. "I thought you were *dead,* Ezra. Do you understand? I need you to admit it. You let me think you were dead. Drowned. After what happened to my father and brothers and mother, you let me think you'd *drowned.*"

"All right. Yes. I know—"

"You do not know. I went to Wellfleet. I walked up and down row after row of sodden, bloated, ghastly corpses. I thought one might be you, or another, or another; I had to lean down and look hard, look close, unsure of my own eyes, but none of them were you. I went home and waited for someone else to find you, for the telegraph to come—" Ida's anger had put a tremor in her voice but it didn't matter; Ezra would only read it as grief.

"I told you, Ida. I didn't *plan* to do it. And look now. I'm here. I'm back. You just have to think of it as a bad dream. Put it out of your mind. Start thinking of the good dream. Us together in Paris."

"You expect me to adjust from the one to the other like that?"

"No, no, I guess . . . well no, I guess I don't. But you've got time; my ticket's for the middle of August." Did he sense a softening in her? She hoped so. He smiled, tentatively, yes, but even so. "Me, I'm already used to the idea because I've been picturing us together in Paris all along."

Oh, Ida doubted that. She doubted there had been any plan for a second ticket at all. She believed that the sight of her had triggered an old lust that had gotten him thinking, *Why not?* Why not this known quantity I've already managed to convince of so much versus starting at the beginning with someone new who would likely never be as naive as this one? Or maybe his thinking only took him as far as his own ticket, his own escape. Or maybe it only took him as far as that bluff.

Ida took a good, deep breath. Then another. The breaths were real, and Ezra, watching her chest rise and fall, seemed to accept that she was in the middle of an honest struggle, if not the one Ida actually battled.

"My own studio, you said."

There. The look on Ezra's face. The triumph. He allowed it to blossom only briefly and then quelled it to begin his list again: studio, castle, clothes, jewels, horses, and carriages—plural this time. In turn Ida played *her* part, listening intently when he spoke of them touring Europe, when he offered to visit those museums she'd always talked of; she studied him and looked away and studied him in turns as if she were coming around one point at a time, as if the sum total of future assets might actually outweigh the sum total of Ezra's past deficits. And when she'd done it, when the light of victory filled Ezra's eyes, Ida bent down to pick up her pack. "I have a driver waiting. You'll send me that ticket?"

"I'll send it. I promise," but as Ida turned, he called after her. "Wait! You never said how you found me here."

Now Ida laughed. "I wasn't looking for *you,* Ezra. You were dead, remember? I found the deed to this bit of land and came here hoping I could sell it. Or did you also forget you left me with nothing? That Ruth owns the farm? That I have no property? No money?"

There Ida saw the first look of chagrin and pounced on it; it wouldn't take long for Ezra to exonerate Ezra. "And needless to say, I don't have money for any train to New York."

Ezra fished in his pocket and pulled out a roll of bills. He peeled off several and handed them to Ida as if he were St. Nicholas himself. "To show my good faith. And to remind you that you've traded a run-down sheep farm for a studio in Paris."

Ida shook her head, smiling as she did it, again a genuine smile that Ezra would be sure to misinterpret. The last look Ida had of him, he stood shading his eyes as if to see her better, or as if to make note of her direction in order to follow her and push her over the bluff a little farther along the track.

28

EITHER LEM HAD SECOND SIGHT or he'd met every boat until Ida walked off one of them; there he was at the dock with the wagon. He peered at her harder than she liked, but no wonder—she was so knotted up that her knees didn't bend and her jaw didn't work. He handed her into the wagon and waited patiently through her yes and no answers to his questions: *Yes*, she found the property; *no*, she hadn't yet made arrangements for sale; *yes*, she was tired from the traveling. Ida knew she should tell Lem about Ezra, but she couldn't, not yet; she needed to calm herself, to think it through. So far she'd managed to think through one thought only: the need to get as far away from Ezra as possible. So Ida asked Lem about the farm and that carried them to the house.

Lem helped her down from the wagon and followed her in with her bag. He dropped it on the table and looked at her one more time. "You all right, Ida?"

"Yes. Tired. As you said. Thank you for minding the farm. Thank you for meeting me."

Lem brushed her thanks away. "Figured you'd either be on that boat or the next one." He turned for the door, turned back. "You had a visitor while you were gone."

Ezra. That was Ida's first irrational thought. Her second more rational one was Hale. But once Lem got through looking at her too hard again he said, "That Barstow."

Ida sat down in the kitchen chair.

"He seemed pretty disappointed at missing you. He said if I

saw you to tell you he's back, which I figured was just about the worst thing I could do, but I'm doing it anyway."

"Thank you."

"You say that today. I could say you won't be thanking me later on, but why trouble myself? You'll do what you want to do, whatever that is. If you even know what that is."

Oh, Ida knew what that was. She wanted to see Henry.

IDA'S KNEES UNLOCKED with the first full rotation of the pedals. Her jaw loosened. She coasted down the hill, taking her usual joy in that flying freedom that even Ezra couldn't diminish. She breezed onto Main Street and thought how like Block Island it was, the summer folk beginning to pour off the steamer in the usual conglomeration of trunks, hats parasols, and gay, proprietary voices. These were people with no cares, Ida thought; these were people without phantom husbands or disappointing lamb counts or recalcitrant paintbrushes. She wove her way through them, not quite believing she'd find Henry in town until she saw his bicycle leaning beside the office door. Ida propped her bicycle beside it, pushed open the door, and was crushed into his arms.

"Oh, Ida." He drew back, smoothed away her hair to look harder at her. "What's wrong?"

"I wasn't sure you'd be back."

Henry laughed. "Neither was I. I sent a letter you probably won't get till tomorrow—"

"I mean *ever.*"

"What? Why? I told you there were complications—"

"She came and took your things."

"What? Who?"

"Your wife."

"My *wife*? Here?" Henry blinked. "Well, of course. I see now. That explains things."

Henry tried to pull Ida close again but this time she was the one who held him away.

"Henry. Listen to me. Ezra's alive." She began to tell her tale, at first stuttering, then lashing the air with her words, but when she'd reached the part about opening her eyes to see Ezra standing over her, she could feel the trembling begin again; she crossed behind the desk and dropped into the chair. "To open my eyes and to see him, the shock of it—"

But something was wrong. The room. The air. She twisted around and saw Henry pacing back and forth behind her, silent. Very well, he would be experiencing his own shock, but Ida needed something more from him than silence. She stood to intercept his track, and at first his eyes were full of all that she needed to see in them: an acknowledgment of her anguish, followed by his own anguish, and last, the full weight of the shock of what Ida was telling him.

Only somehow it didn't look like such a great weight.

"Henry?"

Henry looked at her. Looked away. He began to pace again.

Ida reached out and caught his arm. "Why doesn't this shock you the way it shocked me?"

"It does. Of course it does. It's only—"

"Only *what*?"

Again Henry looked away.

Ida pulled at his arm, drew him around again. And saw.

"You knew."

"No. Not *knew*. Not with complete certainty."

"You *knew*."

"I suspected, Ida. A whiff of suspicion only."

"How? When?"

Henry sat on the corner of the desk, but when Ida didn't re-claim the chair he stood again. "I found a large withdrawal from Ezra's Boston account after the *Portland* went down. At first I attributed it to an accounting error, a delayed transmission due to the storm, much as I attributed Mose's delayed letter to the storm. But when I saw your letter from Ezra, a letter so similarly worded, so exactly timed—"

"When you saw my *letter*? Last winter?"

"I didn't know for a fact. It was a suspicion only. I only grew surer when I discovered some evidence that he might be in trouble, that there were reasons he might have wanted to disap-pear with no—"

"You grew *surer*. And still you said nothing to me."

"Ida, please. It was piece by piece. Your letter. A pamphlet in the office file about mining gold from sea water. Those zinc-lined kettles. Then you showing me the gold, and the discov-ery of an essentially empty office in Boston when it should have been in full operation after such a sudden death—"

When Ida showed him the gold in Boston. In *Boston*. "And the fact that I might not be a widow after all didn't strike you as information of interest to me? It didn't occur to you that I might have some thoughts on what we should do about this?"

Looking at Henry's face, Ida saw that it had not. She whirled for the door. Henry followed.

"Ida. I knew how you felt about Ezra. I knew what you'd gone through with your family. I decided it would only torment you further—"

"*You* decided. You! *I'll* decide my own torment. Oh, I knew this. I knew there was something not right, and it wasn't all your wife. I wanted so badly to trust you and I never could, I never felt I was seeing to the bottom of you. And now I know why." Ida banged out the door. Outside, she spied Perry's bicycle leaning against the building. She wrenched it away and shoved it through the door at Henry. "Give your wife back her bicycle. And her husband."

IDA CLIMBED THE HILL without a hint of a tremble in her now, her rage powering her and clearing her mind. She knew what to do: She would collect her evidence and go to the constable, tell them where Ezra was, what he had done, what he'd *confessed* to doing. She formed the list as she walked: the pamphlet; the card for the assayer who was clearly implicated in some way, judging by his reaction to Ida's name when she'd visited him in Boston. Yes, there Henry had helped her—she must remember to talk of the empty office, the withdrawal of funds; they would call on Henry to confirm, but whether he would do so or not would be his decision to make. He might prefer to protect Mose; in fact, perhaps that accounted for Henry's unwillingness to talk of Mose, for his lack of visible grief for his brother. But what did it matter? According to Ezra, Mose was long gone, while Ezra planned to remain on Block Island until mid-August. Ezra was her concern, not Mose.

And not Henry Barstow.

WHEN IDA TOPPED THE RISE she saw Hattie and Oliver in her garden, pulling radishes out of the ground. Oliver's joy was like a liniment smoothed over sore muscles, so much so that Ida didn't trouble to look at Hattie's face for some time. When Hattie finally caught her eye, she motioned to Ida to follow her a distance away.

"It's Ruth. That detective finally came. Apparently Ezra was involved in a scheme to cheat investors in some sort of scam to mine gold, and they found Ruth's name on the investor list. She's devastated. I tried to calm her but got nowhere—the usual chant—what does some old spinster know about anything?"

Ida peered at Hattie, seeing for the first time the depth of the bitterness in her.

Hattie kept on. "As difficult as she's been with you, she does believe you know things. Would you talk to her?"

"No."

"Please, Ida. She thought the world of that man. That he attempted to cheat her—"

"She made out all right. She got the farm."

"The farm doesn't matter! It's the fact that he tried! Her darling Ezra had tried to cheat her. If she hadn't insisted on his handing over the deed, she'd be a pauper right now."

Ida doubted *pauper* was the accurate word, but Hattie had said other words that struck Ida like darts. *Ezra had tried.* How could he try to cheat his own aunt? How could he try to convince Ida, with three victims of the sea in her family already, that he'd drowned?

And then there was the matter of the larger deception that Ruth—and Hattie—didn't yet know.

"Keep Oliver away," Ida said and set off up the hill.

THE RUTH THAT IDA FOUND was a Ruth Ida had never seen before. She sat at the kitchen table, whitened hands gripping a cup of tea still full to the brim, the flesh on her face sagging against her bones, her eyes red and dull.

Ida sat down. "I saw Hattie down at the—"

"How could he?"

"I don't know, Ruth. I really don't. I didn't know him; I see that now."

Ruth lifted her eyes. "Did he take from you too?"

Ida thought of the disappearance of her family fortune, such as it was. "He didn't need my permission to use my money. That's the way the law goes. But yes, he took from me too."

"He was a lovely boy. Like Oliver. I didn't like Oliver. He was too like Ezra. He made it too hard to excuse Ezra and I always excused Ezra. Every time."

"Until now. So that's a good thing, Ruth. You can stop struggling to excuse him. You can take Oliver into your heart for his own self. You're exactly right—he's a lovely boy."

"He lies."

"Not so much now he knows his father's—" Ida had been about to say *dead*. Dear God, what to tell the boy now? What to tell Ruth? Ida took another look at the old woman, at the reddened veins in her eyes, at the death grip on the mug of tea, surely cold by now. Ruth tried to say something, but her mouth trembled so badly she couldn't speak. Tears welled and leaked. There was nothing Ida could think of that was uglier, more painful to the observer, than an old woman's tears.

Ida couldn't tell her. What purpose would it serve? If the law caught up with Ezra before he left the country, Ruth would have to know, but she didn't need a second shock just now. And Oliver? Someday, it might happen that Oliver too would need to know, but not now, not from Ida's tongue, not when he'd just grown accustomed to the idea of his father being dead; there were only so many twists and turns a five-year-old mind could execute and still keep to the road. Ida got up, collected a clean dish towel, and handed it to Ruth to dry her eyes, but Ruth snatched it and blew her nose instead. She pushed away her tea.

"You've a right to your tears," Ida said. "I've a right to mine. But let's see if we can't get them over with before Hattie brings Oliver home. He doesn't need to know what his father's done."

That brought Ruth's head up. "No." She peered at Ida. "I never once saw you cry. I never once saw you look like you even cared."

"I like to do my crying in private."

Ruth studied Ida some more. "Yes, you would, wouldn't you?" She splayed her hands flat on the table and pushed down; she seemed to struggle to rise but Ida knew better than to lend a hand. "I'm going to wash my face," Ruth said. "If you wouldn't mind staying until Oliver returns, in case I'm unable—"

"Wash your face. I'll be here."

29

IDA WAS IN THE GARDEN with Oliver making a pretext of overseeing his harvest when in fact she was overseeing nothing but her own mind. Ruth was right—Ida shed no tears—but Ruth might have been shocked at the violence of Ida's inner turmoil, the struggle she was having trying to reconcile right and wrong, truth and lies, who paid versus who benefited. If she went to the law the whole pathetic tale would be known; Ruth would learn that Ezra had deceived her a second time in a way that would cut so deep into the old woman's heart the wound couldn't possibly heal. And Oliver would have to live with the knowledge that his father was a criminal who had abandoned his son not once but twice.

And Ida? If Ezra were found and jailed and forced to make restitution to his investors, which was certainly what Dermott Hale was after, the buildings on Main Street and the parcel of land on Block Island might be confiscated. And even if Ezra was locked away, how long would he stay there? At some point he'd be freed, and then what? Would he attempt to reclaim his farm, his life, his *wife*? But even if he did none of those things, even if Ida got away to Boston, would she ever stop looking and listening for him to appear on her doorstep? While if Ida did nothing, if she allowed Ezra to climb aboard the *Umbria* in August, the courts would eventually declare him dead. And to maintain that fiction, to remain safe from the law, Ezra would have to keep away—from the island and from Ida—forever. And all Ida need do was to continue to pretend to the island that she was the widow everyone already believed her to be, to continue to pretend to Ezra that she was exactly as shallow and avaricious as he believed her to be, that she was willing to sit and wait for that second ticket to Paris.

But to let Ezra win . . . Ida floundered. Raged. That Ezra could allow her to think he'd drowned after what she'd been through with her family, that he could prey on his own aunt, proved him so far beneath the low tide mark of humanity that she wasn't sure she could draw her own line in that sand. She wasn't sure she could weigh Ezra free against Ida free and declare them to have come out even. One minute Ida could. The next she could not. Ezra in Paris counting his money, Ida trapped on the Vineyard elbow deep in some sheep's backside, or in Boston unable to afford a new pair of boots, proved a more difficult image for her to ponder than Ezra lying at the bottom of the sea being eaten by crabs.

There Ida left off thinking about Ezra and moved on to Henry. But as it turned out, Henry required a good deal less thought than Ezra; Ida had never allowed herself to fully trust Henry in the first place, so when his deception was proved she had less to regret. Except for that one day, that one afternoon, that one hour that she *had* trusted, almost begged . . . Ida grew hot and cold with mortification in turns. She walked the perimeter of the garden in an effort to recalibrate her thermometer, and just as she reached the door, the phone began to ring. Ida let it ring.

When Hattie came up the hill to collect Oliver she said, "I've been ringing you and ringing you. Can't you hear that phone from out here? Henry Barstow is trying to reach you."

"I'm not interested in talking to Mr. Barstow."

"What? Lem said—"

"You'd best learn not to listen to everything Lem tells you either."

Either? What was Ida rambling on about? Hattie's eyes asked the question a second after Ida's brain asked it, but Ida turned away to avoid answering either of them.

IDA WAS ABOVESTAIRS collecting bed linens for the wash when through the open window she heard the unmistakable sound of bicycle wheels; she looked out and saw the same scene she'd seen once before: Henry, standing on the pedals of his wife's bicycle, pumping his way up the track. Ida stepped back from the window, sat down on the bare mattress. She listened to the knock, the call, the repeat. How many kinds of fool would Ida have to be to open that door? She retreated from the window and went to her studio, but there was Henry again, staring out at her from the unfinished canvas. She went to the window and looked out; Henry was gone, but the bicycle rested against the barn. From the window she could see an envelope tucked into the basket.

Ida took the stairs with caution, half afraid she'd find Henry sitting at her kitchen table. She crossed the empty kitchen, stepped outside, looked down the track: no Henry. She approached the bicycle as if it were a trap, as if when she picked up that envelope a giant spring would close on her fingers and pin her there. *Ida,* Henry had written,

Whatever your feelings regarding me, the bicycle is yours. I made a clean purchase of it. It's not a gift to you but to me—picturing you out on the roads is the most joyful image I'm able to conjure right now, and I beg you won't deny either of us that benefit. Regarding the estate, I'll proceed no further until I hear from you as to what you plan to do about Ezra. I must leave Vineyard Haven on

Sunday for a meeting with another potential buyer, but a
note will always reach me if sent to H. M. Barstow, Inc.,
Union Street, New Bedford. Always—H.

Always. What had that art instructor Cecily Matson said?
When is always *ever* always?
Never.

IDA RODE TO THE OFFICE, but Henry wasn't in it, or in the
apartment, or in the warehouse. She wheeled the bicycle into
the shop where she intended to leave it, but after a minute's re-
flection she changed her mind. One last ride. She set out along
the beach road toward Cottage City, concentrating on the feel
of the wind against her face, the tug at her hair, the pull in her
thighs and calves, sensations she wanted to remember once
they were gone. She'd seen an advertisement in the newspaper
for the new chainless bicycle, priced at seventy-five dollars, but
by the time Ida managed to acquire that much money, she'd be
too old to pedal it.

As Ida drew closer to Cottage City, she spied a scene she felt
a sudden urge to paint: a sap-green field populated with figures
clad in almost every color in her paint box, playing baseball.
Mose Barstow was the one who had loved baseball. He'd loved
the Boston Bean Eaters; he'd loved to tell Ida about the games
while Ezra stood by and yawned. When the Bean Eaters had
won their second straight National League pennant, Ida had
thought Mose would kill himself drinking; she'd been so relieved to see him stagger in behind Ezra she'd forgotten herself
when he grabbed her and kissed her.

Ezra had said something about it later, in bed, as they lay side
by side not touching, not an easy thing to manage considering

the sag in the mattress. "I don't appreciate your free ways, Ida. Time to straighten out. Now."

"*What* ways?"

"Kissing anyone who happens to come through that door. Kissing people who are friends to me, not you."

Ezra had had his fair share of whiskey, and Ida knew better, but she said it anyway. "You wish he'd kissed you instead?"

Ezra thrashed his way out of the bed, leaned over her, hissed hot breath in her face. "I'm warning you, Ida. Watch yourself."

Ida had never been afraid of Ezra and wasn't then, but she was afraid of something. What? That drip drip drip of snowmelt, stretching out for years in front of her.

BUT NOW IDA PULLED her bicycle off the road and into the field to watch the game. It was because of the day; it was because of the fact that this was her last ride; it was because of the fact that she needed to stand on the edge of that field and come to terms with the fact that Mose had also betrayed her. *I liked him*, Ida had told his brother. Perhaps that was why she felt so wounded by Mose; she'd liked him. And what was she to do with that liking now?

It took a number of minor skirmishes between runners and fielders before bat and ball finally connected with a crack like lightning. The ball soared; the figures in the field moved as if of a single mind and on a single plan; chess of a sort, or so Ida imagined it. But a lone figure out in left field was the one who seemed to see where the ball was going first; he lit out like a flame, or rather like a match, a long, slender form topped by a head of hair turning gold in the sun; he stretched out his arm, deftly snagged the ball, and threw it home hard and true.

Henry.

Ida remounted and pedaled back the way she'd come. Before she'd gone a quarter of her route, the sky closed in; the friendly ecru clouds took on an ominous charcoal underbelly; raindrops buried themselves in her scalp. In Boston, the weather never inconvenienced Ida the way it did on the island; Ida could stay inside in Boston, or hop aboard a trolley, or flag down a hack, or just duck inside the Parker House for a cup of tea. Never—or hardly ever—did she have to go out and face up to whatever fell from the sky or blew over the cobbles or bit at the back of her neck.

Ida ducked her head and pedaled harder. She let herself into the office, leaned the bicycle against the desk, and fished for a pencil and paper to leave Henry a note, but when she didn't find any at a first pass she gave up. What words need be added? The bicycle said all she wished.

During the wet walk home Ida remembered other such days where the island weather had defeated her: that soaking day when she'd attempted to teach Oliver his letters; the time she'd trudged out with Ezra's crook to unearth any sheep buried in the drifts; the many, many mornings when she'd been warm and dry inside and had to brave every possible combination of cold and wet to tend to her animals; and of course, those three days of what everyone on the island now called the Portland Gale. But *had* those weather days really defeated her? Hadn't she—and Henry—gotten Oliver to learn the game of chess? Saved a sheep from that snowdrift? Experienced the delicious warming of numb feet in front of a hot fire after slogging through the cold and wet? Survived that gale with farm intact? Ida pulled the collar of her jacket tight and picked up her pace. *Stop being such a whinger,* she told herself. She'd survive this too. She'd survive it all. She was not her mother. And she was just drawing opposite Tilton's Hardware. It was no Parker House, but it was dry. Ida ducked in.

Mr. Tilton took a look at her, disappeared, and returned with a dry towel. Ida wiped her face and neck. "Thank you."

"What are you doing out in this?" Mr. Tilton asked.

"Bicycling."

Tilton shook his head.

"It wasn't raining when I started."

"I should hope not. I never thought you *that* foolish."

Ida studied Mr. Tilton, saw nothing but kindness in his eyes. "How foolish *did* you think me?"

Tilton grinned. Ida had never seen him grin before; it wrinkled his face all the way to the eyes and at once Ida wanted to paint him. "Well, I just never heard of a Boston artist taking up sheep farming," Tilton said.

"Foolish," Ida agreed, grinning back. How could she help it?

But now Tilton sobered. "Of course you didn't plan to do it alone, now did you?" He paused. "I never did say it before and would like to say it now, how sorry I am about your husband. Terrible thing that is."

Oh, how fast a simple exchange could turn treacherous: a *thank you* today became a lie tomorrow. Or not. "It is," Ida answered.

30

ON THE FIRST OFFICIAL DAY of summer Ida stood on the stoop to take it in. She'd slid and slogged through wind, rain, snow, sleet, ice, and mud to keep her farm animals alive; this day the air was so still it might have been a painting except for the hawk coasting on an invisible current far above, the sun warming her face, the catbirds chipping at her from the trees. So, her life wasn't all snowmelt. Ida watched the hawk for another long minute, feeling the urge to paint something, wishing she had that bicycle. Still, it wasn't a long walk to West Chop Light.

Ida set out, enjoying the white shell road that stretched flat and sparkling under her boots. But again, the lighthouse proved to be another favorite spot for the Summer Institute. Ida did an about-turn before the class could spot her and almost succeeded in escaping unnoticed until Cecily Matson rose to examine one of her students' work and spied Ida. She strode toward Ida with purpose, the kind of purpose that Ida suspected would be difficult if not impossible to deny.

"Ida Russell," she said. "I thought there must be a reason you changed your name in the middle of our last meeting, so I did some asking, and lo and behold, my investigation reveals you to be a *real* artist." She held a finger to her lips and looked over her shoulder. "Don't you dare tell them I said that. But I would dearly love you to speak to them. I have little talent at portraits. Surely you'll join us?"

"Perhaps another day."

Matson looked what appeared to be genuinely disappointed,

but she kept on. "Then tell me how you came along with your schooners."

The schooners sat where they'd been left, foremasts too long, water too lifeless. "Another day," Ida said again.

But looking at the water as she walked home, Ida saw something she'd failed to notice earlier. The dark line at the horizon she knew about now, but the closer the water came to shore the livelier it grew, exactly the opposite of Ida's limited seaborne experience. It was the distance that calmed it, the inability to see the detail from shore that took away all that roughness. If only the same could be said about Ezra. And why, why, why must she continually pull every thought back to Ezra?

BECAUSE SHE DIDN'T KNOW what to do about Ezra. Ida wished above all things she could talk to Henry about it; she wished above all things she could never talk to Henry again. But who else might she talk to about Ezra? When Ida crested the hill to spy Lem's wagon parked in front of the barn it felt like the touch of a warm hand. Lem had called himself the best friend she had; Lem enjoyed advising Ida; why not let him advise her about this, then?

Ida stepped into the barn and waited for her eyes to cut through the dusty light, for shapes to define themselves. She spied Lem bent over a hay rake.

"First clear stretch of drying weather we need to get that hay in," he said.

We. In Lem's mind they were a we, at least when it came to the farm, and Ida discovered she didn't mind the thought as much as she once had. Perhaps she'd been going about the thing wrong. Yes, she'd proved she could manage on her own, but wasn't there more to life than just managing? What if she simply stopped trying to decide things for herself and gave herself over to this *ve* concept? After all, Lem wasn't *that* old. Ida let herself drop into a fantasy of waking in the morning to find the ox stall already mucked out, the sheep already checked, the hay already in the hayrack. And thinking of Lem not that old, thinking of things Ida shouldn't be thinking of at all, thinking of waking in the morning, Ida found she could, without a huge stretch of the imagination, back up the fantasy an hour or two earlier until she felt the warm weight of Lem beside her in the bed, felt the loss as he slipped out of it to tend to the farm. She could feel it as if it were real, the heat, the weight, the loss, and overriding it all, the lifting of her worries, the comfort in realizing she needed to decide nothing, that if she let him, Lem would handle it all. Yes, they would fight over the bicycle, the trousers, but how important was that compared to the greater freedom gained by the abdication of her responsibilities? And after all, their biggest argument, Henry Barstow, was gone.

"I need advice," Ida said.

Lem cast her a sideways look. "If it's Barstow, I think you know—"

"I sent Mr. Barstow on his way."

Lem's face changed, lit by a new—or reclaimed—respect, or perhaps . . . perhaps Ida had been reading Lem all wrong. Perhaps Lem's antipathy to Henry had been born out of something more personal than an all-purpose moral code. Perhaps *Lem* had harbored fantasies of his own. There in the dim light of the barn it all seemed so simple to Ida—women were raised to marry and marry well, and if they couldn't marry well they were expected to marry anyway. Love helped, but it had never been required; one matched up one's practical concerns as best one could and made the most of the result, whatever it might be.

Ida rolled a small barrel nearer where Lem was working and

sat down. She pointed to the rake. "Thank you for doing this. Thank you for thinking of it. It would never have occurred to me that such work needed to be done."

Lem straightened, looked at Ida more closely. "That so."

"That so."

"So what advice?"

"I wonder what you thought when Ezra first brought me home."

"That's not advice, that's opinion."

"Opinion, then."

"I thought he did well for himself. I also thought he did wrong."

"Why?"

"I didn't see you settling in. I didn't see you happy. I didn't see an unhappy wife making a happy home."

"You believe I could have made a happy home with Ezra if only I'd tried harder?"

"Ida, what's all this in aid of?"

"I could have," Ida said. "I could have made a happy home *for* Ezra. That's what you mean, isn't it, a happy home *for* Ezra? Because that was my job."

"It's every woman's job. And the man's job is to secure that home and the means to support his family. It's how it's worked for a long time."

"No matter how unhappy I am."

"I want you happy, Ida. Truth is, it worries me how much I want you happy. But let me just say I don't see you so happy now."

"It's Ezra," Ida said. "That's what I wanted to talk to you about. Ezra."

Lem bent over the rake, his face now screened from Ida, much as Henry's had been when she'd tried to tell *him* about Ezra.

Much as Henry's had been. *Wait.* Did *Lem* already know? Why hadn't this possibility occurred to Ida before? Someone had been reporting to Ezra about the investigator; the obvious choice for the job was Lem. And if *Lem* knew, if she had to listen to another man she'd trusted stutter on about why he'd said nothing to Ida, she would lose the last bit of control she'd been clinging to.

Ida stood up. "But the man is dead. What's to talk about now?"

Ida left the barn. She half-expected Lem to come after her, to tell her that he knew the man wasn't dead, that he would have told her if he'd thought it would have made her happier, that he would like to make her happier now . . . And then what? Lem would either tell Ida to leave Ezra be or he would tell Ida to get the constable. And then he would tell her how he'd had his eye on her since she'd first arrived and that was why he so disliked her riding around with Henry Barstow. In the fantasy, Ida would then do whatever Lem told her to do about Ezra, full of nothing but relief at unshouldering the burden, and then she'd say *I could make* you *happy now . . .*

Ida saw the irony—that inside the wild fantasy was a forgiveness of Lem that Ida had not granted Henry. But Ida had never lain with Lem. Ida had never told Lem *I didn't like my own husband much.* And Ida didn't actually *know* Lem knew about Ezra. Or perhaps it came down to something as simple as the fact that at least for one or two brief moments in time Ida *had* trusted Henry . . . Ida was too tired to sort it out. And she was still without someone to talk to about Ezra.

EXHAUSTION DOES DO certain things, good and bad; it may have temporarily derailed her brain but it eventually plunged Ida into a deep sleep that caused her to wake the next morning with a clear plan. Before she talked to anyone about Ezra, she needed to talk to a lawyer, and not an island lawyer but one who had never heard the name Ezra Pease. She needed to go to Boston, and thanks to Ezra she had the money to get there without appealing to Henry. And while she was in Boston she would sell Greave the gold; thanks to Henry she had a better idea of its value, and thanks to Ezra again, she felt justified in laying her claim—at least one ring and one ear bob's worth of nuggets were hers. And maybe once she'd escaped the island, she would be able to see her life from the right end of the telescope again.

FIRST IDA PAID A VISIT to her island lawyer, Malcolm Littlefield, and asked him to put a hold on any more estate work until she contacted him again, to which he responded by handing her a bill that would wipe out her newly acquired funds. Ida next called on Mr. Howes, the new owner of the newspaper store in Vineyard Haven, who had just arrived from Boston, and received from him the name of Dunne & Crane, a well-reputed law firm in town. Mr. Howes then grilled Ida on Vineyard Haven life: Which establishment would she recommend for a simple supper? When does the first hard frost drop down? Did she know anyone who repaired watches? To Ida's surprise she could answer all three questions. She would recommend the Bayside; up to a point in her single dinner there with Ezra, she'd thought it fine. The first hard frost seldom came before November, but to be safe she'd plan on mid-October. She'd noticed a new card on Luce's bulletin board offering clock repair, and if clock and watch could be said to share a similar mechanism . . . Mr. Howes thanked her with a warm smile and a free newspaper.

IDA CALLED LEM and asked him to mind the farm. He sounded different, or maybe he didn't; maybe Ida sounded different and that was the noise that echoed down the wire. Lem agreed to mind the farm, but added, "Don't think I like you traveling alone now any more than I did the last time."

"Oh, I won't think that."

"And, Ida."

"What?"

A pause filled the line. "You know you can ask me for advice anytime?"

"I do." It was just a matter of whether she wanted to hear it.

THE TRIP WAS simpler without Henry but longer, or rather, it seemed longer this time, without someone to chat with on the train. It grew longer still when she found herself dissecting that whole first conversation in an attempt to figure out just how long Henry had been trying to deceive her. All right, he'd never actually outright lied to her, but neither had he shared what he ought with her. He hadn't shared his speculations. Yes, he would argue—or she could imagine him arguing—that speculations were only more untruths, more uncertainties, and besides, they were *his* speculations. But Ezra was Ida's husband, not Henry's. So Ida went, backward and forward, until the city came into view.

It seemed dirtier than Ida had remembered it, a fact that Ida could blame on Henry also; she'd been flustered by his closeness in the car and distracted by the shifts of light in those curious brown eyes as the seamier side of the city outside floated by unseen. But even Mrs. Clarke's boardinghouse seemed seedier than it had when she used to stroll by, Mrs. Clarke less welcoming, as if she'd be happy to take Ida's money but would much prefer it if she—and all single women—slept outside.

Ida dropped her bag and stepped out into the city, avoiding

the dark side streets, Lem's words bouncing between her ears. But as she walked, Ida began to feel that the Boston she once knew might be reclaimed after all; she passed a poster for another suffrage meeting at Horticultural Hall and took note of the time. But when she cut across the avenue in search of Mr. Greave she found the sign in his window removed, the office closed. She inquired in a jewelry shop for someone who might appraise gold and was sent eight blocks to a goldsmith only to be told he didn't trade in "ore."

At the law firm of Dunne & Crane Ida was led into a gentleman's office, but which gentleman it was no one bothered to explain. Either Dunne or Crane left her to sit long enough for her to inventory him from the rigid part in his hair to the cuff links made of tiny padlocks before he troubled to lift his eyes.

"How may I advise you?" he asked in a tone that suggested he was accustomed to his advice being taken.

Ida made an on-the-spot decision not to speak of Ezra's exact crimes, unwilling to risk losing her right to decide for herself what to do about the man. Instead she inquired about the rules for divorcing a husband on the grounds of abandonment. The list of obstacles was long, which even Ida knew meant delay and expense; she tried again.

"And if one's husband were jailed?"

That also seemed to involve an excess of complication and too many unanswerable questions. What was the crime? How long the sentence? Did the crime involve person or property? What was the chance of the verdict being overturned or the sentence commuted? Ida tried one last time. "And if lost at sea?"

Ida watched the lawyer's patience drain away, his suspicions flood in. "Which is it, madam? Are you abandoned, robbed, or widowed? Or is it whichever provides the greater windfall for you? You might save us both time if you go away and make up your mind before asking me to exercise mine."

Ida stood up. "My intention is to determine my recourse as the victim of fraud. And I have a bit of advice for you: when you meet a new client, introduce yourself, so he or she won't make the mistake of calling you again."

"You may go now."

"And you, sir, may stay."

OUTSIDE THE LATE-JUNE AIR had already grown sticky in a way it never seemed to do on the island. Discovering herself to be only a few blocks from the Boston Art Club, Ida decided to stop in and see what had changed in the art world since she'd been gone. The answer: very little. The paintings that lined the walls appeared different only in Ida's perception of them, as she now puzzled over an artist's need to record every seam in a woman's gown and never allow the slightest deviation in expression to show through. She walked from face to face and marveled at the thing she'd never once before troubled to note: Henry was right; nowhere could she find either a laugh or a tear.

Ida hastened back to the boardinghouse and a meal that she downed without pausing to taste it. She retreated to her room, changed into her fresh skirt, dusted off her boots, combed and re-pinned her hair, and set off for the lecture at Horticultural Hall. A block away from the building she could see a crowd of women outside, and at first she assumed the lecture had been sold out, that women were crowding the doors to hear the inspirational words within. But as Ida drew nearer she realized the women outside were carrying signs: YOU DON'T NEED A BALLOT TO CLEAN OUT YOUR SINK, DON'T WASTE USEFUL TIME ON A

USELESS VOTE, OR YOUR MAN VOTES FOR YOU. One sign depicted a cartoon of a man holding two squalling babies while a woman wearing a VOTES FOR WOMEN sash skipped out the door. As Ida watched, a chant welled up: "Men vote, women don't!"

A couple of women stood at a safe distance, observing, not participating. Ida joined them. "Who are they?" Ida asked.

"The Antis," one woman answered. "Otherwise known as the Massachusetts Association Opposed to the Further Extension of Suffrage for Women."

"But . . . why?"

The other woman shrugged. "Why spend all that effort for a few silly votes? What good will it do?"

"And what man would ever give it to them?" the first woman added.

"Us," Ida said.

"Pardon me?"

"Give it to *us*, not them."

"Next it will be free love. Divorce. Birth control. Look there! That's Congressman Dodge's wife holding that sign."

"Well, that explains her position."

Both women looked at her blankly.

Ida walked away.

WHEN THE STEAMER DREW CLOSE to the island and Ida could make out the jury-rigged Union Wharf, she was jolted by a feeling that came absurdly close to affection. She disembarked and went straight to the Seamen's Bethel in hunt of Rose; she needed to tell Rose about the Antis.

Rose stood over a table of men's clothes, dropping items into various piles; she looked surprised to see Ida and perhaps cool, but why not? Ida had never returned to help at the Bethel as she'd promised.

But when Ida explained about the Antis, Rose grew warm enough. "Women? These were all women?"

"Every one."

Rose slumped onto a stool behind the table. "If we can't even count on our own, we're doomed. How many were there?"

Ida did a mental head count. "Twenty? Twenty-five? One was a congressman's wife. Most looked well dressed."

"I guess they know who buys the dresses."

"There's that, I'm sure. But I can't cast stones—I haven't yet been successful with the one person I said I'd speak to."

"I'm not getting the response I'd hoped for either. 'I'm too busy for meetings,' 'I'm not interested,' 'If my husband ever found out,' and so on. But Antis. It's one thing if they just don't care. But *Antis*—"

Ida looked at Rose with new affection. "I'm sorry I haven't come by."

Rose waved Ida's words away. "You have your own troubles."

Without intending to, Ida let loose a great sigh. "More than you know."

Rose touched her ears, a signal clearer than words that she was available for listening, but Ida shook her head. She pointed to Rose's pile of clothes. "I need to do my own sorting first."

31

BUT SOON IDA FOUND IT HARD to sort anything but hay. As was the case with so much to do with farming, when it was time to harvest, it was time to harvest, and everything else must be left by the way. The first good reading on the barometer and the first hot bright sun in a windless sky brought Lem with Bart Robinson and his sickle bar mower. Bart nodded to Ida from his seat atop the sickle bar, but that was all he wasted in terms of a greeting; he flicked the reins and the horses moved down the field, the sickle bar flattening every blade of grass in its path.

The next day the hay that lay in the field was dry on the top but damp on the bottom. Bart returned with a tedder hitched behind the horses this time, scooping and tossing the hay to fluff and dry it. On the third day he came with the dump rake and again scooped up the hay, but this time with the pull of a lever, he left it in evenly spaced windrows across the field.

Now it was up to the men with the pitchforks—the only trouble was there weren't as many men with pitchforks as there had been in previous years. Ida suspected she knew why—they were afraid they wouldn't get paid—and Ida didn't blame them; *she* was afraid they wouldn't get paid. But the barometer had gone down a notch that morning and the formerly gentle breeze had grown argumentative; only two loads safe in the barn and Ida spied a line of black, runny clouds advancing from the horizon. She shouted for Lem, who was driving the wagon, and pointed.

"Call the Bethel, ask for more men," Lem shouted back.

Ida ran to the house to put in the call, but when Hattie came on the line she told her what to say and ran back to the field; they needed Lem on a pitchfork, not on the wagon; if they didn't get the hay in the loft before the rain it would mold, or worse yet, combust. She drove the wagon along the rows, pausing long enough for the men to fork in the hay until it mounded higher than her head and walled her in on both sides; as she headed for the barn she saw three men with pitchforks slung over their shoulders, heads down, trotting toward her. The first two men she didn't recognize. The third was Henry.

The men unloaded the hay, climbed in, and rode with Ida back to the field. Ida recalled those times in her Beacon Hill home when she and her mother had left her father and brothers in the parlor to tend to something in the kitchen; Ida would try to engage her mother in conversation but her mother's ear was always tuned to her father's voice whenever it wafted in from the other room. But it worked the other way as well; Ida had been sitting with her father when her mother left the room and watched her father's eyes following, even lingering on the door she'd passed through. It had seemed to Ida then that an invisible string bound her parents together even when they were apart, and she thought of that now as Henry sat behind her in the wagon. She still felt pulled by that invisible string, no matter how it had frayed.

Once they reached the field, the men vaulted down and began madly forking hay into the wagon; when it reached a certain height one of the men climbed atop the load to receive and place the forkfuls the better to keep them from tumbling. As Ida urged the ox from windrow to windrow she caught glimpses of Henry, his back arcing and straightening with a rhythm that no carriage maker got planing wood. But what on earth had Hattie been thinking in calling Henry Barstow to her aid?

They put away four loads and were a scant few forkfuls into a fifth before the storm broke over them with a rumble and roar. "All right!" Ida shouted over it. "Coffee at the house!" The men piled into the wagon; by the time they reached the farmhouse their clothes sagged on them like fresh-hung wash on a line.

Ida put up the ox and threw a tarpaulin over the hay, thinking of the barn door after the horse had bolted. She hurried in to get the coffee on, but Hattie was already inside, the coffee perking, the table covered with cold chicken and mutton and cheese and pie, only some of those items out of Ida's larder. Despite the drenching, the men were in high spirits, joking and laughing, the kitchen filled with the steaming mass of them, so it took Ida a minute to realize that Henry wasn't there.

When they'd gone, when nothing remained but an empty pantry, Hattie and Ida set themselves side by side at the sink and dove into the dishwashing and drying. Not having to face Hattie eye to eye, it seemed the perfect time to ask Hattie the burning question. "You called Henry?"

"He's walking and breathing, isn't he? And I knew he'd want to help—he was raised on a farm."

Yes he was, and Ida had forgotten that fact, as she'd also forgotten the fact that Hattie was raised on a farm. This farm. Ida turned to Hattie to say something about that, how Hattie was the one person who never seemed to butt into the farm's doings, and was silenced by the sight of tears painting Hattie's cheeks.

"Hattie! What's wrong?"

Hattie smacked at the dampness on her face. "Nothing. I'm tired."

"Well, stop. Sit down. I can finish this." Ida gripped Hattie's elbow to guide her to a chair but Hattie shook her off.

"I'm fine. It's not that kind of tired." She swung around to face Ida. "Doesn't it get to you sometimes? Day in and day out, the same old thing? And what result in the end? Even when you finally get something you've always wanted, even then, there's no happiness in it because you just know it's going to end terribly."

"Hattie. Sit."

Hattie sat. Ida sat. Hattie flapped her hands. "Oh, don't listen to me, Ida. I don't know what I'm saying half the time. And I sure don't know what I'm saying now. It's just . . . I don't know, I can't bear it sometimes."

Ida had no words. She laid a hand on Hattie's wrist and thought of all the things she didn't know about her. What was it Hattie "always wanted"? If working at the telephone exchange and living with her mother wasn't it, what was? What dreams did she secretly harbor? Never before had Ida felt the weight of her own failing so intensely. She had been no friend to Hattie. There had been overtures aplenty, but Ida had ignored them or denied them altogether. And now, when she desperately wanted to offer some sort of comfort, she didn't know how to do it. Ida thought of Rose, how she'd avoided Rose until she hadn't, and how warm, how sympathetic, Rose had been. She thought of Mr. Tilton; Ida had never troubled to speak to him, and then once she did trouble to do it, why, he'd been friendly. Was it Ida all along who had refused to let this island in?

"Everything doesn't end terribly," Ida said, and was taken aback for the second time that afternoon when Hattie burst into laughter.

"Oh, Ida, that you could say that! You of all people! Do you know I could hate Ezra—I mean really hate my own cousin—for what he did to you."

You don't know the half of it, Ida thought, but now wasn't the time. And what *was* the thing to say now? There Ida remembered Rose, the way she'd touched her ears, offering so simple a thing as to listen. "Hattie, please know, anytime you have something burdening you that would be lighter if shared—"

Hattie stood up. "It's already lighter, Ida. Thank you. And don't mind my silliness. But I *am* tired. I'm going home now."

IDA'S MIDDLE-OF-THE-NIGHT LIST GREW. She needed to check in on Hattie; she needed to thank Rose for sending the men from the Bethel; she needed to tell Ruth to pay them; she needed to remember to turn and air that last load of sodden hay that hadn't yet made it to the loft. And she needed to decide what to do about Ezra.

How easy to do nothing about Ezra. Ida could continue to walk among the islanders as the widow Pease and no one would ever know that their former neighbor, friend, nephew, cousin was alive and well on the other side of the Atlantic Ocean. But Ida would know. She thought of Rose, Rose with her ready sympathy, her willing ear, Rose believing Ida to be a widow in need of her deepest concern, her greatest efforts at comfort. How could Ida ever look Rose in the eye again knowing the lie she was living? But did Rose even matter?

Yes. Ida was taken aback to feel that answer hit her like a jolt in her spine. And Mr. Tilton, who'd conversed so sympathetically with Ida, he mattered too. And her new friend Mr. Howes at the newspaper store. Even Chester Luce. And what of Ruth and Hattie and Oliver? How different was she from Henry if she decided on their behalf that they'd rather not know the truth about Ezra? And how could Ida ever look Hattie in the eye and say *Trust me with your troubles* if at the same time she harbored such a monumental lie?

* * *

IT TOOK IDA TWO MORE DAYS to summon the will, to pack up the papers in the order in which they'd come to her: Ezra's letter, the assayer's card, Dermott Hale's card, the gold pamphlet, the deed to the property on Block Island, the letters to Mose. She placed them inside the canvas tote she took to the market and tied it with twine in case of wind; she pondered as she walked what the chances were that Ezra would be apprehended versus Ezra remaining free. *Ezra remaining free.* Was that, after all, Ida's biggest fear, that Ezra would remain free?

TISBURY CLAIMED TWO CONSTABLES; Ezra had approved of one and disapproved of the other, but Ida hadn't paid enough attention to recall which was which. A constable named Ripley ushered Ida into a chair but perched himself on the edge of the desk, hawklike. He even looked something like a hawk: blunt brow, powerful shoulders, salt-and-pepper hair, a wariness behind the eyes, but when he spoke Ida believed she detected a certain gentleness in his tone. It will be all right, she told herself. Again.

"How may I help, ma'am?"

"I'm Mrs. Pease," she began. "I believe I have some evidence of a crime."

"What crime?"

"I'm not sure. Impersonating a dead person? No, that wouldn't be it exactly, impersonating death. Or is that a crime?"

Ripley blinked. "Perhaps you'd like to show me your . . . evidence." He nodded at Ida's package, which she still clutched in her lap. Ida hurried the package onto the desk and untied the string, reviewing the contents in her mind as she laid them out; as she did so she realized that Ezra's not being dead was probably not the larger crime, unless, of course, you were his widow.

Or wife. Dear God, Ida thought, it hadn't occurred to her till now that she was still married to the man. She took a breath, collected herself, went on.

"I'd like to restate the crime if I may. The man in question, my husband, Ezra Pease, *did* impersonate death, but he did so in order to escape prosecution for—" Ida could think of only the one word: "fleecing some investors." She attempted a smile. "I say this well aware of the irony."

Ripley didn't blink.

"Considering he owns—or used to own—a sheep farm."

Still nothing. "I'm having some difficulty following you, ma'am," Ripley said. "What exactly is this crime?"

"I'm sorry. Let me start again." Ida pointed to each item as she spoke, each laid out in the precise order she'd packed them: Ezra's letter, the assayer's card, Hale's card, the gold pamphlet, the deed to the property on Block Island, Mose's letters. Ripley slid from desk to chair and picked up each item as Ida referenced it, read all the words on each. Ida waited as he did so, and only when he'd laid down the final letter to Mose did she resume.

"I went to Block Island. I'd been left without much in the way of assets, and I wanted to find out if that piece of land could be sold. And that's where I found Ezra. Alive. When we all believed he'd drowned."

"And why did you believe he'd drowned?"

Looking back on it later, Ida identified that question as the exact moment when it occurred to her that this must be the constable that Ezra *had* approved of, that it might not end all right after all. She pushed Ezra's letter across the desk. "He said he was on the *Portland*. The *Portland* went down. There were no survivors."

Incredibly, this bit of news seemed immaterial to the constable. He asked the question several more times in several different ways; she didn't actually *know* her husband was on the *Portland,* wasn't that correct? She'd talked to no one who actually *saw* him get cn the *Portland,* correct? His body never came ashore, is that correct?

"His body never came ashore because he didn't drown."

"And you know this how?"

"Because I found him alive and well on Block Island!"

There Ripley chose to smile. "You're sure?"

"Sure of what?"

"That it was your husband? Many months had gone by since—"

"Are you asking if I mistook the identity of a man who shared my bed for two years?"

The constable looked down; he pushed himself back from the desk as if to increase the distance that separated them; he opened and closed a desk drawer to no purpose that Ida could see. Her talk of beds had flustered him. Well, good.

"I'm only suggesting," he went on, "if the man you saw resembled your husband a good deal, and if you were desperately hoping to see your husband alive—"

"I did not go to Block Island in hope of finding my husband alive. Even when I saw him I had trouble believing it could be him. Nothing in either my experience or my being could account for the enormity of such a deceit. But then we spoke. At length. And he *confessed* to his crime. He laid out his plans to escape to Paris and invited me to join him."

Ripley pursed his lips, drummed his fingers on the pamphlet, looked up at Ida. "This crime you refer to—this *Gold from Sea Water* scheme?"

"Yes. And the crime of impersonating death, which, if it isn't a crime, should be."

Ripley sat back and pondered Ida. Ida pondered him. He was

the first to drop his eyes. Well, good again. "You're saying your husband deceived you and then confessed his crime to you and then invited you to go with him and you simply walked away and returned home and came straight to the law to report him. Doesn't it strike you as odd that the fellow didn't suspect you'd do that very thing?"

There, at last, Ripley succeeded in flustering Ida. "I . . . yes. No. I had no intention of actually going to Paris with him, but I let him believe I would. I'd spoken of Paris once . . . He . . . he believed I was like him, that I'd calculate what *I'd* get out of the scheme and never mind who else got cheated. He believed I'd decided it was in my best interest not to turn to the law."

"So. A deception for a deception."

Ida peered at the constable. Was he, could he possibly be, implying that the two deceptions were the same? That she and Ezra were now even? As Ida studied the constable she recalled Ezra's suggestion that someone on the island had alerted him to the fact that a detective was tracking him. Perhaps it wasn't Lem. Perhaps it was this constable. And perhaps the private investigator only got involved because the constable had already refused to do so.

Ida stood up and made to collect her papers, but the constable speared them with a finger. "The evidence stays here. I'll contact you with any developments."

"Well then, you'd best make note; he'll be on an ocean liner called the *Umbria* headed for Europe in the middle of August."

The constable didn't appear to be listening. Again, he tapped the *Gold from Sea Water* pamphlet. "To be clear. You never saw any gold?"

"No," Ida said, but with such difficulty she marveled at the difference among humans, that Ezra could lie without a blink and here Ida left the station with the sweat pouring between her breasts and her heart beating out of her stays. Or it would have been beating out of her stays if she were wearing any. She took a deep breath, at least still able to revel in that particular freedom, and again found herself mourning the loss of the bicycle that had inspired the loosening in the first place.

THE NEXT STEP was now predetermined. Ida had set the police on the trail of a living Ezra; she now needed to tell Ruth and Hattie that Ezra was indeed living. She did spend the walk home hunting for reasons why she might not have to do that, but as she didn't find any, she landed once again facing the two women across the kitchen table. Outside the open window she could hear the shuffle and thunk of Oliver picking up rocks and throwing them against the barn.

This time neither woman shed tears, but the paired faces were riven with pain, hurt, disbelief, and that other kind of grief—the kind that comes when trust dies.

"You're sure," Ruth said, but not as if it was a question.

"I'm sure. But I confess I had trouble believing right away."

"That boy," Ruth said. "That poor, poor boy."

For a minute Ida thought Ruth meant Ezra until she heard again the thunk of stones against the wall, saw Ruth's eyes travel to the window.

"You leave that boy alone," Hattie said with a fierceness Ida had never heard before. "There's no need for him to know."

"The whole island will know." Ruth pointed at Ida. "*She* went to the constable."

"Well, he doesn't need to know right now."

Ida stood up. Hattie stood with her. "I'll walk you down."

* * *

THEY SET OFF down the hill with matching strides. "Are you all right?" Ida asked.

"Well, I'm not surprised," Hattie said. "That he's alive, yes, but what he's done . . . even my mother isn't surprised. I can tell by looking at her. And I remember once after Ezra left the house and Mother discovered she was missing her gold thimble, I remember how she looked then, how Ezra-the-golden-boy myth had already started to crumble. But then when he drowned—" Hattie snorted. "Or she thought he did, that brought back the halo."

"But you. Are you all right?"

"I want you to forget the other day. My mother can be a trial; I don't suppose I have to tell *you*. I got tired, that's all. But I'm the one should be asking you! Dear God, Ida—" Hattie went on about Ezra, things he'd said and done that Hattie now claimed had convinced her, if not Ruth, that all with Ezra wasn't necessarily as it seemed, or rather, were much as they had *seemed*, if not just as they were presented. And Oliver. Hattie had a good deal to say about Ezra's mistreatment of Oliver.

"His grandfather's written, you know. His wife's better, and they're ready to have the boy home, but I'm not going to send him off until we've decided what to tell him about Ezra. But it's not like the boy even knew him. I remember one time—"

Clearly, Hattie intended to keep up the Ezra talk all the way to Ida's door; Ida couldn't blame her—this was new news and big news for Hattie—but Ida was done talking of Ezra. Thinking of Ezra. She decided to attempt a change in subject: the Antis.

"Well," Hattie said, "I can see their point."

Ida stopped walking. "How so?"

"Well, I mean, really. What man will ever allow it? And in truth, how many women do you know who would want to bother with it?"

"A good number. Some of whom you know too."

Hattie peered at Ida. "Well, if you ask my opinion, the men are taking care of it just fine, and I, for one, don't want that responsibility."

"But what if I want that responsibility? If we had the right to vote, I could vote, and you could not vote. Why should I be denied the chance simply because you don't want to?"

"Ida, be practical. Think of how we spend our day now, me with a job and a household to keep up, you with a household and a farm, me with all that extra work I'll be taking on come December."

"What work?"

"Oh. Yes. I've been meaning to tell you. Lem and I are getting married in December and Mother is giving us the farm."

32

IDA WROTE TO HENRY.

I've been to the constable about Ezra but am not confident anything will be done. I've been to my lawyer here and told him to stop work on estate matters on my behalf. He's submitted a bill to me that I'm unable to pay at present. Hattie and Lem are marrying in December, and Ruth is giving them the farm. I plan to leave for Boston right after the livestock sale—I should realize enough from the sale to at least afford a room. I tell you these things only so you'll know.—I.

Henry answered:

Please send me the lawyer's bill or preferably give it to me in person—I will be back on the island at week's end. You have made clear you no longer have any personal interest in me and I will honor your wishes in that regard, but in my role as executor, and considering the new developments, I do feel we should meet to go over the ramifications regarding the "estate."—H.

At the bottom, in a less defined hand, as if induced by either alcohol or fatigue, he'd added:

Twice I tried to tell you. I pushed you away only until I could tell you. But with what words? I had no words. And

finally at Makonikey. It was so much easier just to follow
the joy down.

Joy. That he should use the word that had once defined him
in Ida's mind, the word that had so eluded Ida until she'd discovered that bicycle . . . and, admit it, Henry. Ida fetched the
lawyer's bill and a blank piece of paper, but as she sat staring at
the paper she realized Henry was right. There were no words.
She folded the bill into an envelope, addressed it to the carriage
shop in New Bedford, and set it out on the table to be mailed in
the morning.

AUGUST. THE DAYS CRISP and hot or damp and hot, the sky a
dense blue that Ida could never quite master in paint or a sodden gray mass that she could. The calendar was much on Ida's
mind; two weeks and Ezra would be gone. But August was also
weaning time, and as if to prove a point, the day Ida and Lem
picked to do it was as hot and sticky as any August day got anywhere. Lem assembled the pens again, and Bett and Ida drove
the sheep through two at a time, allowing for Lem to divert the
lambs into the smaller pen. It was tiring and unpleasant work
and the din of the lambs and ewes calling back and forth put
Ida thoroughly out of sorts. She'd said little if anything to Lem
and he'd said less back, but once they'd gotten the sheep sorted
into the two most distant pastures she said, "I'm getting out the
whiskey."

THEY SAT ON THE PORCH and drank without talking. After a
time Ida said, "I suppose I need to say congratulations."
   "Not if you don't want to."

"Well, I don't. What I want to say is you're quite the old secret keeper. I wonder how many other secrets you've got in there."

"No other secrets."

"I suppose Hattie's told you he's alive."

"Yep."

"I suppose you knew all along."

Lem set down his glass. He slid himself sideways in his chair, took Ida's glass from her and set it next to his on the floor. He took her two hands in his and leaned forward as if afraid his words would drift off before they reached her if he left too much room between them. "Ida, what did I tell you? I'm the best friend you have. Would I have kept something like that from you? Would I have let you go on thinking you were a widow when all along—"

"Henry did."

Lem dropped her hands and leaned back. After a time he said, "I guess he had his reasons."

Ida shifted back in her seat. "So. Hattie *and* the farm. Will she keep on at the exchange?"

"Of course not."

"I guess she'll be busy enough with the farm."

Lem took a good swallow. He looked over at Ida once, twice. "Hattie said Ruth was talking about selling the place once you left for Boston. This keeps it in the family."

"But—" She wanted to say but *Hattie*? Even with the drink she knew that wasn't the right thing to do, that she'd already stepped way, way, way out of the bounds of decorum. She changed course to the thought that had been in the forefront of her mind most of the afternoon. "Did you know about the gold from sea water?"

"Not as a fact. I knew he'd gotten something going up there

in Maine that sounded like more than salvage. Something he didn't feel just right about sharing with me."

"You didn't ask him?"

"I don't make a habit of asking after things I don't want to know."

They drank some more. Ida could tell by the way Lem looked at her glass when she refilled it that it concerned him, this woman drinking hard liquor in the middle of the day. She tried to picture Hattie sitting on the porch beside Lem, listening to that din, drinking whiskey, and could not. "I wonder," Ida said. "When you still thought Ezra was dead, did you ever think about asking *me* to marry you?"

Lem chuckled.

"Well, think of it. You could have saved yourself the trouble of getting out the wagon in the middle of the night to go shoot dogs. You could have rolled over and fired out the bedroom window." Oh, she was seriously out of bounds now.

"And what about Boston?"

Yes, what *about* Boston? At the moment it seemed far away. If Lem had asked, and she'd said yes, and if she'd gotten any money from the buildings, she could have given it to Lem, and he could have bought the farm. She could have stayed and helped him work the farm; she'd have been a whole lot better at it than Hattie.

"And besides," Lem went on, "I don't like arguments."

"What would we have to argue about?"

"Well now, let's think back over a few things."

"The bicycle's gone."

"But not those damned trousers."

Ida looked down. It was true she was wearing the trousers now; in truth she wore them so often she hardly noticed anymore when she had them on. Lem would never say anything about the absent stays, the corset that had in fact now become more of a camisole, but she was sure he didn't approve of that either.

"And I know you, Ida. I do something you don't like and you're going to say something about it, just the way you said something about it to Ezra. And I don't like something you're doing, I'm going to say something about that, just like I do now. Pretty soon we'd be fighting out of habit, over things neither of us even gives a hoot about."

"Name me one thing—one *other* thing besides bicycles and trousers—we would ever fight about."

"Well now, Hat tells me you're agitating to vote."

"I'd like you to give me one logical reason why women shouldn't vote. They work for you, grieve for you, lie down for you, bear your children for you, *love you—*"

"See, now?"

Ida started to laugh. She laughed till the tears ran, until they'd turned to real tears, and then she stopped, wiped her eyes, sat up. Yes, Lem had chosen right—in the end Hattie had declined the bicycle, dismissed the trousers, denied any interest in ever placing a vote. She lifted her glass. "Congratulations," she said.

THE MIDDLE OF AUGUST, when Ezra was supposed to sail for France, hung heavy over Ida before it arrived, but once it came and went, Ida felt no different. She didn't know *how* to feel. Was he gone or wasn't he? She was moving the ewes to fresh pasture, intent on looking over the flock with the livestock sale in mind, but she couldn't seem to look past the aggregate, as Henry had called it, in order to focus on the particular; Bett had condensed the sheep into a single mass of iridescent white cloud, and Ida stood as if blinded. After a time, her artist's eye singled out the way the light backlit a translucent pink ear or turned a black eye to a glistening marble, but she was still standing there when Constable Ripley pulled up the hill in his official wagon.

He climbed down and waited at the gate until Ida had settled the flock and corralled Bett, but even when she reached the constable he seemed in no great rush.

"Nice place you've got."

"It's Ruth Pease's farm."

The constable's eyebrows rose. "Is it, now." This seemed to change something in his thinking; he pondered, studied Ida, looked out at the sheep, nodded out at the sea. "I have a couple of questions for you."

Ida crossed her arms and waited.

"When was it you took that trip to Block Island?"

"Near the end of June. The seasonal visitors were just arriving."

The constable nodded again. "I've been making inquiries. Whoever was living in that shack out there at Grace's Point has cleared out and gone. They found a fellow owns a lobster boat admits to hiring himself out to take someone to New York on August the fourteenth. His description of the passenger sounds like Ezra Pease."

"Does it, now."

The constable squinted. "I might recommend you take a look to your attitude, ma'am. You walk in and present as wild a tale as I've heard in my lifetime and then once I take it up you balk at a few questions. I'm here to tell you I looked into your wild tale and right now it's not seeming so wild after all."

All right, fair enough. "Now what?"

"That's the better question. We got on to the shipping lines late, I admit to you, and the ship had sailed, but there was an Ezra Pease on board."

So Ezra was gone. Then why didn't the weight of him leave her? Why did she still feel the crush of it settling into the lines of her face, moving down to her shoulders, her hips, her heels, rooting her to the ground?

The constable must have observed her sinking. He spoke in a more even tone. "I can't see any hope in trying to chase your husband down, Mrs. Pease. You could file for divorce on the grounds of abandonment; in a year's time you should have the paper in hand and be able to move along." He paused. "Or you could wait for that ticket to arrive."

Ida laughed.

"If that ticket does arrive—"

"I'll be sure to let you know."

33

IDA KNEW SHE SHOULD CALL HENRY, but she was begin-
ning to seriously resent that word, *should*. And *why* should she?
Where Ezra was now had nothing to do with him; it wasn't
Mose who'd gotten on that ocean liner. But—oh, she was starting to resent that word too—*but* Henry did have a right to know
that the estate settlement might be delayed again. And Henry
deserved to know that Mose had gone to Australia, that he'd
wanted to send back some of the money. Yes, all right, she would
have to call Henry.

Even as Ida thought it, the phone rang.

"I'm sorry to trouble you," Henry said, "but I have news." He
paused. "News I'd rather not discuss over the phone." So he knew
the risk Hattie posed by now. "Is it convenient for me to stop by?"

"In fact, I was about to call you."

Ida noted a lift in Henry's tone. "Oh?"

Ida looked out the window. The light had yet to mellow and
lengthen; Lem was moving slowly from barn to wagon, not di-
verting to the house as he often did after his work was done.
He's growing old, she thought. She returned her attention to the
phone. "As it happens, I have my own news. But I'll come there.
To the office."

"Very well," Henry said, each word as level as the ground.

THE SHORT WALK SEEMED LONG, made longer by the tug of
Ida's hem on her ankles. She was missing the bicycle more and

more with each step, not just because of the convenience or the thrill of speed but because of the power, of that feeling that she was in charge, that she could manage her own schedule, her own direction, her own life. Silly, but still.

As if to rub Ida's nose in it, as she crossed Main Street she saw that Henry was standing outside the office with his bicycle, talking to a woman near Ida's age, a woman she didn't know. As Ida watched, Henry bent down and rotated the bicycle pedal backward in a gesture Ida knew well.

"And the brake," Henry was saying as she drew near. "Would you like to try it?"

Only then did Ida see it wasn't Henry's bicycle; it was a woman's bicycle, Perry's bicycle. *Her* bicycle. Ida stepped into the shadow of the wall and watched Henry as he explained everything he'd once explained to Ida, watched his hands moving so competently from handlebar to seat to brake. He looked up and spied Ida. He spoke to the woman; she nodded; he handed her what looked like a card and she walked off.

Ida stepped through the office door ahead of Henry. The first things she noticed were two more bicycles, brand-new, one a man's and one a woman's. Ida went for the woman's and examined it with care—no chain, plush leather seat, perky tilt to the handlebars, a shine that could blind the sun.

"I'm sorry, that one's sold," Henry said behind her.

"You're selling bicycles now?"

"Mary Ellen Bishop asked me to find her one. I was rolling it into the shop when that woman out there asked to look at it. I showed her yours instead."

"So that's sold too?"

Henry didn't answer. "So you have news? I haven't eaten since breakfast. May I invite you to share our tales over dinner?"

"What I have to say can't be said in a public dining room."

Henry crossed his arms and looked at her; after a minute he pointed to the stairs. "I'm sorry, but I'm famished. If I don't eat soon—" He began to climb the stairs, lunging at them as if in a hurry to get away from her, and yet he called over his shoulder, "Come. Please."

Ida followed. Henry went straight to the kitchen and began to set out food: half a cold meat pie with dark, rich beef and onions tumbling out of the cut, a partial loaf of bread, a bowl of apples, and a pitcher of cider, the tang of it snaking straight up Ida's nose. He set out two plates and cut Ida a wedge of the pie; she started to protest, but she too had eaten nothing since breakfast, and the top crust was flaky and golden while the bottom was drenched with juice. She bit; it was all she'd hoped it would be and more.

"You made this?'

"Mary Ellen Bishop brought it yesterday morning. I ran into her at Luce's."

Of course, thought Ida. Mary Ellen Bishop was rumored to have broken off an engagement with a banker in Falmouth who had failed to disclose a mistress in Bourne, to whom he'd also failed to disclose his pending marriage. "She mustn't have approved of your shopping list."

"Bread and beer? I can't think why." Henry smiled at her and Ida responded, although they were likely smiling at separate jokes: Henry at bread and beer, Ida at the suddenly disengaged Mary Ellen Bishop digging into Henry Barstow like a tick.

"Best tell her you're married before she starts arriving with breakfast," Ida said.

Henry set down his fork, no longer smiling. "You said you had news."

Ida told him about the visit from Ripley. "It seems unlikely Ezra will be held accountable." She paused. "Or Mose." She told

Henry about Mose planning to return some of the money and was startled to see a violent flash of anger cross his features; only then did Ida realize how deeply Mose had hurt his brother, how hard Henry must have worked to keep that hurt tamped down in front of Ida. Henry got up, retreated to his room, and returned with a stiff envelope.

"Your news would explain this, then. They've attached the property."

Ida picked up the envelope. Put it down. "What—"

"What does it mean? That if they can't recoup the fraudulently obtained money any other way, the property will be sold, and the proceeds divvied up among the investors. This is what I was calling to tell you."

Henry picked up his fork and resumed eating. Ida sat silent. She was sorry about the food; if she didn't have a plate in front of her, if Henry didn't, it would have been easier for her to go. She cast about for a topic. She pointed to the copper kettle leaning against the wall.

"You brought that thing up here?"

"I was trying to figure it out."

"Did you?"

"Not . . . No."

Ida tried again.

"How is the divorce proceeding?"

"It isn't." Henry set down his fork and leaned forward, a new intensity washing over him like a storm surge. "She knows about you. And now she won't divorce. She won't admit you're the reason; she says only that she's changed her mind, that she was being selfish, she could never do that to our girls."

"How did she find out about me?"

"That time when you came to tell me about the lambs. She appeared to have seen something in my face, or heard something in my voice, I don't know. She asked and I told her; what good did lying ever do?" He laughed, but so bitterly it didn't sound like the usual Henry laugh Ida knew. "So now I'm the ogre for proceeding."

"You're proceeding?"

Henry nodded.

"But not because of—"

"Because of you? No. Silly as it may sound, I believe two people need to be on speaking terms in order to—" He cut himself off with another alien laugh.

"Then why?"

"Perhaps in some way it *is* because of you. I saw who she was because of you. But in fact now I'm proceeding because of my children; I didn't want to divorce because I didn't want to be apart from them, but now it seems I'll be apart from them if I don't divorce. She's keeping them from me. When I moved in behind the carriage shop, she took them away to her parents, said she wasn't comfortable alone in the house, said I'd abandoned them and had no right to see them anymore. Of course I do have that right and I also have a good lawyer who will see it's secured."

Henry continued on, more about the fancy Boston lawyer he was quite sure he couldn't afford, but Ida didn't hear the rest. She was running behind, stuck on that one line: *When I moved in behind the carriage shop.*

They had finished eating. Henry got up and carried their dishes to the sink; Ida needed no other opening to get up and go, just as she'd hoped to do for many minutes now, and yet she lingered.

"I'm sorry," she said. "About your children."

He watched her.

"I have to go. Good luck with—" She hesitated.

"Starting life over? I guess you know something about that."

"It's not easy."

"I'm trying to think of it as building a carriage. I work at it piece by piece, the early pieces utilitarian, the later ones decorative, the final ones the touches that say this is a Henry Barstow, this is a thing of—" He stopped.

Value. Integrity. Beauty. The words might have flowed out of Ida's mouth a month ago, but not now.

34

SEPTEMBER AND IT RAINED. And rained. It rained so often and so much that the edges of everything blurred—sky into sea, sea into sand, sheep into ground—and yet the livestock auction loomed. All summer Ida had been eyeing the flock with the sale in mind; she'd mentally marked a handful of the best ewe lambs to be kept for breeders, pegging all the ram lambs for transport—they were just too much trouble. The rest of the ewe lambs and the ewes who were too old for breeding or producing decent wool she also marked for sale. But now the breeding stock would be Lem's to manage, so Ida and Lem stood silent and dripping in their oilskins side by side as he picked and chose. Or she tried to stay silent.

"Not that one," Ida said, pointing to Betty, as Bett shed her into the sale pen.

"She's too puny for breeding."

"She's the one Oliver fed. She's his pet. Take her price out of my sale money if you have to."

Lem shook his head but ordered Bett to shed her again and return her to the field shelter.

"And not that one." Ida pointed to Benjie. "That one Oliver delivered. Castrate him and keep him to settle the ram."

Lem shook his head again, but Benjie too was shed from the sale pen.

NOT A HALF HOUR after Lem had ridden up the hill to Ruth's— and Hattie's—the sky cleared, and Ruth strode down the hill to check out Lem's selections. Ida understood how things would work from now on: whatever she did or said with Lem went straight to Hattie, and from Hattie to Ruth, and God knew how many others in town. But Ida had no reason to object—it wasn't her farm, and Ruth seemed so old, so distracted; she had been since the truth about Ezra had become known.

Ruth pointed to one of the lambs both Lem and Ida had selected for sale, a sturdy thing with a single spot of dark wool that hung on her chest like a jewel. "Keep that one back. I want to give it to Oliver." She pointed out two more. "And those for Lem and Hattie," Ruth said, seeming to forget they'd all be Lem's and Hattie's soon. She peered at Ida for a time, returned her gaze to the sheep, pointed to one that had bolted across the pen and attempted to climb the wall. "That one will be yours."

"Thank you, Ruth, but I'll have no use for a sheep in Boston."

Ruth looked at Ida blankly, as if she'd forgotten what Boston had to do with it. "You've made note? That one for Ezra, those two for Hattie and Lem?"

"You mean Oliver. Oliver and Hattie and Lem. And if you don't mind my suggesting, Oliver would probably like that one over there better. Betty, the one he bottle-fed. That way she'd be right here at the farm when he comes to visit."

"Visit!"

"Hattie told me the grandparents are ready to have him home."

Ruth whirled and headed toward Ida's house. "I need tea."

THE MINUTE THE TEA HIT RUTH'S LIPS, she became talkative in a way Ida hadn't heard in a while. She rambled on with tales of the farm, conflating Ezra and Oliver first, her father and grandfather next, growing angrier as she spoke. No one knew the farm the way she did. It should have been hers when her husband died. For generations it had been kept from her.

Ida spoke carefully. "This is why women need the vote."

Ruth snorted. "A bunch more nincompoops voting. What good will that do?"

Ida decided to leave that subject there. When she next saw Rose she would tell her how her own sex continued to disappoint her, but even if Hattie didn't want her to, Ida was going to attempt to protect her interests there. "The farm is yours now, Ruth. You can do with it as you choose, and you choose to give it to Lem and Hattie, so that's wonderful. It stays in the family. But think how that deed is worded. Make sure what happened to you doesn't happen to Hattie."

Ruth stared blankly at Ida, or perhaps at nothing, it was hard to tell. At last, after a few more sips of tea, the old Ruth surfaced. Or rather, a new one.

"I haven't been kind to you."

"Well, Ruth, I don't suppose I've been all that kind to you."

"You came here with him, such a fancy thing, so above us all, you didn't seem to appreciate how magnificent he was, how much you were intruding."

"I thought he was magnificent too," Ida said. "For a while."

"And the way you talked to him. Good Lord, if my mother had ever spoken to my father in such a tone!"

"I got tired, Ruth. I got tired of having no one listen, of doing nothing but listening, of listening to nothing but lies. Can you understand? You who so enjoy speaking your mind?"

Ruth appeared to consider that, head tipped, brows furrowed, eyes piercing the air between them. "You were right. He wasn't magnificent in the end. What he did to that boy. I'll tell you what I'm going to do, I'm going to put all the money from the livestock sale into a college account for him. That's what I'm going to do."

Ida sat still, waiting for Ruth to come to it on her own, that she couldn't give Oliver *all* the sale money because 20 percent of it was Ida's.

"Of course we won't make what we made last year. You lost a lot of lambs, you know. But that sale money could be a nice start for the boy."

"That sale money less my twenty percent."

Ruth slapped her hand flat on the table. "Do you mean to say you'd take money from that boy's mouth?"

"Ruth, be fair. We signed a paper. I'm going to need that money to—"

Ruth attempted to bolt out of her chair and stumbled. Ida leaped around the table and caught her arm. "Come, I'll walk you home."

"Leave me alone. You never cared a pin for me. I said you were right about Ezra. I don't blame you for talking to him that way. But that boy, what did he ever do to you? He deserves that money. Those folk of his aren't even going to be alive when it's time for him to go to college."

She's old, Ida told herself. *She's confused.* She'll forget all this in the morning. She held her tongue, eased the old woman out the door, up the hill, and into her house with much trouble, in part because Ruth continued to carp at her all the way, in part because Oliver had run out to meet them and was attempting to escort them inside.

As they came through the door, still arm in arm, Hattie looked at them wide-eyed.

"She's tired," Ida said.

"I'm not *tired*," Ruth snapped.

"Well, I am," Ida said.

"*I'm* not," Oliver offered.

Ruth turned to stare at the boy. "Young man, it's time you went home. We can't keep feeding you forever, tripping over you at every turn."

"Mother, please," Hattie said.

"No, Harriet, *you* please. Write the boy's grandfather and tell him to fetch him. I want him gone now."

Oliver banged out the door.

IDA HAD SET OUT HER SUPPER and was looking forward to it—fish stew, cornbread, a baked apple, and a piece of cheddar so sharp it burned—when the phone rang.

"We can't find Oliver," Hattie said. "Is he with you?"

Ida pushed away the stew bowl. "No."

"He went out to dig in the yard. He digs for *hours*. I didn't think of him again till I went to call him for supper, and he was gone."

"Not gone," Ida said. "Just off somewhere else. He likes that tree off the east—"

"He's not in that tree. Lem looked. He's still looking in the woods. Oliver might have gotten lost. I want you to look around there. He loves those foolish sheep, and your dog, and—"

"The ox. I'll look," Ida said. "You hold on."

"He was crying," Hattie said. "When Lem came by he was crying. Lem asked why he was crying, and he said he wasn't crying."

"What did you do?"

"I didn't *do* anything! I was making supper and Mother was storming about and Lem came in and she started in on him, how if he'd agreed to manage the farm in the first place none of this would have happened, you wouldn't be trying to take money from a little boy—"

"Was Oliver in the room then?"

"No, I told you! He was digging in the yard!"

"You're sure?"

Pause. "*Yes.* Sure."

"You looked out and he was still digging?"

"Of course he was still digging. He's always digging. He—"

"You looked out. And he was digging. Or you just assumed he was digging."

"He's *always* digging," Hattie whispered.

Which meant that Hattie hadn't looked, that Oliver could have been gone a long time by now.

"You hold on," Ida said again, and returned the phone to its hook with Hattie's voice still echoing off the walls.

OLIVER WASN'T WITH BETT, or the sheep, or with Ollie in his stall. He wasn't in the hayloft. Ida let the dog out, remembering the time one of Ezra's dogs had led her safely home, but when Bett flew off after yet another squirrel, Ida wasn't hopeful. Not knowing what else to do she looked in all those same places again; only on the second trip to the pasture gate did she realize that Betty was gone. Boy *and* sheep missing seemed better than just boy missing, although Ida wasn't sure why. She stood and tried to think like a small boy. Where would he go with a sheep? Why? Ida hadn't a clue. She set out to circle the pasture. Again.

Dark had begun to drop down and the soft, slushy lump of worry in the middle of Ida's chest had frozen into a solid cube when she spied four disparate shapes coming up the track: tall, thin man; small, tired boy; dogged sheep; sheepish dog. The lump in Ida's chest exploded with love for them all.

"He was looking to play a little chess," Henry said, "but I told him Bessie—"

"*Bett*-ee," Oliver said.

"*Betty* was tired and wanted to go home."

"Is she going to die soon?" Oliver asked.

"Who, Betty?"

"Ruth," Henry said. "She seems to be out of favor just now. I tried to excuse her on the grounds of advanced age—"

"She's a mean old witch and I want her to die soon!"

"Oliver," Ida started, but she had no other words. She looked at Henry.

"It would appear someone doesn't want to go home," he said.

They had reached the house. Ida penned sheep and dog and when she turned around Henry and Oliver had settled onto the stoop.

"Can you wait?" Ida asked. "I should call."

Henry nodded.

Ida went inside and called. Into the whoops and crackles and echoes on the line as Hattie tried to ask Ida questions and answer Ruth's at the same time, Ida said, "I'm giving him some cocoa, then I'll bring him home."

OLIVER AND HENRY sat at the kitchen table while Ida stood over the stove, waiting for the milk to scald. When the first steam rose she added the chocolate and sugar and stirred, listening to the man and boy chatter: Betty, of course, and how he'd taken her because she was hungry; really, really hungry, and there wasn't any milk in the barn, never mind that Betty had been weaned off milk with the rest of the flock the month before.

There Henry waded in. "Did you think I'd have something to feed her?"

Oliver thought. "She likes chess," he tried.

"*You* like chess."

Oliver nodded.

Ida turned around and met Henry's eyes; the eyes no longer looked as solemn or as bitter as they had the last time Ida had seen them. She looked away.

Ida carried three cups of cocoa to the table and sat down in the chair next to Oliver. It was a symbolic gesture: I'm on your side, she wanted to say.

"Here's the problem," Ida began. "You did a wrong thing, running off. I know you didn't plan to worry your aunt Ruth—"

"I did plan it! She's mean mean mean!"

Henry looked a question at Ida. "Ruth said a few things," Ida explained. She returned her gaze to Oliver. "But you did wrong in running away. So we're going to walk up that hill and you're going to apologize to your cousin Hattie and your aunt Ruth, and you're going to promise them that you'll never do it again. Agreed?"

Nothing.

"Oliver."

Oliver looked at Henry. Henry said, "It sounds like the best way out of this mess to me." Oliver thought a good long while, but in the end he gave Ida a nod so small it could have been a twitch and looked away from her to the wall.

"All right," Ida said. "We're done with that subject. Now tell me. Why don't you want to go home?"

Oliver continued to face the wall.

"You can come back, you know. If Aunt Ruth can't take you, you can come visit me. You can stay in my extra room."

"When?"

Too late, Ida remembered she was moving to Boston. Soon. She clawed ahead. "Let me talk to your grandfather when he comes to get you. I've never met him. Tell me something about him."

But *something* was clearly too vague a term. Oliver kicked the chair in silence; she listened to the steady *tick tick tick* of his boot heel against the rungs and realized she'd probably have to touch up that paint, but somehow the thought gave Ida a hopeful feeling, as if she were looking for more things to do to the farmhouse, which she wasn't, since she was leaving it.

"He lives in New York City?" Henry was asking now.

Oliver nodded.

"What kind of work does he do? Or is he at home?"

Oliver thought. "He's famous," he said.

"Really? What did he do to get famous?"

Oliver thought again. "He built a giant castle. Out of gold. And that's where I'm going to live when I go home."

Ida sighed. She'd thought she'd done the boy some good, thought she'd given him some real stories about his father to counteract the old fables, and those fables had indeed died off, but now here they were again, only with the grandfather this time.

Ida's fable fatigue must have shown, or maybe Oliver just heard—and read correctly—that sigh. "Don't you believe me?" he asked.

Ida scraped her chair around to face Oliver head-on. She took him by the shoulders, aware of a frightening intensity in her grip that she only halfheartedly attempted to tamp down. "Oliver. I want you to listen to me carefully. In life, we only believe the people we trust. Do you know what trust is? It's knowing that a person isn't going to tell us lies. Most of the time, people know or find out when someone lies, and once they know, they don't trust that person anymore. They don't believe that person anymore. Do you want to be someone like that, someone people don't trust?"

Again, Oliver thought. "It's not *all* gold," he said. "Just my room."

Ida stood up. "Come along." They walked in subdued silence up the hill, but the kitchen they entered was subdued too, Hattie red-eyed, Lem holding her hand, Ruth, thank God, not in the room.

"Oliver?" Ida prompted, pushing him a little closer to Hattie.

"I'm sorry."

"And?"

"I won't do it again."

"Well, thank Heaven for that," Hattie said, and grabbed Oliver in what started as a hug and turned into a shake and ended in another hug, which Oliver seemed to know better than to dodge.

IDA ENTERED HER OWN KITCHEN to see the three cups rinsed and drying on the sideboard and Henry gone. She was relieved—there were still no words for him—but even so, she'd expected to find him there and finding him not there was unsettling. It put her off-kilter. It forced her to peer around corners as if he might still be lurking. *Fool.*

35

IDA INVITED HATTIE TO TEA; she wanted to keep the conversation from old and young ears. She'd assumed that a quiet word to Hattie would settle the matter of the livestock sale money; it wasn't that she didn't want Oliver to have it, it was just that she couldn't afford to give it away. It seemed this was something that Hattie would understand. She began by attempting to pick up on an old conversation.

"You said to me not long ago that everything ends terribly. But now you're to be married. You can't be thinking that will end terribly?"

"Of course not. I told you. I was tired that day. This is what you asked me here to talk of?"

"No, not entirely."

"You've never asked me to tea before."

"I know."

"But then, I've never asked you. I never thought you'd imagine it a pleasure. My mother—"

"I know."

"So what else do you want to talk about?"

It wasn't starting well. What the devil, then. "I wanted to ask you if you could talk to your mother about my money. The money I've earned and signed a contract for, that she now wants to give to Oliver. You see, don't you, that she can't do that?"

"You want me to talk to my mother about the money? Really?" Hattie looked so shocked Ida wondered for a minute if somewhere somehow she'd gotten something wrong. She *had* worked the sheep all year. She *had* signed a contract. Oliver *could* have the other 80 percent; he *could* go home to a family that wanted him and cared for him.

But Hattie kept on. "You know she's not . . . well."

"If you mean confused, yes I know. This is why I'm talking to you. Unless you're confused too—" Ida said it with a laugh, but even to her own ears it didn't sound chock-full of funny. At a later time Ida was going to have to give some thought to why it was that Hattie had begun to annoy her so.

"I don't think giving money to a boy to start a college fund is—"

Ida cut her off. "Ruth can give him her money. She can't give him mine. This seems like something I shouldn't have to ask my lawyer to explain to you. I wonder if Ruth has a lawyer. Do you know?"

Hattie stood up. "I don't know what's happened to you."

"Let me think on that. Could it be I got tired of liars? Cheats? Thieves? In a word, Peases?"

Hattie flounced off with a parting shot even Ida had to admire for its brutality. "Imagine if your mother and father were alive, what they'd say to you right now."

IDA WENT TO BED taking comfort in the fact that surely she had reached the lowest point to which she could ever succumb, but it turned out she was wrong.

Oliver's grandfather was one of those men whose kindness was apparent within a half hour of his arrival, which eased Ida's mind some. He thanked Ruth, Hattie, and even Ida for looking out for the boy for so long; he took note of Oliver's downcast face and said right away, "I bet it's hard to leave a place as handsome as this farm, but your grandmother has missed you so. I missed you too. We'll just have to come back in the spring and see how much that sheep of yours has grown."

Oliver lifted his chin, pointed at Ida, and said, "We're going to stay with her!" to which Ida only nodded and smiled.

So who was the liar now?

AND DOWN. More raindrops had just pocked the windowpane and Ida had rushed out to wrestle the sheets off the line, but the wind came up along with the rain, and Ida found herself batting the sheets around like a sailor in a gale. She—and the wash— were pretty well soaked through when Constable Ripley pulled up the hill. To her astonishment he leaped out of the wagon, rolled up one of the sheets as if he'd done it a time or two, and dashed it inside. Ida managed to corral the second sheet and they met up on the porch, Ida going in, Ripley going out. He followed her in.

"I have news," Ripley said.

Ida draped the sheets over a pair of chairs, threw a log on the fire, and crossed her arms, waiting for Ripley's news; she was through dishing up tea as if it could wash down trouble. And clearly, this was trouble.

"What news?"

"I told you Ezra Pease got on that ship. Trouble is, he didn't get off on the other side."

"*What?*"

"They had a man waiting on the other side. Pease got on in New York, but no one of that description came off in France. They think—"

Ida threw up her arms. "I don't care what they *think*—"

"They think he checked himself on board and then looped around and got back off."

"Or he simply slipped through the crowd on the other side."

"These aren't newborn babes over there. They said he didn't get off, I'd tend to believe them."

"Or they wouldn't admit it if he sneaked by them."

Ripley went still, considering, reminding Ida of Oliver, the way the boy drew to a halt every time he needed to think something through. "Possible, I suppose. But just to say again, I tend to believe them."

"Or he went overboard." But even as Ida spoke she knew that Ezra had not pitched himself off the deck of the ship; Ezra would never cash in his chips before the game was played out to the end.

Ripley said, "My money says he wants us to think he's in France when he isn't."

A wave of nausea swept through Ida. "Why?"

Ripley shrugged. "Probably still has things cooking here."

"So now what?"

Ripley shrugged. "Keep an ear cocked and an eye out. Let us know if you get wind of anything."

Ida yanked the sheets off the chairs, threw them on the floor, and sat down.

DOWN AND DOWN AND DOWN. She slept with both ears cocked, hearing time and again Ezra's tread on the stairs, waking to imagine him standing at the foot of the bed or peering in the window, which made no sense, as Ida's room was on the second floor. Bett continued at Ida's side, but Ida wasn't at all sure the dog would sound the alarm if her former owner were to appear; mightn't she just walk up and lap his hand? Ida should know.

EZRA HAD NOT DISAPPEARED ONCE BEFORE. "New York," he'd said when Ida had asked, and she'd seen him out the door and down the track, heard the steamer whistle as it left the dock. With Ezra gone it seemed the perfect time to get his wardrobe in order. She mended, scrubbed, bleached, dried, and the next morning she ironed. But the next afternoon she decided she'd spent enough time on Ezra and turned to cleaning out her Winsor & Newton paint box; it was the kind of thing artists did when they wanted to stave off actually having to paint. Once she'd cleaned the box she decided to treat herself to a lemon pudding, not a favorite of Ezra's, but she'd allowed her sugar to run low; she set off for Luce's. After Ida had secured her loaf of sugar she took stock of the day; it was a fine one, the cool air offset by the warmth of a late-day sun, and her legs itched; she set off along the shore awash in the luxury of no destination or chore ahead of her.

There were three of them: Ezra, Mose, and a stranger. At first Ida doubted her eyes, but the dory sat low in the water and made poor progress so she had time to go through the whole game of Ezra-not-Ezra-Ezra and back again, but where she ended was where she began. It was Ezra.

When he came home at week's end, Ida said, "How did you find New York?"

"Much the same."

"Interesting."

Ezra peered at her. "You've got some problem with New York?"

"New York? No."

"Honest to God, Ida—"

"Don't," Ida said. "If you don't want to make yourself more ridiculous than you already are, don't say another thing."

Remarkably, Ezra didn't.

Another drip of that snowmelt.

SO IDA PASSED THE TIME until the livestock sale, which caused the kind of wrench in Ida no self-respecting farmer would allow. She hadn't felt any such thing the year before, but now she thought of these as *her* sheep, had fought so hard for every life; she only realized how possessive she'd become once she watched Bett and Lem drive them down the track. She lingered, feeding Betty corn out of her hand, corn Betty did not need, corn the chickens did need, until she looked down at her hand and saw how pathetic she was. She dashed the last of the corn on the ground for the chickens, fetched the paint can from the barn, and set to work touching up the chairs. After she finished the chairs she even stood on a stool and painted the beam that ran through the middle of the kitchen, but now she was done. There was nothing left to paint. Time to move on. But how? The Main Street property was attached. The farm would go to Hattie and Lem. The sheep money would arrive at the bank where it would sit waiting for Oliver to go to college?

No.

IDA CLIMBED THE hill. She saw Lem's wagon in the yard and was glad, or she supposed she was glad; she expected fair play from Lem, but then again, she'd expected fair play from Hattie. But she hadn't even reached the stoop when Lem came out the door.

"Hattie saw you through the window. Figured it might be best to head you off."

"So you know why I'm here."

"I guess I know."

"I earned that money, Lem."

"I know."

"I'm not leaving here without that money. I *can't* leave without that money."

Lem reached in his pocket, pulled out a folded bill, handed it to Ida. "Best I can do right now."

Ida slapped Lem's hand away. "No. She's the one owes me."

Lem folded the bill away. "Come, I'll drive you home."

"No."

"Ida, please."

"Why are you letting her do this?"

"She's upset about that boy. She never really figured he'd go home, somehow. You reminded her when you said he'd come back to visit, and so she wanted to get it over with, the leaving. And then she felt bad. Or so Hattie says. So she's hell-bent on giving him that money."

"It's not her money, Lem. Not twenty percent of it. I'm not letting her get away with it. If I have to—"

"All right. Give me a week. Now get in."

Ida climbed into the wagon. They jolted in silence down the hill, but when Ida slid to the ground Lem surprised her by getting out too and walking straight to the pasture gate. Ida stood for a minute staring at his back, thinking what she did and didn't know about that back, thinking of the secrets it had managed to conceal, like Hattie. She crossed to the gate and leaned beside him.

"You never said. How did the sale go?"

"Good. Very good. That ram of Ezra's; they were clamoring to get at some of that bloodline." He pointed to the sheep. "Which of them would you put to him this year?"

Ida thought. "Not Betty. You're right about that." She pointed to one more. Its mother had had a narrow pelvis and had almost expired giving birth to that lamb; it looked to Ida like she'd passed that pelvis on. Ida explained her thinking.

"Good," Lem said. "Any more?"

Ida found one more that she'd been watching because its weight had started to drop. She could see now that it didn't seem to be grazing well; she pointed that one out to Lem.

"Let's look."

Ida fetched Bett and separated the sheep. Lem rolled it and opened its mouth for Ida to see. Parrot mouth: another thing you didn't want to pass on.

So yes, in her year of managing the flock, Ida had learned a thing or two.

AS WAS ALWAYS THE WAY as soon as the days began to shorten, the ewes went into heat and the ram began to lift his head to smell the air. Bett drove Betty and the sheep with the narrow pelvis and the poor grazer into the far field and Lem put the ram in with the rest of them. It began, the ewes in heat squatting in front of the ram, the ram circling the field three times a day to service them all. After a week, the ram had lost weight; he'd lose more by the end of his run. Contemplating the end of that run, contemplating her year having come full circle by then, contemplating another winter on the island, Ida saw that the time had come. It was time to leave. Lem's week was up and no money. Ida was done with the lot of them. She would admit if pressed that she was hurt as well as puzzled by Lem's refusal to push her case for her, despite the new circumstance of a future mother-in-law in the picture. Lem was *her* friend. Or so he'd told her time and again.

THIS TIME when Lem came out the door to head her off, Ida said, "Excuse me," and made to swing around him.

"Ida."

"I'm leaving and I need my money."

"What are you saying?"

"I told you the other day. I need it now."

"I mean about the leaving. You're staying to see me married."

"Why, so you can look across the room at me and remind yourself it could have been worse?"

"Don't go forgetting yourself, Ida."

"I want my money, Lem. You get it or I will. I'll bring in the law if I have to."

Lem gazed off at the field, at the ram sniffing up one of the ewes, and the sight seemed to heighten his resolve. "All right, stay for my wedding and—"

"No. No deals. It's my money and I'm not going to bargain for it. Get it for me now or my lawyer will."

Lem shook his head at her, the way her father used to shake his head at her when she begged to go after her brothers.

"Do I need to call my lawyer?"

"No. Jesus, Ida."

Ida started to move off.

"Ida!"

She whipped around.

"I'd take it kindly if you'd stay for my wedding."

"I'd take it kindly to get my money. If I don't have it by Thursday, I make that call."

IDA PULLED THE TRUNK OUT into the middle of the room. It would be an easy pack this time; she'd already returned her Boston clothes to it, and she need fit in only the few things she'd take with her of her island clothes: her bicycling trousers, her bicycling boots, the hat she'd purchased in anticipation of many hours riding in the summer sun. She went to her studio and looked around; she'd had more room here than she'd had in town but had somehow insidiously filled the space anyway—she imagined she could fill four crates with her books and art supplies and completed or not completed paintings. She lingered over the painting of Henry's father, still unfinished, still waiting for that thing that would make him Henry's father and not Henry. She paused at another early painting she'd attempted of the sheep out in the pasture; it wasn't right and while she couldn't see why before, she thought she might see something of it now.

Ida carried the sheep painting downstairs, propped it up on the porch, and looked out over the sheep. She'd made them too round—she saw that right off; Cheviots had corners to them. And the legs—the way the rear legs kicked back; and where the eyes sat and how black they were—she'd gotten that wrong too. But even if she'd gotten the shapes and the legs and the eyes there was nothing *to* the painting; no one in Boston would pay for a picture of a bunch of dirty sheep standing around in a rock-strewn field.

Ida returned to the kitchen. She'd added little to the shelves here just as she'd added little to the parlor and the bedroom; it was as if the farmhouse had absorbed her, as if she would come and go and leave no mark behind. She wandered into the parlor and stopped at Ezra's desk. Well, she'd left something there.

Ida hadn't, after all, burned the letters Ezra had written her. She didn't want the letters, but neither did she want to leave them for Hattie or Lem to find. She rolled back the desk lid just as she'd done so many months ago, but in such a different frame of mind. How she'd suffered trying to grieve for the man then, how free she was of that struggle now. And yet she was still not free of Ezra.

Where *was* he now?

Ida found the letters. This time she didn't stall but opened the stove door and fired them in, not waiting to watch them burn, not willing to give even Ezra's flames another drop of her attention. She returned to the desk, continuing to sort: one pile to keep, one pile to throw, one pile to leave for Hattie and Lem. Hattie and Lem would get the farm book, the business cards, the bill receipts, the papers on the ram. Ida fingered the ram's paper with distaste; most of the sheep Ida had come to respect, even admire—those thousands of years of survival tactics and adaptation bred into them—she'd even developed a certain affection for their silliness and was outright in love with those ears. But that ram! Ida opened the paper, curious to see how much Ezra had paid for the beast; the shock of it unfocused her eyes. And then she saw the date.

Ezra had deeded the farm and its livestock to Ruth before their marriage; he'd bought the ram a year and a half after it. The ram didn't belong to Ruth; it wasn't Ruth's to give to Hattie and Lem.

36

THEY SAT AT RUTH'S KITCHEN TABLE: Ida, Ruth, Hattie, Lem. The ram's papers sat in the middle of the table where each had read them in turn.

Ida pointed to the date. "Ruth, when did Ezra deed you that farm?"

"What are you saying?"

"I'm saying Ezra bought that ram *after* he deeded you the farm."

"Well, it's not yours either," Ruth snapped.

Ida retrieved the paper and set it in front of her, squaring the corners with the edge of the table. "It's not if I tell the law about him, that's certain; he becomes another piece of attached property and ends up in some investor's bank account. But what if I don't tell?"

Silence.

"I told Ezra when he brought you here," Ruth said at last. "I told him he was a fool."

"He was that," Ida said. "And so was I. But not anymore."

Ruth opened her mouth, but Lem cut in. "What's your plan, Ida? No one here can afford to buy that animal off you, if that's what you're thinking."

"A fair exchange."

"Ruth gives you your money and you give us that ram," Hattie said.

"I told you. I'm not a fool anymore. Ruth *gives* me nothing.

I earned that money. She surrenders that money, and I don't remove the ram from the flock until he's finished the season."

"And next year?" Lem asked.

Ida looked out the window. It had started to rain again—sideways—the wind flipping over the leaves in a way Ida knew only too well. Almost a year ago a storm had come along and flipped Ida's life just as it flipped those leaves, and here she was, still, upside down. It was time to right herself.

"Boston's expensive," she said. "And I don't know just what my situation will be. Let's talk about my fee for the ram's services next year."

"I've always said you were a despicable creature," Ruth said.

"An opinion not generally shared," Lem said.

Hattie flashed him a look.

"Ruth," Lem went on, "Ida holds the paper. She can sell that ram right now and ease her way considerably, but think where that leaves your farm. You know as well as I do it was because of that animal we did so well at the sale this year. You also know that the money you're threatening to give to Oliver is Ida's. I'd take the deal being offered here. One more year of that ram's blood strengthens your flock, and your bank account, no matter what comes afterward."

Ruth pointed a bent finger at Ida. "You don't even care if that boy goes to college. Your own husband's son."

Ida stood up. She took two steps toward Ruth and leaned down, the words she'd once said to Ezra fighting for release, but she held them back. Why, though? Why was Ruth free to say whatever she wished, and Ida was not? She took a breath, felt it press against her ribs. "Ruth, a word of advice. Don't make yourself any more ridiculous than you already are. My twenty percent isn't going to keep Oliver from college, but if it did, it wouldn't matter, because it's *my money*. Now, you think on what I've offered and let me know what you decide. Come Tuesday, if I don't have the money, the ram gets packed up and shipped off."

Lem rose. "I'll drive you home."

"IT'S FAIR," IDA SAID.

"It's fair," Lem answered. "She'll come around."

But if she doesn't . . . "Any idea where I can turn some gold nuggets into cash?"

Lem swiveled to get a better look at Ida. "I do, as a matter of fact."

IT WAS THAT EASY. Tuesday Ruth sent Hattie down the hill with Ida's 20 percent, along with a meticulous accounting. Ida had gone with Lem to someone he knew at the bank and received pretty much what Henry had suggested the gold was worth, which turned out to be pretty much what she'd gotten from the sale of the livestock. She'd then taken the cash from the gold and put it into Oliver's college fund.

"Why the hell didn't you just leave your money with Ruth if you were going to do that?" Lem spluttered on the ride home.

"Because it's *my money*. Can you understand that?"

Lem shifted to look at her. "The day I understand you—" He grinned. "But yeah, I guess I do."

"And Oliver is Ezra's son. If Ezra had claimed Oliver, if he *had* drowned, if he'd never launched that gold scheme or signed over the farm to Ruth—" Ida had grown heated, winded. She took a breath, started again. "According to Malcolm Littlefield, if Ezra had been an honest, decent man, Oliver would have inherited half of everything—the business, the properties, the farm."

"So why didn't you just sell that ram and give him that money too?"

"Because," Ida said, "Oliver's not the only one Ezra owes."

WHEN THEY REACHED THE FARM Lem bolted from the wagon. "Bloody hell!"

Ida looked: the ram had knocked flat the hayrack and was butting the pieces across the grass.

As Lem collected his tools from the barn, Ida fetched Bett and her crook and chased the ram into his pen, successfully this time. This she'd learned too—never turn your back on a ram. As Lem set to work repairing the hayrack Ida stood and watched for a time, transfixed by the way the island light had changed again, casting long, slanting fingers across the fields, throwing purple shadows under the sheep. She watched Lem bend to his work and saw in the strain of his back, the earth-brown in his coat, the steel in his hair, something that she believed was worth capturing; she went inside for her paints.

She took out her pad and made a quick sketch but soon moved on to the larger paper; she was deep in her efforts when she felt rather than saw a change in her peripherals. She looked sideways and saw Henry Barstow topping the hill. He had no bicycle this time; he swung along with what at first appeared to be the same old effortless stride, but as he drew nearer Ida could see the determination that powered him forward. He drew up alongside Ida.

"I heard you're leaving for Boston soon."

Ida set her brush down. "Soon."

Henry said nothing. Strange, Ida thought, how one man's presence felt so different from another's: Lem's body beside her in the wagon always felt like a fortress, a wall; Henry's standing beside her felt like the edge of a forest or an ocean, a definite line of demarcation between them but a porous one, a thing either one might step through if only they dared.

I guess he had his reasons, Lem had said.

"Why?" Ida asked. "Why didn't you tell me? And don't say it was because you weren't sure."

Henry's answer came so fast it was as if he'd come up the hill with it already formed. "Because I wanted you to be a widow. I wanted you—I wanted everyone—to think you were a widow so after my divorce I could marry you. That's the real reason why. After that one, *after* that one, I thought, well, she told me she didn't like Ezra much; I thought, wouldn't she *rather* have him dead than alive? Wouldn't she rather have the thing over? I didn't think—" He stopped. "I didn't think. It was wrong of me to decide for you what you'd want to know."

"When were you sure?"

"I don't know. It was too inconceivable. Too cruel, even for Ezra. I kept making excuses for him. That night in your room when you showed me where the gold was hidden, I told you maybe he left it for you to find, but we both knew he didn't. When I put you away from me that night you thought it was because I wasn't sure about my wife, but it was because of Ezra. Only Ezra. What if we'd done this thing with you thinking Ezra was dead and then later you found out he was alive, and I knew? What would you have thought of me then?"

Ida looked at this man and tried to imagine what she would have thought of him, but all she could picture was Ezra in that situation instead of Henry, Ezra in that room. He'd have had her splayed out on that bed in an eye blink and then stuffed the gold in his pants on his way out the door.

"But at Makonikey—"

"At Makonikey you told me you didn't care about my wife *or* about Ezra. You told me about your family. You were so sad. And I wanted to make you not sad." He smiled, but not as if he meant to. "And you were half dressed. And I'd wanted you for so long. So when you told me you didn't care about Ezra, well, I chose to believe it."

Ida picked up her brush; set it down again; she looked out at Lem working and Henry looked too, as if Lem's progress rebuilding the hayrack was the only thing that concerned them. After a time Henry took a step closer to gaze at Ida's painting, and his nearness set off something new in Ida, or rather something old, something that made her recall how she'd missed his presence, his touch, their talks, how these past months she'd been able to grieve more deeply for Henry than she'd ever managed to grieve for Ezra.

The silence grew long. Ida's sketch pad lay on top of her paint box; Henry picked it up and began to flip backward through the pages with nervous fingers, unseeing, or so it seemed to Ida—as if he only turned pages in order to do something with his hands. But when he drew close to the end—or the beginning—he stopped at the image of Lem she'd sketched at Christmas and held it up next to the current painting. Right there Ida saw it; the one that wasn't Lem and the one that was; the one that was the lie and the one that was true. Without words Henry flipped through another few pages, skipping over the still lifes and portraits, stopping at one of an institute student poised with her brush midair, her body alive with concentration and intensity; stopped again at the sheep on a blowy day hunched against the hill, the wind evident in the posture of the trees, the grass, the clouds, the braced posture of the sheep themselves; paused once more at the one of the schooners beating across the Sound.

"Are you sure Boston's where you belong?"

Ida took the sketch pad and closed it. "You're the one who needs to figure out where you belong."

"I belong with you," Henry answered, steadily, calmly, as if it were a fact everyone but Ida had long known.

But before Ida could respond—*if* she could have responded— a commotion broke out among the sheep. Betty had leaped too high or too long and gotten wedged in the fork of a tree; she started to bawl, and the rest of the lambs joined in. Ida opened the gate and started across the field as Lem straightened and began to jog toward the tree from the far side; Ida reached the sheep before Lem, picked up its hind legs and shoved it through. When she turned back to the fence she saw that Henry was no longer leaning against it but had already covered half the distance to the track. She could have called to him. She *should* call to him. She stood frozen until she felt the ground shudder under her and swung around.

Lem had made it only halfway across the pasture and lay curled on the grass, one arm crossed over his chest, the other clawing at his jacket pocket.

"Henry!" Ida screamed and flew.

Lem's face was gray, his lips blue. He'd managed to withdraw a bottle of pills from his pocket and shook one out, put it under his tongue. Ida knelt beside him. "What is it?"

"Nothing."

"No," Ida said. "Do *not* say that to me."

Henry reached them and knelt too. He took the bottle of pills from Lem's hand. "Nitroglycerine. Your heart?"

"Get me up, that's all I need from you."

"You sit. I'll get the wagon. And the doctor."

"The doctor's been. He gave me those pills. There's nothing else he can do. They should work fine in a minute or two."

Henry and Ida shared a look. Henry jogged off for the wagon, returned, helped Lem in. Lem sat breathing heavily, his hand pressed to his chest as if were trying to hold something in, a posture Ida had seen before but only remembered seeing now.

"Just the same," Ida began, "the doctor—"

"Ida, I'd take it kindly if I could just sit on your porch for a spell. This thing should blow off soon."

THEY SAT: HENRY, IDA, LEM, not on the porch but in the parlor, Lem almost forcibly reclined on the sofa. The spell did appear to have blown off—he'd stopped rubbing his chest, his breathing was less labored, his color had returned; he swung his legs over the side and sat up, but stayed in that position, elbows on knees, head down.

"Does Hattie know?" Ida asked.

Lem's head came up, along with a rare display of ire. "Who do you think I am, someone who'd marry a woman without telling her I'll be dead by May?"

"May?"

Lem dropped back on the sofa. "So I'm told. Hat caught me in the middle of a spell, and I told her just that; I told her about May. That's when she said, well, Lem Daggett, we need to get married. Soon."

"*Hattie* said—?"

"Surprise you? Yep, Hattie wants that farm and Ruth won't give it to her lest she's married, so she offered me a deal. We get married, Ruth gives us the farm, and Hattie nurses me through till the end." He coughed, sat up again, shook his head as if in disbelief. "Till May."

Henry and Ida exchanged a look. "Kind of arbitrary, this May," Henry said.

"He added a 'more or less' to it."

"Let's say more, then. Let's say next January. You can see a little more of that new century."

Ida looked at Henry in alarm, but Lem was grinning. "January it is. If that's all right with you, Ida."

"Yes," Ida said, through fury, through shock, through everything she was feeling about this man. She looked again at Henry. Oh, how could she not admit it now? These men.

37

THEY CALLED HATTIE. She arrived and took command. "I'll keep my eyes on you this night if you don't mind," Hattie said when Lem announced his plan to drive himself home. "We're going up that hill, not down."

After they drove off, Henry and Ida returned to the parlor together. Ida sat on the sofa where Lem had so recently sprawled, but she left room for Henry; it seemed the right thing to do. Henry sat down beside her but leaned forward much as Lem had, elbows on knees, staring at the floor.

"He told me more than once," Ida said. "He told me he was the best friend I had."

Henry leaned back and opened his arm. Ida let her head drop onto his shoulder. Idly, as if out of old habit, Henry began to pick the pins out of her disarranged hair and comb it through with his fingers. Ida closed her eyes and sank into the comfort. *Comfort.* Such an unknown thing in her world.

After a time Henry said, "Hattie. Bloody hell."

Ida pushed herself upright. "She wants the farm! *Hattie.* She's never looked at a sheep. She's never come around when work's going on, except once, at the shearing, and she looked like she hated every minute of it."

"Maybe she doesn't want the farm. Maybe that's only what she told Lem. I doubt he'd marry her otherwise, turn her into a nurse and then a widow without something for her at the end."

He's right, Ida thought. Lem would never marry Hattie just to get a nurse; he would never let Hattie do it. And that Henry would see that before Ida did put her to shame. When had she become that person who would first assume everyone was out for his or her own gain? When had she first begun to so ignore Hattie that she knew nothing of that beating heart inside her? Tears stung at Ida's eyes, tears over Lem, yes, but tears for Ida too, and tears for this man who again held her, who wiped her tears off her cheek with his thumb.

"I'm sorry," he said. "You've hurt so much and all I did was hurt you more." He stood up. "I'm going to finish off that hayrack so Lem won't try to do it and then I'm going home."

"Thank you," Ida said.

Henry's smile was bitter. "For the hayrack or for going home?"

"Henry."

He stopped.

"I need to always know."

"Know what?"

"Everything. All of it. The truth of things. I can't go back to always wondering what's being hidden or camouflaged or . . . left out. Just plain left out."

He studied her. "I'm sorry," he said again.

"I know."

IDA WATCHED OUT FOR HATTIE the next morning on her way down the hill to the exchange and stepped out to intercept her.

Hattie saw her and held up a hand. "Don't," she said. "Whatever you're going to say, don't."

"I'm not going to Boston," Ida said.

"You're going."

"Not till after the wedding. Lem asked me not to."

Hattie broke stride, swung to face Ida. "Did he, now."

"A while ago. I just didn't know why till the other day. Just as I didn't understand your tears that day."

Hattie started walking again. "Do what you want, Ida."

"I want to stay for the wedding. If you two don't want to move into the farmhouse before then."

Hattie snorted. "Before the wedding? With my mother? With Lem?"

"Henry Barstow finished the hayrack."

"What hayrack?"

"The ram knocked it out."

"Oh," Hattie said, but she might as well have said, "What ram?" Or come to that, "What farm?"

"I know why you're doing this, Hattie. I know you don't really want this farm. You only said that to Lem so he'd agree to marry you and let you take care of him. You're a good soul."

Hattie laughed. "Oh, Ida, I'm not as good as all that."

"Good enough."

"No, Ida, not even that. I'm marrying Lem Daggett because I've loved that old crab since I was sixteen years old."

IDA MADE HER WAY UP THE HILL. When she walked in, Ruth was standing over the stove and looking a good deal older than she had the last time Ida had seen her, which had been older even than the time before.

"I'd love a cup of tea, thank you for asking," Ida said.

Ruth turned around just far enough to glare at Ida, but she lifted the kettle, filled it at the sink pump, and set it back down on the stove.

"So I suppose you know all there is to know," Ruth said.

"Oh, I doubt it."

"My daughter's marrying a man who'll be dead before she's

figured out how to iron his shirts. She'll be left with a farm she hasn't the first idea how to run. Why? I said. Because I love him, she said. All of a sudden, after ignoring him her whole life, she decides she loves him."

Ida, who'd thought a bit about this a little more and recalled a few moments, said only, "I think maybe she's loved him for a while."

Ruth carried the pair of teacups to the table and slapped them down. "I'm not feeding you."

"That's all right."

"I don't care if it's all right or not. I'm not feeding you is what I said."

Ida gave up. Moved on. "I've come to ask permission to stay on at the farmhouse till the wedding. Hattie says they won't be moving in until afterward, and I thought maybe I could help out. Henry Barstow already mended the hayrack—"

"Henry Barstow! What's he still doing around?"

Ida didn't answer that. "Well?"

Ruth stirred her tea. "It's not as if I could get a tenant in there for only a month. But I'll expect you to take care of the place just as you did before if you stay on."

"I will."

Ruth pushed her cup away. "Lem told me what you did with that gold money. I don't understand you, Ida Pease. All that fuss and bother—"

Ida rose. "I don't care if you understand me, Ruth. Is Oliver coming to the wedding? His grandparents? They can stay with me if they are."

"Oliver will be staying here with me. Don't think you can lure him away with one measly bag of gold."

* * *

AT FIRST LITTLE CHANGED on the farm and then much did. The trick was to find the thing that needed doing before Lem did and then to call in Henry—Henry who had fled his own family farm never to return. He talked Lem into teaching him how to repair stone walls so he could be on hand to do the lifting and came away talking things like gravity and friction and interior fill and exterior facing; he loaded the hayracks so Ida could keep at her paints; he actually picked up the shovel one day before Ida could get to it and mucked out the ox stall.

And Ida found reasons to be where Lem was. She declared that before she left the island she was going to master drawing and painting sheep, to take away with her an honest representation, and so often in the afternoon light she joined the men at the wall with her sketch pad and paint box. She discovered that whether or not they were working on a wall, where Lem was Henry often was, and that the two men had worked out a game where Henry pretended he'd just stopped by over estate business with Ida. But Lem let Henry do the lifting, the fetching, the carrying, and while Henry loped this way and that Ida and Lem talked.

"He's not a bad fellow."

"No."

"Shame about his wife, though."

"And my husband."

Lem made a disgusted snort, much like the ram's. "If I get him in shotgun range—"

"Then you'd go to jail, and what would I do?"

Lem set down the sketch he'd been studying. "As we're talking about that, what *will* you do, Ida?"

Ida wanted to say *I'm here as long as you are and then I'm gone,* but she knew Lem wouldn't like either half of that sentence. Instead she said, "Vote."

And just as she'd planned, Lem tipped back his head and laughed.

LEM GREW THINNER, paler, more winded; the pills in the bottle dwindled and needed to be refilled. The doctor went up and down the hill, but as Lem had predicted, he made no great difference in things as far as Ida could tell. She—and Henry and Hattie—learned to recognize the subtle changes in Lem's skin and breathing and fabricated restful things that needed his attention, like the splicing of a rope or a review of accounts or even just keeping Ruth company at teatime. The whiskey seemed to help, or at least it helped Ida. Over the whiskey bottle they argued about everything they'd always argued about, but without the teeth in it, if in fact there ever had been teeth in it. Once, when they'd fallen silent and Ida had taken a longer than usual drink, Lem pointed at her glass. "It doesn't help anything, you know. Fact of the matter—" But when Lem saw the tears in her eyes he let it go.

IN BETWEEN THE FARMWORK and chatting with Lem, Ida continued to study the sheep. She took note of the fact that although every sheep had a neck, the neck didn't always show. She learned that even the Cheviot's white face wasn't white, just as she'd learned that muslin and linen and paper weren't white. She learned that the black eyes weren't black. She learned, at last, to paint them as they seemed and not as they were.

LEM AND HATTIE married standing before the fireplace in Ruth's house, everyone struggling to harvest smiles for the occasion, to ignore the physical wasting in Lem and the grief in Hattie's eyes. The only one oblivious of the second gathering soon to come was Oliver, who careened around the wedding feast as if he were Bett working the flock. Ironically, of all the guests, Ruth was the one who shined, hobbling from group to group to greet the guests personally, to inquire at each stop if everyone had food and drink and a comfortable enough chair.

"You might like to be closer to the fire," she told Oliver's grandmother. "I don't think that plate is full enough for a strapping fellow like you," she told George Amaral. "Wait there and I'll fill your glass," she told Henry, who happened to be standing talking to Ida at the time.

"I'll do it, Ruth," Ida said, but Ruth had already hustled off. Ida followed her into the kitchen. "You should sit and rest," Ida said.

"It's *my* daughter's wedding," Ruth snapped back, and burst into tears.

LATER, MUCH LATER than was wise for the players, the party began to disintegrate, and Lem found a moment to fall into the chair next to Ida.

"Change of plans," he said. "Last night Ruth fell on the stairs, and Hat doesn't want to leave her here alone. But Ruth doesn't want to move, of course. So I'm going to move in here, at least for now."

Ida looked at Lem. Lem looked at Ida. "So that farmhouse is going to sit empty till we get a manager in. I asked you to stay for my wedding and you stayed for it. Now I need to ask you to stay for one more thing."

"You don't need to ask me anything, Lem. I'm here."

"Till I'm gone."

Was this why Lem didn't fight harder for Ida to get her money? Because he wanted her to stay around till he was gone? Ida's eyes filled. "Till you're gone."

"Or till Hattie gets in a manager."

"All right, till then. Just don't push your luck too far, my friend."

"Maybe all along you've been the best friend *I* had."

"No," Ida said, "you got it the right way around the first time."

IT TURNED OUT Lem had less time, not more, or maybe he just got tired of the life that had been left him. Hattie and Ruth hovered over him ceaselessly, chirping at him to take his nap, tucking an afghan around him every time he moved. Ida stayed on at the farm, doing her part to annoy Lem further by chasing him off every time he tried to lift a bucket, Henry appearing as if by transubstantiation every time Lem tried to bang a nail. It was Ida who found Lem facedown in the pasture one morning at dawn, a saw in his hand and a partially cut dead tree limb bobbing over him like a dark hand.

AGAINST RUTH'S OBJECTIONS, Hattie declined to hold a funeral for Lem.

"We're going to remember him as a bridegroom, not a corpse," she said, and held fast to it, no matter how loud and long her mother railed. The family gathered at the grave to watch him into the ground in silence and then moved on. But having seen what grief wasn't, Ida was quick to identify what it was when it slammed her between the eyes: she was heartbroken; bereft; immobilized. Ida had promised Lem she would stay till Hattie found a manager for the farm, but in February Hattie told her it was time for her to get gone.

"I can't hire a manager if I have no house for him," she said. "And I want him in place before lambing season arrives."

IDA ARRANGED for her old room at Mrs. Clarke's boarding-house and sat down to write to Helen Ballou. *I return to town,* she said. *I'd love to meet and show you some work, perhaps get some advice on what might sell.* She finished loading her trunk and packed up her crates of artwork, and by the time she was ready to leave, a return letter had come from Helen.

Call when you arrive. We'll meet. I wouldn't presume to advise you on your work, but one of the instructors here, a Mr. Parmenter, has connections at the Guild. We'll start there.

Ruth and Hattie loaded up the carriage and drove her to the dock.

"Well, good-bye," said Ruth, "do come again," as if Ida had been visiting for the weekend.

"Oh, Ida," Hattie said, but left it at that.

Henry said nothing because Henry wasn't there.

38

HELEN BALLOU MADE GOOD; Ida hadn't been in town a week when an appointment had been arranged with the fabled Mr. Parmenter. Ida had kept the painting of Lem repairing the hay-rack for herself but set aside for Mr. Parmenter the one she felt would be more apt to please: the Christmas portrait. Mr. Parmenter didn't know Lem and wouldn't have the first idea that it was nothing like the real man, and there *was* a fair amount of technical skill in the skin, the cloth, the reflected firelight. And as it was her only acceptable portrait, it would have to do. She also included two still lifes: a vase of lilacs reflected in the gloss of the parlor table and the still life of the bowl of apples. To Ida the lilacs appeared imprisoned in the table gloss, but she'd gotten the gloss just right, as well as the complexity in the colors of the flowers; the apples looked contrived and untouchable to her, as if no one could ever eat one for fear of disturbing the composition, but this was what the Guild liked to show: portraits and still lifes. At the last minute Ida included one that Henry had paused over—the sheep huddled against the storm—at the least it would serve to show Mr. Parmenter why she'd gotten so little done in her three years gone.

MR. PARMENTER'S STUDIO looked much like Mr. Morris's, and as Ida stepped inside she felt a brief lapse in her resolve, but only a moment later she rallied, as if Mr. Morris had placed a firm hand under her elbow and eased her along. Mr. Parmenter himself was un-Morris-like in every way; heavy instead of gaunt, ruddy instead of pale, unflappable instead of excitable, spare with his words instead of effusive.

Ida set out her paintings and set in to apologize. "I've been living on a sheep farm, running a sheep farm, in fact, so I'm afraid I don't have many portraits or still lifes to show."

Mr. Parmenter pointed to the painting of the sheep. "That's because your life wasn't still. This is the one for the Guild."

THE GUILD JURY accepted the sheep. Mr. Parmenter himself bought the one of the institute student because "this is how I want my students to draw." Elated, Ida walked the city, reclaiming it as her own despite the many changes, despite the initial sensation that came at her from nowhere of feeling dirty, hemmed in. But with the money from that sale Ida resumed her classes, signing on not with the notorious Mr. Wirth but with Mr. Parmenter. It was, she told herself, the least she could do.

The sheep painting sold, and Ida was asked to replace it with another; she chose the schooners beating across the Sound. One day in class she found herself turning the muscled back of an athletic young model into Ruth as she climbed the hill, her back as stiff as her opinions, every muscle in her body bent on driving her stick into the ground. But the thing that Mr. Parmenter remarked on first was that golden light in the sky—Ida had finally come close to capturing it with the faintest wash of yellow, orange, and burnt sienna—and when he was laid up after a fall from his horse he asked Ida to take over his class.

"Remember," she told the group, "there is only one way to make light. Have some dark to put it on."

*   *   *

IN JULY HATTIE WROTE.

Mother is grown more forgetful. She thinks at times you're
still at the farmhouse and at other times that Lem is alive.
She complains the pair of you never attend her anymore.
The new manager has lost six lambs and two ewes. I'm
working at the farm more and more—it's a way to keep
Lem with me. Bett allows me to direct her now, which is
quite a feather in my cap, as I see the thing. Henry Barstow
has bought the salvage building from the bank and opened
a bicycle shop. He repairs carriages in the old warehouse.
He helped with the haying again this year. Write and tell
me how you fare.

Ida wrote back. *I'm most glad to hear from you. I fare well;
I've sold the occasional painting and I teach too. Indeed, this is
where I belong,* but then she remembered that it was Henry and
not Hattie who had doubted her. She crumpled the paper and
started again.

I think of you all. I went sketching in the park the other
day and drew a dog that looked remarkably like Betty. Yes,
Betty, the sheep, not Bett, the dog.

In October Hattie wrote again:

We did well at the sale this year. Please advise what I owe
for that ram. It's quite unfortunate that nature demands
we keep him, as he's as unpleasant a creature as I've ever
known.

Ida answered:

Perhaps in exchange for the ram you might rent me
a room—ironically, my island paintings seem to sell
best—my teacher tells me it's because they're honest. So I
have in mind a working visit— It's not that I begin to forget
the island, it's that I begin to remember too well.

Ida crumpled that page too and began again, leaving off after
the words *working visit.*
Hattie responded:

Do come. In exchange for the beast's proclivities we will
keep a room available day and night all year long. You are
much missed—by all.

In March, before Ida had answered the previous letter, Hattie
wrote again.

Our new villain, that is to say our new manager, has had
words with Ruth and up and quit just as we head into
lambing time. What do you think of another kind of
working visit to the island? The farmhouse is available
now . . .

Ida packed her bag.

SHE STEPPED OFF THE BOAT onto the rebuilt wharf and
looked for Lem and his wagon, an old habit that had refused to
die with the man. Another old habit: casting her eye down Main
Street for the salvage company sign, now replaced with one that
read H. M. BARSTOW, INC. Ida hefted her bag and was about
to direct her trunk into a waiting hack when Henry Barstow

pulled up in a two-wheeled gig, clearly a Barstow from stem to stern with its simple, clean lines. He swung to the ground, scooped up Ida's trunk, and heaved it aboard: he helped her in, and they started up the hill.

"You're looking well," he said.

"And you." But he wasn't, exactly. He looked older; drawn; or more like, drawn *down.*

"Are you bicycling?" he asked.

"No."

They fell silent.

Henry carried Ida's bag inside. Hattie had left a waxy green fountain of periwinkle in a canning jar in the middle of the kitchen table, the table still bearing up well under Ida's paint; through the pantry door she could see that someone had stocked the shelves.

"How long do you stay?" Henry asked.

"Till lambing winds down. Or until Hattie finds another manager."

Henry nodded. "Things are going well?"

"My island work is selling. I hope to restock while I'm here. I'm taking classes again. I even teach sometimes."

"How to draw nude men?"

"How to *draw,*" Ida snapped.

"I only meant to joke. Apparently I don't know how anymore." He hefted her trunk and carried it up the stairs. When he came back down he looked different.

"Henry, what are you *doing* here?"

"Hattie asked me to meet you."

"No, I mean on this island."

He shrugged. "The cars haven't yet arrived here. The bicyclists have. Those concrete roads out at Cottage City. That shell road out to West Chop. The word is spreading. And there's nothing for me in New Bedford now that my wife has taken the girls to Connecticut."

My wife. "Still no divorce, then?"

Henry shook his head, a violent yank left to right. "But she allowed the girls to visit last summer. They loved it here." He centered his gaze, looked long at Ida. "You needn't worry that I'll be hovering. I just have to say, it's good to see you back." He jerked his head up the hill. "They missed you." He went to the door, stopped again, "Oh, I almost forgot. I left you something in the barn. Leave it if you don't want it—I'll collect it later on."

IDA WENT OUT to greet Bett and look over the sheep; so many new ones, but sprinkled throughout Ida was able to spot a few old friends, Queen proud among them; she looked to be heavy with impending birth, and Ida was glad she was here to see her through. She moved along the fence to the barn and stepped into the dust and gloom, ambushed by a sudden sense of loss. But over what, an ox stall waiting to be mucked out? Ida didn't think so. She turned to leave and spied her old bicycle, basket attached, leaning against the corn bin.

THE REST OF IDA'S REINTRODUCTION was hurried and informal; Hattie and Ruth had barely made their respectively substantial and imperceptible fusses when the lambs began to arrive. Ida had found Ezra's old canvas pants on the peg where she'd left them and slipped them on like old friends; she coached Hattie as needed, hearing Lem's voice in her head as she did so: *gentle pressure . . . if you pull, she'll push . . . ease it . . . ease it* but in truth Hattie took to the task far better than Ida had dreamed. After a particularly grueling day of one turned lamb and two sets of twins, they sat together at the kitchen table and talked of Lem.

"I wonder what he'd say if he could see us now," Hattie began.

"Ida, get out of those pants."

"Ida, don't even think of getting on that bicycle."

"Vote? *You?*"

They fell silent. "I would have, you know," Hattie said after a time. "All of it. The pants. The bicycle. The voting. I didn't care what Mother thought, but I knew how he felt, and I cared what he thought. I kept on hoping—"

Ida stood up. "Come on."

HATTIE WAS SHORTER and plumper than Ida but managed to worm into Ida's bicycling trousers anyway. The trouble was, once they got to the bicycle they couldn't stop laughing. They laughed when Hattie was upright, and they laughed when she was on the ground. They laughed when they were just standing beside the bicycle staring at it. They laughed when Ruth came barreling down the hill to scold. And they laughed—oh how they laughed—when Hattie finally sailed off down the track and up again, whole. They went to Henry's bicycle shop together and shamelessly asked for a second loaner; Ida would never have done so on her own, but with Hattie by her side she didn't mind. While they were there another woman came in inquiring about a bicycle, and turned to Ida, where she was standing by as Henry adjusted Hattie's seat for her.

"Do you ride one of these?" she asked.

"I do."

"What do you like about it?"

"The freedom," Ida said. "The means to make my own way from here to there."

"Yes!" the woman said, so thoughtfully that an idea occurred to Ida.

"Do you live here?"

"Summers. Out by the lagoon."

"I wonder if you'd be interested in joining a group lobbying for women's suffrage?"

The woman peered at Ida. "Here?"

"Yes, here. It has to happen everywhere, doesn't it?"

"I . . . Yes, yes, it does. Yes. I would."

So Ida now had two to bring to Rose. And as she watched Henry and Hattie another thought occurred: she'd ask Henry if she could put up a poster in his shop. If a woman was brave enough to get on a bicycle, she was brave enough to speak out for the right to vote. Or so it would seem.

HATTIE BOUGHT MATERIAL and Ida made her her own bicycling skirt. They didn't ride far—they couldn't, not when lambs kept arriving—but they did make it to West Chop and back again, and another day they rode through town as far as the lagoon. When they got to the top of the hill again, they dismounted and went straight to the fence to look over the sheep.

"We could do it, you know," Hattie said.

"The vote?"

"No. I mean yes, that too. But I meant this farm. My sheep. Your ram. We could do this. An even split down the middle. You'd have time to paint summer and fall but you'd be here to help with the lambing, shearing—"

"No," Ida said. "Boston's where I belong." But again, it was Henry's challenge she was answering.

* * *

AND YET, as lambing season wound down, Ida thought more about what Hattie had said. She rode out alone with her sketch pad and paint box and captured a single horse and carriage on the road to West Chop, the horizon its destination, and just above the horizon that light that Ida had seen nowhere in Boston no matter how she'd hunted for it over buildings, harbors, fields. She rode the other way to Cottage City and then out along the county road and came home with a basket full of more promise than she'd found in Boston in a year's time. She thought this and then she thought no, this wasn't for her, she couldn't come back with him here, and then she thought, late at night, alone, *or could I?*

SHE CALLED HIM. "Thank you for the loan of the bicycle. I wonder how much it would cost to purchase it."

She could feel the weight of Henry's thoughts down the line. "That painting of my father. Did you ever finish it?"

Ida had. She'd even carried it with her to the island, and yet she'd never given it to Henry, because it was too Henry. Too hers. "You'd have to see it. To decide if you like it."

"All right, I will. Now?"

Ida swallowed, nodded, realized Henry couldn't hear a nod and said, "Now. Yes."

THEY SAT ON EITHER SIDE of the whiskey bottle—another bottle—and looked at each other. It was all they seemed able to do. After a time Ida fetched the painting and Henry said, "The bicycle and fifty dollars," and Ida said, "The bicycle only," and Henry said, "The bicycle and twenty-five," and Ida nodded.

After a time Henry said, "Here I sit across from you, where

I've wanted to be forever it would seem, and yet I don't know what to say to you. I just don't know what I could say in fairness to you. I'm not free, Ida."

"I know."

"I'm not free and I don't know what we can do."

"Well," Ida said, "you could stay."

IT WAS DRIER THAN BEFORE: no sodden clothes, no tears. It was slower, more considered. Ida watched their clothes drift to the floor like fall leaves, layering one over the other—boots, stockings, trousers, skirt, blouse, shirt. They lay on a clean bed, not a moldy banquette, and reached across all that lay between them until there was nothing there but each other, until Henry's hands began to do all that she'd dreamed they could do and more. Ida felt she'd been long acquainted with Henry's hands, but not the rest of him, not even on that banquette, and it took them a long time to learn all they needed to learn of each other. All, at least for now.

After they'd reached stillness and had lain there luxuriating in that stasis a good while, Henry shifted. "It's near dark. I'd best—"

"No," Ida said. "Don't go."

"You know what you're going to get if come morning my gig's still sitting out there?"

"I don't care."

"You're sure?"

A lightness filled Ida, a thing she at first couldn't identify until it came to her that what she was feeling was joy, the joy that could only come from knowing, at last, when to care and when not to. "I'm sure."

39

MAY AGAIN. NEW LAMBS. FRESH GREEN. An occasional blue sky. A decisive wind. Ida was in the garden watering Oliver's freshly planted seeds; he'd come to visit recently but the excitement hadn't been Bett or Betty or Ollie but the new dog he now had waiting at home, a dog he'd named Henry, who was *really really really* going to miss him while he was gone. Oliver had planted more radishes and squash and peas and raced around trailing Betty for a time but hadn't dug a single useless hole. Ida had been somewhat sad about that.

She heard the wagon climbing the hill and thought of Lem, as she often did, but of course it wasn't Lem but Chester Luce's new delivery boy, bringing Ida's recent order along with the mail, which wasn't part of his job, but "just to save you the trip, Mrs. Barstow." Of course she wasn't Mrs. Barstow, but Henry had never actually gone home after the night when Ida had asked him to stay, and after a time people just assumed she was, or if she wasn't, well, it was nobody's business but their own. Ruth, of course, had her own ideas about whose business it was. "It's a lie," she said. "A flat-out, outrageous lie."

Well, of all the lies Ida had come to know, this was one she could live with.

The boy carried the packages and a single letter inside, set them on the kitchen table, and returned to his wagon. Ida picked up the letter and opened it.

* * *

WHEN HENRY CAME IN Ida was sitting at the kitchen table staring at the square of pasteboard she'd propped against the jam jar in the middle of the table. He'd come in singing. *Buffalo Gals, won't you come out tonight, come out tonight, come out tonight . . .* It was good to hear Henry singing again, to know that he felt all right sharing his voice with Ida now, but he broke off midstream when he saw her sitting and staring so. He came up behind her, rested a hand on the back of her neck, and leaned over to read the pasteboard. Ida read with him, again: a one-way passage on the RMS *Umbria,* New York to Liverpool, August the twenty-fifth.

Henry sat down. "So."

Ida said nothing.

"So, he *is* over there."

Ida stood up. "I best get moving; I teach a class at three o'clock."

"Ida."

Ida sat back down. Henry lifted his hand, rested it over hers where she'd flattened it against the table.

"I was always wondering," Ida said. "If he never got on that boat, if his intent was only to get everyone looking for him elsewhere, couldn't he show up here anytime? What if he did show up here and tried to claim—" She swung her arm wide, indicating the house, the farm, Henry. Her life.

"But now you know he did get on that boat. So this is good news."

Ida smiled at Henry. "Yes. Good news." She watched him ponder, decide, say it.

"Aren't you at all tempted? Paris? Your own studio? No more trekking back and forth to Boston to sell your work? No more instructing vacationing teachers in how to teach their students to draw a pear?"

Ida turned over her hand and threaded her fingers through Henry's, felt the answering pressure. "I belong with you," she said.

After a time—a long time—Henry picked up the ticket. "So what do we do with this? Take it to the constable?"

"No. If we do that, they'll be waiting for him on the other side. They'll arrest him and bring him home. Sooner or later he'll get out of jail and then—" Ida shivered.

Henry held tighter to her hand for a second and then let it go. He stood up and crossed to the stove with the ticket.

"Don't," Ida said.

"What? Change your mind already?"

"No. I want to keep it."

Henry peered at her. "Insurance?"

How to explain? "It's proof he told the truth to me at least once," she said. "He said he'd send a ticket and he did. It's proof that in his eyes I'm worth that at least."

"That you're *worth*—" Henry stopped, his eyes dark, his mouth tight; he set the ticket back where it had rested against the jam jar.

Ida collected her paint supplies and her straw hat and crossed to the door but stopped there; she turned around and looked at Henry. He sat facing away from her, but she could see how the tightness had traveled from his mouth to his jaw and around to the back of his neck.

Worth.

What was Ida saying? Why was she still, again, trying to see herself through Ezra's eyes, trying to find her own worth inside a worthless being? Like an avalanche, the last of the snow that had lingered on the roof of Ida's mind thundered to the ground and slithered away. She set down her paints, reversed her steps, laid a hand on Henry's neck just as he'd laid his hand

on hers. They did this often, whenever they could: the touching, the reminding that they were together, that they were connected. One. That touching meant everything to Ida but even
it wasn't the measure of her worth; Ida's worth could be traced
only through the memory of who she'd once been and then lost
and had at last regained, in the promise of who she would yet
become. She reached around Henry, snatched up the ticket,
opened the stove lid, and fired it in.

ACKNOWLEDGMENTS

I have to start with Jim Athearn of Morning Glory Farm on Martha's Vineyard. For some strange reason known only to Jim, he responded to a cold email inquiry about sheep farms on Martha's Vineyard, and off we went. Jim organized an all-island sheep farm tour, which turned into an all-island history tour, and history being a shared favorite subject of ours, we've been kibitzing ever since. Jim also graciously agreed to proof the manuscript for bloopers—despite my many visits to the Vineyard, I've spent most of my life on Cape Cod, and I knew better than to assume that what's true on the Cape is true on the island. For example, did you know that on Cape Cod we call them spring peepers and on Martha's Vineyard they call them pinkletinks? Or that what we call shadblow they call wild pear? Or that it's always better to harvest your hay when it's "in the bud"? Jim set me straight.

I also have Jim to thank for introducing me to the "Painter who Farms," Allen Whiting. I may have fallen in love with the beauty of Clarissa Allen's sheep farm in Chilmark, but when it comes to sheep, Allen Whiting's historic Cheviots are the ones that own my heart. Allen graciously spent an afternoon talking sheep with me as we stood knee deep in newborn lambs. I even got to bottle-feed one—I guess that explains my love affair with those Cheviots. Allen and I also exchanged books, a deal in which I came out far ahead: he got a paperback edition of *The Widow's War* and I got a gorgeous hardcover coffee table version of *The Artist at Sixty*.

I first met Andy Rice at the Taylor-Bray Farm Sheep Festival in Yarmouth Port here on Cape Cod. To watch Andy shear a sheep is to watch an artist at work; to listen to him talk sheep is to enter into a whole new wonderful world of entertainment. An additional bonus was the reading list he provided, and I suspect I now know more about sheep and sheep dogs than any non–sheep farmer on earth.

Archivist Bow Van Riper at the Martha's Vineyard Museum gave generously of his time while I sank into the museum's collections of all things Portland Gale, Summer Institute, Gold Hoax, and artist Amelia Watson, whose watercolors of Vineyard sheep got me hooked on my setting. The folks at Vineyard Haven Public Library allowed me to sit spinning through microfiche of the old *Vineyard Gazettes* for hours and answered every call for various obscure bits of information. I am grateful.

Artist Odin Kaeselau Smith managed to stop laughing long enough to teach me what I needed to know to make Ida's struggles at the palette (hopefully) ring true; her words are sprinkled throughout these pages. Artist Geoffrey Smith graciously allowed himself to be cornered at a Christmas party to discuss the differences between landscape painting and portrait painting. William Morris Hunt's words can also be found within these pages; he was one of the first artists to offer classes to women at the Museum School in Boston in the late-nineteenth century.

Thanks also to Paul Daley, who provided the proper rifle, figuratively speaking, and to Bill and Patsy Roberts, who read—and in Patsy's case, reread—the manuscript and offered much useful feedback.

My editor Jennifer Brehl is a true partner. We dance to the same tune, but she always knows when I'm off a note. It's been wonderful to get to work with assistant editor Nate Lanman—his sure but light footprint can be found throughout these pages. My agent Kris Dahl helped me shape my tale by refusing to accept "a sheep farm on Martha's Vineyard" as the answer to that annoying question "What's this book about?" She also reminded me my sheep were characters too, and suggested that we share an odd affection for farm animals. I would also like to thank copy editor Victoria Mathews, production editor Dale Rohrbaugh, and especially Mumtaz Mustafa, for her persistence and patience with the cover design. It is much appreciated. My family of readers, Jan Carlson, Diane Carlson, Ellie Leaning, and Nancy Carlson always see what I never seem to while simultaneously providing the necessary enthusiasm to drive the project forward. Jan also accompanied me to art classes and provided that needed impetus. My husband, Tom, critiqued, encouraged, and chauffeured, each of those things many times over. He also made sure I kept painting, and I now have two whole paintings of sheep that I haven't (yet) thrown out.

One last thank-you, and it's a big one—to my readers, you can't imagine how you inspire me when I mention there's a new book coming and you respond with a chorus of "When?" Many a day it's sent me back to the desk instead of out for a beach walk.